ROSIE FROST

FROST

& the Falcon Queen

ALSO BY GERI HALLIWELL-HORNER

If Only

ROSIE FROST
& the Falcon Queen

Geri Halliwell-Horner

PHILOMEL

PHILOMEL
An imprint of Penguin Random House LLC, New York

First published in the United States of America by Philomel,
an imprint of Penguin Random House LLC, 2023

Copyright © 2023 by Geri Halliwell-Horner

Philomel is a registered trademark of Penguin Random House LLC.
The Penguin colophon is a registered trademark of Penguin Books Limited.
Rosie Frost is a registered trademark of Geri Halliwell-Horner.

Visit us online at PenguinRandomHouse.com.

Library of Congress Cataloging-in-Publication Data is available.

ISBN 9780593623343 (hardcover)
ISBN 9780593690727 (international edition)

1st Printing

Printed in the United States of America

LSCC

Edited by Jill Santopolo and Linas Alsenas
Editorial contributions by Joseph Elliott and Claire Baldwin
Design by Lily Kim Qian
Interior art created by Pieter van Loon
Illustration on p. 305 created by Lily Kim Qian
Text set in Sabon LT Pro

THE WORLD NEEDS A NEW HERO . . .

TO SKYE, BLUEBELL, OLIVIA
& MONTY

BLOODSTONE
· ISLAND ·

Queen
Nike

Volcan
Crag

Ms. Parr's
Cottage

Wildcat
Woods

Konik
Ponies

Bell
Tower

Heverbridge
School

Ivy
Dome

Hemlock's
Tower

Black
Lake

N
W E
S

Prologue

EVERY BRICK FOR HER

JUNE 1ST, 1563—BLOODSTONE ISLAND.

The crowd's murmurs rose into excited chatter as four black horses pulled the golden state carriage over the drawbridge. She was coming. The island's wintry wind blew cold and hard in their faces as they watched it approach.

Their queen peered out from behind the red velvet curtain of the carriage window, the hood of her dark cloak framing her skin, which was so white it almost glowed. Tendrils of her hair, reddish and long, escaped and danced in the wind.

Hidden within the carriage, she clutched a small purple book with a golden bird embossed on its cover. "Thank you," she softly whispered, then touched the ruby and diamond ring she was wearing. It contained a miniature enameled portrait of her mother, Anne Boleyn. The carriage went on through an iron gateway and trundled up the long path to the blood-red brick mansion beyond. A vast, opulent lake stretched all the way along the side of the path, and she watched the winter sunlight glisten off its surface as they went past.

The nineteen men from her Privy Council had already arrived, along with those selected members of Parliament who had also been summoned to meet with their sovereign here. All dressed in their best clothes, they fell to their knees as her carriage came to a stop in front of them.

She stepped slowly down, the light catching the diamonds embroidered into the lustrous white velvet fabric of her gown. Strings of pearls lay heavy around her throat, and one large ruby orb hung from her jeweled belt.

"Her Majesty Queen Elizabeth," a groundsman announced, and bowed.

She smiled graciously at the old man, and a flicker of memory came to her. Of seeing his face before, when she'd visited once as a girl.

The crowd remained silent, expectant, waiting on her word, while she scanned the enormous building and extensive grounds. She then looked up at the sky and closed her eyes, breathing out slowly. *Finally* . . . Everything she had wanted, finished at last. There would be redemption for her mother. A large white falcon flew over the iron gates, past the many turrets, then over the crowd, eventually swooping down to rest obediently on a guard's gloved hand.

She cleared her throat and cast her eye over the men before her. Always, so many men. She thought of the petitions for her to marry that had come flooding in upon her succession to the throne. A foreign king, duke, or prince—but she didn't want any of them. Her eyes sharp and firm, she began, "I say unto you all that, since I first considered myself born to serve almighty God, I have happily chosen this life. I am wedded to my country; I am already bound unto a husband, which is the kingdom of England."

Her words pierced the cold air as her council listened intently. She raised her chin.

"You wish me to produce an heir to our throne. Well, here we will now have one. Today, as your sovereign, I give birth to life everlasting. My lineage shall transcend flesh and blood. This school, which I open today, will be a place to nurture the great minds, the hearts of polymaths, and the future leaders of our land. The children to come from within these walls will be my legacy, my successors, my heirs, and it is they who will go on to serve our kingdom. This school will house only the greatest of students, and of course, all of my father's allies and descendants are welcome."

Many of her advisors nodded appreciatively, while others conferred with their neighbors, the discussions growing in volume.

"Silence. I am not finished." She raised her voice above the din. "My mother's death was not in vain. She will live on, through our endurance, courage, power, and freedom. And every student here will embody the principles my mother taught me."

The men frowned. Mention of Anne Boleyn had been forbidden since her execution.

Elizabeth's lips folded in tightly.

Her voice grew stronger, darker. "I cast out the shadows, the lies about her. My mother's name, her blood, lives on in me, and not just in flesh, but through ideas. The truth will out. Her power will spread, through the scholars and students who come here, shining out in their craftsmanship and philosophies."

There was a doubtful murmuring from some of the men.

"I am your queen, and those who defy me in this venture will feel my wrath." Her eyes were thunderous. The voices quieted.

She then smiled, her posture firm, and looked out across the crowd, who were listening to their commanding monarch with absolute attention again.

"Here, on Bloodstone Island, greatness can flourish. It is England's own Garden of Eden, a place where all of God's creatures live undisturbed by the hand of man. All who study here shall come to appreciate God's divine majesty through the observance of his diverse creations. And the students will grow strong living by the foundational principles bestowed on me by my own blessed mother, the Falcon Queen: *Animo, Imperium, Libertas,*" she declared.

The crowd cheered. "*Animo, Imperium, Libertas!*" they repeated.

"So I declare my school now officially open."

A large glass bottle with gold ornate trim smashed ceremoniously against the red brick of the building.

She turned her back on the mansion and looked over toward the estate's entrance. Glinting in the sunlight was a monumental white-and-gold falcon, its wings spread wide, poised over the top of the huge iron gates. It hovered, regal and grand, the proud protector of the building beyond and all its inhabitants. In its talons it gripped a metal sign, engraved with bronze writing:

WELCOME TO HEVERBRIDGE SCHOOL

"Thank you, Mama," she whispered, still clutching the small purple book. "This is all for you."

Chapter One

W hy did being left out hurt so much? Rosie Frost had always felt like she didn't belong. All her thirteen years it had been that way, and she didn't know why.

She was sitting alone on the edge of the flimsy school table, her rucksack neatly tucked under her worn-out old boots. Most of the other students were huddled together at the other end of the same long table. All of them packed together in the sterile classroom, under a low polystyrene-squared ceiling and fluorescent lighting.

Rosie chewed on the end of her plastic pen, accidentally grinding it on her braces, which made a cracking sound louder than it should have.

"Oi, weirdo," Simon called out. "What do gingers and

extinct dinosaurs have in common?" The boy paused, then continued, "Not enough!"

The others around him laughed, and Rosie self-consciously tucked her unruly ginger hair back down into the neck of her oversized hoodie. The giggling continued, longer than it normally would. She looked up. What was going on? And then she spotted the writing on the whiteboard.

JANE EYRE—SHUT UP U TURD, SAME TO U ROSIE FROST—NO ONE LIKES A KNOW-IT-ALL

Rosie flinched. She never meant to be a know-it-all; she just found books interesting, and she couldn't help it if she knew the answer when the teacher called on her. She certainly didn't think she was clever in some extraordinary way, and she didn't mean to make anyone else look bad, but somehow it always ended up that way.

"So who was it? Who was it?" stammered the teacher, Miss Metcalf, her clunky earrings jangling. "Which one of you wrote this?"

"Well, they have a point," someone called out.

The spidery writing on the whiteboard seemed to scowl over the classroom.

"And where is my book? It was right here. Who took it?" Miss Metcalf demanded, folding her arms.

The late November rain lashed at the thin windows of the cold classroom, as though it was trying to point out the true culprit.

"I said, who wrote this filth, and *who* has my book?! That cost money, and this school has just had budget cuts."

Still more giggles sounded from the other end of the table. Miss Metcalf sighed, scanning the room.

"It was Frost, that wannabe Hermione. It's 'er," called out a boy with a gruff voice, his red cap pulled down over his eyes as he nodded toward Rosie. "The weirdo wants the attention," he taunted, straining to stretch his leg out and kick Rosie's chair.

If only I could stand up to these bullies, thought Rosie. She flinched, tempted to kick him back.

No, don't do it.

Say nothing, do nothing—silence is your shield. Keep calm; it's your armor. Then you don't have to apologize for the words you haven't said, things you haven't done, her mum always advised her.

Rosie really did feel like the odd one out here. Apart from one other person in her class, she was probably the only one who had bothered to do the homework. But she didn't have the teacher's book. She slowly placed her hand in her hoodie pocket, reaching for her phone, then looked down and sent a pineapple emoji: 🍍

This was her and her mum's "Batman" code. A secret signal, her mum had called it. *Just send me one whenever you need to, so no matter what happens, you'll know someone's got your back*, she'd said. Long ago, apparently a pineapple was a symbol of friendship. (It was also both of their favorite pizza topping.)

Those bullies will make you stronger. People are just threatened by anyone different or smarter, her mum always reminded her, after every rubbish day at school. One time, Rosie had accidentally leaned on her phone and sent a succession of pineapples. Her mum had immediately turned up at the school with a worried look on her face, informing the teacher that Rosie had "an important dental appointment" that she'd forgotten about before. But Rosie was okay; it had just been a false alarm.

One day, when the time is right, you'll go to an amazing school, for exceptional students. That's where you belong. Once you're there, none of this will matter. I promise, her mum had said.

Miss Metcalf looked at Rosie and raised her eyebrows, and right now, Rosie certainly didn't feel *exceptional*. Rosie swallowed as she looked up at the words on the board, her mouth dry, then glanced at the other students. Who *had* taken the teacher's book? It could have been Jayden, who hadn't been able to answer Miss Metcalf's questions yesterday about the chapters they were meant to have read. Or maybe Becky, who got called out for being on her phone during yesterday's lesson. Rosie scanned the room to see if she could spot the book, but it didn't seem to be anywhere.

Still silence, then a few murmurs and more sniggers came from the back.

"If no one owns up, then I shall have no choice but to hold the whole class back after school for detention."

Everyone groaned.

"And—and—I will ring your parents." The room went quiet.

Miss Metcalf paced the room like a hawk eyeing its prey. "I want it back, now."

"She's the book thief," Jayden called out, pointing at Rosie. "Just admit you did it. We know you've got it."

"Yeah," said Jayden's best friend, Wayne, smug in his brand-new trainers.

Rosie sent another pineapple emoji. 🍍 No reply yet, though. Her mum was probably busy.

"Yeah, little girl, loser, trying to be all clever with her big words." Connor, the third boy in their trio, kicked Rosie's rucksack, and the contents spilled over the floor.

Miss Metcalf walked over toward Rosie. "Well?"

Rosie's face went red. Wayne nodded down toward Rosie's rucksack, directing Miss Metcalf to take a look. And there it was, on the floor. Miss Metcalf reached down and picked up her missing copy of *Jane Eyre*.

What?! No, it wasn't me! Someone must have planted it—it was a setup. Rosie's eyes began to fill up, hot with tears.

She blinked. No crying, not here, not in front of this lot.

"Detention for ya," sniggered Jayden.

Don't let them get to you, she heard her mum's voice in her head again. She swallowed hard. *Never let them see your tears.*

But she couldn't take the blame for this. She had to be back home on time today, for her mum. Mum had been too quiet this morning, so Rosie knew that she needed her, and was expecting her, and Rosie had promised she'd pick up milk, and . . . and . . .

Suddenly there was a knock on the window of the door. The school secretary entered, then whispered something to Miss Metcalf, whose face turned gray. She then looked down at Rosie, frowning as she listened to the secretary. Once they'd finished, Miss Metcalf cleared her throat and said, "Rosie Frost, would you please go to the head's office immediately."

What the . . . ?!!! But it wasn't me, it wasn't me! Rosie's stomach tightened. She reached for her phone in her pocket; quickly looking down stealth-like, she sent her mum another pineapple emoji: 🍍

Then she stood up, her chair scraping back on the linoleum flooring. All eyes were on her as she followed the secretary out of the room. This clearly wasn't her week.

Rosie entered the stark, sparsely furnished headmaster's office with its gray tin filing cabinets, drawers half-open with papers spilling out. The headmaster nodded to her as she entered, his face giving away nothing.

Tick, tick, tick, the clock on the wall tutted, cutting through the silence.

"Have a seat," he said eventually.

Rosie sat on the hard plastic chair in front of his desk. The muscles in her legs tightened; whether it was the comfort of a rhythm or just nerves, her foot began to tap.

The headmaster was pale and balding, with translucent-looking skin almost blending into his office's gray walls. He cleared his throat.

"Life doesn't always go how we hope." He coughed. "Sometimes it's just best to say it how it is."

The clock ticked, as though in agreement. Rosie bit her lip. What was he going on about?

"I didn't do anything," she blurted out.

A woman police officer and a man in a gray suit entered the office.

Rosie's heart started to beat double-quick. Oh no, was she being arrested? Expelled? Because of Miss Metcalf's book?!

The police officer took off her hat. Her face said nothing.

The man beside her was holding a paper file and a small red leather briefcase. Rosie hadn't seen him before; he wasn't from the school. The police officer nodded at the headmaster, who nodded back, as if acknowledging that they should proceed.

"First, I must tell you my name is Chief Inspector Clarke," the police officer began, her voice calm, staring directly at Rosie.

"And my name is Colin Fletcher. I am a lawyer," said the man in the gray suit, smoothing down his floppy hair.

"There's no easy way round this . . . I have some bad news for you," Chief Inspector Clarke said, clearing her throat. "I have been instructed to tell you . . ."

No! Oh no, this isn't fair. The punishment did not fit the crime. Besides, she wasn't even guilty! Her mum would be so disappointed; she couldn't handle it right now.

"I'm sorry to tell you . . ." Chief Inspector Clarke said. "Your mother . . ." She stopped again mid-sentence.

Will be so disappointed, I know. Please don't tell her.

"It wasn't me!" snapped Rosie.

"She passed away this morning," said the officer, placing a hand on Rosie's shoulder.

Rosie frowned. What was she saying? *What?* She laughed nervously. "What?"

"Your mother is dead," interrupted the lawyer. His eyes studied her, grave and stern.

Rosie felt a tremble start to build in her legs. "Stop this, what, no, I'm in trouble, that's why I'm here. Because I'm in trouble, okay? I took the book!"

Rosie pulled out her phone and sent more 🍍 emojis to her mum. His words hammered into her skull. But she wouldn't listen to this. What kind of sicko would say such a thing?

"We have been given strict instructions how to proceed, from her letter of final wishes. You are to leave immediately for Bloodstone Island, and will be taken home now so you can pack up all the things you need. Everything has been taken care of."

"No way. I can't just *leave*." Rosie shook her head. *Bloodstone Island? What?*

"This is a lot for you to take in, but it's for the best. It's what your mum had instructed," said the policewoman, her eyes softening.

"I don't believe any of this. Where is she?" Rosie demanded. She felt sick, like she was delirious with fever, not understanding the words spoken to her.

"There will be a coroner's inquest, and then we will have more answers."

"We have a cat, no, I need to take care of Muffin," Rosie stammered. Her head was pounding. *Oh no, not now.* She felt a tingling in her nose, and the room swayed. Oh no, was it coming? No, not now, this was *not* the time. She touched her nose with the back of her hand, then glanced down, checking for the warning sign, the first tiny red drop. Nothing, thank God. She sighed with relief. She'd had nosebleeds all her life—every time she got stressed it would look like a horror movie. But her mum always said, *Just breathe through it, you'll be fine.* Thank goodness it hadn't happened. *What was he saying about my mum? Where is my mum?* The words seemed to have left her.

She breathed in deeply and kept tapping her foot and somehow managed to gain control of herself.

"I'm sorry, Rosie, this must be very upsetting for you."

The adults just looked at her, pity in their eyes.

Rosie swallowed hard. *No, no, no . . .* This couldn't be true. Who was this man, anyway? An army of emoji pineapples would be texted back from her mum any minute now. She was just busy.

"And just to be very clear, you are not to open *this* yet," the lawyer said as he presented a small red leather case. "It holds something very special that your mother felt was important for you to have. Something which, in her words, will reveal to you who you really are."

Who I am? I know who I am, and I want my mum! She pressed down hard on her phone and sent another line of pineapple emojis: 🍍🍍🍍🍍🍍🍍🍍🍍🍍🍍. Still, there was no reply.

"But, I repeat, it's imperative you don't open this case until you arrive at Bloodstone Island, and *only* open it with Miss Churchill," he said, holding it out to her. "Bloodstone is a beautiful, unique place, with a school educating exceptional young students."

What was he talking about?? She took the little red case from him, her hands shaking. A numbness began to creep through her whole body, and her cheeks went clammy. Suddenly a trickle of red fluid oozed from her nose.

"I think you also need this," he said, passing her a tissue, pointing at his own nose.

Rosie Frost dabbed her nose with the tissue and stared down at the little spot of crimson, glaring. The warning—it was coming. No, this couldn't be happening. The room began to spin.

She didn't want this, not now, but most of all she didn't want to go to some island she'd never heard of. She just wanted her mum.

Chapter Two

THE JOURNEY TO BLOODSTONE ISLAND

WEDNESDAY, NOVEMBER 30TH. LATE AFTERNOON.

TWO DAYS BEFORE THE BLACK LAKE CHALLENGE.

The helicopter jerked and dipped, causing Rosie's stomach to flip. She still felt like she was in a daze. What the hell was going on? After mopping up the residue of an epic nosebleed that looked like a crime scene, she'd been taken home to pack a suitcase of essentials and give her cat, Muffin, to Mrs. Yates across the hall. Then the lawyer, Mr. Colin Fletcher, drove her to a helipad and tucked her aboard, waving goodbye from the tarmac. They'd been flying for half an hour now, and the ride had been torture.

Oh no, please, I feel . . . I feel . . .

Stop! Rosie shouted in her mind. But it was too late. She couldn't hold it in any longer; she vomited into a brown paper bag, heaving up the Crunchy Nut Cornflakes she'd eaten for her breakfast. She was glad she hadn't had anything for lunch.

"Sorry about that," yelled the pilot over the whir of the rotor blades. "Not long now." Rosie wiped her face with the back of her hand, folded over the top of the paper bag, and then tucked it away on the floor between her feet. She wrinkled her nose and knocked back some water. The acrid taste lingered in her mouth, clinging to the metal of her braces.

Rosie stared ahead, rolling the numbers on the combination lock of the old red leather case back and forth, back and forth. She clutched it tightly to her chest as though it were her favorite teddy, the one packed safely in her suitcase. She rolled her fingers over the numbers of the lock again. She had already tried her and her mum's birthdays and googled how to crack combination codes on her phone. Nothing worked.

The lawyer had told Rosie in the car that Miss Churchill was the only person who knew the combination and could explain the case's contents. The case was heavy and old, and presumably contained something that had belonged to her mother. Rosie had no idea what it could be. As far as she knew, her mother hadn't owned anything valuable. They certainly weren't the sort of people to have fancy family heirlooms. Her mother had been a freelance writer, with other jobs to help ends meet, and she had even been forced to sell the little jewelry she ever had to pay the bills when things got really tight. Almost everything Rosie had from her old life was gone, even her ginger cat.

Whatever was in the case, Rosie prayed it would give her some answers about what had really happened to her mother and why she was headed to this mysterious island now.

The helicopter jolted again, and the little case dropped from Rosie's arms to the floor, making a clunking sound. Did the contents just break? Rosie unclipped her safety harness and quickly snatched it up to her chest again, then belted herself back in.

They were now flying over vast blue waters, and in the distance, a vague lump of landmass crept into view. *That must be it. Bloodstone Island.* It was a small island off the southwest coast of England, just at the end where it dipped its toe into the Atlantic, the lawyer had explained. The island looked dark and mysterious in the distance, shrouded in wintry mist against the backdrop of the raw setting sun.

The pilot turned the helicopter sharply to the right, and they began their descent. The island came racing up to meet them, the ocean's foamy waves crashing onto its southern cliffs. The landing was bumpy and rattled Rosie's teeth. Her nails dug into her palms until the vehicle finally came to a standstill.

"This is your stop," said the pilot, looking over his

shoulder at her. The blades of the helicopter were still turning; the pilot clearly had no intention of staying longer than he needed to.

"That's my shift done for the day. Out you get, kiddo."

"Where do I go from here?" Rosie asked.

"Just follow that path." The pilot pointed to a track leading into the trees. "That'll take you all the way to the front door."

Rosie unclipped her straps, took off the headset she'd been given to wear, and opened the door. Still clutching the battered burnt-red briefcase under one arm, she stepped out onto the grass. The rotor blades blasted even louder outside the cabin, and she ducked, worried they might slice off the top of her head.

"Everyone always ducks!" laughed the pilot.

Rosie pursed her lips and tried to stand tall, frowning at the pilot. She pulled her main suitcase out of the cabin but didn't know what to do with the little paper bag of vomit. What was sick bag protocol? She left it where it was on the floor, silently apologizing to whoever would find it later, and pushed the door shut. When she was a few steps away, the pilot gave her a quick salute and then turned his attention back to the controls. The noise of the engine intensified to a high-pitched whine as the helicopter lifted off the ground, causing the wind to whip up Rosie's hair. Strands of rusty copper lashed across her face, obscuring her view. A moment later, the helicopter and its pilot were gone, and Rosie was alone.

She looked around. The sun whispered a few final rays of light through the dusky sky, just enough for Rosie to see where she was going. The late November air was cold and dense, stinging Rosie's face. The gravel track was just ahead, exactly where the pilot had pointed, so she made her way there and started walking down it. The ground squelched with mud, and loose stones kept getting caught in the squeaky wheels of her suitcase, but she continued along the path, sighing heavily and pulling her belongings behind her. The large trees with their huge branches overwhelmed her, and something about them and the rugged bushes in the undergrowth felt . . . off. They weren't like the plants at home. "Ow." She flinched as a spiky leaf spitefully brushed against her skin. Her body stiffened.

"Hmmm la la, hmmm la la, I'm okay, okay," she hummed, trying to distract herself.

I wish you were here with me, Mum, thought Rosie as her fingers lightly touched the leathery green leaves.

She wanted to hold her mother's hand, to see her face, to tell her how much she loved her. Rosie wished more than anything her mum were still here, still with her. She always made everything all right.

But even thinking about her mother felt like falling into an endless hole, a drop into darkness.

Why is this happening? Why have you sent me here? Why??

This particular school, on this particular island.

The thought that she'd never see her mum again was like a stabbing pain that ripped through her heart.

A short while later, Rosie could see the track came to an abrupt end at an iron gateway. Beyond the gates was a long driveway and an enormous redbrick mansion, and beside the driveway a huge black lake loomed. Her eyes widened—even from a far distance, its dominant presence, defiant in the moonlight, demanded her attention. It was the biggest lake Rosie had ever seen. It stretched all the way from the entrance to the building. This was it; there was no turning back now. She had nowhere else to go, after all. She put her hood up, then yanked her suitcase and dragged it toward the gateway. The battered little red case remained safely tucked under her arm.

Rosie frowned, hating how she was stumbling along like a nervous fawn. Being abandoned on this island in the middle of who-knows-where wasn't exactly what she'd had in mind. *Bloodstone Island.* Rosie had never even heard of the place until this morning.

Rosie looked down at her Flik Flak Swatch watch. She was far too old to wear it but couldn't bear to take it off. It had been a birthday present from her mother, one she had found again this afternoon when she was packing her suitcase and put on immediately. Rosie tightened the strap.

"Just get on with it," she whispered to herself, taking a resolving breath. *Be strong.* That's what her mum would have wanted.

She refused to act like the scared little orphans she had read about. Oliver Twist, Cosette, Mowgli, Cinderella—each one had been vulnerable and alone. She didn't have to be *that* kind of orphan. She didn't want to be pitied; she didn't want anyone to feel sorry for her. Ever.

She would not cry, even if this really was her future. Besides, they were all in silly stories; Cinderella got pumpkin carriages and princess dresses. No, this was real life.

Prince Charming wasn't coming to save her.

Neither was her mum.

All she had now was herself.

Chapter Three

ROSIE'S INITIATION

WEDNESDAY, NOVEMBER 30TH. EVENING.

TWO DAYS BEFORE THE BLACK LAKE CHALLENGE.

The closer Rosie got to the mansion, the bigger and more menacing it looked. It was lit with numerous uplights, and shadows snaked across its blood-red walls. She shook her head and carried on walking toward the gateway. She was so lost in thought that she didn't notice the giant bird until it was swooping down upon her. Rosie flinched and let out a gasp.

But the bird didn't move, and Rosie scoffed at her own foolishness; it wasn't real. She craned her neck to look at it. Glinting in the moonlight above her was a monumental white-and-gold falcon, its wings spread wide, poised over the top of a pair of huge iron gates. It was regal and imposing, like it was guarding the building beyond. The bird's talons gripped a metal sign, engraved with weathered bronze writing.

WELCOME TO HEVERBRIDGE SCHOOL

The gates were slightly ajar, as if daring Rosie to enter. She squeezed her way through, and then crossed an actual drawbridge (complete with creaky planks), which stretched across a murky, narrow moat below. It was as though she'd traveled back in time. There up ahead was the black lake with the icy dominance. Alongside the lake was a strict path leading up to a semicircular courtyard presenting the huge mansion.

Rosie kicked at the gravel, trying to scrape the mud from her boots. Up close, the building's windows were huge, and its mighty wooden doors looked like the mouth of a monster ready to swallow her.

She clutched the burnt-red briefcase, then climbed the three stone steps to the entrance and rang the doorbell. It clanged like something from an old horror film. There was also a strange smell in the air, like rust and candles.

Rosie waited, her feet freezing. She peered through the nearest window, but it was too dark to see inside. Was anyone coming? She reached for the doorbell again but paused. A faint click-clacking sound could be heard from inside the building. The footsteps got louder and then the large doors creaked open.

"Rosemary Frost?" came a commanding voice from

within. "My name is Mr. Hemlock, and I've been expecting you. You lucky little barnacle . . . Don't just stand there gawping." He closed the door as soon as she was through, banishing the cold. Inside, the polished stone floor gleamed, and an old leathery aroma lingered. The large windows were shrouded in heavy tapestry curtains, and a vast globe chandelier dripping with old glass hung proudly in the middle of the dark hallway. A little white rabbit hopped through an arched doorway, then scampered up a large sweeping staircase.

Mr. Hemlock strutted toward the other side of the large hall in the direction of the staircase. Rosie quickly followed him. Something about Mr. Hemlock made her feel small and insignificant. He was very striking: tall and slim with a strong jaw and dressed in an immaculately tailored suit. His cream patent shoes were so shiny you could see your face in them, and they clacked when he walked, as if he was slapping the floor. He ran one hand over his slick hair, which was champagne blond and fashioned into a neat side parting.

"Are you going to be something more than a puerile impingement on our school?" he said in a clipped, posh voice.

Rosie stared back blankly, not really understanding the question.

"Forgive me," he said with a thin smile, his words softening. "I'm just curious, what kind of student are you?"

"Er, um . . . I was told to ask for Miss Churchill," Rosie blurted. "She's the only one who can open this for me." She held up the old red case. Her heart thumped in anticipation. What was in it? Finally, she would know.

"Interesting. Let me take that for you," he purred, reaching into Rosie's arms for the old case.

Rosie took a step back, holding the case away from him. "I was told I have to open it with Miss Churchill, no one else. It contains something very important. I've strict instructions it can only be her."

The man tilted his head. "I'm afraid Miss Churchill is away at the moment. Don't worry, I'll take care of it for you. It'll be safer with me."

Her stomach tightened. *You're not taking this. It's my mum's. No.*

"I'm the acting head of the school. Perhaps you failed to notice my badge." He raised his eyebrows and tapped the lapel of his suit jacket with a slender finger. A prominent badge pinned to it read MR. HEMLOCK: DEPUTY HEAD.

"Here at Heverbridge, we have the highest standards of pupil obedience, so I hope we won't be having any trouble from you." His lips pinched together, clearly irritated that she wasn't immediately compliant to his instruction. "This is an elite academy. You are extremely privileged to be here," he added.

The grand mansion's pillars loomed over her, dark and foreboding. Rosie didn't feel privileged. She wanted to be back in London, in her little flat on the corner of the block. With her mum, and with Muffin too. It might not have been much, but she'd been happy there, sort of.

Hemlock proceeded to prattle on about the Heverbridge core values. The whiff of intense aftershave emanating from him flushed over her. What was he going on about? "Blah . . . Heverbridge, standards . . . blah." She gripped the red case, her legs beginning to weaken, the long journey suddenly feeling heavy upon her. *I'm exhausted.* If he was the deputy head, maybe he *would* be able to help her with the case instead of Miss Churchill?

Hemlock turned mid-sentence as a girl stepped through one of the doors that led into the hallway. She seemed roughly the same age as Rosie, with silky dark hair flowing down her back in a flawless cascade. *She looks like she's from a hair advert*, thought Rosie. The girl stopped short when she spotted Rosie and Hemlock.

"Ottilie, what are you doing wandering about?" Hemlock asked her.

"Miss Eliot asked me to check she'd locked the library, sir," the girl replied.

"Well, you can do me a favor instead. This is Rosie.

She's new here, on a *scholarship*. The lucky girl." He smiled. "Perhaps you would be so kind as to show Rosie to her room, and give a little tour, point out places she needs to know about on the way?"

"Of course, Mr. Hemlock," said Ottilie, flashing him a perfect smile.

"Very good," said Hemlock. "Ah, and, Rosie, you've missed dinner. I hope you've already eaten?"

Rosie's stomach rumbled. She hadn't eaten anything since breakfast, and she'd vomited most of that up in the helicopter. She shook her head.

"You poor thing, you must be so hungry." Then, with a tight smile, he leaned forward and smoothly plucked the leather case out of Rosie's hands.

Without really knowing why, Rosie let him take it. She was numb and couldn't find any words left in her to argue further.

"I shall bid you adieu." With that, Hemlock turned on his heel and disappeared down the hall, taking Rosie's little case with him.

No, no! That's my mum's. Please.

Rosie froze. Her heart was beating fast and panicky, her head beginning to spin.

Something inside her felt this was wrong. She glanced down at her phone, longing more than anything just to see a pineapple emoji text back. The case had the answers she needed about why she was here, she was sure. But what had happened to her mother? Why did she die? The lawyer had used long medical terms she didn't understand. Where was her mother's body now? Even though Rosie had been told that her mum was dead, she hadn't actually seen her. There had been so much confusion, and the lawyer had said it had all been left to a coroner's inquest. Someone was going to give a report on why she died, which put a halt to proceedings, meaning there wouldn't be a funeral for a long time. So was she in the morgue? In a freezer somewhere? Whatever the answer, Rosie had never had the chance to say a proper goodbye.

Rosie closed her eyes, the intense pain of this thought shooting through her, her heart aching.

"This way," said Ottilie, sauntering off up a wide staircase encased in old stone banisters carved with cunning foxes and snarling wolves. Rosie looked down the hallway where Mr. Hemlock had disappeared with her case. The man was deputy head. He could be trusted with it, right? Right? She sighed, then followed Ottilie and started hauling her suitcase up the stairs, one bump at a time.

"So where are you from?" Ottilie asked, watching Rosie struggle without offering to help.

Say nothing, do nothing—silence is your shield. Keep calm; it's your armor. Then you don't have to apologize for the words you haven't said, things you haven't done. Rosie would follow her mum's advice. She would keep to herself, stay quiet, mind her own business. She didn't want to do anything she would regret. And, even more importantly, she didn't want anyone to find out she was an orphan, with no other family. That was a miserable label she wouldn't allow.

Ottilie stared at her. "Where are you from?" she said, slower this time, as if perhaps Rosie didn't understand before.

Okay, maybe I should be polite. "London," Rosie said, taking deep breaths as she stepped up the steep staircase.

"Cool. My family's from Spain originally—the Aragons," she said, as if it should mean something to Rosie. "I'm an *Aragon*—Aragon-*Windsor*. My father's German and my mother's Spanish, so I can speak both languages, as well as Russian and a bit of Latin. It's the Aragon-Windsor protocol to be polyglots."

Polyglots? Rosie frowned.

"It means speaking several languages."

Polygloats, more like.

"It gets you further in life. What languages do you speak?"

"Um . . . just English, really," Rosie said, somehow feeling ashamed.

"Oh . . . is that all? You poor thing. How basic. Well, you haven't had the funds for tutors, I suppose, obviously, with you being on a scholarship." Ottilie stuck out her lower lip. "You got lucky, then, didn't you? Like all the other little sponge—I mean, *scholarshippers* coming here! Education is everything!" Then she took the last few steps two at a time.

Once Rosie got to the top, Ottilie glanced down at the mud that was caked on Rosie's boots, then marched off, forcing Rosie to jog after her, still hauling her suitcase along.

Rosie tried her best to keep up, her cheeks flushed from the vigorous workout.

"Oh, come on, slow coach—just kidding." Ottilie winked. "It's not your fault. No one can keep up with me; I'm a genetic triple threat, slay vibes." She smirked, clicking her fingers.

Did this girl say her name was Aragon? Or Arrogant?

"Down there are the science labs, that corridor leads to the food tech kitchens and the art studio, up there are the senior offices and the Sovereign Hall . . ." Ottilie said with a quick pragmatic tone, pointing left and right as she walked. Rosie stared at the tall ceilings and dark wood-paneled walls. Everywhere she looked—the staircases, the pillars that lined the corridors—there were engravings of the most incredible plants and animals. Stone monkeys chased each other along the top of the walls, and chiseled ivy curled up the banisters. Hummingbirds peeked out of crevices, and badgers prowled in the corners. There were bats and sunflowers, parakeets and foxgloves, mice scurrying along the skirting board and lizards curled around the light fittings. So much to take in, and all of it so perfectly engraved and lifelike.

"Rosie? . . . Rosie?" Ottilie was staring at her.

"Yes?"

"Were you even listening to me?"

Rosie nodded. This was a lie; she'd zoned out, still trying to catch her breath from all the stairs. And she was done with small talk from Miss Polygloating Arrogant gobby girl.

"Hmmm. Well, don't blame me when you get lost on your first day." Ottilie flicked her hair off her shoulder. They'd stopped outside a set of double doors engraved with two mighty falcons surrounded by a wreath of twisted thorns and delicate flowers. Ottilie looked at the doors, then at Rosie, and a small smile played across her face. "Anyway, as I was saying—*if you'd been listening*—this is the Falcon Queen gallery. Want to see inside?"

Rosie shrugged. "Sure."

"You can leave your case here. We'll come back this way."

Rosie leaned her suitcase against the wall outside the thick wooden doors, grateful to have a rest from lugging it around. She followed Ottilie into a long room with wide floorboards and a huge stained glass window at the far end. The ceiling was carved with more animals and leaf patterns, except these had been painted white and overlapped each other, layer upon layer, like an upside-down wedding cake. Slim windows ran down the length of one wall, and the opposite contained a row of paintings, with a stone fireplace in the middle. A glass cabinet stood down at the other end with a golden trophy lit up inside it. The rest of the room was completely bare, the floor one long, empty space.

Great place for skateboarding, Rosie thought.

Rosie wandered down the long room, admiring the paintings. They were all portraits of women, each one painted in a slightly different style, and adorned with exquisite gold frames.

"They're the Falcon Queens," Ottilie announced. "You've heard of them, surely. They're like superheroes. We had a whole lecture on them at the start of term. There've been loads of amazing students of all genders here, but Heverbridge has *always* made sure strong women are properly celebrated too, in honor of the founder of the school. That one's Emmeline Pankhurst, the suffragist who helped women get the vote. That's Mary Seacole. She was this awesome nurse during the Crimean War. And next to her is Charlotte Brontë—you know, the author?"

Yes, she wrote Jane Eyre—*another poor orphan,*

thought Rosie. She nodded. If only the worst thing that had happened to her this morning was that she'd been accused of stealing that book. She'd do anything to have her old life back, even with the bullies, if it meant she had her mum back. It felt like a lifetime ago. The next portrait was the largest of all, hung above the big, hollow fireplace. Rosie recognized the woman straightaway. She had coppery red hair and ivory skin and was wearing a beautiful silk dress covered in delicate embroidery. Several strings of the finest pearls hung around her neck. Dangling from a chain at her waist was a gleaming red orb, about the size of a small tangerine. Rosie couldn't take her eyes off it. The orb seemed to call to her, as though it wanted her to know its secrets.

"So that's obviously Queen Elizabeth I," said Ottilie. "Even you must know that one. This school belonged to her; she built it in memory of her mother." Rosie nodded once more, interested in spite of herself.

"I bet you don't know that at one point she was thrown into prison? Like, an actual prison?"

Rosie shrugged. She found most things about history pretty boring, but maybe that was because her last history teacher had just made her learn a load of dates and droned on about politicians not getting on.

"There was serious beef between the half sisters Elizabeth and Mary—same dad, Henry, different mums," Ottilie explained, as if she was telling her the latest of last night's soap drama. "Henry was married to Catherine of Aragon, Mary's mum. I'm an actual descendant." She smiled. "But then he divorced her for a younger model, Anne, Elizabeth's mum, and because he wanted a son." She rolled her eyes.

"Anyway, when Mary became queen, she threw Elizabeth into prison," Ottilie said. "Mary chucked her half sister into the Tower of London and kept her there for nearly a year. Not much of a sisterhood, if you ask me."

Rosie half frowned, half smiled, then nodded again. She moved on to the next painting, which looked different from all the rest. It was the oldest by far, and the paint was starting to crack, covering the woman's face in tiny imperfections. The background was dark, an ominous black. The woman's rich, damask green dress stood out against it, as did a gold *B* hanging from a necklace at her throat. In her left hand was a blood-red rose, which she held over her heart. She had a pert mouth and sad eyes which seemed to follow Rosie wherever she moved.

Rosie stopped and stared at her.

"That's Elizabeth I's mother, Anne Boleyn. She was executed, you know? Got her head chopped off. By her husband, Henry."

"Why?" Rosie was really listening now. This one had gotten her attention.

"Back in the day, any woman who had something to say, or who was smart, was labeled a witch or branded a rotten orange. King Henry had a right-hand man called Cromwell, who was a snake, and he was threatened by her clever opinions. He lied, saying bad stuff about her to get her out of the way. Henry was tired of her anyway and wanted another new wife, so Cromwell's lies were a convenient way to get rid of her. Basically, she was murdered by a misogynistic pig. That's my opinion, anyway. *And*, unfortunately, some of those Cromwell snakes go to this school." She curled her lip in disgust.

Ottilie pulled out her slimline, rose-gold iPhone and used the camera to admire her reflection. "Rumor has it, her ghost haunts this gallery, and she can be heard at night wailing from the rooftops. A headless queen! Can you imagine?" Ottilie took a lip balm from her pocket and proceeded to smear shimmering pink gloss over her lips. "Since we're here . . ."

She positioned herself in front of the portrait of Anne Boleyn, stretched out her arm, and clicked her phone multiple times, pouting like a lumpsucker fish. Rosie tried not to roll her eyes.

"Hashtag Quuueeeeeen Ottilie Aragon-Windsor," said Ottilie once she'd finally finished snapping. "My fans are going to *love* that. Okay, let's get out of here; the dust is clogging my pores."

Rosie sighed with relief and walked wearily toward the exit, but as they reached the doors, Ottilie let out a gasp.

"My lip balm! I must have dropped it when I was taking a photo. Be an angel and go grab it for me, would you? I've got to upload this pic for my fans . . ." Her head was already buried in her phone by the time she'd finished speaking.

Rosie frowned. Why couldn't Ottilie get it herself? But Rosie walked back down the gallery anyway. *Be nice, Rosie; it's your first day.*

Her footsteps echoed as she made her way down the empty hall, but there was no sign of the lip gloss.

"I can't see it anywhere. Are you sure you . . . ?" she called out, her voice echoing in the gallery.

Rosie turned just in time to see the double doors shut, with Ottilie on the other side of them. Then came the heavy clunk of a key turning in the lock.

What the . . . ?

Rosie ran to the doors and tried to open them, but they wouldn't budge. "Ottilie?" Rosie called. "Ottilie, what are you doing?"

"Ha ha!" Ottilie laughed from the other side of the doors. "Think of this as your initiation," she said. "Welcome to Heverbridge. Hope the ghosts don't come out to haunt you . . . Sweet dreams, you little sponger!"

And with that, Ottilie left Rosie locked in the gallery.

At first, Rosie thought it was some sort of joke, that Ottilie would return and they'd both laugh about the funny prank. But as the seconds turned into minutes and Ottilie still didn't reappear, Rosie punched the door in frustration.

She wasn't coming back.

Who would do that? How could she be so cruel? And what did she mean, *sponger*?

Rosie banged on the doors as hard as she could, but they were so thick it barely made a sound. "Hello?! Help me!" she shouted. No answer. The walls were too thick. She leaned up to the high windows and pulled at the handles. All locked. She glanced at her shoe—perhaps she could throw it at the glass? But when she looked down through the window, it was three stories up. Far too high to jump. How *dare* Ottilie lock her in, like a prisoner? Rosie didn't even have her suitcase with her. Ottilie had probably made her leave it outside on purpose. And of course, she'd left her mobile in the front pocket, so she couldn't phone for help. Who would she call anyway, even if she could?

Rosie stomped back down the gallery, her hands clenched into two tight fists. Were the women in the portraits looking down at her, mocking her as she passed— or worse, pitying her? She stopped by the portrait of Anne Boleyn. Once again, she thought how sad her eyes looked.

She shivered. Was this gallery really haunted by Anne

Boleyn's ghost? No, Rosie didn't believe in ghosts. Another lie Ottilie had made up, just to scare her.

Well, she'd have to try harder, because Rosie Frost didn't scare *that* easily. "Oh well," she sighed as she tied her hair back. If she had to spend the night in this weird gallery, so be it. She lay down in a corner and rested her head on her hands, scanning the high ceiling. She shook her head. She'd never wanted to come to this school in the first place. All she wanted was to be back in London in her little flat with her mum, laughing about nothing or listening to music, singing their favorite songs together or debating something silly, like which were the best toppings to go on a pizza. (Pineapple, obviously.)

Rosie hadn't shed a tear since her mum had died. People had told her it was all right to cry: the police officer, the lawyer in the gray suit, the social worker they'd made her see at the flat just before she left . . . She knew she was allowed to cry; she just hadn't been able to. Maybe it was for her mum . . .

No crying, Rosie Frost. Never let them see your tears; it's a sign of weakness.

She'd spent so much of her time trying to seem happy for her mum's sake, she started to wonder whether she'd forgotten how to cry. Well, she wasn't about to start now, just because of some cruel prank. She had dealt with worse—those bullies back at her old school, her old life.

Her old life. No, this wasn't the time to think about that. Anger bubbled through her veins. She hated this place, with its strange plants, weird teachers, and that scratchy witch girl. Did her mum really want to send her here?

The large room was cold and empty; all she could hear was her own breathing. Rosie curled up on the hard wooden floor and closed her eyes. The damp November chill crept over her skin, making her shiver. She pulled her knees tighter into her chest and wrapped her arms around herself.

From their paintings on the wall, the Falcon Queens watched as she drifted into a restless sleep.

Chapter Four

THE FALCON QUEEN

Rosie woke with a start, a jolt of fear rushing through her. Thunder rumbled in the distance, and a brief flash of lightning lit up the gallery. She sat up and looked around, blinking away sleep. *Where am I?*

The women in the portraits stared down at her. She was in the Falcon Queen gallery, locked in like a prisoner. Rain started to lash at the paned windows, casting eerie shadows across the length of the hall. Something in the room had changed; the air was different. It was colder and felt heavy, as if condensed by an unknown weight. Rosie rubbed her arms, then glanced at her wrist, at the Flik Flak Swatch watch. Rosie could just about make out the time: 3:00 a.m. That creepy hour of no-man's-land, lost somewhere in between the magic of a cozy evening and the promise of the morning yet to come. Rosie suddenly felt very alone.

A rich scent drifted toward her. It was sweet, like dark red velvet plum roses. They'd always been her mother's favorite flower, one hybrid in particular known as the "Deep Secret," which was often found growing in pockets of frost.

Just like this rose, us Frosts can endure the harshest weather, Rosie's mother had often told her, reassuring her with the fact that whatever life threw at them, their family somehow always got through it. The smell in the room grew stronger, now mixed with a curious blend of cloves and spices. It was opulent and intense. Rosie looked around to see where it was coming from.

Eerrrrrrrrrrrrrrrrrrrk.

A creaking echoed from the other end of the gallery, followed by what sounded like a person whispering.

"Is someone there?" Rosie called out. Her chest tightened. No one answered. She peered into the shadows, but it was too dark to make anything out.

The gallery fell quiet again, the only sound being the rain as it rattled against the windowpanes. If there *was* someone in the gallery with her, maybe they'd unlocked the door to come in; maybe she'd finally be able to get out. Rosie stood up and crept toward the entrance, all the while squinting into the darkness for any signs of movement.

The smell of cloves and velvet plum roses still hung thick in the air, but the room was empty, and when she reached the door, she found it still locked. She had definitely heard someone, though, hadn't she? Unless it was Ottilie playing tricks on her again, trying to scare her.

Eerrrrrrrrrrrrrrrrrrrrrk.

The same sound echoed again, this time accompanied by a repeated tap-tapping noise . . . *Footsteps!*

Who's there? Everything is fine; everything is fine.

"Hello?" Rosie called. Her throat was tight, and her voice came out raspy. "Hello?" she said again.

A cold rush of wind bristled Rosie's hair. Her skin prickled, as if someone had just brushed past her.

"Who's there?" she said.

She turned around, then back again, which was when the woman walked straight out of the wall, into the center of the room. Rosie covered her mouth to hold back a gasp. Her heart was racing at the speed of a galloping horse. It wasn't possible. *This is not real . . . This is not real . . . I am just dreaming.*

The woman remained focused on what she was doing. She knelt in the middle of the room, in front of the large fireplace, and started muttering to herself. There was another flash of lightning, and Rosie glimpsed her deep, dark eyes, which had the same power as the storm outside. The woman then hung her head low, and smoky tendrils danced around her like mist on the ocean. Where the light from the windows hit the woman's body, she looked almost . . . see-through. Rosie dug her nails into her palms, trying to wake herself up, but she could feel the sharp pinch in her skin, telling her she wasn't dreaming. She shook her head, but deep down she knew the truth: she was looking at a ghost.

Anyone else might have screamed or called for help or looked for somewhere to hide, but Rosie did none of those things. She stood absolutely silent and watched.

The ghost muttered once again, followed by a fierce sigh. The rain pounded harder against the windows, as if warning Rosie to run away. She should have run, but the room was locked anyway. There was no escape. Instead, she started taking a few slow steps toward the figure. She could barely breathe. What did a ghost look like close up?

The woman was wearing an old-fashioned dark green velvet gown, and her long hair was covered by a dark head-dress with a trim of gold and pearls. She held something tightly in her pale, almost translucent hands, but Rosie couldn't make out what it was.

"Lies, lies, lies! My imprisonment is so strange to me. Never did a king have a wife more loyal in all duty . . ." The words fell out of her like a jumble of scattered thoughts. Her voice was strong and impassioned, and heavy with grief.

"Unworthy stain, so foul a blot. Let me have a lawful

trial, for my truth shall fear no open flame." The woman looked through the windows at the night sky, her face full of rage.

A cold chill ran through Rosie's body. Were ghosts dangerous? Could this one hurt her? The woman gripped whatever it was in her hands even tighter.

Rosie paused, then looked around the room. Maybe if she just pretended she wasn't there (the rabbit philosophy— keep still and you're invisible), the ghost would eventually disappear. Yes, Rosie could do that. Although now that she'd resolved not to make any noise, her throat was starting to tickle. She swallowed, but it only made it worse. She couldn't stop herself: she coughed—a short, sharp cough that demanded attention.

The woman whipped her head around, startled, and looked straight into Rosie's face.

Rosie froze, not daring to move a muscle. The woman was pale and her mouth small, with heart-shaped lips. Suddenly Rosie knew exactly who it was she was looking at: the ghost of Queen Anne Boleyn. *(And she still had her head on!)*

The queen stared at her with such intensity it was as if she was penetrating Rosie's soul. Rosie's heart began to thump, her skin clammy with sweat. Now what should she do? She wanted to run, but her feet were glued to the spot. Should she bow? Or curtsy? She was standing before a queen, after all, albeit a dead one, and she didn't want to anger her. She already looked fierce enough—an angry ghost, who might attack her at any moment! How did you fight a ghost?

Rosie slowly lowered her body, then looked down at the floor stiffly. It was something halfway between a bow and a curtsy, which came out more like an awkward bottom-dip.

Anne Boleyn rose to her feet and Rosie gasped. She was petite and delicate, but her presence was arresting. That, and the fact that she was transparent. She shimmered with an almost holy light as the obedient mist still floated around the edges of her dress.

They stood staring at each other for a couple of heartbeats, and then the ghost did something entirely unexpected: she smiled. A smile so full of love and warmth that Rosie breathed out, her fear melting away.

"Dear child, you've come," Anne Boleyn said. "I always knew you would."

Rosie glanced over her shoulder. Was she talking to her? The ghost was looking at Rosie, but also looking through her as if she was seeing something else.

"Um . . . hi," said Rosie, not knowing what else to say. What *did* you say to a ghost who also happened to be royalty? All Rosie knew was that she didn't want to get on the wrong side of her.

"This is for you, my lambkin." Queen Anne held out the object she'd been clutching. It was a small book with a purple cover, sealed with a metal clasp. The edges were sprayed gold and there was an image on the front, slightly obscured between Anne Boleyn's fingers. But Rosie could just about make out a crest featuring a mighty falcon, inked in gold.

"For me?" Rosie stammered, unsure whether she should trust a ghost.

"Of course," said Queen Anne gently. "It will teach you everything you need to know, to withstand any trials. *Animo, Imperium, Libertas,*" she declared. "Everything I wish I could have taught you myself. You will become one of the greatest Falcon Queens.

"Although it breaks my heart to leave you, I am not long for this world . . . So take it. Please, it's yours. Take it." She stretched her arm toward Rosie, the book quivering in her grasp.

Rosie paused, unsure.

"Any challenge you face, remember rule number one: Have courage," said Queen Anne. "Make the choice thou fearest the most."

Rosie raised her hands and caught her breath as she took the book from her, looking down at it in amazement. It felt solid and real. Anne Boleyn then let out a gasp, causing Rosie to glance back up. As she did so, the ghost disappeared, leaving nothing behind but a swirl of delicate mist. When Rosie looked back at her trembling hands, the little purple book was gone too.

Rosie blinked, then blinked again, her mouth open like a stunned fish's. *Did that really just happen?*

"Hello?" she said to the empty room. "Anne? . . . Queen Boleyn?"

She chuckled and shook her head. This was ridiculous. A minute ago, everything had seemed so real—the queen, the book, the conversation they'd had—but now . . .

The storm outside still snarled against the windows.

I'm not thinking straight. It must be lack of sleep, Rosie thought. Something about this building, about being trapped in such a strange place, was making her see and hear things that weren't there. That was the only explanation.

But it had felt so real . . .

Rosie walked across to the portrait of Anne Boleyn and looked deep into her eyes. "What was in that book?" Rosie asked her. "And why were you trying to give it to me?"

Chapter Five

THE FIRST DAY OF SCHOOL

THURSDAY, DECEMBER 1ST. ONE DAY BEFORE

THE BLACK LAKE CHALLENGE.

The next time Rosie woke up in the Falcon Queen gallery, it was early morning. She squinted at the winter sunlight which gushed through the windows, flooding her face with a comforting heat. The storm had passed, and the world felt safe once again. Well, sort of, given that she'd spent the night on the floor. Rosie stretched. Her body was full of cricks and aches.

Time to get out of here.

As she made her way toward the door, she kept her eyes on the windows or the floor, anywhere other than the portraits. *Don't look at her.* But the memory of Anne Boleyn's ghost clung to Rosie like a strange dream. It didn't happen; it wasn't real. *It* wasn't *real, okay?* That was the end of it.

The doors were still locked, but Rosie could hear voices in other parts of the building: children chatting and running down distant corridors. The school was awake, which surely meant someone would pass this way soon.

She didn't have to wait long. As soon as she heard footsteps approaching, she yelled, "Hey, I'm in here!" at the top of her voice and banged on the door until her palms turned red. Whoever it was stopped outside and turned the key.

"Ottilie? Is that you?" Rosie asked, thinking she must have come either to apologize (unlikely) or gloat (much more likely).

The door opened, and a boy was standing on the other side. He was tall and solidly built, with bright eyes and a friendly face with floppy sandy hair, dressed in muddy football gear.

"Oh, hi," said the boy with a curious frown. "What are you doing in there? Were you trapped?"

"Sort of," Rosie admitted.

"How did you manage that?"

"Long story . . . Thanks for letting me out."

Rosie stepped out of the gallery and was relieved to find her suitcase still leaning against the wall where she'd left it.

"I'm Charlie," said the boy. "Are you new?"

"Yeah, I arrived last night. I'm Rosie."

"And you got yourself locked in the Falcon Queen gallery? On your first night here? Blimey."

"Not a great start, I know."

"Well, lucky for you, I rescued you just in time for breakfast." Charlie gave her a broad smile. "You hungry?"

"A bit." Rosie's stomach rumbled, which Charlie was polite enough to ignore.

"Then follow me—food awaits!" Without further discussion, he picked up her suitcase and started wheeling it down the corridor, one finger raised in the air like some sort of valiant soldier.

After a quick pit stop at the toilet (Rosie was bursting—Charlie waited outside for her, guarding her case), they marched swiftly on toward the promise of breakfast. The rooms and hallways they passed through were vast, but as she walked up the mighty stone staircase leading to the Sovereign Hall, then through the gaping doorway, her mouth dropped open. The room was spectacular—the kind you could easily imagine kings and queens having lavish banquets in. Wooden panels engraved to look like a dense forest covered its walls. The pine trees rose higher than any Rosie had seen in real life, their tips meeting the high ceiling, which was by far the most impressive feature of the room. It was decorated with thousands upon thousands of stone birds: swallows and swans, pheasants and geese flocking among kingfishers and owls, herons and swifts. They were all twisting and swooping, frozen mid-flight as they peered down at the students beneath them. The largest bird of all, right in the middle of the ceiling, was another proud falcon, its wings outstretched as it flew across a giant winter moon.

"Impressive, eh?" said Charlie.

Rosie nodded.

"They call it *The Celestial Rising*," he said. "It was based on a design by that dude called Leonardo Definchy—something like that—in the early fifteenth century. Or maybe the sixteenth . . . I'm no good with dates. Either way, he was a brilliant artist, and invented stuff as well. It's pretty cool, right? But not as cool as the mound of sausages I'm about to eat!"

Rosie followed Charlie toward the canteen at the far end of the room. They had to pick their way through other students who were milling about with empty trays. Charlie still had Rosie's suitcase and pushed it in front of him, edging people out of the way.

The majority of students were sitting at the many wooden tables which ran down the length of the room. Unlike Charlie, still in his muddy football gear, they all wore the same neat uniform: crisp gold shirts and navy blazers. Some of them turned to stare at Rosie as she passed. The scruffy clothes she'd been forced to sleep in made her stand out like a grubby rock in a pristine blue ocean. She should have changed her clothes when she went to the bathroom, although even if she had, she'd still have looked different from everyone else. She needed to get herself some school uniforms, soon.

Rosie kept her head down and took a deep breath. The room smelled of ancient oak, mixed with wafts of baked beans and grease coming from the kitchens. Breakfast was a self-service buffet laid out on four long tables. Charlie was already loading up a plate with toast and sausages.

"How much does it all cost?" Rosie asked Charlie. She pulled out the five-pound note from her pocket.

"It's all free, of course," Charlie replied. "It's covered in the school fees. Tuck in."

Rosie hesitated. *You little sponger.* That's what Ottilie had said.

"What does someone mean when they say 'sponger'?"

"Why, who said that?" Charlie frowned.

"Oh, no one." Rosie didn't want to get into it.

"Well, it's a complete dis, a put-down for people on scholarships, said by snobs who think if someone doesn't pay to come here, they're sponging off everyone else. Bang out of order." He furrowed his brow, clearly irritated.

"So who decides about scholarships?" asked Rosie.

"Well, firstly, you gotta be super bright to get into this school, full stop. It helps if you get recommended, especially by someone who went here . . . And then, if you can't afford to come, you apply for a scholarship, and there's a board of important people who decide."

Hemlock had said she was on a scholarship. But how? She wasn't super bright, at least not compared to someone like Ottilie; she didn't know anyone who had gone here; and she certainly couldn't afford to come. Her stomach grumbled, which was a bigger concern. She grabbed a plate and spooned some beans onto it, as well as scrambled eggs and giant tomatoes dripping in butter. And then one more spoonful of beans and two slices of toast for good measure.

Once they'd both squeezed as much onto their plates as they could, they made their way to one of the tables and sat opposite each other on the heavy mahogany benches.

"So you got here last night, right?"

Rosie nodded, shoveling in a mouthful of scrambled eggs. She licked her teeth, then gingerly picked at her braces, just in case.

"By chopper?"

"Yeah, I was gonna ask about that too. How does everyone get around?" Rosie scooped up some beans.

Charlie swallowed before he said, "Most people walk or use bikes. There's limited buggies and cars—mostly service vehicles."

Rosie hadn't seen many roads on the helicopter ride, so she guessed it made sense.

"What do we do if we want to leave?"

"Wow, new girl wants to leave already, does she?"

Rosie frowned and shrugged. "No, I just wondered. They can't helicopter everyone on and off all the time, surely? There must be nearly five hundred pupils here."

"More like eight hundred, actually, but you're right. The chopper's only for after-hours drop-offs. And for the flashy kids. For the rest of us, there's a ferry that runs twice a week. It's mainly for supplies and whatnot, but it takes passengers too. Or if you're really adventurous, you could swim. We're not that far from the mainland—it'd only take about ten hours, if you manage to navigate the choppy tides and deadly currents . . ."

I'll stick to the boat, thanks.

Charlie picked up a sausage from his plate, folded it in two, and shoved the whole thing in his mouth.

"So what brings you here?" Charlie asked her, his mouth still full. "We don't often get pupils joining halfway through the term."

"I was told I had to come," Rosie said, looking down at her plate. *Okay, remember to be polite, but only small talk*, she reminded herself. *Silence is your strength.*

Charlie swallowed. "By who?"

"A lawyer," Rosie answered quietly.

"A lawyer? Get you, swanky pants. How come?"

The hairs on the back of Rosie's neck bristled. She

looked up at the large bird with expanded wings on the ceiling.

Because my mum died, I've never met my dad, I don't have any family, and I was told this was my only option. But I'm not going to tell you that. I don't want a Little Orphan Annie label, thanks. The thought that her mum was dead made a stabbing pain pinch at her throat, and her eyes felt hot.

Remember, no crying, Rosie Frost. Be strong. She swallowed, then cleared her throat.

"I don't want to talk about it," Rosie said with a sharper edge than she'd intended, folding her arms. She stared at her food, which no longer looked as appetizing.

"Not everyone here is as mean as whoever it was who locked you in the gallery, you know. In fact, lots of people are really nice." Charlie smiled.

"Like you?" She bit her lip, trying hard not to smile back at him. She was really starting to break her minimum-chat code with Charlie.

"Maybe." Charlie grinned.

A stodgy silence then filled the space between them as Rosie forked at her cold hash browns. See, this confirmed it: talking and making friends meant probing questions—questions she had no intention of answering.

"What are the teachers like here?" she asked, desperate to change the subject.

"They're all right," Charlie said. "Some are quite weird."

"What about the head, Miss Churchill?"

"She's a bit of a legend, to be honest, one of the best headmistresses in the school's history. She's super old—a proper crinkly—but has spent most of her life traveling the world, saving endangered animals. She's really made this school stand for that, and kept up the island as a conservation area, as it has become over the centuries. She's devoted to educating like-minded people to go into the world and spread the same message," he said, biting into his toast. "It's pretty cool; there're loads of rare animals here, some really bizarre. Miss Churchill goes away a lot on conservationy-type expeditions, though, and only comes back for very short visits. Haven't seen her in ages. Mr. Hemlock pretty much runs things these days."

"I met him yesterday, when I first arrived." *When he stole my briefcase.* The panicky heartbeat thrummed in her chest again. She had to find him today and get it back.

"He loves himself a bit, and all the mums think he's some sort of suave gent. Even my mum does." Charlie frowned. "He's a right pillock, if you ask me. He once caught me nodding off in the middle of his lesson and gave me detention for a *month*. It's not my fault his lessons are as exciting as my nan's dog breaking wind."

Rosie gave half a smirk.

"Wow, you're a tough nut to crack, aren't you, Rosie Frost?" said Charlie with a laugh. "Most people think I'm hilarious. Might have to start calling you Frosty."

Rosie gave a gentle shrug. He *was* funny, but laughter didn't come easy to her these days. And she'd never really been into cool banter anyway. Rosie had always felt a bit of an outsider with other schoolkids. She didn't feel confident enough. Always too brainy, not cool or particularly sporty. She *would* occasionally play football with the other kids from the block, but her real focus had always been to make her mum happy. They had their music—music was always their go-to for celebrations or when they were down or scared. Her mum seemed sad so much of the time, especially lately. Which had made Rosie sad too.

She looked at Charlie. He had a warm, kind face, like someone she might trust, even though she'd only met him about an hour ago. But the gloom that lurked like a dark cloud in the pit of her stomach gripped her, making friendship and laughter all but impossible.

Brrrrrrrrrrr, warned the school bell; lessons were about to start.

"I'd better get changed; I'll be back in a min. I'll show you to your room, help you with that case. Wait here," said Charlie, running off.

But the corridor outside became a chaotic riot, crammed with excited students. As Rosie tried to walk toward the first flight of stairs, pulling her suitcase along, it was as though she were a tiny fish being pushed downstream by a tide of salmon, a hundred or more pupils rushing and pushing her in the opposite direction.

She stopped a young girl with long brown hair.

"What's going on?" Rosie asked her. "Where's everyone going?"

"It's sign-up day!" squeaked the girl. "For the Falcon Queen games." Without another word, the girl dived back into the crowd and was swept away.

Chapter Six

SIGN-UP

THURSDAY, DECEMBER 1ST. ONE DAY BEFORE

THE BLACK LAKE CHALLENGE.

*T*he Falcon Queen *games?* Pushing up against the fast current of students was impossible, so Rosie figured she might as well see what all the fuss was about. The swarm of pupils went down the flight of stairs and then converged around a vast noticeboard in the central atrium. Rosie hung back, peering over the many heads. The air was buzzing with frenzied chatter.

She saw Charlie get to the front of the crowd, writing something on a long piece of paper that was pinned to the noticeboard. He then pushed his way back through and up the stairs to where Rosie was standing. His floppy hair bounced as he took the stairs two at a time.

"Hey, Frosty, you gonna sign up?" he asked.

"Sign up for what, exactly?"

"The Falcon Queen games. It's just been announced! I think you should enter," said Charlie, smiling and giving her a nudge. "The tasks are designed to test for the school's three core values: *Animo, Imperium, Libertas*—courage, power, and freedom."

Animo, Imperium, Libertas. The three words the ghost of Anne Boleyn had said to her.

"There are three challenges altogether," Charlie went on. "The winner is crowned the 'Falcon Queen's champion.' It only happens every seven years! The champion gets to make a new school rule! And you get to sit on the throne at the Bloodstone Banquet—this fancy-pants meal they throw during the winter solstice—right next to Miss Churchill."

Rosie's heart skipped a beat. "Miss Churchill? She's back?"

"Not yet, but she'll be here for the night of the banquet. It's her favorite day, apparently, so she never misses it. The champion gets to go with her on one of her special animal expeditions as well. Miss Churchill also has to approve the champion's new rule. And there's a legend that if it's *really* special, it could become part of the Falcon Queen's Rules, but that hasn't happened in living memory, and in fact some say the actual Falcon Queen's rule book has been lost. So, cool prize, eh? I reckon a good rule is extra desserts, ban cold mash."

He smirked. "What rule would you make . . . ?"

Hang on, back up, what rule would Rosie make? If she actually *won*, she'd get to make a rule?! Something like *All confiscated personal belongings should be returned!* And if she could sit next to Miss Churchill at the banquet, she could be sure she'd have the opportunity to talk with her about how Rosie's case had been stolen from her, and get her to open it.

There was just one way to be sure of making that happen: Rosie had to enter the Falcon Queen games. And she had to win.

"When do the Falcon Queen games start?" Rosie asked.

Charlie smiled. "The first challenge is tomorrow."

"Tomorrow?!" That wasn't a lot of time to prepare . . .

"Don't worry, I'll help you!" said Charlie, flexing his muscles and grabbing her suitcase.

"I don't need help," Rosie snapped, pulling the case back from him. "Sorry. Thanks, Charlie," she then said more gently. "I'll be fine. You get to class; I can manage myself."

"All right. And if you're up for it, there is gonna be a game of *Miracles and Monsters* after school . . ."

"Huh?" Rosie had no idea what he was talking about.

"It's a legendary board game . . . Come. We all play it. It's gonna be epic, everyone is going . . . Laters, Frosty," Charlie called as he headed off.

This school was intense, that's for sure . . . Rosie waited until most of the other pupils had dispersed and then approached the noticeboard.

Any challenge you face, remember rule number one: Have courage. Make the choice thou fearest the most. The final words that ghost Anne Boleyn had said to her kept going round and round in her head. Rosie bit her lip.

I'm scared, she thought. Then she took a deep breath and blew out heavily.

"Courage," a voice whispered.

Rosie froze. The scent of velvet plum roses tickled her nose, accompanied by a waft of cloves and spices. Rosie's skin prickled from a cold breeze, and she could feel someone's presence, as though they were right next to her. She looked from side to side, but the hall was now empty.

"Real courage is going forth despite being afraid."

Rosie wondered, was she just hearing things? Maybe she was just tired? But she recognized the elegant tone of the voice from the night before in the gallery. *Is it . . . ? No, it couldn't be.*

"Okay, thank you," Rosie said politely. Speaking aloud felt awkward when no one was actually there.

She stared at the gold-trimmed poster. Beneath it was a sign-up sheet which already contained around a hundred names. Charlie's was near the top, and she recognized

Ottilie's further down, spelled out in beautiful, perfect handwriting.

Rosie sighed. She had no idea what the challenges would involve, and she would almost certainly be up against people smarter and more athletic than she was. But this was her chance to meet Miss Churchill and get her mum's case back.

She took a pen out of her pocket and chewed on its lid.

This is a terrible idea, thought Rosie.

"Courage," the voice whispered again. This ghost queen was getting quite pushy.

Okay, Queenie, I'm listening. You think I'm good enough to go for it?

Did Anne Boleyn *really* believe that?

Or was it that Rosie just wanted the ghost queen to leave her alone?

Whichever it was, Rosie took a deep breath and added her name to the bottom of the list. All she could do was give it a go, at least. But as she studied the large gold-trimmed letters on the poster, the prospect of the competition—whatever she might have to do in it—grew overwhelming in her mind. Because not only did she have to compete in the Falcon Queen games, she had to win.

Chapter Seven

THE BLACK LAKE CHALLENGE

FRIDAY, DECEMBER 2ND. DAY OF THE BLACK LAKE CHALLENGE.

What the hell am I doing here? thought Rosie. Her feet were freezing, the damp sneaking in through the holes in her old boots.

The previous day had gone by too quickly, a blur of classes and faces and names she couldn't possibly remember. She'd finally found her bedroom, which was simple but still nicer than her cramped bedroom at home. And she got to meet her roommate, an interesting girl named Bina who liked wrestling and talking, a lot. Bina was nice enough, and she seemed like she might be a nice friend, if Rosie were looking for one. But no, she didn't want or need a friend. Friendship meant questions, which she didn't want to answer. It was safer to be on her own.

Besides, right now there was no time for friendly chitchat;

the first Falcon Queen challenge was in fifteen minutes. She pulled on her thick, coarse socks—this place was cold, no matter how many layers she put on, and the damp chill of winter crept under her skin. Rosie squinted as she stepped outside into the Friday morning sunlight. She dug her hands into her pockets as she stepped across a frozen puddle, her black boots forming crystal spikes in the ice. Down toward the front gates of Heverbridge, the other contestants chatted and pushed one another, laughing, egging each other on. With only her icy puffs of breath for company, with her head down, she focused on her old black boots; they were the one thing that reminded her of home. She took what felt like the longest walk ever down the stretched driveway from the main building, the Black Lake glistening in the distance like it was waiting, just for her.

This was it; there was no turning back now.

The whole school was gathered around the lake's edge. They'd been summoned earlier this morning by an announcement over the school loudspeaker, informing all pupils that the first of the Falcon Queen games would take place, and that all participants—as well as those wishing to watch—should report to Black Lake on the Heverbridge grounds by eleven o'clock sharp.

Rosie spotted Charlie through the crowd, and then realized he was making his way over to her. His nose was red from the cold.

"Hi," Rosie said, pulling the turtleneck of her jumper higher up over her chin. Her skin was also beginning to pinch with the chill. She had purposely kept her distance since their first meeting yesterday.

"Hi," said Charlie. "You signed up. Wasn't sure you would."

Rosie shrugged. "So, what do we have to do for each of these Falcon Queen challenges?"

Charlie looked out at the lake. "Dunno, it changes every time, but they're supposed to be pretty intense."

"Really?" said Rosie. "How hard?" She bit her lip. Her heart began to pound. Her veins flooded with cortisol, like that feeling of dread when the school nurse held up a needle for a shot; you knew it was coming, but . . . oh God, what had she got herself into?

Maybe she could say she needed the loo, make a run for it.

"Don't worry, I'll protect you!" said Charlie, laughing and flexing his biceps.

"I don't need protecting," Rosie snapped.

"All right, Frosty, I get it."

Rosie bit her lip again.

Charlie smiled, as if to show there were no hard feelings.

"Look . . ." Rosie said, "I just wanted to say—"

"What?" Charlie interrupted. "I get it, you don't wanna be mates."

"Why would you think that?" Rosie grimaced slightly.

"Well, you've sorta lived up to your name, Frosty." Charlie smirked at her and raised his eyebrows. "'S all right, I can take a hint or two, or five." He grinned.

"No, it's not that; it's just . . . I dunno. Complicated," said Rosie. Why was she so bad at this?

The truth was, she wasn't very good at being friends, at sharing things about herself and her life. She didn't want pity and she didn't want to talk about what happened. She didn't want to feel sad; she was too angry for that. It was bubbling away like a monster beneath the surface, waiting to erupt. *How could she just die so suddenly? And leave me alone, with no one?* Silence would be her defense.

Charlie wiped his runny nose on the edge of his sleeve. "So, you ready for today?"

"No," Rosie replied. "I don't even know what I'm supposed to be ready for."

"Said like a true champion!" Charlie grinned. It was nice to see him smile, and Rosie was glad they were talking, despite herself.

As well as the students dotted around the lake, there were several stern-looking people dressed like Navy SEAL officers, each of whom was holding some sort of giant electric drill.

"Who are they?" Rosie asked, nodding in their direction.

"Ice guards," Charlie replied.

"Ice guards? What's an ice guard?"

"They must be here in case someone falls in. The water is about five degrees Celsius, so it can be totally lethal. You can survive for about fifteen minutes. A few years ago, a boy fell in and got hypothermia. He nearly died."

"Hypo-*what*-ia?" Rosie had read a lot of books but hadn't come across that word before.

"It's not good," Charlie said gravely.

"And the drill things they're holding?" Rosie swallowed.

"For drilling, I guess." He shrugged. "In case someone gets trapped underneath the ice?"

"Trapped under the ice! What kind of challenge is this?!" Her heart began to thump again, only harder, thumping in rebellion as if to say, *Get out of here now!* She wasn't scared. That would be an understatement. She was terrified. *This place is absurd!* Before Charlie had a chance to say anything more, a hush rippled through the crowd.

A man's clipped voice boomed through a megaphone. "Good morning. What lies ahead is unknown, but I smell both victory and defeat among you."

It's him. The one who took my mother's case . . . Hemlock.

He was standing on a podium on one side of the frozen lake, wearing a tailored suede coat that hugged his trim frame and made him look even more angular than when

Rosie had first met him. His hair was neat, and his white teeth caught the sun whenever he attempted a smile.

"As you know, today is the first day of the Falcon Queen games—a Heverbridge tradition that goes back centuries. To win is the highest achievement at Heverbridge. Several alumni who have won have gone on to achieve greatness; it is the launchpad of our most celebrated students, those who have become actual Falcon Queens *and* Kings in their own right. They are honored in our galleries. Only every seven years does it happen; this is based on Elizabethan scientists' belief that every seven years there is cellular inner transformation . . . Today we honor the Falcon Queen who believed deeply in transformation, the founder of this great school—Queen Elizabeth I—and her mother, Anne Boleyn, the original Falcon Queen, who loved Bloodstone Island."

Right on cue, a white falcon appeared overhead, screeching loudly as it circled above the students. Hemlock looked up and watched it, his mouth pouting as though he'd just sucked on a bitter lemon.

"This will be the first of a total of three challenges," Hemlock continued, "each representing one of Heverbridge's core values: courage, power, and freedom." He stood with his shoulders back and chest out. *"Animo, Imperium, Libertas!"*

"Animo, Imperium, Libertas!" the crowd chanted back.

"Whoever gets through all three, triumphing over their fellow students, will be crowned the Falcon Queen's champion by our beloved headmistress, Miss Churchill, who as you all know is still away at the moment. But she will be back in time for the final celebrations. Until she returns, it is my honor to launch these prestigious games."

The crowd erupted with excited chatter. "This is gonna be awesome!"

Hemlock coughed. "Silence," he commanded, and then leaned into the lectern.

"Today is the Black Lake challenge, which will demand your courage. Designed to be as sharp as an executioner's blade, this first challenge exposes the foolish and shows no mercy. If you're not afraid, you should be, for most of you *will* fail. One hundred and twelve pupils have chosen to enter the games; only thirty of you may continue to the next stage of the competition."

Rosie's stomach lurched. Okay, all she had to do was make sure she was one of the thirty to get through to the next round. How hard could it be?

Who the hell are you trying to kid?

Hemlock raised a remote control and pressed a button. There was a whirring sound as a large screen emerged from a metal crate on the far side of the lake. Once the screen had reached its full height, the noise stopped and a digital number thirty blinked onto the screen.

"To complete today's challenge, you must simply cross the frozen lake in front of you, by any means possible," Hemlock said. "Only the first thirty pupils to reach the other side will proceed to the second round."

Goose bumps broke out all over Rosie's skin. Yes, the lake was frozen, but that didn't mean it was safe. She'd been warned multiple times as a child not to walk over frozen lakes; ice was never as thick as it looked from above.

This place is outrageous. How on earth am I meant to do this?! thought Rosie.

"What if we fall in?" someone shouted.

"Then I suggest you swim," Hemlock replied in a droll tone. "The cold will cut you like Rombard, the executioner. I should remind you that participation is not compulsory, even if you have already signed up. This challenge filters the courageous from the cowards. If you do not have the *courage* to try, you may step aside now, and make your way around the lake to watch with the other spectators. Everyone else, line up along the shoreline and wait for my whistle."

A few of the students started to step back.

"I see a few spineless snowflakes have had second thoughts," muttered Hemlock smugly.

"What do you think?" Charlie asked Rosie.

"It sounds impossible . . ." Rosie replied.

"Sounds cool to me; we'll be fine!"

"Well, good luck!" She gave Charlie a quick glance,

then the two of them went to find suitable spots among the other participants. Most were older pupils, including several sixth formers. Surely they'd be at an advantage with their long legs and athletic physiques? Although, thinking about it, the year sevens who'd been brave enough to enter might be better off, having smaller, lighter bodies.

The surface of the ice was hard and rough, like the back of a sleeping leviathan, lying in wait, ready to engulf her. Was she really going to do this? The number thirty glared at her from the screen on the other side of the lake. She had no choice; she wasn't going to back out now. *I need my mum's case back*. The ends of her fingers tingled with nerves.

Rosie took in a deep breath and suddenly smelled something vaguely familiar. She sniffed again. *Could it be . . . ?* There was a hint of velvet plum roses tinged with spicy cloves in the air. A moment later, the smell was gone. Rosie shook her head but was sure she hadn't imagined it.

Courage . . . The Falcon Queen's words echoed in her mind.

Okay, focus. She needed to think tactics. Should she race across as quickly as possible or be more cautious in her approach? The inky black water beneath the ice looked like a deadly abyss waiting to suck her into its depths.

A short distance away, Ottilie Aragon-Windsor flicked her long, silky dark hair and rolled her shoulders, as if about to enjoy a nice, calming bath. She caught Rosie's eye and gave her a glare. Rosie forced herself to smile back, as sickeningly sweet as she could muster. *Wow*, Rosie thought, *Ottilie really is your first-class "mean girl."* She gritted her teeth, thinking about what Ottilie had done to her on her first night here.

"Let the challengers be swift and the Black Lake be merciful," Hemlock said through the megaphone as he eyeballed them all. "On your marks. Get set . . ."

The shrill sound of his whistle echoed across the lake, and the pupils launched themselves onto the ice to begin their frantic dash for the other side. Along with them, Charlie bounded off at a high speed, his arms spread wide for balance. The fast approach had its disadvantages, though. Already, several people had slipped and fallen, landing with a hard thump. Some even deliberately pushed others to take out the competition. Two boys were locked in a scrap not far from the shore, and other tussles were breaking out all over the ice. Ottilie somehow glided past them all, like an Olympic champion, with effortless grace. Or perhaps no one dared touch her.

Rosie took her first step onto the ice and nearly lost her balance straightaway. The old, worn-out boots she was wearing didn't have very good grip. She crouched down and started inching along on her hands and knees instead.

The ice began to creak and groan, complaining at the number of people on its surface.

The sounds grew louder, like angry floorboards in a haunted house. Then came the first almighty *CRACK!*

Ahead of Rosie, someone disappeared into the freezing water. They would surely get hypothermia, as Charlie had said. How was this allowed in a school? The cracks started to spread across the breadth of the lake, toward Rosie.

CRACK! SPLASH! THWACK!

More people plummeted through the shattering ice into the water, and their arms thrashed about as they tried to haul themselves out again.

Still on her hands and knees, Rosie was making good progress. Fast enough to overtake the more cautious pupils, yet slow enough to navigate the cracks and holes that had appeared. This had also pushed her more into the middle of the lake, and she was halfway across now, where the ice was thinnest. *Be very careful here*, she urged herself.

BZZZZZZ!

Rosie flinched as a buzzer blasted. It had come from the digital screen, which was now showing the number twenty-nine.

"Congratulations, Jackson Sterling. The first contestant to successfully cross the lake!" Hemlock's voice blared through the megaphone.

Rosie watched as more pupils quickly followed, scrambling off the ice. Each time they did, the screen buzzed and the number dropped again. Only twenty-four more places, and there were still plenty of people ahead of her, frantically speeding their way toward the finish line. She pushed on, winding around those still struggling to keep their balance or others who were filled with such intense determination they would take her down if she got too close. Then she heard a familiar voice, yelling.

"Help! I can't get out!"

It was Charlie! He'd fallen into the water a short distance from her and was struggling to claw his way back onto the ice.

BZZZZZZ! BZZZZZZ!

Rosie looked at the finish line. The number twenty shone back at her. Ten people had now completed the challenge, including Ottilie, who was striking a victory pose for her phone camera.

BZZZZZZ! Nineteen . . .

BZZZZZZ! Eighteen . . .

The buzzer continued to screech, as if echoing Rosie's nerves.

"Help!" Charlie yelled again.

BZZZZZZ! . . . BZZZZZZ! . . . BZZZZZZ!

Fifteen!

Half the places were gone. If she stopped to help Charlie, she would never make it through to the next round. Charlie would have to get himself out. She crawled away from him, trying to make up for lost time.

BZZZZZZ!

Then Rosie stopped.

No, Charlie, who'd been kind to her since she arrived, even after she'd pushed him away. Could she abandon him now?

"I'm coming," she called back as she turned around and crawled over to him. Charlie's face was tight with panic and starting to turn blue.

"I'm stuck," he said. "My foot's caught in the reeds."

Rosie paused at the edge of the crack, whipped off her coat, and threw one end of it toward him.

"Here, grab hold of this. I'll pull you free."

BZZZZZZ! Rosie glanced at the screen, and then immediately wished she hadn't; only thirteen places left.

It took Charlie three attempts to grab the coat sleeve, and then he pulled on it so hard that Rosie was dragged across the ice.

BZZZZZZ!

Rosie dug her boots down into the ice to try to get some grip, but it was too slippery. She continued to slide toward the hole, finally plummeting into the water next to Charlie.

"Aaah," she gasped, the cold water engulfing her. It was unlike anything she had ever experienced. A million insects biting her at the same time, on every part of her body. Her head broke the surface and she shook the icy droplets from her hair. Her breath was racing out of her in uncontrollable gasps. She flapped her arms and shouted hoarsely to get the attention of one of the ice guards, but they were all busy rescuing other students on the far side of the lake. She grabbed hold of Charlie's jacket shoulder and tried to pull him toward the thicker ice, but he really was stuck.

"G-go without me, Frosty," he said, his teeth chattering.

The screen buzzed and the number eleven glared at them. The competition was really on now. Pupils were scrambling aggressively, which only made them slip more, while others were literally wrestling each other to the ground.

"You're gonna lose—go!"

Rosie shook her head. "I can't leave you here to freeze."

The intense cold was beginning to seep into Rosie's bones, making her limbs feel sluggish and heavy. She had to be quick. She took a deep breath and dived back under the water, pushing herself through the slimy algae, feeling for Charlie's trapped foot. The sinister weed was hornwort—she'd seen it on a wildlife program—and it was wrapped around his ankle, like the tentacles of a hungry octopus. Rosie pulled at it, but it wouldn't budge. She pulled harder. It was no use, and she couldn't hold her breath any longer. She kicked back to the surface and sucked in a greedy lungful of air.

Charlie was worryingly silent. His face was now stark

white and his breathing shallow. She had to get him out of the water. Fast.

"Help us!" she called out.

The ice guards were still busy pulling someone else out of the water; they couldn't hear her. *Okay, it's up to me.*

Rosie took another almighty breath and dived back into the darkness. The army of evil weeds closed in around her, twisting themselves around her own legs too. She started to lose herself among the swirls of their creepy caresses as she snatched at the leathery tentacles around Charlie's ankle again and again. But the leaves slipped through her numb fingers and the vines wouldn't break. Above her, a slice of bright light rippled across the surface. The dull buzz of the descending numbers continued, but it felt like it was a thousand miles away. Her lungs ached and her head was pounding. It was too much; the last of her energy was dissolving and her mind began to drift and go fuzzy.

A flash of white silk drifted past her. It was a pale woman with red hair billowing in the water . . . lifeless. The body twisted in the algae and Rosie could only just make it out, the white dress glowing through the dark slime. The woman was holding a single red rose, rich and opulent, and one she knew well. A Deep Secret rose.

It couldn't be.

Mum?

Rosie reached out as her mother disappeared deeper into the water.

No, don't leave me, Mum. I need you. Where are you?

Just like this rose, us Frosts can endure the harshest weather. Rosie could feel herself fading. She closed her eyes and sank down toward the bottom of the lake. Maybe she could join her mother, wherever she was. Then the scent of velvet plum roses, mixed with cloves and spice, entered her nostrils. But that was impossible. She was underwater— how could she smell anything?

"Courage. *Animo.* Make the choice thou fearest the most," a voice whispered through the reeds.

Rosie opened her eyes again, and a new surge of strength flooded her muscles. She began to kick hard, swimming back up toward Charlie and the light of the surface. As she went, she ripped at the vines with a newfound determination, and Charlie's foot finally wriggled free of the hornwort.

Rosie erupted out of the water and heaved in several desperate breaths.

"I b-broke the w-weeds," she said to Charlie as he gasped for air beside her, barely able to get the words out, her teeth chattering. *BZZZZZZ! BZZZZZZ!* "Now I'm going to p-push you out, but you need to help, okay?"

Charlie gave her a frozen nod, and Rosie braced herself, then went under once more.

She pushed Charlie's backside from beneath, feeling only slightly self-conscious that she was touching a boy's bottom. The weight eased as Charlie pulled himself back onto the ice.

As soon as he was out, Charlie snapped back to life and reached in to help Rosie. One pull and she was out too. She collapsed onto the ice, wheezing like a washed-up seal.

The screen buzzed again and Rosie gasped. *Focus, Rosie, focus . . . Oh no, only five places left!* Several contestants were locked in a messy scuffle over by the finish line—kicking and tripping each other up in their desperation to win.

"Come on," said Charlie, "we can still make it."

BZZZZZZ!

In all honesty, Rosie was now giving up any hope of getting through the challenge—she was just grateful to be alive. But Charlie helped her to her feet and, supporting one another, they hobbled toward the finish line.

There still seemed to be lots of people ahead of them, all dashing for the final handful of places.

BZZZZZZ!

One pupil pulled another contestant back by her hood, while she swung a punch at his head. Everyone was scrambling and fighting. It was utter chaos.

They finally made it to the shore, and Rosie threw herself forward across the finish line, collapsing onto the ground beside Charlie. Her eyes blurred. How many pupils had made it ahead of her? It looked like a lot more than thirty. They were too late.

She was shivering all over and felt like there was a hailstorm in her lungs. A couple of teachers approached with heated blankets and steaming mugs of sweet tea, then someone led her and Charlie to a large bonfire, where other pupils who'd fallen in were recovering, a cluster of drowned rats who all smelled of the dank Black Lake. Rosie didn't care; the warmth was a dreamy comfort. She closed her eyes and clamped her teeth together until they gradually stopped rattling.

"Well, well, well, aren't you just full of surprises?"

Rosie opened her eyes. Hemlock was standing over her with a clipboard in his hands.

"Sir?" she asked.

"You were the thirtieth participant to reach the shore. Congratulations, Miss Frost. You're through to the next round."

Chapter Eight

LITTLE TIMMY

Rosie had showered and put on warm clothing, and was now standing on the outskirts of the group of students milling about the classroom where they'd just had a motivational debrief with Mr. Johnston, the PE teacher, and where the school nurse was checking everyone who had fallen in for hypothermia.

"A couple of us are going to the games room. We're gonna celebrate that we're through to the next round. Wanna come?" Charlie's beaming face interrupted Rosie's thoughts. Three of their classmates stood behind him—a boy and two girls. Rosie had seen Charlie chatting to loads of different people after the Black Lake challenge; making friends clearly came easily to him.

"Er, well, I'm not sure . . ." She dug her hands into her pockets. More people meant more questions about where she came from. "Actually, no thanks," she replied. "I've got things to do. I've got to see Mr. Hemlock, got to pick up my uniforms." That part was true; there hadn't been time since she arrived to pick them up.

"Suit yourself. See you around, Frosty," he said. Then the four of them left the classroom, laughing as Charlie pouted his lips, with shoulders back, doing an impression of an uptight Mr. Hemlock.

Rosie was the only person left in the classroom.

She peered around the door. The hall was empty now too, Charlie and the others gone. "Damn it," she whispered under her breath. Her mum was her best friend in her old life. It was going to be a long year if she didn't make any friends, but it was safer this way. Besides, it was too late now. And Rosie had something more pressing on her mind.

There was no way she could go through another Falcon Queen challenge.

I need to see Hemlock.

She wandered through the door into the long corridor, which looked the same as all the others. Last night her roommate, Bina, had casually mentioned where his office was, but there was no one around now to guide Rosie. The corridor was lit by several chandeliers which hung sporadically from the ceiling, the light reflecting off the polished floor, which was made up of black and white marble squares, similar to a chessboard. A grand staircase spiraled up on the opposite side of the hall. The place smelled musty, and a radiator groaned. Behind the sprawling staircase, Rosie followed the corridor to the East Wing, until she passed a slender archway. This was it. Above the archway she saw a gold plaque labeled MR. F. HEMLOCK-C. ESQ., DEPUTY HEAD screwed into the stonework.

She stepped through the archway and crept up the spiral staircase on the other side. Looking out a slim arrow-slit window, she realized she must be in one of the mansion's many turrets. *I bet only the most important teachers get offices in turrets*, she thought.

About five steps away from the office door, she stopped.

Was there any point in doing this? Yes, she had a plan, this was it, and she was going to get her case back. *Stick to the plan, Rosie, stick to the plan.*

She walked up the last few steps to his office. The door was slightly ajar, and she could hear Hemlock's voice sliding out through the crack. By his tone, it sounded as though he was on the phone with someone important. Rosie looked to her left and right. She shouldn't eavesdrop— especially not on the deputy head—but no one was about. She pinned herself behind the door.

"You have my assurance, no one will ever know," he was saying. "With Churchill away, we can do whatever we like." There was a pause while the other person on the phone spoke, then Hemlock continued. "No, I know . . . Well, I don't give a damn about the wildcats, or anything else on this island, for that matter . . . That's what I'm saying . . . Yes, of course . . . No, I understand. That's why we're using the Isambard Foundation—no one will suspect a thing . . . So we are in agreement? Excellent . . . If the little *Felis silvestris* get caught in the way of our venture, so be it," he said with nonchalance. "It will be done. Trust me, the pleasure is all mine. Thank you. Goodbye."

Wildcats? Isambard Foundation?

There was the dull clatter of a receiver being put down.

What on earth had she just overheard? It was impossible to know exactly, but it sounded an awful lot like Hemlock was up to something terrible behind Miss Churchill's back. Where were there wildcats? She'd been told that this was an island of conservation, with all sorts of rare and endangered species brought to live freely and safely here. Hemlock clearly didn't seem to share this love of nature, however.

Calm. Stay calm. A little shaky, Rosie breathed out, then knocked firmly on the door. It was time to get her briefcase back.

"Enter," came Mr. Hemlock's stern voice from inside.

Rosie pushed the door open and stepped into the turret room.

The office was big and strangely bare, immaculate even, like a minimalist art gallery. The only furniture was a bookshelf which was almost devoid of any books, two chairs, and a grand steel desk. On a pedestal in one corner, half-hidden in shadow, was a stuffed bird trapped in a glass box. It was about three feet tall, with gray downy feathers and a black bill. Its eyes were startled, as if saying, *What? Why me?*

Hemlock was sitting behind the desk, wearing a sharp charcoal suit which again accentuated his slender form. Squatting awkwardly on his lap was a skinny gray cat with leopard-print markings. It looked like a supermodel cat compared to her fat ginger cat, Muffin. It tolerated the occasional absentminded caress from Hemlock while eyeing the goldfish that swam in circles around a large glass bowl on the desk. The fish seemed to stare miserably out, trapped in its spherical prison.

"Good afternoon, Miss Frost," said Hemlock with a vanilla tone. If he was surprised to see her, he didn't show it. He nodded to the hard steel chair in front of his desk. "Sit."

Rosie perched on the edge of the chair, feeling like a criminal who was about to be interrogated.

"The name Frost was often given to those born in winter. Also to those said to be wicked. Which, I presume, is true of you?"

"Erm . . . well." Rosie wasn't quite sure how to answer. *If in doubt, say nothing. Silence is your shield.*

"Well? Why are you here?"

"Erm . . ." What *had* she planned to say exactly? "I . . . um . . ." Her skin began to sweat under his stare. "Mr. Gripen told me to come to you for school uniforms . . ." she eventually spluttered.

"How foolish of me," Hemlock said, without a hint of sympathy. "I shall ensure someone brings everything necessary to your room."

"Thank you."

"Is that all?"

Rosie's eyes drifted to the oil painting behind Hemlock's head. It depicted two brown birds lying lifeless beside a duck and another half-plucked larger bird she didn't recognize. It was such a sad scene, a massacre of innocence and beauty. Why would anyone want that in their office?

"Art is everything," Hemlock mused, following Rosie's gaze. "Everlasting and perfect. Take this bird, for instance." He nodded at the taxidermied animal on the pedestal. "The poor dodo—its whole life seen as fat, flightless, clueless, and clumsy." He smoothed down his perfectly cut suit as he spoke. "And in a flash, gone, extinct, just because some ridiculous pigs invaded its island. Didn't stand a chance." He continued, "And yet here it is, frozen for the rest of time in all its beauty, revered, and we all feel bad for it.

Interesting how we flawed beings appreciate things so much more once they're gone."

Rosie nodded. *Poor thing.* But there was no beauty in it or the painting. She then looked to a second painting in the room, hanging on the wall to her right. It was huge and depicted Hemlock next to an ugly-looking bird which was almost as tall as he was and the size of an emu, but it had a bright blue head and a crooked beak. Alongside it, Hemlock was standing with his shoulders back, a wide smile on his face. Rosie looked at the Hemlock in the painting, then back at the Hemlock in front of her. Her chest tightened, trapped as she was between the two of them.

"That was done by the artist David Hockney," said Hemlock proudly. "Worth an absolute fortune. His last painting sold for seventeen million . . . He's a family friend."

Rosie turned away from the painting and finally looked Hemlock square in the eyes. "I want my case back . . . please," she said.

"Do you know why you're at this school, Miss Frost?" Hemlock asked, ignoring her question.

"The lawyer said I had to come."

"But why Heverbridge? This isn't some charity for poor, unfortunate orphans. This is a school for the elite; we don't let just anyone through our doors."

"I didn't really ask. Everything happened so quickly after . . ." Rosie stopped.

After my mum died. The words were left unspoken, but they still made Rosie's insides turn to stone.

"That was inconsiderate of me. I am sorry for what happened to your mother," said Hemlock, lowering his head. "I'm sure it must have been very hard for you." He cleared his throat. "But let's get reacquainted," he said with a mild tone, his hands clasped together. "I believe in hard work. You feel better when you work for things . . . not leaning on entitlement. That's how one truly succeeds in life. You are extremely fortunate to have ended up here. I suggest you remember that."

Words Rosie's mum spoke months before popped into her mind: *When the time is right, you'll go to an amazing school, for exceptional students. That's where you belong . . .* Was this the school her mother had meant? Had she planned for Rosie to go here all along?

High above them, a large moth bashed into the highest window again and again, trying to escape. *Stick to the plan, stick to the plan*, thought Rosie.

"I will. I'm very grateful. But please, can I have my case back?" Rosie said again, with as much assertiveness as she could muster.

Hemlock's face hardened. He opened his desk drawer and took out a sharp steel knife. "What case?" he asked, the words clipped and sharp.

Rosie swallowed.

"The one you took from me when I first arrived," she said. "The little red one. The one I must open with Miss Churchill."

Hemlock bared his teeth as he looked at his reflection in the blade. "I don't remember any case."

Rosie felt like she'd been punched in the stomach.

Hemlock gave her a sly grin, then took a shiny green apple from the drawer and started to peel off the skin in one long, twirling loop.

"It was from my mother. She left it to me in her will. It's important."

"I'm sorry, my dear, but I have no idea what you're talking about."

Rosie could feel her blood beginning to boil. "You do know! You took it from me. I need to see Miss Churchill; the lawyer said she knows about it. You stole—"

Hemlock raised his hand and gave Rosie such a stern look that it cut her off mid-sentence.

"Heverbridge is a school where excellence thrives. We do not tolerate delinquents, and we certainly don't tolerate liars. Because that's what you'll be known as. Is that what you want to be? Frost the wicked liar?"

"I'm not lying!"

For a long while neither of them spoke. The only sound was Rosie's breath, which raged out of her nose in furious bursts.

Hemlock dropped the apple peel into the bin and pushed the cat off his lap. The cat responded with a noxious hiss, flicking its tail in disdain before settling down at Hemlock's feet.

"I don't like cats," said Hemlock. "Apart from my little Valenka here. They're vicious creatures, and also proud ones. They have no great love for us humans, yet they tolerate us. Why? Because they know who is in charge, who holds the power. And they know that, ultimately, they need to play by the rules we have set for them."

Hemlock reached for the fishbowl and slid it toward himself. The goldfish sloshed about inside.

"Miss Churchill loves all her animals, even this little *piscis*," he said, his mouth twinging with disgust. "I've never been much of a fan, but I promised to feed him while she is away, and if he's important to Miss Churchill, he is important to me. And he's so well behaved. Little Timmy doesn't want much. But if I do not feed little Timmy, poor little Timmy will die."

He opened a drawer, pulled out a small pot of fish food, and sprinkled a few flakes into the bowl. The fish hungrily darted up and sucked at the flakes.

"There. Now little Timmy is happy, so my power over him is absolute. He needs me." Hemlock interlocked his fingers and rested his elbows on the desk. "But Valenka here must also be fed. Her life is also in my hands." He shrugged, then scooped the goldfish out of the bowl. The fish flapped about, gasping for air, as he held it by its tail and dangled it above the cat. "Those are the rules of life."

Rosie stared at Hemlock in horror. The cat stared intently at the fish.

"As you can see, Miss Frost, we all are captive servants to the rules. Whoever has the power gets to make the rules . . ." He let out a brittle laugh and then threw the goldfish onto the floor.

Valenka pounced and swallowed it whole. Rosie gasped.

"In this school, that would be me. I make the rules and I have the power. You would be wise not to forget it. *Ne t'inquiète pas. Sois une bonne fille; sois une bonne fille.*" He smiled.

Rosie stiffened. He was telling her to be a good girl. Her mum would playfully say things like that to her in French, which was sweet and funny, but when Mr. Hemlock said it, he just sounded like an uptight creep.

I just want my case. Where is Miss Churchill?

"*All* my students at Heverbridge matter to me, though, and I can see your mother's missing case is concerning to you. And what's important to *you* is important to *me.*"

What does he mean, missing? He just denied all knowledge of it. This guy is such a weirdo.

"Just be a good girl, and all will be fine. You might then find something jogs my memory," said Hemlock.

Chapter Nine

SKIDMARK

FRIDAY, DECEMBER 2ND. AFTER SEEING HEMLOCK.

Rosie stumbled down the turret's winding steps, then leaned against the wall in the main corridor. Her legs were like lead, her stomach hollow. Had Hemlock just threatened her? Why would he deny having her mother's case? And why would he take it in the first place? Either way, one thing was clear: she wasn't going to get her case back just by asking for it. It looked like she was going to have to continue in the Falcon Queen games after all. Yes, definitely her new rule . . . *Return all pupils' confiscated belongings!*

She would worry about all of that later. Right now, all Rosie wanted to do was sleep. So much had happened since she'd arrived on this island, and now she could add the weird encounter with Hemlock to the list. She thought again about the conversation she'd overheard before she entered the office. What was it Hemlock had said—that he didn't give a damn about the wildcats, or if they got caught in the way? What could be his aim? She pulled out her phone to google the Isambard Foundation, but their website came up with an UNDER CONSTRUCTION notice. She couldn't find any other online information about the company.

As Rosie headed back to her room, a numbness began to creep through her whole body, and her cheeks went clammy. Her head was pounding. *Oh no, not now.*

The first sign of epistaxis. In familiar terms, a nosebleed. It wasn't dangerous, just one of those things that happened to people. For Rosie, it normally happened when she was tired or stressed. The biggest problem she had with it, though, was the hemophobia. Rosie suffered from an intense fear of blood. She was the complete opposite of a vampire; as soon as she saw a tiny peep of the crimson red, the dizziness took hold and a feeling came over her that she was about to pass out or die.

Blood, oh no . . . The room began to spin. Hot liquid trickled down from the top of her nostrils.

"Is there a toilet nearby?" Rosie asked a passing student, quickly pinching her nose.

Her voice sounded like a Dalek's from *Doctor Who*.

"Sure, there's one right next to the Sovereign Hall. This way."

The girl led Rosie, running, through a maze of twisting corridors and wooden staircases, then stopped outside the girls' toilets.

"Thank you," Rosie said.

Rosie swung the door open into a large green-tiled room, by far the biggest toilet she had ever been in. It looked like something out of a grand 1960s hotel—probably fancy at the time, but now rather gaudy and out-dated. Like the rest of the building, the tiles were adorned with leaf patterns and small animals.

Rosie rushed into one of the toilet cubicles and snatched up some loo roll, then quickly stuffed it up her nose and leaned forward. Another thing her mum had taught her to do during a nosebleed.

Her heart pounded and the room spun. Three large oval mirrors were mounted above equally spaced sinks, which had wide china basins and dusty brass taps. The spouts of the taps, rising up from the sinks like the necks of snooty swans, began to blur. There was a tightness in her chest.

Breathe, breathe. It's just a little one, she told herself. *It will pass.* She closed her eyes, not daring to catch a glimpse of the crimson red. And luckily it *was* just a small one, compared to others she'd had before. She cleaned her nose and face and threw the last of the evidence in the bin, keeping her eyes firmly on something else other than the blood.

Then, standing in front of the nearest sink, she looked at herself in the mirror.

No blood. All gone.

Her heart rate settled. Dizziness subsided. A pale face stared back at her with dark circles under its eyes.

That last day, before she had set off for school, she and her mum had stood side by side in front of the bathroom mirror. They had the same heart-shaped face and cherub lips that looked like they'd been stained with dark cherries. Rosie's rusty-copper hair was wild and tangled, a mayhem of waves around her face.

Her mum had said it was cute and made her look friendly—what she called a "happy mess"—but Rosie wasn't a fan.

But they make fun of me, she'd complained to her mum.

They don't even know you. And that's their issue, not yours. We never know what's going on with someone until we really get to know them, her mum replied, stroking Rosie's ginger waves. *"Don't judge a book by its cover." They shouldn't, and you shouldn't, either.*

Really, Mum?! Those pointless sayings don't help. Rosie pulled away.

Her mum looked at Rosie in the mirror and placed her hands on her shoulders.

Look deeper. There's always more on the inside. Her

eyes were fueled with something Rosie didn't recognize.

That doesn't mean anything. Rosie shrugged, and then left for school.

That was the last thing she had said to her mum.

She splashed water onto her cheeks and retied the escaping strands of her hair into a careless ponytail. As she turned to leave the bathroom, the door opened and two girls walked in, mid-conversation.

Rosie's heart sank. One of them was Ottilie, who had given her such a cruel welcome on her first night at the school.

". . . yeah, but Daddy wants me to be a forensic pathologist," said Ottilie as she squirted anti-bac gel on her hands. "I said to him, 'Eww, Daddy, no. I don't wanna touch *dead* people . . .' And anyway—" She looked at Rosie and stopped. "Oh. It's you. Hi!" Ottilie said, flicking her long hair and twiddling it round her fingers as if the two of them were long-lost siblings.

Rosie clenched her jaw, glaring at her, and said nothing. Ottilie's heavily glossed lips flashed her a sickly grin.

"Oh, Rosie, you're not still cross about the other night, are you?" Ottilie asked with another flick of her shiny hair. "It was just a bit of fun. I knew you'd be able to take it. It was kind of your initiation ceremony. Everyone gets one. Rosie's new here," she explained to her friend. "Rosie, this is Jamila."

"So nice to meet you," said Jamila, not looking up from her phone. She was standing with one hand on her hip. Her pouting lips were painted a bold orange, which stood out strikingly against her dark skin tone.

Ottilie glanced down at the bin and noticed the crimson-stained toilet paper. "That explains Miss Cranky. It's her *moon* time. Poor you," she said. "Let's forget all about the other night and start again, shall we?" Ottilie looked at Rosie pointedly. "Friends?"

Ottilie held out her hand for Rosie to shake. Her nails were perfectly manicured and painted a soft pomegranate pink.

Rosie hesitated. Was this some sort of trap? Another way for Ottilie to humiliate her?

"Come on, I'm not a piranha; I won't bite." Ottilie laughed, as if finding herself hilarious.

"Haaa!" Jamila joined in a few seconds later, a bit behind in the conversation and far louder than the joke warranted.

Rosie took Ottilie's hand and shook it.

"There. Now we're friends," said Ottilie, releasing Rosie's hand. "We're going to have a *lot* of fun together, I can tell."

I don't think so. You're a female dog. That's what Mum would have called you. Rosie gave a weak smile. Her eyes flitted to the bathroom door, and she started to move toward it, but the two girls were blocking her way.

"I have to go . . ." she stammered.

"Of course," said Ottilie. "See you around, Rosie Frost."

Ottilie finally stepped aside, and Rosie walked past, her head lowered. As her hand reached for the handle, there was a scream from behind.

"Ewwww, skidmarks!" Ottilie shrieked from inside one of the toilet cubicles. "Rosie, was that you?"

A burst of heat rushed to Rosie's cheeks. "What? No." She hadn't even used the toilet.

Ottilie stepped out of the cubicle with hands on hips, glaring at Rosie like she was the toilet's law enforcement.

"There's pooey skidmarks all over the inside of that toilet bowl," Ottilie said. "And it *really* stinks."

"Skidmarks are the worst," said Jamila, popping some gum in her mouth. "They make me feel all . . . skiddy."

"It's called a toilet brush," Ottilie said to Rosie. "You should really learn to use one. Hygiene, darling, you know?"

"It wasn't . . . I didn't . . ." said Rosie.

Ottilie burst out laughing, and then so did Jamila. "Jokes, Rosie! Or should we call you *Skidmark*? You are way too easy to wind up."

Rosie looked at the door, her feet feeling suddenly heavy, like blocks of concrete.

"She entered the Falcon Queen games too." Ottilie smirked at Jamila, then looked to Rosie. "The whole point of the Falcon Queen games is to find a *champion*. No offense, darling, but it's really not for the likes of you."

"Nahhh, no skidmarks allowed," said Jamila with an emphatic shake of her head.

"I'm surprised they let spongers even enter," said Ottilie.

Spongers. Rosie now knew what that meant. And it wasn't nice.

"Well done, I heard you actually managed to make it through the Black Lake challenge! Well, *only* just . . ." she said to Jamila, and then turned back to Rosie. "But you must be thrilled. Although, the very last one to make it, poor thing." She applied some lip gloss and smirked. "Don't worry. You'll certainly be cut in the next round. Really, bless you for trying."

Ottilie stopped laughing then, her face suddenly serious and intense. "One last thing before you go, *Skidmark*," she said, her eyes boring into Rosie's. "If you ever tell anyone about what happened the other night, I'll make sure that you regret it."

Back in Rosie's room, there was still no sign of her roommate—they'd barely even spoken since Rosie arrived. Maybe Rosie had been a bit too standoffish? Or actually, was Bina just avoiding her? She needed some time to herself anyway. In the past, Rosie had always loved using down-time to get cozy in her pj's and make up songs, but she hadn't done that in ages. That was in her previous life, before her well of inspiration had dried up and deserted her, along with her mother.

She turned to a blank page in her unicorn notebook and picked up a pencil from her bedside table. Instead of writing a song, she found herself starting a letter.

Dear Mum,

Where are you???!!! How could you just leave me?? I still can't believe you're gone. Are you really dead? I kept hoping it was just a bad dream, that something was going to change, or that Prince Charming was going to swoop in and save me. But that only ever happens in fairy tales, right? Besides who wants a "true love" kiss, while you're sleeping? Ugh, no thanks. Brainless stories for little girls. I know not to believe in those anymore. I thought I saw you at the bottom of the Black Lake today. Was I dreaming? I feel so alone. If you are really dead, haunt me more.

Are you in heaven? Or is that just made up as well, to make us feel less scared?

You told me never to give up—to keep shining bright—but how can I do that here? This place is so strange, filled with scratchy girls (female dogs, you'd call them), mean teachers, and wild animals. It's also haunted.

What made you so sad? Was it me? I'm sorry, Mum, if it was.

Is that why I have been sent here, Mum? I don't fit in. I can't cry. I just need to punch something. I won't, of course. I don't know what to say; I don't know what to feel. And what's so important about that case you gave me—why would a weirdo teacher want to steal it? Why couldn't I just open it?

There's so much that doesn't make sense. I don't know anything . . . except I miss you. Please help. 🍍

Rosie x

P.S. 1. Please don't be annoyed at me. Doreen Yates (I know what you're thinking: "Our worst neighbor!") is now looking after Muffin. I had no choice (and she does like cats).

P.S. 2. I signed up for something called the Falcon Queen games. I got through the first challenge, which was a nightmare.

Chapter Ten

WILDCAT, WILD GIRL

SATURDAY, DECEMBER 3RD. LATE MORNING. THE DAY AFTER THE BLACK LAKE CHALLENGE.

Rosie lay in bed, completely exhausted from yesterday's Falcon Queen challenge. They had been given the morning off because of it. *They normally have school on Saturdays?! Who does that?* She'd spent most of the morning staring at the ceiling or scrolling mindlessly through her phone. She googled "Falcon Queen games." No results. And nothing on the school itself—or even Bloodstone Island—either. How on earth was she going to get through the next challenge, whatever that might be?

Thankfully Bina still seemed to be avoiding her. She was always up and out before Rosie, or asleep when she came back to her room. She'd told Rosie she preferred hanging out in the wrestling room with her teammates, and otherwise spent time in the library. Rosie looked at the poster over Bina's bed with the slogan CAN YOU SMELL WHAT THE ROCK IS COOKING? So she clearly liked The Rock.

Most of the students had gone to the games room, which, according to Charlie, was infamous for its all-day table tennis competitions, or they were reading books and playing board games in the Blue Room. Rosie's plan was to waste a whole day in bed and hide from the world.

Her mother always used to tell her that if she was in a slump, the best thing she could do was go outside in the fresh air and find some nature. There hadn't been much nature to find around the London block where they used to live, unless you counted the weeds that came through the cracks in the courtyard or the mice that sometimes visited the hallways (which her cat, Muffin, would sometimes gift to Rosie). Despite her often-dark moods, Rosie's mum had always found the beauty in the everyday, though. A setting sun, a rainbow, a catchy melody, or just laughing and eating cake.

Rosie got herself up off the bed, threw on her warmest coat, then grabbed a leftover sausage roll from yesterday, wrapped it up, and put it in her pocket.

As she sped through the corridors, head down, she managed to avoid talking to anyone and slipped out through one of the mansion's side doors. She stepped through the archway, the smell of pine trees and cold air hitting her.

Other than the Black Lake challenge, it was the first time she'd been outside since she'd arrived. The winter breeze felt cool and clean on her face. She pulled her hood up over her unruly hair and made her way into one of the school's gardens.

During her first few days, she'd glimpsed a bit of what was outside through the mansion's many windows, as well as when she did the Black Lake challenge—although she'd been very distracted that day—so she had an idea of what to expect. She was still taken aback by just how big the grounds were, though. They seemed to spread as far as she could see in all directions. Should she take the fields down to the wetlands, or go over the bridge into the meadows? She settled on crossing an expansive lawn and made her way into the wooded area opposite. As she got closer, next to the path, she saw a sign in bold red letters:

NO STUDENTS BEYOND THIS POINT.

Rosie peered past the sign . . .

The wind rustled through the dense trees, making their inviting branches swish like they were calling her, the elusive woodland enticing her to enter. What was *beyond* this point? Rosie looked left and right and quickly walked past the sign into the woods.

Once again, as when she'd first arrived, the intensity of the lush vegetation, the unusual plants and trees, filled her senses. She stepped under the twisted branches of a tree with bright copper bark, then past a bush with tiny heart-shaped flowers. Spiky vines hung from the tallest trees and blood-red moss covered their giant trunks. The path she was following was lined with mottled lilies and ink-black hollyhocks. Although Rosie didn't know much about plants, she imagined these were the kind of flowers that you'd only see in hot, exotic places, or at the very least in summertime here. She touched their silky petals, and her fingers came away damp and slightly sticky. It was all so strange.

She trundled on, looking up at the trees as she went. There was something . . . different about them. Some of the leaves looked *too* big, and the trunks *too* old, like they belonged to another world or a different time. Despite the fact that it was now winter, most of the trees were still thick with leaves, and wildflowers littered the ground. There were more trees that towered with shimmering crimson bark, plants with stripy leaves the size of coffee tables, and trunks that looped in circles and tied themselves in knots. The flowers were also unlike any Rosie had seen before: some burst through the bushes like bloodshot eyes, while others hung in the air like alien dragonflies. Everything was big and bold. What was this place? It was like something out of a Grimm's fairy tale or *Jurassic Park*.

A small bird zipped toward her out of nowhere, stopping just inches from her face. A hummingbird! Rosie had never seen one before. It was tiny—about the size of her thumb—and had the most electric green feathers. A moment later, it was gone.

Now that she looked more closely, there were all sorts of other unusual animals around her too. Some sort of deer with curly horns was spying on her through the trees, and a giant dragonfly pranced over the crushed leaves that covered the forest floor.

It wasn't long before the woods grew even thicker with vegetation and she had to push her way through the bushes, raising her arms as she went. Strange animal chirrups, whoops, and cries sounded all around her.

She shivered. *That's enough nature for one day*, she thought. She turned around and started to pick her way back toward the mansion, her steps crunching through ferns and the spongy mosses on the forest floor.

Then Rosie stopped. An eerie silence had settled over the woods.

She suddenly had an overwhelming feeling that someone—or some*thing*—was watching her. Was it that deer again? She peered into the dense trees, the leaves shifting suspiciously in the breeze.

"Hello?" she called, a slight tremor in her voice.

Two silver eyes, tinged with flecks of gold, appeared through the shrubs. They stared at her, unblinking. Rosie took a step backward. The eyes then caught the sun and shone like pure mercury. What was this creature? The long grass rustled as it slinked toward her.

"Stay away," said Rosie. Her heart started racing and she took another step back.

The animal emerged from the undergrowth a couple of meters in front of her. It was a large cat, bigger than a domestic cat, its ears upright and alert, with a thick tail, unlike any cat Rosie had seen before. Its tawny fur was covered in thin, parallel tiger stripes and muted black spots.

It's okay. It's just a cat, like Muffin back home. A big one, but still just a cat. Rosie knelt down.

"Hey, puss-puss," she said, holding out her hand. Its ears pricked up, and it hissed, snarling with sharp teeth.

Rosie flinched and jumped back. Then it arched its back, fur standing on end.

Actually, it was more than just a cat; it was a wildcat.

"I won't hurt you. I get it, you're just scared. I know what that feels like," she said. "Are you hungry? Here." She pulled the sausage roll from her pocket and threw a piece of it on the ground near the wildcat.

The animal poked the meat with its little pink nose and then gobbled it down in three greedy bites.

"Wow, you *were* hungry," said Rosie. The wildcat looked at her with its bright mercury eyes, as if pleading for more. She ripped off other pieces and threw them on the ground, but closer to herself each time. Slowly it crept toward her, eating each one.

"You want some more?" She threw it the last piece. "That's all I got. Sorry."

The cat moved closer, then sniffed her fingers and mewed, its piercing silver eyes fixed on Rosie. She had the sudden impression that this wildcat was trying to tell her something.

"What do you want, hey?" Rosie asked.

The cat licked its nose with its little pink tongue, then stepped closer still.

"I used to have a cat."

Did wildcats purr?

"You wanna be friends?" Rosie said, resisting the urge to stroke it.

The wildcat twitched its ears in response.

"That's all I've got, Mercury, I promise." With those silver eyes, "Mercury" seemed like an appropriate name for the cat.

Mercury tentatively rubbed his head against Rosie's calf, as if thanking her for the food. She stayed completely still.

"I won't hurt you, I promise," she whispered, slowly reaching her hand out to stroke him.

The cat looked at her with suspicion.

A cat purring was her old life . . . her old life. If only she could have it back. He really was the most beautiful creature; his glossy coat shimmered orange, brown, and bronze, and his piercing eyes were full of intelligence.

Well, I don't give a damn about the wildcats, or anything else on this island . . . Hemlock's words echoed through Rosie's head. Would he really allow these special creatures to be harmed? What "venture" might they get caught in the middle of?

Mercury walked off, then suddenly became a stealthy predator, slowly prowling, ready to pounce, before nosing something down on the ground. What was it? Rosie looked closer and saw it was white, with the light that trickled in through the canopy above reflecting off it. She bent down and picked it up. It was a plastic key card like the ones used to open security doors in important buildings. In one corner was a large *I* inside two interlocking circles. Beneath that were the words

PROFESSOR J. ISAMBARD

THE ISAMBARD FOUNDATION

The company Hemlock had mentioned! And now a wildcat had led her to this key card with that very name on it. It was all too much to be a coincidence, surely.

Without really knowing why, Rosie picked up the key card and slipped it into her pocket.

Mercury knocked his head into Rosie's shin and meowed. He then walked away, looking back over his shoulder as if waiting for Rosie to follow.

She really should be getting back, but Mercury meowed again, louder this time.

Rosie made her decision and followed the wildcat deeper into the forest.

After half an hour of Rosie's scrambling through thick vines and twisted roots, the forest started to thin, and then the trees gave way altogether. From where she stood at the top of a steep hill, Rosie had an incredible view of the island spread out before her.

It was amazing . . . She couldn't believe they were so near England. Everything was luscious and full of life, bursting with every shade of green imaginable. To the east, a large herd of white ponies with gray-taupe manes grazed in the wetlands; to the north, what looked like a huge volcano sat nestled in a snow-tipped cluster of mountains. The sky was full of birds—albatrosses, pelicans, and plenty more whose names Rosie didn't know. A flock of red geese passed over her head in an arrow formation, honking as they went.

Mercury meowed, drawing Rosie's focus to the valley in front of her. A small stream led all the way down to a dense wooded area at the bottom of it. In stark contrast to the rest of the island, the woods there were completely enclosed by a high metal wall. Painted at various points along it—stark white against the dark gray of the metal— was the letter *I* inside two interlocking circles, the same logo as on the key card she'd found. Looking down on the compound from above, Rosie could also make out a square metal building inside it, tucked away between the trees. What was going on in there?

"Is this what you wanted me to see?" she asked Mercury.

The wildcat meowed. Something about this place didn't feel right.

I wonder where the entry door is.

She looked at the key card again and then scanned the high metal walls. "Let's go take a look, Mercury," she said.

The wildcat meowed once more and set off toward the enclosed area. Rosie was about to follow when she suddenly heard someone behind her.

"Hey."

She quickly shoved the key card into her pocket and turned around.

He was leaning against a tree, like he was some kind of rock star. Rosie recognized him at once: it was Jackson Sterling, the boy who had crossed the lake first in the challenge yesterday. He was about Rosie's age and *yes*, he was hot, with warm brown eyes and light brown skin. His slouchy jeans and Abercrombie jumper weren't exactly for outdoors, but they made him look cool, in a boy band–swagger kind of way.

A burst of heat shot to Rosie's cheeks.

She was suddenly aware of how sweaty she was, and how much dirt was under her fingernails.

"Wild girl all alone?"

"Er." Rosie looked down the slope. Mercury had disappeared.

"You shouldn't be here, you know," said the boy.

"Nor should you."

Both were clearly breaking school rules being there. "So what are you doin' out here, then?" he asked.

Rosie shrugged. *Remember, silence is the best defense.* She shuffled her feet awkwardly, adjusting her hood tighter around her face.

But the pause felt too uncomfortable. She cleared her throat.

"Just taking in the view. I only got to the island a few days ago. What are *you* doing here?" asked Rosie.

"Like you, gettin' away from everything. Inspiration, for my lyrics." He curled up some paper and put it in his back jeans pocket.

"Oh," was all Rosie could think to reply.

" 'I am so clever that sometimes I don't understand a single word of what I am saying,' " the boy said with a shrug.

"What?"

"I'm just kidding. It's an Oscar Wilde quote."

"Of course," said Rosie. Although she knew who Oscar

Wilde was, she'd never met anyone who'd quoted him before.

"I'm Jackson. What's your name, wild girl?"

"Rosie." She gave a small smile, being careful not to show her braces, and her cheeks flushed again. Why was she feeling this awkward?

"I'd be careful wandering this far from the estate, though, if I were you," said Jackson. "There are more dangerous predators on this island than they let on."

Predators, thought Rosie, *like the deputy head*. She glanced back at the enclosed area at the bottom of the valley.

"What's in there?" she asked, pointing at the metal walls.

"That's Wildcat Woods," said Jackson, "where the wildcats live."

"Why is it fenced off?" Rosie asked, hoping he might be able to explain what was going on here, make this island less of a mystery.

"There's an environmental company that's come over to do research on the wildcats, I think. It must be something to do with them." Jackson shrugged.

"The Isambard Foundation?" Rosie asked, realizing too late maybe she wasn't supposed to know that information.

Jackson shrugged again. "I don't know what they're called. Could be." He stretched his arms wide and yawned. "Wanna head back?"

"No, I'm fine. Thanks." Rosie frowned.

"I wouldn't stay here by yourself. Like I said, there're predators." Jackson's eyes looked dead serious. Rosie sighed, then reluctantly followed Jackson back through the forest, toward the school. For a long while, they trekked through the dense woodland, pushing through saplings, under canopies of trees . . . both saying nothing. The air was crisp; just their breathing and crunching footsteps filled the easy silence between them.

"See you around, Rosie," said Jackson as they reached the main building.

"Okay, bye," said Rosie. She stopped, waiting for him to go, and then glanced back in the direction of the woods. Something very strange was going on. Whatever it was, Hemlock was definitely not working on a project to help conserve the wildcats, of that she was sure.

As she crossed the lawn, a large white bird with gold-tipped wings swooped above her, before soaring high into the sky again. Rosie watched it circle a couple of times and then went inside.

Chapter Eleven

. . . WHO IS SHE?

Once back in her room, Rosie dumped her outdoor clothes in a pile on the floor, took out her phone, and googled "*Felis silvestris.*" It came up with pictures of wildcats, exactly like Mercury, the one she'd just seen.

She then looked up the Isambard Foundation again, but their website still came up as under construction, so Rosie tried "Professor J. Isambard" instead. Most of the articles were about a famous engineer called Isambard Brunel—not useful. There was a Miss Isambard who worked as a primary school teacher in Ohio, and another who sold homemade chutneys out of her garden shed. Rosie kept scrolling. Then she found it: an article about a woman called Professor Jane Isambard, who worked as a conservationist and animal rights activist, specializing in the breeding patterns of endangered animals. She had to be the one. The article spoke about her past work and achievements, describing her as one of the most influential people in her field. At the bottom there was a photo of her in which she was looking straight at the camera through a pair of thin-rimmed glasses. She had a kind smile and was wearing a pretty blouse with a slim-fitted skirt. Her glossy brown hair turned up at the edges. She had the "Miss Honey from *Matilda*" vibe. Beneath the photo, a quote from her read, *We are just tenants on this planet. The world is our back garden, and it's up to us to look after it.*

If Professor Isambard was such a great environmentalist, why would she be working with Hemlock?

When Rosie had confronted Hemlock about her case, he'd made it cruelly clear that he was in charge while Miss Churchill was away, and he would not stand for any trouble. And as far as Rosie could gather, Miss Churchill wouldn't be back until the Bloodstone Banquet.

With Churchill away, we can do whatever we like.

Hemlock was obviously using Miss Churchill's absence to plot something bad. Rosie paced her bedroom and sighed heavily in frustration. If she did say something, who would believe a friendless new girl like her?

Dear Mum,

I met a wildcat today. Pretty cute. I think Hemlock is up
to something shady that could hurt them, though. There's this
compound here in the woods, which looks weird. I also met this
boy called Jackson. Loves himself a bit. He's one of those ones
you warned me about, I can tell.

He'd be great material for one of my songs—I'd call it "Hot
but KNOWS IT." But I can't write, not without you by my side.
It doesn't feel right. I wish we could have one of our special
days: write, sing, bake. Pineapple upside-down cake? That would
have cheered you up, I know it.

I saw a big white bird, swooping down from the sky. It's
a falcon. I googled it. I had this strange thought—that it was
you, protecting me, watching over me . . . I know that sounds
silly, but I can't help it. Is that you? It feels like everywhere I
go, I'm lost. I'm scared. But that ghost queen said rule one is
have courage . . . so . . .

Okay, going to get a bite to eat; I'm starving.

Rosie x

P.S. I miss your hugs.
XXXX 🍍

Chapter Twelve

SMELLY AND AGGRESSIVE

SATURDAY, DECEMBER 3RD. AROUND 5:00 P.M.

THE DAY AFTER THE BLACK LAKE CHALLENGE.

I t was teatime and Rosie's stomach grumbled. She was ravenous after her long walk in the woods and had barely eaten all day. She made her way to the Sovereign Hall and sat on her own in the vast room, the thousands of stone birds on the high ceiling looming above her. Her bones still felt cold from her plunge in the icy lake yesterday too. She hadn't seen Charlie since just after the games and wondered if he was recovering okay. All around, groups of friends laughed and joked, while Rosie just absently poked at her shepherd's pie with her fork and made the peas roll around her plate.

The bench opposite her was dragged back with a screech, and then someone placed themselves very deliberately on top of it. Rosie looked up to find Ottilie beaming at her from across the table. Jamila, who had been with her in the bathroom, sat on one side of her, and a suave-looking boy who Rosie had heard was called Ishaan sat on the other.

"Rosie, hi!" Ottilie said with sugared enthusiasm. "Have you been preparing yourself to lose the next challenge?" She said this with condescending glee. "You don't seem to be athletic, exactly, so well done for getting this far. I bet you're exhausted."

Rosie glanced around her, rolling her eyes. She placed her knife and fork together on her plate. If there was one person she wasn't in the mood for, it was Ottilie Aragon-Windsor.

Just get up and walk away; dinner is over.

No, why should she?

Just say nothing.

"Ooh, do I detect a hint of hostility, Rosie? I'm only trying to be nice. The least you can do is be nice back. Right, guys?"

Jamila shook her head from side to side, then clicked her tongue, while Ishaan touched up his quiff with a delicate hand.

"So I heard the teachers say your real name is Rosemary," Ottilie went on. "That's so cute. Like something you'd stick up a chicken's bum at Christmas!" Ottilie laughed, and Jamila and Ishaan dutifully joined in.

Rosie gripped the sides of her chair and gritted her teeth.

"Oh, don't look so fierce, Rosie, I was only teasing," said Ottilie. "It's better than *Skidmark*, isn't it?"

"Yeah, you should learn how to take a joke, girl," said Ishaan. "Especially when they're funny." He glanced admiringly at Ottilie.

"I don't like skidmarks, and I don't trust people who leave them," said Jamila, a bit behind in the conversation.

Rosie sat there and still didn't reply. She knew if she did, Ottilie would twist whatever she said against her.

"Look, I brought you some pudding. Maybe that will cheer you up," said Ottilie, sliding a bowl of jam roly-poly across the table toward Rosie.

Rosie eyed the dessert, picked up a spoon, then stopped.

"Don't worry, I haven't poisoned it," said Ottilie, as if reading Rosie's mind.

Vanilla sponge was one of Rosie's favorites, and it did smell good.

Maybe just a bite . . . like a peace offering, a reset.

Rosie looked at Ottilie, who nodded.

Was this a peaceful statement between them? She certainly didn't want to provoke her.

Perhaps if she ate some, Ottilie would finally go away. *Maybe she'll even be nice if I take a bite? Just a bite . . .*

She casually dug into the soft pudding. It oozed with strawberry jam and didn't look like there was anything nasty hidden in it. She took a small scoop and slowly put it in her mouth, the sweet sponge melting on her tongue.

"Couldn't resist, could you, *Roly-poly!*" said Ottilie, shaking her head. Rosie swallowed. *What did she just call me?*

"It's okay, some of us are just built differently than others," Ottilie said, looking down at Rosie's tummy.

Rosie instinctively sucked in her stomach.

"You need to get some more willpower, darling." Ottilie smirked. "I'd have thought you of all people would be sticking to salads, nothing fatty."

Rosie stopped chewing.

"Although a little extra padding helped her in the cold lake." She smirked at Ishaan.

Rosie plopped the spoon back in the bowl. She wanted to spit out the mouthful of pudding but forced it down. It was now hard and clumpy.

I would love to wipe that smug smile off your face, Rosie thought.

"Oh, Rosie." Ottilie leaned in and lowered her voice, like she was revealing a secret. "I couldn't help noticing that you're sitting by yourself. Again." Ishaan snickered and Jamila kissed her teeth. "Can I be honest—girl to girl? You really need to take better care of your personal hygiene. Everyone's talking about it. You're never going to get any real friends with BO that bad." She tilted her head and gave a pitying pout. "I thought it best to tell you to your face. I guess your mum hasn't taught you about deodorant yet."

Rosie slammed her hand down on the table. "Don't you dare talk about my mum!" she blurted out.

"Oooh, someone's hit a nerve," said Ishaan.

"Smelly *and* aggressive. Not a good look, babe," said Jamila.

Rosie tried to control her breathing, which was still storming out of her nostrils.

Ottilie leaned back and swept her immaculate hair off her shoulders. "Rosie, darling, there's something you should know. I'm an Aragon-Windsor; I can talk about anyone I want, however I want, including you and your stupid mum."

Rosie stood up, fists clenched.

"Hey, what's up?" A gentle hand landed on her shoulder. Charlie. Kind, considerate Charlie.

"Nothing," Rosie replied. "I was just leaving."

"Thank goodness your boyfriend turned up in time. Another sponger," said Ottilie, picking a speck of dust off her jacket sleeve. That word again: "sponger." "The two spongers, sponging together. I suppose you *spongers* have to stick together, sponging your way through the games."

"What did you call us?" Rosie asked. Heat poured through her veins, waking up the sleeping monster within her.

"Let's go," said Charlie, steering Rosie away.

"No, I wanna know what she meant," said Rosie, knowing full well what "sponger" meant.

"Oh, come on, everyone knows you're both charity cases," said Ottilie. "Neither of you deserves to be here. What shall we call you? *No* hope and *no* chance. Come on, you have no chance of winning in the games. Have some dignity and give up now. Spongers were born losers, and that's all you'll ever be."

"The queen has spoken!" declared Ishaan.

That was it. *Ottilie, you are gonna pay.*

Rosie trembled, hot rage shooting through her as she grabbed a fistful of her shepherd's pie and threw it at Ottilie Aragon-Windsor's face. It hit with a satisfying *thwack*, the soggier parts rebounding and spattering Jamila and Ishaan. Jamila screamed. Ishaan raised his hands to protect his quiff, a look of horror on his face. Ottilie froze, her gaze fixed on Rosie as mashed potato dripped from her nose and congealed meat juice soaked into her hair.

The Sovereign Hall went silent with fear and trepidation. Everyone stared, and Rosie's hands were shaking. Had she really just done that? To the immaculate Ottilie Aragon-Windsor?

Brown sludge dripped down Ottilie's once-pristine

uniform. She sneered at Rosie, like a tiger about to devour its prey, then pounced across the table. Rosie raised her hands to defend herself as Charlie grabbed Ottilie around the waist and tried to pull her back. All at once, they were a mess of wild limbs, scratching nails, and smushed shepherd's pie.

"FIGHT! FIGHT! FIGHT!" the other pupils cheered.

"What is the meaning of this?" A searing voice tore through Ottilie's screeches.

Everyone stopped.

Mr. Hemlock stood over them with a thunderous frown.

"She, she . . . that girl is wild!" said Ottilie, pointing at Rosie. "She threw shepherd's pie at me!" she whined. "How dare she degrade me!"

"All three of you. My office. Now," said Hemlock.

"But, but . . ." Ottilie looked back at Jamila and Ishaan for support, but they were too busy worrying about their own appearances.

Rosie sniggered. Yep, she was in big trouble, but watching Ottilie lose it might just have made it all worth it.

Twenty minutes later she was standing with Charlie and Ottilie in Hemlock's prison-like turret office, staring at the empty bowl where Timmy the fish used to live. She'd already scanned the room for her case, but there was no sign of it. Valenka the skinny cat purred aggressively at Hemlock's feet. The Hockney painting of Hemlock and the giant bird loomed over them.

"Explain," said Hemlock.

"She started it; *she* incited violence!" said Ottilie, her hair still crusty and colored with streaks of brown.

"Well, *she* was bang out of order," said Charlie.

"She ought to be kicked out of the school. It was all her fault," snapped back Ottilie.

Rosie said nothing. *Silence; always fall back on that.*

Hemlock held up his hand. "One at a time. Charlie, you first."

Ottilie and Charlie told their version of events—with lots of tuts and scoffs from Ottilie when Charlie spoke—and then Hemlock ordered them into silence once again.

Rosie still said nothing.

"I can see I am not going to get a true picture of precisely what happened," he said, "so I have no choice but to punish all three of you."

"But that's not fair," whined Ottilie.

"Charlie had nothing to do with it," declared Rosie.

"Silence." Hemlock eyeballed all three of them. He folded his arms and there was a heavy silence as Hemlock patted his finger to his lips, pondering.

"The Gutter Club." He spat the words out. "Perfect, that's where you shall go. Have you heard about it?"

They all shook their heads.

"Well, it's Ms. Parr's early-morning conservation group. She has asked me to find her some victims, I mean *volunteers*." He smirked. "I can't think of anything worse, personally. All three of you will report to her at the Ivy Dome every day of the week promptly at six thirty a.m., starting tomorrow. And Ms. Parr will probably need you for the rest of the term. So consider yourself volunteered for the Gutter Club until further notice."

"But—" Ottilie began.

"Please, Miss Aragon-Windsor," said Hemlock, "finish that sentence and give me a reason to extend your punishment to the rest of the year."

Ottilie closed her mouth and screwed up her face. It looked like she was chewing a wasp.

"I had half a mind to dismiss you all from the Falcon Queen games."

That would be a relief, thought Rosie. *Oh God—no.* She had to push on with it, as a way to get her mum's case back and speak with Miss Churchill.

"But you can consider yourselves lucky," said Hemlock. He gave a dismissive wave of his hand. "You may leave."

Ottilie stormed out, closely followed by Charlie.

"Miss Frost," Hemlock called after her as she was about to step through the door. Rosie turned to face him. "One more thing. We have standards at this school, and conduct is everything. You have not had a good start to your time at Heverbridge. I don't care who you are or how you got your place here, you need to control your temper."

What did he mean, *I don't care who you are*? She was just ordinary Rosie from the back end of London. Why on earth *did* she get a scholarship?

At that moment, his phone started buzzing. He held up his hand, commanding her to stay put, then turned his back to her.

"Professor Isambard, how lovely to hear from you! Yes, all is in hand . . ." Despite what he said, Hemlock sighed as if speaking to her was an inconvenience. "I can't really speak now, but I hope you have everything you need in the conservation area too . . . In that case, I'll leave you to your work. Goodbye."

Hemlock hung up the phone and tightened his lips. He was glaring at Rosie.

Rosie blinked, then quickly looked down at the floor, her anger bubbling. She blurted out, "Why are you denying you took my case? It's very important to me. I must talk to Miss Churchill immediately about it."

Hemlock looked at her like an outraged chief of police. Oh no, she shouldn't have spoken up again.

"We've been through this before. I don't remember any case. What you 'must' do is be a good girl, and that *may* help with my recollection of such things. But I do not have to explain myself to you. And if you ever go running to one of your teachers and start telling lies about me, stirring up trouble, it will not go well for you or them. I hold the ultimate authority here to fire whomever I please. Instantly." He tilted his head and frowned. "Oh. I've just had a terrible thought: What would happen to you if you were expelled? Do you have anywhere else to go?"

Rosie froze. Where *would* she go?

Hemlock suddenly softened, composing himself perfectly again. "Grief can make one rage, Rosemary." He sighed. "As your only ally in this school, I suggest you just toe the line, and be sure to keep your nose out of things that don't concern you. Like I said before, *ne t'inquiète pas; sois une bonne fille.* Be a good girl. Have I made myself clear?"

Rosie gave a weak nod.

"Then I think we're done. Close the door on your way out."

Dear Mum,

I did something you wouldn't have been proud of. I can see you frowning at me from wherever you are. You should have heard what Ottilie said, though—she behaves like she's some sort of queen, and she called me fat. Who does she think she is?? It made me so angry, it felt like my rage just took over me.

Besides, "my body, __my__ business!" Right? That's what you told me.

I know I shouldn't have done it, but it felt good at the time. I'm sorry I let you down. 🍍🍍

And then there's Mr. Hemlock, who's a lying creep. I think he's also lying to this woman, Professor Isambard, and is going to do something bad. So that's making me angry too, because I don't know what I should do about it . . . And he wants me to "be a good girl"?????!!!!!!! No way!

He said if I try to talk to anyone, he'll have them fired. And he'll expel me—then where would I go?? Foster care? I don't want new parents. Why am I even here, Mum? Did you choose this place for me? I have no power, no say. It's not fair.

I've been feeling angry a lot since you went away. Maybe at you. I can't help it. But it's tiring being like this all the time. I wish I could feel something else for a change. I miss you. I want my case back, and I don't want to carry on with the games. This place is just irrational, awful. Nothing makes sense. What else can I do? I want YOU back. 🍍🍍🍍

Rosie x

P.S. That ghost queen seems to have gone now, which is good.

Chapter Thirteen

THE LITTLE PURPLE BOOK

SATURDAY, DECEMBER 3RD. EVENING.

THE DAY AFTER THE BLACK LAKE CHALLENGE.

With weary feet, Rosie made her way to her bedroom, then paused outside her door. The sound of terrible singing was coming from inside. That was all she needed—forced small talk with her hardly there roommate.

Rosie had decided that, with Bina, she would follow the golden rule her mum had once told her: when seated next to a passenger you don't know on an airplane, don't engage in any real conversation, otherwise you could get stuck with them talking the entire way. And with a roommate it wasn't just for a flight, but forever (or school forever). Polite but respectful silence, that was the best way.

She opened the door without knocking—it was her room, too, after all.

"I LLLLOOOOOOOOOOOOOOOOOOOOOOVE YOU . . ."

On the far side of the room, with her back to the doorway, Rosie's roommate had her headphones on and was singing some big ballad from the '90s. By the sounds of it, she was making half the words up, or filling gaps with expressive *ooh*s and *aah*s.

For a brief moment, Rosie thought back to the songs she used to sing with her mum—the ones they'd write together, sitting side by side at their old piano with its chipped keys.

No, that's your old life. Rosie shook her head as if to drive away the memory and watched her roommate sort through her dirty laundry. As she did, Bina's knees jiggled to the music, and one of her arms suddenly shot out as though she was a diva onstage.

Rosie closed the door and the girl flinched. She turned and whipped off her headphones, her eyes wide with horror.

"Oh! I didn't know you were there," she said.

Bina was short with plump cheeks and round glasses, and her face was framed with an electric-blue hijab.

She looked at Rosie, then bit her lower lip and cringed. "Sometimes I get a bit carried away . . ."

"It's fine." Rosie shrugged.

"Finally, we can really talk." Bina sighed with relief. "You looked a bit, well, tired when you arrived, so I was giving you space for settling-in time, but now we can start to get to know each other. I promise not to sing *allllll* the time, Rosie, although I sometimes forget when I've got my headphones on." Bina spoke rapid-fire, like a battery-powered rabbit on steroids. "So, ultimate question to decide whether we can be friends . . ."

Oh no. What the hell is she going to ask?

"Who do you prefer: The Rock or 'Stone Cold' Steve Austin?"

"Um . . . ?"

Bina's jaw dropped dramatically. "Oh, Rosie, you have a *lot* to learn. I can teach you all about wrestlers. Lucky you have me to educate you. And, of course, we have to discuss Mariah versus Whitney. The nineties was the golden age of pop music and divas, you know? They don't make songs like that anymore."

With bright eyes, Bina pulled out her phone and pressed a few buttons. A song started playing through a speaker on Bina's desk.

She swayed in time with the music, mouthing the occasional lyric. "Well? What do you think?"

Rosie and her mum had listened to music all the time. They liked really old stuff, like the Beatles, the Bee Gees, and Joni Mitchell.

"I like it," said Rosie, sitting down on her bed. Her eyes felt heavy; all she wanted to do was sleep.

Bina's face fell. "Oh no, I did it again, didn't I?"

"Did what?"

Bina pounced on her speaker and turned down the volume. "Sorry, I'm boring you. I get a bit overexcited sometimes. My mum tells me I need to talk less and listen more. The strongest muscle in the body is the tongue; I'm living proof." Bina sighed. "I was doing so well before; the truth is, I was trying to give you a bit of space before you got 'the full Bina.'"

Rosie smiled gratefully, though. Bina seemed nice.

"I could put on something a bit more chill," Bina offered. "Like Eternal? Or . . . some of East 17's tracks are severely underrated." She already had her phone out and was scanning through options. She then looked up at Rosie's baffled face. "No, no; you're right. We can listen to music another time."

Rosie quickly hid her notebook containing the letters to her mum under her pillow, and at the same time noticed Bina was busy putting a green papier-mâché shell with a prickly spine on her back, which made her look sort of like a homemade crocodile.

She pulled out a headband with some antennae and gave a satisfied "Aha!"

"What's with the outfit?" Rosie asked.

Bina beamed. "*Miracles and Monsters*–themed party. Everyone's going!" she said. "It's an all-evening marathon, looking for the hidden treasure. I've got my lucky dice. Join us, if you like!"

"No thanks, but you look great," said Rosie, without even considering whether she might like to.

"Thanks. I made these myself," Bina said, placing the antennae on her head. "Okay, see you later, then. If you change your mind, we'll be in the games room. I've *so* got to get my detective hat on—tonight we solve the case!"

With her bag of lucky dice clutched firmly in her hand, Bina bounded out of the room.

Solve the case.

"Bina!" Rosie called after her.

Bina's head popped back into the doorway. "Yes?"

"Where's Miss Churchill's office?" Rosie felt a plan brewing.

"Oh, uh, it's up on the third floor of the West Wing, next to the observatory. Why?"

"Just wondered."

"Okay, laters!"

And with that, Bina was gone, leaving Rosie alone with her thoughts once again. *Tonight we solve the case*, Bina had said.

Maybe it's me who needs to get my detective hat on.

The one thing Rosie knew was that she needed to speak to Miss Churchill, urgently. It seemed far too long to wait until she got back for the banquet, and the headmistress was the only person who could do something about the fact that Hemlock had stolen her briefcase. Why was he being so twisted about it? She also had to warn Miss Churchill about the suspicious conversation she'd overheard outside Hemlock's office yesterday. Perhaps she could even ask about Professor Isambard and the Isambard Foundation, and find out how they fit into everything.

There might be something in Miss Churchill's office— some clue—that would reveal where she was now, or how Rosie could get in contact with her.

It was a long shot, but worth a try.

Rosie hadn't been to the observatory before (she didn't even know what an observatory was—something to do with space?), but she knew roughly where it was, so it didn't take long to find. And next to it, just as Bina had said, was a sturdy-looking door with a gold plaque on it reading MISS CHURCHILL—HEADMISTRESS. Should she just go in? Miss Churchill was away, after all.

Rosie chewed on her bottom lip as she eyed the brass doorknob. She stopped.

Think like a detective. Knock first, right? That's the smart thing to do . . . just in case she's in there? Rosie knocked on the door . . . No answer . . . She knocked again. No answer.

Okay, good. She looked left and right: all clear.

She really shouldn't, but . . . her palm was sweaty as

she turned the metal doorknob. She twisted it slowly . . .
It wouldn't turn . . . She shook it slightly. Damn it, it was
locked.

Okay, Detective Frost. What should you do now? She
looked left and right again—still no one around—then
crouched and peered into the lock. Rats, the key was still
in there. (The office was empty, so there must have been
a side door somewhere, which was probably locked from
the outside.) *Think, Detective Rosie, think.*

Rosie reached inside her rucksack and took out a pencil
and paper. She slid the paper under the door, then poked
the pencil through the lock, pushing the key back the other
way; it clunked onto the floor. She then pulled the piece of
paper through the gap under the door. Bingo! It worked! It
had the key on it!

Who knew Doreen, her "criminal neighbor," would be
so useful; once, when Rosie was locked out, Doreen had
shown her how to break into Rosie's own flat.

She turned the key. It was stiff, but with a sharp twist
and clunk, it turned. With one last look down the corridor to check no one was watching, Rosie pushed open the
door and slipped inside.

Miss Churchill's office was nothing like Mr. Hemlock's.
Where his had been pristine and sparse, Miss Churchill's
was bright and full to bursting with books. Thick leather-
bound volumes filled numerous bookcases and spilled out

into piles all over the floor. Yellowing papers, curled at their edges, covered a solid oak desk, the feet of which were carved to look like those of a lion. There were drawers at each end of it, with a large gap in the middle for the leather seat. Plants filled every nook and cranny of the room, spilling down from the tops of the bookcases, clambering over the desk, and squashed together on the windowsills. One particularly intrepid specimen had grown up the entire height of the room and was now inching its way across the ceiling, its vines stretching out toward the light fitting like poisoned veins.

Rosie pushed the door closed and tried to steady her breathing. What was she doing? If anyone found her in here, she would be in serious trouble.

My case. I just want my case back.

Come on, get back to being the detective.

Was there even a possibility Hemlock might actually have put the case in here for safekeeping, waiting for Miss Churchill's return? No, that would be too much luck.

It didn't seem like she'd used this office for a long time; a heavy smell of dust hung in the air, and lots of the plants had wilted leaves and dry soil, as if they hadn't been watered in a while.

Rosie wandered over to the far wall. It was covered in framed photographs and certificates. The pictures all featured the same woman, who Rosie presumed must be Miss

Churchill. Even though Charlie had described her as a crinkly, she was still a lot older than Rosie had imagined—maybe as old as eighty.

There were some black-and-white photos showing her as a young woman too, though. Each picture was taken in a different location, all over the world. In one, Miss Churchill was in the depths of a rain forest, next to a voluminous orangutan; in another, she was alone in the desert plains, surrounded by curious meerkats. A third showed her on the edge of an active volcano, admiring some sort of giant lizard. In every photo, she had the same sort of vibe as the old man John Hammond in the movie *Jurassic Park*, and she always had the same glint in her eye: awe at her surroundings and the wonder of the planet.

But if she was off on another adventure to places as remote as these pictures implied, it would probably make her very difficult to contact.

The books on the shelves all had similarly complex titles: *The Economics of Ecosystem, On the Origin of Species* . . . After a while, the words started to jumble together for Rosie.

Next, Rosie crossed over to the desk and scanned the scattered papers that covered it, being careful not to disturb anything. The pages were printouts of various documents and journals, with titles such as *Precious Minerals* and *Biodiversity Conservation*. The margins were filled with notes, written in a sprawling, spidery handwriting, most of which Rosie either couldn't read or didn't understand. She searched for an address or a contact number, anything that might hint at Miss Churchill's current whereabouts. There was nothing of real interest, except for a photo of another orangutan hugging its baby and a large map of Borneo with the words *Act now! Stop deforestation!* scrawled across it.

Rosie was about to move on when she spotted a familiar face in one of the framed photos. Standing next to an elderly Miss Churchill, with one arm around her shoulder, was a woman dressed in a pretty blouse and skirt, with glasses and brown hair turned up at the edges. The woman with the Miss Honey vibe from the Isambard Foundation—Professor Jane Isambard! So she and Miss Churchill were friends. The photo had been taken outdoors, but there were no clues as to where, or how the two women knew each other.

Beside the photo was a strange-looking plant: yellow with large flowers like trumpets. The smell around it was sweet and light. Next to this sat a metal watering can, half-filled with water. Rosie didn't care much for gardening, but it seemed a shame for all the plants to die just because Miss Churchill wasn't here to water them. If she was caught, perhaps she could even pretend that was why she'd come. She picked up the can and began to water the strange-looking flowers. The water trickled from the old watering can slowly into the thirsty soil. Rosie sighed with impatience, glancing around the room, then something red on top of the towering box shelf caught her eye. She could only see the corner of it, but it was a burnt-red leather . . . her case?! Excitement and relief washed over her. She'd found it!

Rosie climbed onto a footstool and stood on tiptoes, stretching her arms up, but her fingers only just touched the middle shelves. Instead, she placed one foot on the shelf as well as one on the desk, and then pulled herself onto the old wooden slats. Using the shelf like a ladder, she gradually pulled herself higher and higher up, until she could just about reach the red leather corner . . . Her fingers closed around it and she tugged, loosening it from the books around it. Yes! The red object came loose, surging toward her, but the shelf began to wobble. *Oh no; no!* Rosie quickly grabbed on to the old bookshelf tightly. This only made it worse as she put more weight on it, and the brackets holding it to the wall started to come loose. The towering shelf creaked, leaning more toward her as it came farther away from the wall. Rosie still desperately clung on, even when the red leather object smacked her on the head and crashed to the floor. It felt like a slow-motion movie scene as the shelf, along with Rosie and a mountain of books, tumbled to the floor.

"Ow . . ." Rosie lay in a heap covered in dusty old books. She groaned, and then saw the red leather "case" right next to her on the floor. It was, in fact, a large red leather-bound textbook on poisonous plants.

Luckily, the shelf had fallen over the stool and desk, which had stopped it from smashing over Rosie's head. But it was still covering her like a cage. She tried to heave it upward, but it wouldn't budge. Damn it, she was trapped in a hovel of old books. That would teach her for trying to play detective. So much for finding the case *or* Miss Churchill's contact details.

She needed to get out of here, fast. If she were caught in this mess, she would definitely be expelled. Perhaps if she moved enough of the books away from her, pushing them through the mound, she'd be able to crawl her way out. As she started to push volumes away, one of them caught her attention: a small book poking out from under the heavy dictionaries. As well as being a lot smaller than all the other books, it had a purple spine and gold edges. In fact, it looked an awful lot like . . .

It couldn't be, could it?

Her heart beating fast, Rosie stretched her fingers toward the book and eased it out of its space. She blew the dust off the old cover.

"What the . . . ?" she gasped.

On the front, there was a crest featuring a mighty falcon in golden ink. There was no mistaking it—this was the same book that the ghost of Anne Boleyn had tried to give her. And now here it was in Miss Churchill's office! What on earth did that mean?

This is for you. Take it . . . Anne Boleyn's words echoed in her mind.

Eooorrrrr. The heavy office door opened, and Rosie quickly slipped the book into the pocket of her hoodie.

"What the?!" a voice gasped.

Rosie glimpsed familiar sandy hair.

"What the hell are you doing?" said Charlie, peering down at her through the slats.

"Watering the plants?" Rosie shrugged. "So what are *you* doing here?"

"Bina said you were asking about Miss Churchill's office, and I thought I'd come find you, in case . . ." he replied. With an almighty push, he heaved the large bookshelf back up against the wall as though it weighed nothing at all, freeing Rosie.

Charlie is *strong.*

"Protein shakes and burgers." He grinned.

There was a slight pause as Rosie stood up and brushed herself down, and then she said, "Sorry for getting you in trouble with Hemlock."

"Don't worry about it. That Ottilie's a right cow. She's got the 'Aragon chip on the shoulder.'"

"What do you mean?" Rosie frowned.

"This school accepts all the descendants of the important

Tudor families. But it was originally started from the Boleyn heritage, Queen Elizabeth's mum."

Yeah, she knew that.

Charlie continued, "Ottilie's family's ancestors are Aragons—who despised the Boleyns. But it's a good school, kind of the best, actually, so she had to come. Even though it was centuries ago, Ottilie hates the fact she goes to a school that was built by her family's 'frenemies.' So that's why she always wants to be top dog, 'to honor her family's heritage' and prove they're better."

"Sounds like a lot of pressure," Rosie said. *Who cares where you're from or what your name is?*

"It's the Aragon pride. That's why she's so 'me me me me.' She deserved a pieing, to bring her back down a peg or two," he said as he started to put some of the books back on the shelf. "Anyway, I don't mind about all the trouble. You got *me* out of trouble in that lake. It would've been really bad if I hadn't made it through the first round."

"Why? To make a new rule?"

Does he want extra dessert that badly?

"I'm a sponger like you, remember. I've got to do well here. I've gotta prove myself. Even my dad doesn't quite believe I got in. He says, 'You're gonna get kicked out any minute, son.' He doesn't believe in me. It's like I don't belong here."

She knew how that felt, to not belong. It was horrible.

Who's my dad? Why's it only just us? she'd asked her mum one time, years ago.

We're fine with just us. It's better this way, her mum had said, then turned up the TV.

But Rosie always wondered; the not-knowing left her feeling frustrated, different from everyone. Although one thing her mum did was believe in her.

"I'm sorry," said Rosie, handing Charlie a book to place back on the shelf.

Charlie shrugged. "So, um, I guess that's why I really came to find you here. To say thanks. With everything that happened afterward, I didn't really get a chance to say it properly. Thanks, Frosty. I'm not used to girls saving me. But I guess I'll have to get used to it. And it's all right, 'cause it's you."

"Uh, you're welcome, I think," said Rosie.

She climbed over the mountains of dictionaries and joined him in putting all the books back on the shelf.

"So what are you doing here, anyway? I'm not stupid, you know. You weren't here to water the plants. We're mates now; tell the truth."

Rosie stopped and walked around the desk. "Call it research." She turned the framed photo of Professor Isambard toward him. "Do you know who this is?"

"Yeah, she's that nice conservation woman, loves

animals. She comes by school now and then. She's friends with Churchill, I think. Why?"

"Can you keep a secret?"

"Of course."

Rosie looked at Charlie. She had to confide in someone, and Charlie was her best option right now.

"I think something's going on with Mr. Hemlock. He's doing something behind her back, and Miss Churchill's." She told him about the conversation she'd overheard outside Hemlock's office, and about the metal wall she'd seen around Wildcat Woods, the supposed "conservation" area.

"So you think the wildcats could get hurt? Become victims of whatever it is he's planning?" Charlie had paused midway in putting one of the books on the shelf.

"I don't know what to think," Rosie said with a shrug, "but something bad is going on inside those walls, and Hemlock is behind it."

Charlie picked up more books and then turned to Rosie. "This Isambard Foundation you mentioned—how do they fit into it all?"

Rosie still wasn't completely sure, but she had some ideas. "They're here to monitor the wildcats, I think. That's what Jackson said. I googled the company, but their website's under construction, so it's hard to know for sure. Hemlock said something about *using* them, so my guess is that he's invited Professor Isambard here as like a smoke screen, to hide whatever it is he's really up to."

"Wow, quite the conspiracy you've brewed up," said Charlie.

"You don't believe me, do you?" Rosie looked down at the mess on the floor. She never should have told him.

"Of course I believe you. The question is, what should we do about it?"

Rosie smiled. It felt good to have someone back her up. To believe her no matter what. Just like her mum. Not that Charlie was like her mum, of course. But still, it felt nice. "I've thought about going to a teacher, but Hemlock's smart. He'd deny everything and cover his tracks."

"So you need clear proof," said Charlie, reaching down to grab a massive dictionary. "How are you gonna get that?"

"Dunno." Rosie shrugged, putting another book on the shelf. Suddenly there was a rattling of the door handle.

"This bloody door!!" said a flustered voice from the corridor outside.

Rosie and Charlie froze. "What the?!" mouthed Charlie.

"This bloody key! Why won't you open?!" the familiar voice demanded as he forced the key in the wrong direction. It was obvious who this was. There was a scuffling sound as he shook the handle. Then the office door made the same familiar clunk.

The door opened. "She left it open? The incompetence." He sighed.

Mr. Hemlock came through as the door opened, stroking a white rabbit with black circles around its eyes. "Don't make me chase you again! You could end up in the chef's stew. Being cute won't save you from him! You're lucky I like you." It was Ada, Miss Churchill's house rabbit.

"What on earth is going on!?" he shouted, scanning the explosion of books on the floor. "Aww, for God's sake."

Ada, who was still dangling from his arms, suddenly kicked out and scratched him. Little brown pellets dropped onto his pristine, shiny cream shoes as the rabbit jumped down and promptly ran under the desk.

Charlie froze.

"What the hell are you doing here? Aren't you in enough trouble? Now vandalizing an office, Miss Churchill's, no less!"

"Er, well . . ." Charlie grimaced, his eyes darting around.

Out the corner of his eye, he glimpsed Rosie's shoe. She was hiding under the wide oak desk, along with the rabbit. Rosie held her breath and stroked the trembling Ada.

Hemlock came farther into the room.

"I was watering the plants, and then the shelf collapsed . . ." Charlie picked up the watering can and leaned closer to the yellow trumpet flowers.

Hemlock paused and stared at Charlie suspiciously, then scanned the room. "Who on earth asked you to water the plants?"

"Er . . . I was told by . . . erm, Ms. Parr? You know, with the Gutter Club? You'd sent us to her . . . I started early."

Hemlock looked at the empty can and the wet soil, which seemed to indicate Charlie was telling the truth.

"That woman is a bloody nightmare. Miss Churchill asked *me* to do it, not Ms. Parr. I suppose it was Parr who left the door open. *I* look after all things important to Miss Churchill, including her silly bunnies such as Ada here, who has chewed through my computer wires because Miss Churchill insists on them roaming free around the building. Where has that damn rodent gone?" Ada was now right by Rosie's shoes, nibbling at her laces. Hemlock started to approach the desk.

"Well, yeah, she said Miss Churchill had asked her to check as well, just in case." Charlie was babbling, quickly trying to think of something believable. He moved slightly to the left to cover any view of Rosie. "I suppose 'cause she knew you'd have far more important things to deal with than plants and rabbits, being in charge of everything. I'm sorry if I made a mistake."

Hemlock's face softened. He then turned sharply and was about to reach down to pick up Ada from under the desk when Charlie intervened.

"Be careful," he said, grabbing Hemlock and swerving him in the other direction, away from the desk. "Sir, the shelf could fall again, on you. It nearly killed me. I was pretty lucky."

Rosie then quickly pushed Ada out from under the desk toward Charlie, who picked her up.

"Well, you can leave it all to me. I'll clean up everything." He stroked Ada. "And I can take her back to Ms. Parr."

Hemlock looked at Ada, then at Charlie. Was he up to the task?

"Very well, and that bunny is fortunate, poor little thing. She could be lapin à la cocotte if the chef gets hold of her," he said, and then walked out the door.

Rosie waited for a bit, making sure it was now safe, and then crawled out from under the desk.

"What is he up to? Why would he be coming in here with the rabbit?"

"Something weird, that's for sure," said Charlie, putting Ada down and starting to restack the books. "We need to go."

Once the last book was back in place, Charlie and Rosie bolted out of the office with Ada, closing the door firmly behind them. On the way back to their rooms, Rosie also told Charlie about Hemlock taking her case, and how he had then denied ever having it.

"All sounds very suspicious. He's definitely a creep, and that's well out of order," said Charlie. "But we need to find some proof against him. I wonder what's gonna be the next Falcon Queen challenge. See ya tomorrow." He winked and walked off in the direction of the boys' rooms.

Oh goodness, *another* challenge. What the hell *was* it going to be? And Hemlock the creep. It was a lot to think about.

Rosie hadn't told Charlie about the book she'd found, or the ghost of Anne Boleyn. That seemed too much.

The whole way back to her room, the little book felt like a hot coal burning a hole in her pocket. She kept her head down as she passed anyone, as though they might be able to tell she'd stolen something from the headmistress's office.

Yet she didn't feel like a thief.

Anne Boleyn had said the book was for her, and that was exactly how it had felt when she picked it up in Miss Churchill's office—like it belonged to her. Even so, she was relieved to arrive at her bedroom without anyone questioning the guilty look on her face.

Bina wasn't back from the games room yet. Rosie shut the door and leaned against it, sliding down, and sat on the floor. Taking a deep breath, she then pulled out the book. It was old, its edges frayed, and it smelled of wet soil and dust. Rosie ran her fingers over the emblem of the bird. It looked powerful and dignified, as though it had all the answers to every question she'd ever wanted to ask.

Below the crest, also in gold, were the words "*Animo, Imperium, Libertas.*" Courage, power, and freedom—the same values that would be tested for in the Falcon Queen games. She pulled at the cover, but there was a little padlock guarding it like a secret diary, with no sign of a key. She crawled on her knees over to her bedside drawer and took out a pair of tweezers, then jammed them into the lock, but they were too big. Okay, back to full detective mode. She tried a hairpin next, wiggling it around until her wrist ached, but the lock still didn't open. It wasn't as easy as they made it look in spy movies.

What else could she do? Rosie grabbed hold of the front and back covers of the book and heaved, gritting her teeth as she pulled as hard as she could to pry them apart. But the clasp held firm. For God's sake! One more thing she couldn't open, just like the case!

You're just annoying, thought Rosie, flinging the book across the room, where it landed facedown, defiant.

She stared at it and huffed. But the book remained a mystery, its secrets hidden.

Chapter Fourteen

THE KEY

SATURDAY, DECEMBER 3RD. EVENING. AFTER MISS CHURCHILL'S
OFFICE. THE DAY AFTER THE BLACK LAKE CHALLENGE.

It was a miserable evening. The rain lashed at the bedroom windows with merciless strikes. Bina was still in the games room playing her *Miracles and Monsters* marathon, and Rosie was sitting at her desk, chewing on her pen. She sighed.

Okay, time to make a list of all that's happened and find a solution, she thought, still in detective mode. Rosie took out her unicorn notebook and began to write.

- Shepherd's pie fight with Ottilie—Aragon/arrogant cow deserved it
- Hemlock—weirdo creep—"be a good girl." Get lost!
- Professor Isambard—nice conservationist, friend of Miss Churchill's

- No case—where is it??? What has Hemlock done with it?
- 🍍
- Bina—roommate . . . nice, but full-on

To-do list

- Find proof to show Miss Churchill about weirdo Hemlock—what if all my detective skills are dead?
- Win dreaded Falcon Queen games. Everyone's talking about what the next challenge will be. All the ideas seem absurd. I can't face another one! What if I lose?
- Open the little book. Found Anne Boleyn's book—can't open it—duh

Note

- No Churchill, no case—what if I'm just a loser?
- Haven't heard from ghost Queenie since the lake

She tapped her fingers on the defiant little book, which refused to be opened.

It will teach you everything you need to know. That's what the ghost of Anne Boleyn had told her right before she disappeared.

If only that were true. There was so much Rosie didn't know, like why she'd ended up at this school, what was in her burnt-red briefcase, what to do about the whole Hemlock-and-the-wildcats situation . . . The list went on and on.

And most of all, what had really happened to her mother.

All things considered, Rosie could really do with some guidance right now.

Maybe some wisdom from a real queen was exactly what Rosie needed, and she would only find that by opening this little purple book.

She attempted to pry apart the covers again, but it wouldn't budge.

"How do I open you?" she asked the book. She tapped the cover as though she was knocking for entry and scrunched her mouth up in thought.

Then, as if it was the most obvious solution in the world, Rosie knew what she had to do. Return to the Falcon Queen gallery, wait for Anne Boleyn to appear, and then ask her for the key. Simple, right?

The idea was so ludicrous it almost made Rosie laugh out loud. Half her brain was telling her that she was being ridiculous—making plans to creep around at night, chasing after a ghost—but the little purple book in her hands now was exactly the one she'd seen before, the ghostly offering, meaning the vision of Anne Boleyn had to have been real too, right? Whether she was ridiculous or not, there were also questions about this school that needed answering, and Rosie felt sure the answers were trapped inside the little purple book.

Everything about the island, its strange animals and

weird plants, felt out of this world. Her only other previous nature experiences consisted of a day trip to London Zoo when she was ten, and once planting a sunflower in a pot on their flat's balcony. Little as that was, Rosie could still see that the usual laws of nature didn't seem to apply to Bloodstone Island—the things that grew here that would never survive elsewhere in Britain—and she was at a loss what to make of it all.

She pushed her diary aside and stood up, knocking over her chair. She should go now, while the majority of the school—including Bina—was preoccupied with *Miracles and Monsters*. It gave her the perfect opportunity to spend the night in the Falcon Queen gallery without anyone noticing.

Rosie put the book into her backpack, and then crammed the bag with anything else that might be useful: extra clothes to keep her warm, a torch, a couple of towels to use as a blanket and pillow, and two bags of bacon Frazzles (her favorite) in case she got hungry. Next, Rosie shoved a load of clothes under her duvet to make it look like she was in bed. It'd be late by the time Bina came back, and she never turned on the light if she thought Rosie was asleep. With any luck, she wouldn't notice that Rosie wasn't there.

Rosie then made her way stealth-like to the Falcon Queen gallery. Just as she'd hoped, she didn't pass a single person. The only sign of life was Freda—one of Miss Churchill's other floppy-eared house rabbits—who she passed just around the corner from the gallery, nibbling on the edge of an expensive-looking rug.

After a heavy push, the doors to the gallery swung open. Inside it was dark and cold, as if someone had sucked out all the air. Moonlight shone through the slim windows, casting rectangular strips of light down the length of the room. Rosie removed the door key from its lock—there was no way she was going to let herself be locked in again—and shut the doors. She was on her own. But sort of not, at the same time, with the Falcon Queens peering down at her from their portraits on the wall. This time Rosie felt comforted by them, as if these women were looking out for her. She scanned their names—Amy Johnson, Charlotte Cooper, Ada Lovelace—half wondering who they were and what they'd done to deserve a place in the gallery. Maybe she'd look them up one day. (Bina said there was also a gallery of the Falcon *Kings* on the other side of the school. There was so much to take in.)

As she passed the portrait of Elizabeth I, Rosie's eyes were once again drawn to the gleaming red orb depicted at the queen's waist. It was almost hypnotizing.

Rosie shook her head. Right now, she was most interested in Anne Boleyn and whether her ghost would reappear. Rosie chewed on her lip and shivered. What if the queen suddenly turned into a murderous ghoul and tried to attack her?

Stop. No. Everything would be okay. She'd only ever helped her before. This was just a fact-finding mission. The last time the ghost had appeared, it'd been the middle of the night (3:00 a.m., to be precise). Rosie knew very little about ghosts—despite having met one—but assumed it always had to be late for one to appear. She put on her extra clothes, ate both packs of Frazzles, and made herself a makeshift bed out of the towels she'd brought.

Rosie thought once again how ridiculous this whole situation was. Lying on the floor, wrapped in a towel, waiting for a ghost to appear. It sure sounded bizarre when you put it like that. But she was here now, so she just closed her eyes and waited.

When she next opened them, it felt like only a few minutes had passed, but it must have been much longer. The moonlight was gone, and the room was almost pitch-black. What was it that had woken her? Rosie squinted at her Flik Flak Swatch watch, trying to make out the time. She'd cracked it during the Black Lake challenge and it still hadn't quite dried out.

2:59.

Eerrrrrrrrrrrrrrrrrrrrk.

The same creaking sound as before broke the silence in the room, followed by the tap-tapping of erratic footsteps.

Then the rich smell of spice and velvet plum roses wafted toward Rosie. Anne Boleyn was coming.

An icy chill ran down Rosie's back. Now that she was in the presence of a spectral being once again, she wondered if it had been such a good idea to come here. In some of the movies Rosie had seen, ghosts were cruel and unpredictable; they possessed people and took over their lives. What if the ghost of Anne Boleyn tried to do that to her?

Rosie breathed, pulled out the purple book from her rucksack, and got to her feet. She considered turning on her torch but decided against it. Maybe she could use the light as a weapon, though, if things took a turn for the worse. The spicy floral scent grew more intense and then, just as before, the ghost drifted in through the wall.

It took Rosie's breath away to see her again. Anne Boleyn was dressed exactly the same as last time, in the delicate headdress and dark gown, with thin wisps of mist drifting away from its hem. An eerie glow followed her as she paced the room, her hands clasped tightly in prayer. She hadn't yet noticed Rosie, but Rosie could sense the woman's dread, which seeped from her like a damp breeze creeping under a locked door.

"Give me strength, oh Lord, for they cometh for me. My own fate is set . . ." the ghost whispered in a gentle voice. "Mine enemies hath turned the king against me."

Rosie took a deep breath and then gave a timid cough

to get the ghost's attention. It worked; the queen stopped pacing and turned toward her. Tears spilled down her cheeks like tiny, desperate jewels. *The queen is crying?* The impassioned resolve Rosie had witnessed last time had completely dissolved, exposing a fragile young woman, full of vulnerability.

"Are you okay?" Rosie said softly.

"You came back, my darling child," said Anne Boleyn, wiping away her tears.

"Yes, um . . ." Rosie stammered. "I, uhh . . . I found this." She held up the book. "But it's locked and I don't have the key."

"The book. The rules. I wrote it for you," replied the ghost with relief.

"For me? Really? Why?" Rosie still couldn't believe it was true. "I don't even belong here."

The ghost gave her a look so full of love that it made Rosie's heart ache. It was the same look her mother used to give her whenever she was proud.

"Because you are my blood, child. My family, my bloodline. That's why you're here, of course," said the queen.

What? That couldn't be right. Rosie had sometimes watched a TV show called *Find Your Family*, where they discovered relatives from the past, and in one episode a soap actor turned out to be related to ancient royalty, but that was a one-off. This was all a bit much. She was just a normal girl from a downbeat flat in inner-city London; there was no royalty to Rosie Frost.

"You belong here, more than anyone," Queen Anne went on. "Deep down they are afraid of you. That's why they attack; they know you have power. The book will help you."

"Who's afraid of me? What power?" Surely she didn't mean Ottilie? Nothing the ghost was saying made any sense.

"It is time for you to stand up for yourself. Follow the Falcon Queen's rules. *Animo, Imperium, Libertas.* Let them be your guide, and then you will find your courage, power, and freedom."

Rosie brushed her fingers over the gold embossed bird on the book's cover. What secrets lay inside it? "But it's locked," Rosie said again.

The ghost of Anne Boleyn frowned. "I have many enemies, men who spread vicious lies about me—'the smiling vipers,' I call them. People who are kind to your face and pretend to be your allies, but then stab you in the back. These vipers wanted the key, but I refused to let them have it. I should have been discerning with my words; it was my downfall." Anne Boleyn turned her head sharply, her eyes frightened. "They're coming," she said. "I have to go." She bowed her head and touched her heart.

"How do I open it? Where's the key?" asked Rosie quickly.

"Dear child, in this wicked world, what is it that really guides us? Le coeur, le coeur."

She placed her hand on her heart.

Rosie looked at her blankly.

"Your heart," she whispered, reaching out toward Rosie.

And with that, the ghost disappeared, leaving nothing but a shimmer of mist in the air and a lingering smell of rich red roses.

Rosie's knees suddenly went weak. She lowered herself onto the floor before her legs failed her completely and took a moment to catch her breath. The whole exchange had been so surreal.

Over the course of their brief conversation, Anne Boleyn had revealed a lot, but none of it was very clear, and Rosie still had no idea how to unlock the little purple book.

My heart? This queen has watched way too many Disney movies, thought Rosie. *Thanks, Your Majesty; really useful.* Unless . . .

Rosie reached into her breast pocket. Maybe it could be there, by some magic? She peered inside: nothing. She then checked her other pockets. No magic, no key; just a snotty old tissue, a piece of chewing gum covered in fluff, and her cruddy old phone. She looked at the phone. Zero messages (unsurprising, who would message her?) and only 4 percent battery. She cursed herself for not remembering to bring her charger. Well, she might as well use that 4 percent. Even though Rosie wasn't usually interested in history or dead people, questions about what Anne Boleyn had been like, and why she'd died, were rolling around in her mind.

She opened the phone's web browser and clicked on the first article that came up. She learned that Anne had been Henry VIII's second wife—the king famously known for having six (even Rosie knew that much). Back then, the pope didn't approve of the marriage, so Henry left the Catholic Church (very controversial) and declared himself head of the Church of England. Anne Boleyn was smart and ambitious and heavily influential in politics—something that was not approved of for women at that time. She gave birth to a daughter, Elizabeth, but then had three miscarriages. Henry was desperate for a male heir.

When Anne lost a baby which turned out to be a boy, Henry was furious. He had already started courting one of Anne's maids, Jane Seymour, but in order to marry her, he needed Anne out of the way. So a creep named Thomas Cromwell, the king's advisor and Anne's number one enemy—he didn't like Anne's opinions or ambitions—helped him do this. Thomas Cromwell spread rumors about Anne being unfaithful and told people she was plotting against the king. She was found guilty of all charges and beheaded.

At that moment, Rosie's phone flashed black, and then shut down; the battery was dead.

What a tragic end to such an incredible woman, thought Rosie. Now that she'd met the queen's ghost, she was no longer just some name in a history book or a painting hung in a gallery; she was a real person with hopes and dreams and feelings, as well as being a mother to a two-year-old daughter. And at such a young age, all that was snatched away from her.

Like my mum. Even though she didn't have the answers she so desperately wanted about her mother's death, Rosie felt a connection between the two women: both had been headstrong and independent, and both had died before their time, leaving a young daughter behind.

Rosie crossed her legs and stared up at the portrait of Anne Boleyn. "Sorry for what happened to you," Rosie said.

She half expected the portrait to reply (stranger things had happened in this room, after all), but the picture just stared back at her with its sad eyes and sullen mouth.

Could there be any truth in what Queen Anne had said about Rosie being part of her bloodline? It was absurd, impossible.

Nothing is impossible! This proves it! her mum had

declared years before with the biggest smile on her face. When Rosie was eight years old, her mum had run around the kitchen jumping with joy, flapping around the acceptance letter she'd received from a national newspaper, for an article she'd written and submitted on the off chance they might like it. Her mum had scooped up Rosie, spinning her around. *Follow your dreams, Rosie! Believe in yourself! No matter how obscure or slim the odds. Give it a try; just do your best*, she'd said.

If Rosie *was* somehow related to Anne Boleyn, it might explain why she'd ended up at Heverbridge. Mr. Hemlock had said she was on scholarship. Charlie had said you had to be either super talented or have some kind of connection with the school—or both.

Maybe Hemlock was lying about her scholarship, just like he'd lied about her mum's case, and maybe there was some distant, rich relative who'd decided to sponsor her education there? Hemlock had made it clear that this school wasn't some charity for poor, unfortunate orphans, after all. But not all the pupils could be descended from royalty; that would be ridiculous. This school might be for the super clever, but she didn't feel like she was. God, it was confusing. If only she knew why she was sent here.

She stood up to take a closer look at the queen, searching for any hint of family resemblance (aware, as she was doing so, of how preposterous that was). Up close, the cracks in the paint shattered Anne Boleyn's face, splitting her lips and cheeks. The golden *B* pendant at her throat was broken into pieces, and the rose in her hand was riddled with tiny fractures.

Rosie gasped.

The rose in the portrait was hovering right over Anne Boleyn's heart.

Could this be the heart that the ghost was talking about? There was only one way to find out.

Rosie grabbed hold of the frame and heaved. It took all her strength to lift it. As it unhooked from its fastenings, Rosie remembered with a jolt of panic that some paintings in galleries were alarmed. She held her breath, but no sound came. She slid the portrait onto the ground and ran her finger over the wall, looking for any signs of a hidden panel or secret button.

Nothing.

Next, Rosie turned the painting around and scanned its back.

The key was small, but she spotted it straightaway, sewn into the canvas directly behind the rose and Anne Boleyn's heart. *Le coeur! Of course.* She gave it a gentle tug, and it came off the canvas. Rosie then grabbed for the little purple book and inserted the key into its lock.

With a satisfying click, the lock turned and the book opened.

The moon shone sharply through the window, a spotlight piercing down onto the purple book. Energy flooded through Rosie as her eyes pored over the faded gold paper and she read the title: *The Falcon Queen's Rules*.

She hungrily turned the pages. Seeing the now-familiar words "*Animo, Imperium, Libertas*" laid out in the old script filled her with a deep comfort, as though a glow had been turned on within her. Beneath this was some faded ink handwriting, as if someone had been keeping a diary, or making notes. The spidery words were very pale and hard to work out.

This might take a while.

Chapter Fifteen

THE GUTTER CLUB

SUNDAY, DECEMBER 4TH. 6:15 A.M.

*B*ZZZZZ! *BZZZZZ! BZZZZZ!*
Rosie sat bolt upright in bed, sweating all over. Why was the screen still buzzing?

Was she still in the lake? How many places were left?

BZZZZZ! BZZZZZ!

Oh, it was her phone alarm, vibrating on her bedside table, showing 6:15 a.m.

Rosie breathed a sigh of relief and slapped the alarm off. She picked up the little purple book from where it still lay open on her chest and tucked it under her pillow, then buried herself back under her covers. It had been the early hours when she'd crept into bed after her meeting with the queen and kept her tired eyes open for as long as possible after that, looking through the book. She was exhausted.

A short while later, someone started shaking her with gentle hands. "Rosie? Rosie? You're going to be late."

Late for what? It was Sunday; normal people have a day off on Sundays, a lie-in. She kept her eyes closed and turned her body away.

"Let me sleep," said Rosie, nestling her head deeper into the warm pillow.

"Don't you have to be somewhere this morning?" Bina asked.

Oh no. Rosie had totally forgotten—Hemlock's punishment for the shepherd's pie fight. She sat up.

"Thanks, Bina, I forgot."

Rosie glanced at her watch. 6:21. She had to be at the Ivy Dome in *nine minutes*. She leaped out of bed and yanked some clothes out of her wardrobe. Coat hangers clattered to the floor.

"I'm a bit jealous, to be honest," said Bina, sitting on the edge of her bed.

"Jealous? Of what?" Rosie glanced out the window. It was still dark, the lethargic winter sun struggling to pierce through the slug-gray sky, and it looked like it might pour with rain at any moment.

"The Conservation Club, of course. It sounds fun."

Oh, you mean the Gutter Club?

Bina pressed play on her wireless speaker ("Killing Me Softly" by the Fugees) and started bopping her head.

"I'm sure you'd be more than welcome to join us if you wanted to," said Rosie, pulling on a pair of old jeans.

"I would, but I've got my Kfab group. You know, my wrestling. I'll teach you some moves sometime. Today we're focusing on The Rock's Rock Bottom! Come join us later, if you like?"

"Maybe," said Rosie, knowing full well that she wouldn't. She zipped up her coat and then pulled on her tatty old wellies. "Bye." Rosie darted through the door without looking back.

"Have fun!" Bina called after her.

Rosie raced down the corridor and took the stairs two at a time. Her wellies pinched at the sides of her feet. Her mum had bought them for her from a charity shop years ago and they no longer fit, but they were the only waterproof option Rosie had; if she was going to spend the whole morning outdoors, they would be better than her leaky boots.

She was also going to have to spend the morning with Ottilie Aragon-Windsor. Her stomach twisted with anxiety. Just imagine if Rosie *was* somehow related to Anne Boleyn (of course, another ridiculous idea). Ottilie would hate her even more. What if she and Ottilie got into another fight? She'd be in big trouble if they did. *Frost. Someone wicked.* That's what Hemlock had said, and maybe he was right.

Rosie shivered as the damp winter wind crept down the neck of her shirt. She wished she could be back in bed right now, reading the little purple book, safe under the covers. It was as though the book was calling her back, its mysteries to be decoded. *But what do the queen's scribblings all mean?* She kicked the last of the frosted leaves as she crossed the lawn toward the Ivy Dome.

The Ivy Dome was a circular bandstand which was occasionally used for outdoor performances, apparently. Thick green ivy wound up each of the stand's marble pillars and entirely covered its roof, giving the structure its name. Rosie trudged over to it through the crisp grass, and the freezing morning breeze nipped at her cheeks. Three figures were already there, waiting for her: Ottilie, Charlie, and a woman who must be Ms. Parr. Ottilie stared daggers at Rosie as she approached.

"You're late," said Ms. Parr with a grimace, which emphasized the wrinkles at the corners of her eyes. Ms. Parr was the school's groundskeeper. Rosie had never met her before, but according to Bina, she lived in a little cottage on the other side of the Heverbridge estate. She'd been on the island her whole life and, also according to Bina, had never once left. She had a stern nose and a ruddy face, her dark brown hair flecked with gray and tied back in a loose bun. Rosie noticed that her hiking boots were caked in layers of dried as well as fresh mud, and she wore a sage-green body-warmer over a short-sleeved T-shirt, leaving her strong arms exposed. Some pupils called her "Parr Moody"—she wasn't known for being especially friendly.

"So here we are," said Ms. Parr. "I presume you all know each other?"

"Yep," said Charlie. He winked at Rosie, who smiled back at him.

"Yeah, I know her, the Skidmark." Ottilie *hmph*ed and looked at her nails.

"Do not let any unwholesome talk come out of your mouth," snapped Ms. Parr.

Ottilie frowned and didn't look up.

"Good," said Ms. Parr. "Let's get started. You know why you're here?"

Silence.

"You're here to work."

Ottilie threw a scowling glance across at Rosie.

"I see." Ms. Parr looked from Rosie to Ottilie, taking in the bad vibe between them. "For the moment, all seems painful rather than pleasant, but later this will yield the peaceful fruit of righteousness to those who have been trained by it. And yes, this morning you shall be trained by it."

Rosie had no clue what she was saying at first, and then it twigged. She was talking about punishment.

"Firstly, please could everyone put on the protective gear." Ms. Parr threw each of them a bright green, high-viz waistcoat.

"I'm not wearing this!" cringed Ottilie, holding it in disgust. "And matching with those sponge— I mean, with *them*." She frowned.

"You will all wear the same protective clothing. This isn't a request."

"So what exactly do we have to do?" said someone from behind her.

Rosie turned. That someone was folding his arms, leaning up against a tree and casually taking it all in, smirking. Rosie bit her lip and quickly looked away, a surge of butterflies erupting in her stomach. It was Jackson Sterling, the boy she'd bumped into by Wildcat Woods yesterday.

Why is he here? wondered Rosie. Was he being punished for something, like the rest of them?

"Workmanship," said Ms. Parr abruptly. "Follow me. We have lots to do, and we're going somewhere extra special."

Ms. Parr led the four of them, all wearing their oversized high-viz waistcoats, away from the Ivy Dome.

"We look like we're in an awful nineties boy band wearing these," muttered Ottilie.

They headed down a skinny path that wound through an overgrown field. Ottilie smothered her hands in anti-bac gel as they went and tutted as her shoes got covered in muck.

"These are Praaaada!" she squealed, after stepping in something which looked a lot like horse poo.

Rosie grinned. Perhaps the Gutter Club was going to be fun after all. She dropped back and Charlie sidled up next to her.

"So, um, I guess I oughta thank you again," she said. "For not ratting on me in Miss Churchill's office."

"Like I said, we're mates now. Spongers stick together. And if one of us wins the Falcon Queen games, the spongers will rule the school." He smirked. "Doughnuts on the lunch menu every day—that will be my rule."

"Sounds good." Rosie smiled, but she wasn't ready to share her rule with Charlie. She just wanted her case back.

She wondered what the next challenge might be. "Have you heard anything about the next round?" she asked him.

He shook his head. "My mate told me that during the last Falcon Queen games, they only gave them a few hours' notice before the second challenge. So it could happen at any moment."

Rosie rolled her eyes. Of course this school would do something like that.

They carried on marching along the path, following Ms. Parr into a thick forest.

"Come on! Nearly there!"

Ms. Parr charged forward, directly trailed by Jackson,

who swaggered on without a care in the world, then Ottilie, pouting with pure disgust.

As the morning sun finally awakened, dappled light filtering through the trees, Rosie looked up and spotted a tiny cinnamon-colored bird. It was peering at her from its peaceful perch on a low branch.

"That's a Socorro dove," said Ms. Parr, who had looked back and stopped when she saw Rosie staring at it. "It's extinct everywhere in the world except here."

The groundskeeper plowed on through the undergrowth, addressing all four of them as she went. "As I'm sure you know, Bloodstone Island is a small haven—a place of safety for nature. Safe from the destruction of man's greed, that is." The frown on her forehead was a deep one. "Due to its unique climate and uniquely complex ecosystem, the island is home to some of the rarest and most impressive plants in the world. And animals too, making it a conservation hot spot and nature lover's dream. We have some of the last animals of their species living here: beavers, pine martens, wolves, wildcats."

Wildcats . . . Should I tell her what I overheard Hemlock say? No, no way. She's too scary. And everything Rosie knew was so vague, Ms. Parr wouldn't believe her without proof.

"Then there're the Konik ponies—a breed of small horses that are very nearly extinct, and whose soft brown manes turn white in winter. They've been part of this island's history for centuries. Legend says they have magical senses, and respond harshly to anyone they consider wicked, serving only the brave."

There're a lot of legends on this island, thought Rosie. She was far too old for such nonsense, even if those ponies she'd seen yesterday were very cute. But "unique climate" and "complex ecosystem" only seemed to go so far to explain all the strange things she had already seen here. There was some other inexplicable element at play in this special place which Rosie couldn't work out.

"So how does this all grow here? Some of this wildlife is unreal. I've never seen anything like it," Rosie said.

Ms. Parr continued, "You're quite right; what has been achieved here is astonishing. Queen Elizabeth believed in the power of Mother Nature, and it was one of her subjects, an explorer, who discovered a secret here. This island has the most powerfully enriched soil on the planet, where nature can thrive to its full potential, even in winter. The minerals and fossils found in its land are so rare they make Bloodstone Island the most precious jewel on Earth, a hidden treasure. Queen Elizabeth, a forward thinker, knew this and supported its welfare and protection. It was her mother Queen Anne Boleyn's favorite place on Earth."

My ghost queen. Rosie's ears pricked up.

"That's why Elizabeth originally created the school

here in her honor: in part to safeguard Bloodstone Island, and because she had special memories with her mother here. And it is the perfect place to set up a school for polymaths to be inspired, learning from nature's diversity and educating like-minded people to go out into the world and spread the same message of wildlife conservation."

So her ghost queen had loved it here.

"The Konik ponies' grazing has also helped create ideal living conditions for a host of other wildlife such as geese, spoonbills, bitterns, and corncrakes. Amazing when you see the whole ecosystem working together in perfect harmony, the way it's supposed to."

"Hang on, rewind a minute—did you say *wolves*?" Ottilie demanded, her hands on her hips.

"I did indeed," Ms. Parr replied.

"Here? In this forest?" Ottilie looked incredulous.

"Yes, they have been extinct in the United Kingdom since around 1800; however, they still exist here on Bloodstone," she said proudly.

"What if they attack us?" Ottilie frowned, rubbing her temples.

Ms. Parr shook her head. "You don't need to worry about that. Wolves are very cautious animals; if they see you, they'll do their best to avoid you."

"I can relate to that," Rosie muttered, which made Charlie laugh out loud.

"And most animals will be wary of you in that high-viz jacket. Ottilie, please put it back on." Ms. Parr glared at Ottilie. She'd already told her twice this morning. Ottilie rolled her eyes and hung it over her shoulders.

"Wolves I can deal with," Charlie muttered. "But spiders . . . Hate 'em."

"Okay, here we are." Ms. Parr stopped. They'd come to a large open space and what looked like the beginnings of an empty pond, half dug out. Beside it was a large old barn.

Ms. Parr picked up two shovels and handed one each to Rosie and Jackson. Rosie looked at it flatly. What did she want them to do?

"You can start digging." She nodded to both Rosie and Jackson. "Yes, it's going to be a pond. We are providing a sanctuary for the Daubentons. You and you"—she pointed at Charlie and Ottilie this time—"can start shoveling this into the wheelbarrows." She pointed to a large mound of brown stuff. "Then spread it over there."

"What *is* that?" asked Ottilie, cringing.

"Alpaca dung. It attracts the beetles. Needs spreading evenly."

Ottilie looked at Ms. Parr, screwing up her face in horror. "I'm not doing that."

"As I said before, what all seems painful rather than pleasant now will later yield the peaceful fruit of righteousness to those who have been trained by it. And yes, this morning you shall be trained by it." Ms. Parr nodded firmly.

Subtext: "Get on with it, you uptight cow," thought Rosie.

"*And* the horseshoes love beetles."

Ottilie grimaced. "I've no idea what you mean, but FYI, I am not touching anything dirty." She pulled out some more anti-bac gel and wiped her hands.

"Well, you can spread the guano instead." Ms. Parr nodded toward some little brown pellets in a bucket.

"Guano?"

"Soil enrichment. High in nitrogen and phosphorus. Great fertilizer."

Ottilie spoke into her phone. "What is 'guano'?"

"Here's some information," said an electronic voice from the phone. Ottilie looked at the screen, then looked up with an open mouth . . .

"BAT POO! I am not touching bat sh—"

"Excrement," said Ms. Parr, promptly cutting her off. "Or perhaps 'feces' is the word you're looking for?"

"Hello, COVID??!! SARS??!!!!!" snapped back Ottilie.

Rosie had to bite her lip to keep from laughing. Of course, digging a hole wasn't exactly her idea of fun, but seeing Ottilie freak out made it kind of worth it.

"Daubentons and horseshoes are indeed bats. Bats

have been given such a bad reputation, what with vampire movies and now being blamed for a virus, but they should be treasured as an important part of ecosystems all over the world. They need our help," Ms. Parr snapped. "They're under threat due to habitat loss because of *us*. And yet *they* are valuable to us. Their excrement is fantastic soil enrichment, fueled with minerals which will help all the other wildlife here. So I suggest you pick up that shovel and start spreading."

Ms. Parr gave Ottilie a look that could have turned her to stone. Ottilie said nothing more and picked up the shovel slowly.

"Use these." Charlie handed her his gloves.

She glared at Rosie. "You're gonna pay for this, taking me down to your disgusting level." She spat the words out.

Under Ms. Parr's supervision, the four of them spent the morning shoveling and digging. Despite the smell, Rosie started to quite enjoy it.

"There are worse jobs in the world. Maggot farmer," mused Charlie. "Vomit collector."

"Proctologist," said Jackson.

He pulled a cute face at Rosie, then raised one eyebrow and tilted his head. He *was* funny and ironic, but he knew it. She bit her lip and tried not to grin. *Hide the braces*, thought Rosie. The butterflies lightly fluttered in her stomach—this boy was annoyingly distracting.

Charlie and Jackson's endless banter made Rosie laugh, while Ottilie's anger only brewed as she slowly shoveled small bits of alpaca dung. But only when Ms. Parr was watching. Otherwise, she spent most of the time on her iPhone, scrolling through her Instagram feed, doing as little work as possible. She didn't say another word to Rosie, perhaps biding her time, like a coiled snake waiting for the perfect moment to strike.

Toward the end of the early morning session, Ms. Parr walked up to Rosie and said, "Before you go, I have one more thing." She gave Rosie a small bag of food. "For the foxes and badgers. Fine to scatter it around there." Ms. Parr indicated an area just through the trees. "Follow the stone path toward the evergreens."

Rosie nodded and set off into the surrounding woods, clutching the small bag of peanuts, fruit, and scraps of meat. Every few paces, she dropped a handful into the undergrowth. The voices of the others drifted into the background and, before long, Rosie found herself alone among the trees. Just as she was about to empty the last few pieces from the bag, she spotted two little ears poking out from behind a prickly bush. Then a pair of gold-flecked eyes joined them and held her in their stare. "Hello, Mercury!"

The wildcat twitched his ears in response.

"It's so good to see you! Are you hungry? Here." Rosie took out the remaining scraps of chicken from the bag and threw them on the ground near the wildcat. The animal crept out of his hiding place with a stealthy prowl, sniffed the meat, and then devoured it in one big bite.

"That's the last of it, I'm afraid."

Mercury knocked his head into Rosie's shin and meowed. He then walked away, looking back over his shoulder as if waiting for Rosie to follow again, just like before.

She really should be getting back to the others—they'd be wondering where she was.

Mercury meowed again, louder this time.

Okay, a little while longer couldn't hurt. She followed the wildcat deeper into the forest.

After several minutes of their scrambling through thick vines, Mercury meowed, drawing Rosie's attention to the valley in front of her. She was back at the compound she'd seen yesterday.

"Is this what you wanted me to see *again*?" she asked Mercury.

His glossy coat shimmered orange, brown, and bronze, and his piercing eyes were full of intelligence. The wildcat set off toward the enclosed area, meowing as he went, and Rosie followed.

Suddenly a heavy whirring sound rumbled through the trees. She looked down the hill, toward the source of the noise. The compound's steel door had opened, and a large digger was entering with boxes of crates. What was that doing there? She could just about read the letters *ANF* on one of the boxes, but the rest of the word was covered with a sheet.

Anfibian? No, that was with *mph*: amp*h*ibian. She pulled out her phone and googled words starting with "anf." "Anfractuous"? Or "anfora," which was high-quality tableware in Mexico? Strange, but could it be something to do with that?

Through the trees in the distance, a man in a hard hat was looking down at a clipboard, taking notes. He looked up as another man approached, and Rosie quickly pinned herself behind a tree, out of sight. She recognized this second man immediately, his finely cut blue suit out of place among the woodland environment. She slowly peered back around the tree to see Hemlock patting the first man's shoulder, then strutting into the compound. The gate slammed firmly shut behind him. What *was* he doing in there? Something really didn't feel right.

Mercury meowed as if in agreement, as well as to say, *Keep up, girl, let's go.*

Rosie pulled up her hood, stepping forward. "Aaaah," she gasped as a hand suddenly touched her arm.

"Hey, wild girl, you playing hide-and-seek?" It was Jackson.

"How did you know I was here?" she asked, looking into the trees. Mercury had gone.

"Followed the bread crumbs," he said, holding up a scrap of bacon. "You still checking out that view?"

"Well, that view's a bonus of the Gutter Club." She shrugged.

" 'We are all in the gutter, but some of us are looking at the stars,' " Jackson said with a smirk.

"Another Oscar Wilde quote?" Rosie asked. What was it with this guy and Oscar Wilde?

"Yep. The man's a legend," replied Jackson, smiling. It was an almost perfect smile.

A warm feeling flushed over her, and butterflies, again.

"What?" She flinched as the whirring sound of the digger erupted in the distance, interrupting her thoughts.

Don't get distracted by good teeth, she scolded herself.

"What are they doing down there?" She nodded at the compound.

"No idea. Sorry to break it to you, but Ms. Parr says we're done for the day."

Rosie sighed and followed Jackson back toward the others, glancing round at the compound as she went. Whatever Hemlock was up to behind Miss Churchill's back, that was definitely where it was happening, she was sure of it. Like Charlie said, she needed proof, though, and that wouldn't be so easy to come by.

Chapter Sixteen

FROSTBITE

TUESDAY, DECEMBER 6TH.

Rosie was in the middle of double science, but wild-cats, Hemlock, the compound, the digger, crates—everything she'd seen Sunday morning flooded through her mind. Hemlock had made it very clear that he would fire anyone she "told tales" to, but if she somehow found enough evidence against him, surely that couldn't be ignored by everyone? She still had the key card she'd found in the forest—did she dare use it and risk expulsion if she was caught?

Questions and worries continued to swirl through her mind.

Today in science, they were supposed to be emulating volcanic eruptions. The elements needed for the experiment were spread out on her desk, but Rosie just stared at them blankly. It didn't help that the chemistry room stank—a pungent antiseptic smell that seeped through the lab like a spiteful virus, waiting to infect them.

At the desk in front of her, Ottilie was preening her hair, while Ishaan looked on admiringly.

"You've got such great shine and thickness," he said, touching the ends of Ottilie's hair as she used her phone as a mirror.

"I know, right? Daddy bought me this new conditioner. It has rare organic ingredients, imported all the way from Guacamole in South America."

"I love guacamole too, with nachos," said Jamila.

"You mean 'Guatemala,' right?" Ishaan asked, unsure whether to correct her or not.

"That's what I said," said Ottilie. "The point is, it's really expensive. But it's *so* worth it. Image is everything, after all. We have to take care of our appearance, don't you agree?" She gave a sly glance over her shoulder at Rosie.

Rosie looked away and focused on the experiment.

"Be careful with sulfuric acid, my darlings—the fumes in this reaction can be very irritating to the eyes," said Mademoiselle Curie Labouisse from the front of the class. Rosie's science teacher was French Polish, a descendant of the late Nobel Prize winner Marie Curie. Her accent got thicker whenever she became excited, which was usually when she was discussing something to do with science. She had dyed blond hair, in perfect waves like Marilyn Monroe, her lips were painted with bright red lipstick, and she wore a pristine crisp white shirt and tight pencil skirt, like she was a couture fashion magazine editor rather than a science teacher. She insisted on everyone calling her the full mademoiselle, Mademoiselle Curie Labouisse.

Ottilie started filming herself on her phone, pouting into the camera as if she were a Hollywood movie star strutting the red carpet. Jamila popped up behind her and gave a peace sign.

"Hi, my STEM-loving angels!" Ottilie said into the camera. "It's your STEM queen here. You know what it stands for: science, technology, engineering, and *me*! So today we're exploring *exothermic reactions*—so fabby. They're basically reactions that release energy, usually in the form of heat or light. I'm using sugar and sulfuric acid, but you can try this at home using baking soda and vinegar. Volca*no*? More like hashtag volcan*yes*. I thought of that myself." She gave a smug wink to the camera.

Is this girl for real?

"No phones allowed in class, my darlings," said Mademoiselle Curie Labouisse.

"But I'm live-streaming science!" Ottilie said, batting her eyelashes. "This is important."

Ottilie presented her petri dish to the camera for her

two thousand followers to see. She added a few drops of acid to her sugar lumps, which then turned black and started to bubble and fizz. "Look, angels! The wonder of science."

"Never let the social media be your master, *ma cherie.* It's not good for you," tutted Mademoiselle Curie Labouisse, approaching Ottilie's desk. "Turn camera off! Unless I can be in the video too?" She ruffled her hair and gave Ottilie a look.

"Eww, no, miss; this is for the *current* generation. You'll lose me at least a hundred followers." Ottilie frowned and put down her phone.

"So rude, this girl," said Mademoiselle Curie Labouisse. "But also so clever. Look, class: the perfect reaction." She held up Ottilie's petri dish for the whole class to see.

Rosie rolled her eyes. She was fed up with Ottilie Aragon-Windsor being so good at everything. She'd show her and make an even better exo-whatever reaction. She added a handful of extra sugar cubes to her petri dish and then poured on a small amount of the sulfuric acid. Nothing happened, so she added some more, and then a bit more.

Suddenly the petri dish erupted and a syrupy black mass exploded all over the desk.

"Aaaah!" Rosie winced and jumped back. Smoke billowed into the air.

"Too much, too much!" said Mademoiselle Curie Labouisse. "Someone fetch baking soda."

"It's a real volcano!" shouted Ishaan, raising his hands to protect his hair.

"I got the baking soda," said Ottilie. She opened the lid and threw the entire contents at Rosie, a large portion of which hit her square in the face.

"Oops, I'm so sorry!" Ottilie said, placing her hand on her chest. Then she whipped out her phone and took a photo.

Rosie stood there, gritting her teeth at Ottilie. She was covered in black goo and white powder, and the whole class was staring at her. Someone stifled a giggle.

"Oh dear, dear me," said Mademoiselle Curie Labouisse. "A catastrophic disaster!"

Rosie trembled with anger. *What the hell?* She clenched her fists. Oh no, this was it.

Rosie Frost was about to lose it. She breathed in furiously.

The familiar scent of velvet plum roses and spice wafted around her, and she blinked. Could anyone else smell that?

Rosie took a deep breath and slowly unclenched her fists. "Can I go to the toilets, please, mademoiselle?"

"Yes, I think this is a good idea," said Mademoiselle Curie Labouisse.

"The sponger needs a sponge," sneered Ottilie.

Rosie scurried out of the chemistry lab, feeling the eyes of everyone in her class on her back. She was in such a fluster that she took a wrong turn and ended up lost, in a corridor she'd never been in before. She was about to turn back when she heard the familiar click-clacking of Hemlock's shoes coming from the other direction. She didn't want anyone seeing her like this, especially not Hemlock, who might use it as further proof that she didn't deserve a place at the school. Rosie dived behind a stone pillar just as Hemlock turned the corner. The pillar was engraved with a large python twisting around it, as well as a proud fox peering through some majestic vines.

"How is your work going?" Hemlock asked, sounding a little bored.

"Very well, thank you," a female voice replied. "I can't thank you enough for allowing us to come here."

"My pleasure, Jane."

Jane? Isn't that Professor Isambard's name?

"Oh, look, a bunny!" said the woman.

Rosie peered out from behind the pillar. Freda, one of Miss Churchill's long-eared rabbits, had hopped into the corridor, and the woman with Hemlock was crouching down to stroke her. Rosie couldn't see her face, but she had the same glossy brown hair turned up at the edges that Rosie had seen in the photos online and in Miss Churchill's office.

It *was* Professor Isambard!

"Bunnies," Hemlock said. "Sweet little things. Anyway, I must be on my way. I have a rather busy schedule. I trust you know your way out from here?"

"I do. Thank you for your time, Mr. Hemlock," said Professor Isambard without looking up from the rabbit.

"And you for yours."

Rosie's brain was whirring. The compound with the Isambard Foundation logo on it was clearly what Hemlock had granted the professor for her conservation research, but Rosie was sure he was using it as a cover somehow. Dare she say something to Professor Isambard now?

"You're a friendly one, aren't you?" Professor Isambard was saying to Freda while stroking her behind her floppy ears.

Rosie looked an absolute state, but this might be her only opportunity to speak with the woman. She stepped out from behind the pillar.

"Professor Isambard?" she said.

The woman looked up in her direction. "Oh, hello. Goodness, are you all right?"

"Yeah, I'm fine." Rosie gave a meek smile. "Science experiment gone wrong . . ."

The woman stood up. She was neat and composed, with a delicate frame and the thin-rimmed glasses she'd had on in the pictures. "How did you know my name?" the professor asked her.

"Um . . . I heard Mr. Hemlock say it a minute ago," Rosie spluttered. "You work for the Isambard Foundation, right?" Rosie already knew that, of course, from her name as well as the key card.

"I do indeed. As it happens, I'm the CEO." Professor Isambard gave Rosie a cheeky grin and wrinkled her nose. "That means I'm the boss."

"And you're working in Wildcat Woods?"

"You certainly know a lot about me." Professor Isambard smiled.

"I'm a big fan of conservation," Rosie quickly replied.

"That's great. My team and I are gathering information on the seasonal habits of wildcats. They're such incredible creatures; we're very fortunate to be able to study them here."

Rosie chewed on her bottom lip, wondering whether to risk her next question. "What about Mr. Hemlock?" she asked.

"The deputy head? What about him?"

She wasn't quite sure how to say it. "Is he working with you too?"

"Yes. I just popped in to check soil alkali levels. He's been wonderfully accommodating, making sure we have everything we need. The soil here is amazing, unbelievable, really."

She has no idea he's up to something, thought Rosie.

"That's nice. So do you think he *likes* animals?" Rosie stroked Freda. "And cats?"

"Er, of course. We all do, that's why we're here. I see that you do too." She smiled again.

"It's just that . . . erm . . ."

The professor was being used and misled by Hemlock, and she had a right to know. But Rosie had no proof, and she couldn't run the risk of Isambard reporting everything back to Hemlock himself.

Then Rosie spotted a drop of crimson on Freda's fur. *Oh no, is that blooood?*

Her heartbeat began to escalate. *Oh no—it was probably the stress of suppressing her own volcanic eruption with Ottilie that brought this one on.*

Professor Isambard looked at her watch. "I need to go now, but are you okay? I think you might need this," she said, like a kind mum. "When my son was your age, he used to get them too, every time he was overwhelmed or stressed. Don't worry, he grew out of it." She handed her a white cotton handkerchief.

Rosie could now feel the hot liquid dripping down her nostril cavity. "Thank you," she said, quickly holding it to her nose.

I wish blood didn't always make me panic like this!

Her mind suddenly became infused with dread, mixed

in with the comforting, crisp scent of sweet limes from Professor Isambard's perfume.

"Your hanky. I'll ruin it," she said as the dizzy feeling began to engulf her.

"Keep it, get yourself to a loo, and pinch your nose. Head forward." The professor looked at her with a concerned, kindly expression, placing a hand on Rosie's shoulder.

"Yes, I'll do that. It's all fine, thank you. It's all fine." Rosie pinched her nose.

She looked down at the pristine white cotton with the initials *J. I.* neatly embroidered onto it, now flecked with red spots.

The hall is spinning. Oh goodness, she was about to faint. *I'm going to die . . . Breathe, breathe.*

Rosie turned and ran down the hall toward the toilets, still holding the posh hanky to her nostrils. Had she just blown her only chance of making an ally against Hemlock? Once she made it to the bathroom, she cleaned herself up as best as she could, washing her face and scrubbing the handkerchief. The nosebleed eventually stopped and her heart rate returned to normal, the floor no longer moving. *Okay, all good.*

She looked again at the embroidered handkerchief. It had been so nice of Professor Isambard to give it to her. At least Rosie now felt even more confident that the Isambard

Foundation was really doing what Jackson had told her it was. Which meant it was just Hemlock she had to worry about. Professor Isambard might be completely naive about Hemlock, but he did seem to have an ability to manipulate people. Either way, she needed evidence of what he was up to, and for that, she needed to get inside the compound.

Rosie leaned further into the basin and splashed her face with water again.

"Be careful . . ."

"What?" said Rosie. Nothing.

"Beware . . ." The warning word echoed in the toilets. Rosie stiffened.

"Hello?" Once again, she smelled the deep, rich scent of roses.

Rosie looked around, but there was no one there. She then looked back to her reflection in the mirror and gasped.

Standing behind her in the mirror was a woman in an old-fashioned green velvet gown, shimmering in golden light. Her long hair was covered by a dark headdress with a trim of gold and pearls.

THE QUEEN IS IN THE SCHOOL TOILET?!

Would anyone else be able to see her?

"Er, hello," said Rosie, still looking into the mirror but with one eye on the door, worried someone might come in. "Is everything all right, Your Highness?" asked Rosie, nodding into a respectful half curtsy.

"This court is a nest of vipers. Be careful. Temper thy fire. Beware of the smiling viper." She shook her head, then stared at Rosie once again like a mother to her child.

"You belong here more than anyone. They know you have power, and the rules will teach you everything you need to know," she said firmly. "Your doubts are your traitors."

She turned, swishing her heavy gown.

Rosie quickly looked around, but no one was there.

Silence. *Did that just happen?*

How long Rosie stood there afterward, she couldn't say. She was stunned, and this was weird and happening way too often. The ghost of Anne Boleyn was officially haunting her. The rules . . . the little purple book—she'd left it under her pillow. She felt an urgent need to go back and study it right now, but it would have to wait until later.

She shook out her shoulders and gave her copper hair a vigorous ruffle. It was still peppered with white baking soda, but she could live with that. She'd have a shower as soon as school finished for the day.

As she left the bathroom, the lunch bell rang, so Rosie went straight up to the Sovereign Hall rather than return to science class. She was waiting in line to collect her food when she felt Charlie tap her on the shoulder.

"You okay?" he asked with a genuinely concerned

expression. He'd been in her science class too, and had seen everything that had happened.

"I'm fine."

"Okay, as long as you are," he said, then left to join the back of the queue.

Rosie loaded up her plate with a burger and chips, and a side dollop of spicy beans. She sat down at a table on her own.

Bina walked past. "You all right?" she asked too.

News about the experiment must have traveled quickly.

"It was my fault," said Rosie. "I added a bit too much science."

"Don't worry, I told everyone to delete it," she said, placing her tray next to Rosie's. "I threatened to do The Rock's Rock Bottom on them otherwise.'

Suddenly Jackson was joining them, placing himself opposite. What could *he* want? Rosie ran her tongue along her braces and smoothed down her frizzy hair, conscious of how dusty it still was.

Bina glanced up at Jackson, then stopped talking, looked at the floor, and started adjusting her hijab.

"Hey, Rosie," Jackson said.

"Hi."

"I've got to go . . ." Bina said quietly, like she was shy. She then gave Rosie's arm an affectionate squeeze and walked off toward some friends.

Eh? What did she mean, she told everyone to delete it? And why was she being so weird around Jackson, acting shy? Bina's never shy.

"Are you all right?" Jackson asked, gazing intensely at Rosie.

"Yeah. Why does everyone keep asking me that?" Rosie tried to twist her hair back, in the hope it would look a little less of a powdery wreck.

"Haven't you seen?" he asked.

"Seen what?" she said, wishing she had a hair tie on her wrist.

Jackson pulled out his phone and scrolled down a couple of pages. "I hate to be the one to break it to you, but you've gone viral . . ." He turned his phone toward her.

She gasped. *What the . . . ?!*

It was a close-up of Rosie's face, covered in baking soda and smears of black.

Surrounding the image were the words:

#FILTH #SPONGE #CLEANUP

The photo Ottilie had taken. Rage bubbled inside her. *How could she have done this?*

That queen had been right. Ottilie Aragon-Windsor: "the smiling viper."

I'm gonna kill her.

No doubt the meme had been shared around the whole school. Everyone was laughing at her.

"Here, I got you this," said Jackson. He reached into his blazer pocket and pulled out a carton of banana milkshake. "I wasn't sure which was your favorite, so I brought two." From his other pocket, he removed a strawberry milkshake. He placed them both on the table in front of Rosie. "You can choose."

"I'll take the strawberry," said Rosie tentatively. "Thanks."

She popped the straw into the carton and sipped at the sweet milk.

"The image was just a cheap laugh. Everyone will have forgotten about it by tomorrow." Jackson smiled at her. It was a kind smile.

Rosie sincerely doubted the photo would be forgotten but nodded anyway. He was trying to be nice. She drained the last of her strawberry milk, the empty carton making a harsh slurpy sound. Jackson looked at her and, as she looked back at him, she felt a flush creeping into her face, and butterflies again tingling in her stomach, despite her simmering anger. She quickly looked down.

" 'There is only one thing in life worse than being talked about, and that is not being talked about,' " said Jackson.

"Is there any scenario you *don't* have a quote for?" She rolled her eyes. He was just so annoying. *In that kind of "annoying," sort of funny way.*

Rosie scanned the Sovereign Hall and saw everyone looking at their phones and laughing.

"Can't argue with Oscar Wilde." Jackson took a chip off her plate.

"Well, he's wrong; I'd prefer not to be talked about at all, thank you. Not everyone wants to be famous, like you," she snapped.

Who was Jackson Sterling, anyway, giving it all the big I am quotes? Of course, he was the winner of the first round of the Falcon Queen games. How would he know how it felt to be labeled a joke and a sponger? He was the kind of guy—cute, athletic, charming—who always got away with everything. It was infuriating. Even Bina went all funny around him.

"And leave my chips alone," she said. She clunked her knife and fork onto her plate of half-eaten food. *I wish these butterflies would get lost, along with Jackson Sterling.*

"Wow, Frostbite. I'm sorry, I didn't mean to offend you." He looked at her with his big brown eyes, all hurt.

"No, it's just . . . It doesn't matter. Thanks for the milkshake."

Rosie scurried out of the Sovereign Hall, leaving Jackson staring after her. She went straight to her bedroom and collapsed onto her bed.

What was she doing? Jackson was only trying to be friendly, and she'd pushed him away. Why was she always so awkward around him, or weirdly irritated by him? She was acting just like a spiteful cabbage.

Jackson Sterling *was* annoying. Or maybe she was just mean and Hemlock was right: anyone named Frost *was* wicked.

When the bell rang for the start of afternoon lessons, Rosie couldn't face leaving the safety of her bedroom. Everyone was laughing at her. "Clean up, ya filthy sponger" was the main theme of their jokes.

She lay on her bed and stared at the ceiling. She typed Pizza? to her mum's phone, then a row of 🍍 🍍 🍍 🍍. Of course, there was no reply.

If she could delete this day, she would. It was at times like this, when she'd had a problem, her mum would always have told her what to do. She longed for her to hold her, and to reassure her that everything was going to be all right. But the only person who seemed to have her back now was a dead queen.

The rules will teach you everything you need to know.

She pulled the purple book out from under her pillow, opened the cover, and glided her fingers over the yellowed pages. She stared at the first rule:

Have courage; make the choice thou fearest the most.

Under the rule, which was marked in a strongly defined dark ink, there were faded words scrawled across the page. The same spidery writing she'd been trying to decipher since first opening the book. Perhaps thoughts written in haste. She couldn't make any sense of them. Maybe the queen had written this part when she was in trouble and her time was running out?

But what did these rules really mean? *Tell me, Queenie.*

Despite her confusion around its contents, the little purple rule book was the only thing that felt solid and real in Rosie's life right now.

She pulled her knees in and curled up like the tiny child she felt she was at that moment, imagining her mother's arms wrapped tightly around her. Clutching the book to her chest with closed eyes, she whispered, "Courage, show me courage."

Chapter Seventeen

PROOF

It's like footie. Everyone moans about a bad game, then people forget about it quickly," said Charlie, kicking a ball toward her.

He was trying to make her feel better. All afternoon she'd seen other students laughing about her. "There she goes, the filthy sponger." "Need a sponge, sponger, ya definitely filthy," they sniggered and hissed as she walked by.

Charlie and Rosie had been paired together for PE, so they were outside on the school playing fields, running up and down with the football.

"Look, loads of players get called names during a match. You just gotta shut 'em up and score, and then you're the hero."

Rosie frowned. *Not everything is about football . . .*

"I mean win the *next* game, the next challenge."

"Oh, I see."

A jolt of panic struck her in the belly. He meant the next Falcon Queen challenge.

It had to be in the next two weeks, before the winter solstice, and she still had no clue what it would be.

She could pull out. But what would Charlie say? Rosie kicked the ball back and frowned.

"Yeah, I've thought about it a bit, I s'pose," she said. "After last time, I'm not exactly looking forward to it."

"Don't worry. It's like when they take a penalty: you can tell they're brickin' it, all eyes on them, but they go for it anyway. The ones with heart always score. Besides, you'll be fine. *I* can protect *you* this time." He raised his arms like a valiant knight, then kicked the ball hard at Rosie.

It'd been a long time since Rosie had played football. She used to play with the other kids in the car park outside their flat in London, but that felt like a lifetime ago. She breathed heavily as she ran after Charlie up the field.

"I told you, I don't need protecting," she panted.

Charlie held up his hands. "I know, Frosty, I know."

Urgh! Why was she always being so defensive, when all Charlie was doing was trying to be nice?

"So you're here on a scholarship, are you?" Rosie called out.

"Yeah, but I'm rubbish at writin', or any clever stuff. I got some other skills, but I don't like to brag." He winked, then started doing keepy-uppies with the ball. "I'll show 'em all one day. My parents could never afford this place. It costs about a gazillion pounds a term. What about you?"

It was a good question and still a mystery to Rosie. She'd been thinking a lot about it. Everything had happened so quickly after her mother's death. She couldn't afford to come, either, so was it a scholarship as Hemlock had said? But she didn't feel she had a super talent to get one. The other explanation was that someone was paying for her to be here. But who? She didn't know anyone with that kind of money. It all came back again to her missing red case. With Miss Churchill's help, she was sure she'd find the answers she needed in there.

Then there was the strange revelation from Anne Boleyn's ghost. Could she really be connected to the school through her ancestry?

Nah, now she really was daydreaming. She was just plain, simple Rosie. Girls like her never turned out to be someone special. But then, who did the ghost queen think she was? And why? Maybe it was just her hair color; that was probably it. The queen was just confused. *Get your head out of the clouds, Rosie.*

"Wow, I thought my chat was half-decent, but I have totally lost you!" Charlie kicked the ball toward her.

"Sorry," said Rosie. She hadn't realized how long she'd been quiet, trying to figure out an answer to his question. And she still didn't have one. Charlie knew about the stolen red case, but he still didn't know about her mum, and she wanted to keep it that way. It was too much to explain.

"Just thinking about . . . the wildcats. And how to stop that scheming creep Hemlock. You said we need proof. What if we went out one night to find it?"

"Went where?" Charlie headed the ball when she sent it back his way.

"Back to Wildcat Woods, to the compound."

"But what if we're caught?" said Charlie. "I've seen people get expelled for less, and I can't afford to lose my scholarship."

And I can't afford to lose my only place to live, thought Rosie.

"We won't get caught," she replied. "Besides, you owe me. I saved you from drowning, remember?"

"What, saving you from Churchill's office doesn't get me anything?" he exclaimed, laughing. "Now, don't get me wrong, I'm very grateful for not dying, as you know. But what you're talking about is risky. I mean, *ris-ky*."

A whistle blew, indicating the end of the lesson.

"Everyone in," shouted Mr. Johnston, their PE teacher. "Balls back to me."

"Reckon I can get it in from here?" said Charlie, nodding toward the goal, which was ten meters away.

"Even *I* could get it in from here," said Rosie. She'd been quite a good striker, when she'd last played.

Charlie pulled back his head, unconvinced.

"You feeling that tough, are ya? I like it. Okay, how about this: Take the penalty. If you get it in, I'll come with you to snoop around the compound. You miss, you agree your plan is totally bananas—no offense—and we both stay away from that place."

Rosie bit her lip, eyeing up the distance to the goal. "You're on."

"Suddenly she's got game." Charlie smirked, strutting over to the goal.

Rosie placed the football on the frozen ground and took a few strides backward. The winter air crept down the back of her PE shirt. Charlie stood firm with legs bent, arms out, ready in position. The goalposts suddenly looked much farther away than before . . . She took a breath, ran to the ball, and kicked it with all her might. The ball careened through the air in the direction of the goal. Charlie flung himself to the left as the ball hit the right-hand post and ricocheted into the back of the net.

Charlie's mouth dropped open. "Nice one, Frosty!" he said. "I'm impressed."

Rosie shrugged. "Let's say tonight, then, shall we?"

✳ ✳ ✳

It was forbidden for any pupil to leave their room after eleven o'clock. It was also forbidden to be on the school grounds at night, and it was certainly forbidden to go near the Wildcat Woods compound. Rosie and Charlie were about to break a shed-load of rules. If they were caught, it would mean immediate expulsion. What was the alternative, though? Let Hemlock carry out whatever it was he was up to? No, she had to do something.

Rosie tucked the rule book into the side pocket of her rucksack. She didn't know why, but she wanted to bring it with her, sort of just in case. She might not understand it all yet, but she could feel the power of the words, ready to guide her.

Charlie had agreed to meet Rosie at midnight, by the bins outside the kitchen toilets (very glamorous). Rosie had gone to bed fully dressed and was now sweltering under the heavy duvet. Bina was snoring softly in the bed next to her. *11:55*. It was time to go.

Rosie slipped out from under the covers without making a sound and pulled on the wellies she'd left by the side of her bed. She picked up her backpack and crept toward the door, slowly opening it. *Eeeeeer . . .* The hinges creaked like a sneering witch. Light from the corridor pooled into the room.

Suddenly an arm swung over her shoulder, then the weight of someone's body slammed her down on the floor.

"Aaaaah!" screamed Rosie, landing flat on her back.

"YOU JUST SMELLED WHAT THE ROCK IS COOKING!" said the person looming over her.

"Bina!" gasped Rosie. "What are you doing??! Get off me!"

"Oh my God! Rosie!" she said, catching her breath. "I thought you were an intruder. It was The Rock's Rock Bottom wrestling move. Sorry, I got carried away; I've just learned it. Did I hurt you?"

"I'm fine," Rosie said from the floor.

"Anyway, never mind what *I'm* doing. What are *you* doing? Where are you going?" said Bina, still pinning her down.

"Um . . . just to the toilet," said Rosie, looking straight up at her.

"In your wellies? Tell me the truth . . ."

Busted. She could trust Bina, right? "Can you keep a secret?"

"I swear it on my life," said Bina, getting up and taking Rosie's hand. "And on the life of my hero, The Rock." She smiled, pulling Rosie up. She put her hand on her heart and pointed to the poster of the smoldering wrestler in his red pants on the wall.

"I can teach you the move, if you like? It's his most famous. The trick is you stay tight together but stay loose;

bounce together and no one breaks anything."

"Er, okay," said Rosie.

"But first, tell me where you're going?" Bina asked.

Rosie sat on the edge of Bina's bed, rubbing her own back, and then told her about Hemlock and her plan to go down to the compound to find evidence against him and save the wildcats. "And Charlie is coming too."

"The boy you saved from the lake?" asked Bina.

"Yeah," said Rosie.

"I'll come too. I'll show you the move when we get back," said Bina. "We'll be just like the Goonies! It's a great movie from the nineties." As though that needed clarifying.

"But if we get caught—" Rosie didn't want Bina to get in trouble.

"If we get caught, you'll need me more than ever. I'm top of the debating society, remember, so I can talk my way out of anything."

That was definitely true. Rosie glanced at her watch, and then back at Bina. "Okay, but we've gotta be quick."

"Is anyone else going to be there? That boy Jackson, from the Gutter Club?" Bina asked.

"No, why?" Rosie answered.

"Doesn't matter," said Bina, putting on her hijab.

Ten minutes later, they were outside and found Charlie crouched behind the big metal bins.

"Could've warned me you were gonna be late," said

Charlie. His hands were tucked under his armpits for warmth.

"Sorry," said Rosie. "Bina's coming too."

"Oh, okay. Hi," Charlie said to Bina. She gave him a tiny wave in return. "Let's get going, shall we?"

It was a clear night. Rosie led the way as they slunk from the central mansion, keeping low and running from shadow to shadow to avoid the moonlight exposing them to anyone who might happen to be awake and looking out one of the school windows. They passed the cottages where the teachers lived and the converted church at the end of the row which belonged to Hemlock, then carried on in the direction of Wildcat Woods.

They pushed forward at a steady pace, keeping the chill of the night at bay, winding through the woods where Rosie and Charlie had spent their first day at the Gutter Club, and then down the slope to the compound. No one spoke, and there were just the crisp leaves crunching beneath their feet. As they drew nearer to the compound, its wall loomed high above them.

The moonlight made the gray metal shine.

"There's a door a bit farther around. I saw Hemlock go in through it, and there was a digger," whispered Rosie. Charlie and Bina nodded and followed her around the curve of the wall.

The door was more like a gate—at least three meters

wide with wheels at the bottom, so it could swing open easily and let vehicles through. It had a horizontal slot at eye level, and the three of them peered through it together. All they could see was an endless expanse of dark trees, which seemed to go on for miles, and the edge of a square metal building on one side.

Rosie grabbed hold of the gate's metal handle and gave it a hard tug. It didn't move.

She tugged again. Nothing. It was locked, of course.

"What now?" asked Bina.

"We'll have to climb over," said Charlie. He put his hands through the viewing slot and pulled himself up until his foot was wedged into the hole. He then reached for the top of the gate but was half a meter short. He hung there for a few moments, wondering what to do next, then lost his grip and fell.

"Ow! Yeah . . . That hurt," said Charlie from the ground.

"We could try this. It's a key card, I think," said Rosie. She whipped out the plastic card belonging to Professor Isambard.

"Where did you get that?" asked Bina.

"I found it in the woods," Rosie answered.

"And you didn't think to tell me before—instead, I land like a doughnut. Cheers," said Charlie.

"Sorry," said Rosie.

Rosie pressed the card to the small screen next to the door. A light turned from red to green. This time, when Rosie pulled the handle, the gate swung wide open. "We're in!"

Just as the three of them were about to enter the compound, a flash of tawny brown darted between their legs.

"Mercury?" said Rosie. The wildcat turned back to look at her, the gold flecks in his silver eyes catching in the starlight. "No, you don't want to be in there!"

The wildcat mewed at the trees inside the compound—a wild and passionate cry. A moment later, two heads emerged from the bushes. They had silver eyes and tawny fur, just like Mercury, but were half the size. Little wildcats—Mercury's babies! Mercury was female, and a mum!

This must have been what Mercury was so desperate for: to find her way back to her cubs. Had she been locked out, perhaps when someone was passing through the gate?

She'd been trying to tell Rosie all along—showing her the location of the key card and then, later, leading her to the compound. These cats were amazing, super intelligent.

But by opening the gate, Rosie had inadvertently led her straight into danger.

"You need to come back out again," Rosie told her. "Bring your babies with you. It's not safe for you in here."

With a flippant flick of her tail, Mercury turned her

back on them and sauntered deeper into the compound, followed by her cubs.

"Wildcats!" gasped Bina, her eyes like saucers.

"Yes," said Rosie. "I've met the adult one before—I call her Mercury. But I've got a horrible feeling we just let her into somewhere really dangerous."

"There's loads more of them living in these woods. This is their home," said Bina.

"One reason to find out what Hemlock's up to in there," said Charlie.

The three of them stepped through the gate and let it swing shut behind them. It made a thunderous clatter as it closed. Rosie winced.

"This way," she said.

The Wildcat Woods were dense, with evergreen pine trees spread throughout the vast area. Rosie peered into the darkness and imagined hundreds of hidden wildcats staring back at her.

The three of them made their way toward the metal building as the brittle ground crunched beneath their feet. Their heavy breathing filled the air. The building was a temporary one, like those used by construction companies working on a new project. It was large, though, the size of a house, and made out of corrugated metal panels.

Charlie was the first to reach its door. He tried to open it, but it refused to budge. "Locked," he whispered.

There was no screen on which to use the key card again, just a keypad of numbers.

Was this where Hemlock had gone after coming through the gate? They did a loop of it. There was only one window, and it was high above their heads.

"Bina, if me and Charlie lift you, d'you think you could look through that window?" Rosie asked.

"I'll try," said Bina, cringing.

"Put your foot on here," said Charlie, linking his hands together to form a little platform.

"And take this," said Rosie, handing her a torch from her bag. Bina took the torch and placed her foot on Charlie's hands.

"On three," said Charlie. "One, two, three."

At the same time, Bina jumped and Charlie pushed, causing Bina to shoot up into the air. She steadied herself by slapping the side of the building, causing a loud clang.

"Shhh!" said Rosie.

She caught Bina's other foot, which was flailing about all over the place, and between them they pushed Bina higher until she was level with the window.

"Okay, that's high enough," said Bina, gripping the window ledge. She clicked on the torch and shone it through the glass.

"Well?" said Rosie, her arms straining as she tried to keep Bina's leg steady. "What can you see?"

"Not much, really," said Bina. "There's a computer and lots of technical equipment, like some sort of control panel. A desk with some papers on it and—*oops!*"

Bina wobbled and nearly fell. The light from the torch flickered skyward as she readjusted her position.

"Careful with that torch!" said Rosie. "Someone might see the light."

"Sorry," said Bina. She placed her foot further along on Charlie's shoulder, putting the torch in her mouth and holding it between her teeth.

"Can you see anything else?" said Charlie. "Don't think I can hold on much longer."

Bina shone the torch back through the window.

"Just a load of wooden crates," she said. "Big ones, all stacked up in the corner. I can't tell what's inside them."

Rosie's arms started shaking. "Okay, come down."

"Wait," said Bina. "There's something written on the crates. It's hard to make out." She repositioned the torch and squinted into the darkness. Then she let out a gasp.

"What? What is it?" said Charlie.

"Lower me down."

Bina was lowered and then half fell to the ground.

"What did you see?" Rosie asked.

"I'm not entirely sure," said Bina. "The writing on the crates . . . it looked like a chemical formula. NH_4NO_3."

"What on earth could that be?" Rosie asked no one in particular.

"Ammonium nitrate," Charlie replied, as if it was the most obvious answer in the world.

"Ammoni-what?" Rosie asked.

"When mixed with fuel oil to make ANFO, it causes a chemical reaction that blows things up. It's big-time demolition. Explosives."

Rosie and Bina exchanged a glance, clearly both wondering how Charlie knew so much about it. Charlie shrugged. "*Minecraft* war zone weapons challenge. Shell shock on level five."

"ANFO?" She slapped her forehead. "I saw boxes with the letters *ANF* being brought in here by the large digger the other morning. I thought it meant 'anfora,' ceramic bowls!"

"So you're telling us there are explosives in there?!" said Bina. "Presuming they're Hemlock's, why would he want to blow anything up?"

Before anyone could answer, there was a loud clunk in the direction of the perimeter gate. The sound of it reverberated through the woods.

Rosie's mouth fell open. "Oh no," she said. Someone else had entered the compound.

Chapter Eighteen

GONERS

Quick, hide!" said Rosie, her voice a strained whisper. "The trees, behind that digger. Run, then get flat on the ground and cover yourselves."

The three of them ran as far as they could, darted behind an excavator with caterpillar treads, and then dropped down quickly among the thick pine trees, not daring to breathe.

Had someone followed them here? Or seen the light from the torch? Whoever it was must have a key card, since they'd been able to get through the gate.

The sound of approaching footsteps grew louder. The steps were slow and meticulously placed, as if the person was searching for something as they walked.

Charlie lifted his chin a little and mouthed, "Run for it?"

Rosie shook her head. If they ran now, they'd definitely be seen. An icy wind swirled around them. Bina shivered.

"Shhhhhh," whispered Rosie, putting her finger to her lips.

Bina clenched her jaw tight to stop her teeth from chattering.

"There you are," said a voice. It was Hemlock.

Rosie's heart stopped beating. There was no way out of this one. Hemlock had caught them, and they were all going to be expelled.

"I've been trying to get hold of you," Hemlock said.

What?

"Why didn't you answer sooner?"

Relief flooded through Rosie as she realized Hemlock wasn't talking to them; he was on the phone. "I'm at the site. We've had a security breach. Either that, or the system is playing up. An alert came through saying someone entered via the main gate at twelve forty-seven." There was a brief pause while the other person spoke. "I know that no one should be here that late, that's why I've come down . . . Well, there's no sign of anyone, but I'm going to sweep the area and check the container . . . No, this changes nothing; we proceed as planned . . . Yes, the evening of the winter solstice . . . It's fine; everyone will be too distracted by the games. They won't hear anything with the fireworks going off at the end of the Bloodstone Banquet . . . Okay, well, stay by your phone just in case. I'll call when I've finished looking around."

Hemlock hung up without saying goodbye, then proceeded toward the metal building.

Rosie's body tightened. She rose onto her knees and risked a glance from behind the giant wheel. She saw Hemlock take out a long metal key and open the door. Once he was inside, the door clicking shut behind him, she let out a long breath.

"We need to leave," said Rosie. "Right now, while he's distracted."

The others nodded, and a thin layer of sweat glistened on Charlie's forehead, despite the cold. With one final look back at the metal building, the three of them sprinted as quietly as they could to the entrance gate, pressed the release button, and didn't stop running through the woods until they were back at the school building.

Only once they were upstairs, safe inside Rosie and Bina's room with the door shut, did any of them risk speaking again.

"Whoa! That was *full-on*!" Charlie said. "Thank God! I thought we were goners."

For once, Bina had very little to say.

"Well, you were right," Charlie continued. "Hemlock is definitely up to something dodgy in there. And with explosives too. What do you think he's planning on blowing up?"

"It must be something in that area," said Rosie, "for the wildcats to be in danger." She felt a pang of grief at the thought of Mercury and her babies trapped inside the compound.

"There's proof now. We need to tell someone. A teacher, or the police?" said Bina.

"The police would need a search warrant, and they don't have enough 'reasonable grounds' for that," said Charlie. "And as soon as Hemlock gets wind of it, he'll hide any evidence."

"We should've taken a photo, damn it," said Rosie, kicking the bed. She should have insisted on that straight-away, before Hemlock had turned up and interrupted them. "We'll have to go back another time." She reached into her trouser pocket for the key card. "Oh no."

"What?" Charlie asked.

"The key card," said Rosie. "It's not in my pocket." She turned her pockets inside out and checked all the ones in her jacket too. "It must've fallen out while we were crouching behind the tree or something."

"Even if you did still have it, we couldn't go back," said Charlie. "Not now that we know opening the gate sends an alert straight to Hemlock."

"If we can't tell the police, what about a teacher?" Bina asked.

"You think they'd believe us over him?" said Charlie.

"Probably not," said Rosie. "Besides, Hemlock told me if I ran to any of the staff, or encouraged them to question him, he'd have them fired."

"What?! He's such a tyrant, controlling everything on this island. We have to find some way of breaking his power over everyone," said Charlie.

Rosie frowned. It looked like it all came back to the Falcon Queen games again. "You said Miss Churchill will definitely be returning for the Bloodstone Banquet, right? At the end of the Falcon Queen games?" Charlie nodded. "Well, if one of us was crowned champion, not only would we get access to her straightaway, but we'd have the respect of the whole school. We'd be in a much stronger position to expose Hemlock and persuade Miss Churchill to stop him."

"And you'd get to make a rule for the school," said Bina.

"But the banquet is always held on the winter solstice— the twenty-first of December," said Charlie, "and Hemlock said he was doing whatever he's got planned that night! It doesn't give Miss Churchill very long to put a stop to it."

"What other choice do we have?" Rosie asked. The thought of putting herself through two more challenges made her feel sick with nerves, but it had to be done. There was also her mother's case, and finally getting the answers she was so desperate for from it. Hemlock was at the root of it all, preventing her, for some unknown reason, from having what was rightfully hers. She had to stop him somehow.

The three of them were silent, Rosie staring at the wall, deep in thought, and Charlie pacing around the room. What else could they do?

"Okay, Frosty, looks like there's no other option. One of us has to win," said Charlie. "And I heard a rumor they're announcing what the second challenge will be tomorrow. Although I'm *far* too pumped to get any sleep tonight."

After Charlie left, Rosie changed into her football kit pajamas.

"Come on, let's practice The Rock's Rock Bottom?" Bina placed her hand on Rosie's shoulder, then her waist, and went to push her.

"Maybe tomorrow." Rosie yawned, stepping back. "After everything that's happened, I'm shattered." She then crawled into bed.

"Okay, tomorrow then. But I'm holding you to it! You will master it. 'Blood, sweat, and respect. First two you give, last one you earn.' I promise," said Bina, snuggling under her covers. "Night, Rosie."

"Night."

So hopefully tomorrow Rosie would finally find out exactly what the next challenge would involve. Who knew what fresh torments it might bring? She clutched the hard cover of the little purple book, then placed it safely under her pillow. As she drifted off into a deep, heavy sleep, she gently stroked the golden leaves printed down its spine.

Something seemed to be changing within her, although she couldn't say what exactly. But now she had her rule book to guide her, and there was no other choice but to go for it.

Chapter Nineteen

THE SECOND FALCON QUEEN CHALLENGE

Rosie swallowed a yawn. What with spying in the night and getting up at the crack of dawn for the Gutter Club, it was going to be an effort to keep her eyes open today. Apparently the task for this morning would be digging up worms and making vermicompost.

"Oh, well done. You've cleaned up nicely," said Ottilie when she arrived and spotted Rosie.

"I know you did it, and yeah, maybe I'm a filthy sponger, but at least I'm not a mean-girl little witch . . ." Rosie said, referring to the cruel meme from yesterday. "What's wrong with you?" Rosie gritted her teeth.

"That will teach you for dragging me into this. Anyway, it's more like what is wrong with *you*? You going to hit me again? Go on, please; then we'll finally be rid of a sponger.

Do us all a favor." Ottilie smiled and put her face close to Rosie's.

Rosie trembled. *I'm gonna wipe that smug smile off your witch face.*

"The white falcon!" called out Ms. Parr.

A shadow passed overhead, causing Rosie to look up. In the sky just above her, a majestic bird swooped and swerved, effortlessly beating its enormous wings. It looked like the same bird she'd seen on her first weekend here— the one she'd imagined was her mother watching over her. Its chest was white, flecked with shining bronze and golden speckles.

"It's the only one on the whole island, as far as we know. I call her Queen Nike," Ms. Parr said proudly.

"Nike like the trainers?" asked Charlie. "I didn't know you were the sporty type, miss."

"No, not like the trainers, Charlie," said Ms. Parr. "Nike is the goddess of victory in Greek mythology—the 'Winged Goddess.' I thought it sounded apt for such a regal bird. There's been a white falcon here for as long as anyone can remember, perhaps as far back as the times of the original Falcon Queen, Anne Boleyn."

Rosie's ears pricked up.

"Why was she called that?" Rosie asked.

"The nickname originally came from the falcon on her family crest, but she also kept a white falcon as a pet. At this school, the term 'Falcon Queen' has come to mean someone courageous and strong, who stands up for what they believe in and stands by their friends. Falcon Queens stand together."

Like all the women in the Falcon Queen gallery, thought Rosie.

"And what about the lads, then? Don't we get a mention?" said Charlie.

"Yes, and boys. Everyone stands by this, Falcon Kings too," Ms. Parr said. "Whoever you are, standing together makes you stronger.

"However, there's an old saying," she continued. "'As the falcon flies, Heverbridge thrives.' As long as there is a falcon here, the queen's spirit remains strong at Heverbridge. 'But if the falcon falls, judgment calls,' which means something bad will happen to Heverbridge. So keep an eye out for our friend Queen Nike—we wouldn't want anything terrible to happen to her."

Ms. Parr looked at Ottilie, then Rosie. "Love prospers when a fault is forgiven, but dwelling on it separates friends."

Ottilie grimaced at Rosie. "She is *not* my friend."

The falcon looped around the field one final time and then flew into the forest, out of sight. *Of course*, thought Rosie. Just like the bird on the Heverbridge crest and on the front of the little purple book. *Temper thy fire* was what the queen had said. She couldn't let Ottilie get to her anymore.

The wintry sun beamed down on her, as if with approval, as Rosie strode ahead. She decided it was best to avoid Ottilie as much as possible from now on. The last thing she needed was to be back in Hemlock's office—or expelled.

Later that morning, after the Gutter Club, Hemlock stood in front of the whole school, behind the grand wooden lectern that was elevated on a small stage at the far end of the Sovereign Hall. Although his suit was sharp and his hair was neat, his eyes were a little blotchy and red.

Prowling around in the middle of the night will do that to you, thought Rosie.

Not that she could talk, since that was exactly what she'd done too. She was so tired she'd forgotten to take off her high-viz jacket. She shrugged it off her shoulders.

"Good morning," Hemlock said, his voice amplified and made slightly tinny by the microphone he was speaking into. The conversations throughout the room died down. "It gives me pleasure to announce that the second round of the Falcon Queen games . . ."

Rosie stiffened. What was it going be this time, another death-defying experience? She could call social services.

". . . will take place next Saturday. For this challenge,

you will be split into teams." He paused, and the crowd murmured with curiosity.

Rosie's thoughts started racing. What if she was put with people she didn't know or didn't like?

"It is called the Court of Reform and celebrates Anne Boleyn's dynamism. She believed in improvement, restoration, and the ability to inspire change," Hemlock went on. "So this challenge will test for the second Heverbridge core value: power. In this case, the power to inspire.

"A week from Saturday—that's ten days from now—there will be a show in the school theater, featuring performances from all seven teams. The performances may take any form you like, but must feature every member of the team equally.

"The presentations will be judged, and the two teams deemed most worthy will be put through to the final challenge. Those who don't make it through will face Crumwell's Shame Trap, and trust me, that is not something any of you wish to experience."

An outbreak of excited chatter rippled across the room. Rosie chewed on the side of her nail. She didn't know what to think. This sounded strangely easy.

It's just showbiz. Easy-peasy, right? How hard can it be?

At least it sounded less life-and-death than the Black Lake challenge had been. But she was not a natural performer, so the thought of having to do something in front of the whole school still terrified her. Also, what did Hemlock mean by "Crumwell's Shame Trap"? Whatever it was, it didn't sound good.

"Silence," Hemlock boomed into the microphone. A bubbling quiet descended once again. "The teams have been posted on the noticeboard in the central atrium. Good luck to you all."

Assembly over, all the pupils started to gather up their bags.

Hemlock cleared his throat. "One final matter, before you leave," he said. "A reminder that it is *strictly forbidden* for *any pupil* to be outside after dark. Even during the day, you have no reason to be farther afield than the main school campus, so anyone found outside at night, or anywhere they shouldn't be, will have me to deal with, and the punishment shall be severe. I hope that is understood."

Rosie frowned, her stomach sinking. Was he looking directly at her? She lowered her eyes, suddenly finding her shoelaces remarkably interesting.

As soon as assembly was over, all students were supposed to go straight to their first lesson, but the majority raced to the atrium instead to check out the teams posting. Rosie followed them and pushed her way through the crowd, stretching her neck. There were too many tall pupils in front of her, though, so she could only see the backs of heads. It was like being in the middle of a crowded marketplace among a load of frantic bargain hunters, all pushing to the front of the queue.

"NO WAY! You have *got* to be kidding me!" Ottilie's cry of dismay pierced through the other chatter.

By the time Rosie had made it to the front, Ottilie was no longer there, but she could still hear her complaining to Jamila and Ishaan as they headed off to class. "Do they know who I am?!"

In the middle of the noticeboard, covering the majority of the other posters, was a large piece of cream paper with a gold trim.

THE FALCON QUEEN GAMES—

CHALLENGE II: THE COURT OF REFORM

Underneath were thirty names, split into groups of four or five. Rosie scanned them all for her own and finally found it. *No, no, no.* This was some sort of joke.

Group 5

- Ottilie Aragon-Windsor
- Rosie Frost
- Charlie Saint
- Jackson Sterling

What?! So she was going to have to work with Ottilie again. Great. This was about as bad as it got. Ottilie couldn't even look at her without sneering; how were they ever going to actually perform together? At least Charlie was in her group too. And Jackson. It seemed like a big coincidence that the four of them from the Gutter Club had been put in the same team, but perhaps it was one of Hemlock's cruel jokes—forcing them to work together when he knew there had already been a big bust-up between them. Whatever the reason, being placed in a team with Ottilie meant Rosie's chances of making it through to the final round were now zero to none.

The next day at the Gutter Club, the debate of what they should do for the second challenge continued. "Let's just put our cards on the table," said Ottilie as Ms. Parr led them across a frozen field to the place they'd be working that morning. This was the first time the four of them had seen each other since yesterday, after the announcement of the groups. "I love honesty, so here goes: I don't care about any of you deadbeat losers. But I *do* care about getting through to the next round because *I want to win.*"

She put her hands on her hips, then threw a shady look at Jackson. "Actually, correction: I *will be* the winner of the whole Falcon Queen games. I've visualized it.

"You guys are lucky: I'm a born winner, so by being with me, it gives you all a better chance of being a runner-up. I asked Hemlock if I could switch teams, but he won't let me, so it looks like I'm stuck with you. I'm prepared to put aside the despicable behavior of certain individuals"—she looked pointedly in Rosie's direction—"*for now*, and focus on how we're going to win this thing. Okay?"

Charlie clapped his hands and wiped an imaginary tear from his eye. "Wow," he said. "That was beautiful. Team spirit in full effect. You should become a coach."

"Ha, ha, very funny," said Ottilie. "People who can't, coach. Daddy says I've got the brains and the beauty to be anything I want to be, *actually*. I'm like Oprah. I actually have talent. Meanwhile, I'm baffled why some people are even at this school." She shrugged, then eyebrowed Charlie.

"Hey!" said Rosie, leaping to Charlie's defense.

"Guys, chill!" said Jackson. "Arguing isn't going to get us anywhere."

"That's what I was saying," said Ottilie, "if any of you were listening . . . So are we going to come up with a plan to win this thing or not?"

"I suppose so," said Rosie, scowling at Ottilie.

"I'm in," said Jackson.

Charlie nodded. "Me too."

"Great," said Ottilie. "So Anne Boleyn believed in integration of cultures, so I was thinking we should do some kind of contemporary dance routine. Daddy took me to see Cirque du Soleil last summer and it was really dreamy, but also totally edgy. I love that combo." She flicked her hair.

"I'm not really much of a dancer," said Rosie.

"Me neither," said Charlie. "I'm not wearing a skin-tight leotard."

"Well, what other ideas have you got, then?" said Ottilie with a huff.

"I could show off my football skills," said Charlie. "My record is three hundred and fourteen keepy-uppies without dropping the ball."

"Well done, you, I'm *so* impressed," Ottilie said. "And meanwhile the rest of us can stand at the sides of the stage and cheer on an empty-headed loser kneeing a ball a few times? That's *truly* groundbreaking . . . I don't think so. The Court of Reform is a creative opportunity to push boundaries for collective expression."

"We could read poems by some cool beat poets?" suggested Jackson. "That'd be easy enough."

"Yawn," said Ottilie, rolling her eyes. "We'd never win doing that."

"What about baking something live onstage and giving it to the judges? Like . . . pineapple upside-down cake is simple, yet visually brilliant," said Rosie. Her mum's recipe was amazing. They used to make it together to celebrate their victories, big or small.

"I love your darling naivete," said Ottilie. "But absolutely not. They'd think we were trying to bribe them and end up deducting points. It's a terrible idea."

The discussion went on in a similar fashion for the next twenty minutes, with Ottilie either ridiculing or dismissing all of their suggestions.

"We're here," Ms. Parr interrupted, and came to a halt. They were standing in open grassland dotted with large knobby trees. Clumps of sandy grass poked through the hard ground all around them.

"Ottilie, would you please put your protective jacket back on." Ottilie rolled her eyes and let it sort of hang off her shoulder, as usual.

"You'll need to have your wits about you today," Ms. Parr told them with a stern look on her face.

"Why?" said Ottilie. "Where are we?"

Ms. Parr looked at all four of them in turn, as if sizing up their worth. "This," she said, "is where the Komodo dragons live."

Chapter Twenty

DRAGONS

"W ait a minute," said Rosie. "You're saying there are Komodo dragons—those giant lizard things—living on this island?"

"That is correct," replied Ms. Parr.

"What?!" said Ottilie, looking all around her. "Don't they, like, eat people?"

"They can eat almost their entire body weight in one meal," said Ms. Parr, "but very rarely eat humans."

Rosie also took a couple of glances over her shoulder. "Very rarely" was not quite rare enough.

"I read on Twitter that a Komodo dragon once ate Sharon Stone's husband's foot," said Ottilie.

"Well, I don't know about that," said Ms. Parr, "but

what I do know is that they're an endangered species, which is why they need our help. The lack of egg-laying females, habitat destruction, and human poaching has threatened their population."

"I thought they only lived in Africa," said Charlie.

"Indonesia, actually," said Ms. Parr. "And yes, this island holds the only wild population of them outside the Indonesian Archipelago. Technically they're a different subgenus, since they evolved here to endure the colder climate, but they're from the same family."

"Wow, this island keeps getting more amazing and absurd all at once," said Rosie, looking around in search of hints of Komodo dragons.

"I think what you mean is that it keeps getting more and more special," said Ms. Parr. "Komodo dragons are one of the most incredible creatures on earth and an endangered species. They're descendants of gigantic lizards that roamed the earth over four million years ago. Fully grown adults can be as long as a small car and run up to thirteen miles per hour. They have an acute sense of smell and enough venom in their jaws to bring down a tiger."

"Wooow, impressive." Charlie whistled, while Rosie continued to scan the undergrowth and bushes, clenching her jaw.

"Don't worry, though," Ms. Parr continued. "We're unlikely to encounter any adults today. These dragons, they like hot climates but can stand the harshest weathers, they're highly resourceful and intelligent, and they usually spend the winter on the other side of the mountain. So you won't see any around here. Although occasionally they are spotted at the top of the volcano, the Volcan Crag. It's the highest point on the whole island—you can just make out the summit from here. There's a graveyard at the base of it too." She pointed above them to a snowy peak in the distance. "The Volcan Crag is also known as the Soul's Gateway. The high altitude combined with the unusual gases it emits can make some people hallucinate—either beautiful dreams or their worst fears . . ."

Sounds bizarre to me, thought Rosie. The more she heard, the more strange and magical this island felt compared to everything she'd ever known on the busy mainland. All those people going about their business on the streets of London had no idea what they were missing, and yet here it all was. All this wonder, just off their shores, just a little way out across the ocean.

"Anyway, I digress . . ." said Ms. Parr. "It's the young Komodos we're interested in today, and they're above your heads." She gestured toward the trees around them.

"They live in trees?" asked Jackson, peering into the tree nearest him.

"That's right," said Ms. Parr. "When a baby Komodo dragon is born, it quickly scurries up the nearest tree, out of the way of predators—including adult Komodos, which would happily gobble it up given half the chance. Komodo dragons have cannibalistic tendencies."

"Eat your babies . . . nice." Charlie cringed.

"So the young lizards stay in their trees for about four years, living off beetles, grasshoppers, snails, and birds' eggs, until they're big enough to come down and fend for themselves. That's all well and good in the summer, when food is plentiful, but times are hard during the long winter months. Which is why we're here."

Ms. Parr reached into her rucksack and pulled out a large plastic container. She unclipped the lip to reveal hundreds of snails clambering over one another inside.

"Komodo dragons do not hibernate, and due to climate change they are now listed as endangered. Our job today will be to place these little fellas all over the trees—on the highest branches you can reach—to give the baby Komodos a little extra food to keep them going."

"Cool!" said Charlie, picking up a handful of snails as if they were sweets in a pick 'n' mix.

"I am literally *not* touching a snail," said Ottilie. "Eww. I saw on TikTok once that snail slime gives you diarrhea. I'll leave it to Dora the Explorer to do it." She scowled at Rosie, then pulled out a bottle of Gucci apple blossom from her mini-rucksack. "Also, they really stink. Anyway, I've been on safari—my dad took me three times. We saw the big five, no stupid snails and pathetic dragons." She squirted the perfume all over her neck and wrists. "Actually, just to be sure . . ." she said, doing an extra burst in the direction of the snails.

She took off her high-viz jacket, screwed it up, and discreetly dropped it behind a tree, then waved her hands around and sniffed her wrist. "All gone," she sighed, next taking out her iPhone and starting to scroll through her socials. Ms. Parr had already walked on, ignoring her. She'd become used to Ottilie not joining in.

Rosie picked up a couple of snails by their shells and walked over to the nearest tree, plonking them on one of the branches. She searched through the star-shaped leaves for any signs of a baby dragon.

As the group spread out to ensure all the trees got their share of the snails, Rosie kept scanning her surroundings to make sure there weren't any giant lizards sneaking up on her.

"I'm not nervous, I'm not nervous," she whispered to herself. She started singing—quietly at first, then a little louder, thinking the sound might help keep any prowling dragons away too.

"*Show me the way. Where should I go?*"

"You've got a really nice voice."

Rosie gasped and turned, dropping the snail she was about to place.

"Sorry." Jackson smiled at her, and she sighed with relief. It was just Jackson. A wave of flutters rose up in her stomach.

"Oh. You've got one of the, um . . ." He pointed at her face. "On your neck." Rosie flinched and swiped the snail to the ground.

"What was the song?" Jackson asked her.

"What song?" She was still preoccupied with cleaning the snail goop off her neck.

"The one you were singing," he said. "I didn't recognize it."

"Oh, it was nothing."

"It must have a name," said Jackson. "I liked it."

"It was a thing I started years ago, but I never finished it. It's nothing, really . . ."

"Wait, you wrote that? That's so cool." Jackson's eyes sparkled. "That's it; that's what we should do for the Court of Reform."

"What is?" Rosie was so distracted by the snails and the Komodo dragons that she was only half listening to him.

"You should write a song for us to perform. I like singing, and I know Ottilie likes the sound of her own voice. As for Charlie . . . Well, we can just give him a tambourine or something. It'll be awesome!" It was the most animated Rosie had ever seen him.

"I dunno . . ." said Rosie. It had been a long time since she'd written anything, and without her mum's encouragement, it didn't feel the same. "Do you think Ottilie will go for it?"

"Only one way to find out." Jackson started walking away.

They wandered back to where Ottilie was standing, Instagramming her face with a "cheeky pixie" filter, which she probably thought made her look cute but actually made her look like a bug-eyed alien.

"Charlie, come over here; we've got an idea!" Jackson put forward his plan.

"I like it!" said Charlie. "I've always wanted to be in a band. Do I get to smash a guitar at the end of the performance?"

"Maybe it'd be safer if you played the triangle," said Rosie.

"Rock 'n' roll!" Charlie stuck out his tongue and made horn signs with his hands.

The three of them then turned to Ottilie.

Silence.

Rosie glanced at the others, waiting for her cutting disapproval.

Ottilie twiddled a strand of her hair around her finger and pursed her lips.

"Fine," she eventually said. "On one condition: I'm the lead singer and I get the final say."

"Oh no!" said Charlie, shaking his head. "No, no!"

"Why not? I'm the lead or nothing at all," Ottilie snapped.

"No, it's not that," said Charlie. "Look." He pointed across the frozen grassland, some distance away.

Rosie gasped. A Komodo dragon ten feet long, the size of a large crocodile, was slinking toward them.

Ottilie screamed. "What do we do?"

"Where's Ms. Parr?" said Jackson.

They looked around, but the groundskeeper was nowhere to be seen.

"Quick—climb a tree!" said Rosie. "It's what the baby Komodos do, which must mean the adults can't climb."

"But this coat is Louis Vuitton," Ottilie shrilled.

"Well, it's either get your fancy coat dirty or get eaten by a lizard. The choice is yours." Rosie was already scanning for a suitable tree.

The Komodo dragon took another few steps forward. Its long tongue snaked out of its mouth and then whipped back in again. Was it tasting the air, sensing their fear?

Suddenly it turned its head to the side, opened its jaws, and started tearing into something bright green. It was Ottilie's high-viz jacket.

"Oh dear, it's probably got your scent now," Rosie said to Ottilie.

"Or your BO," Ottilie quipped back.

"This one," said Jackson, running to a nearby tree and pulling himself up with ease.

He reached down and hoisted Ottilie up, while Charlie and Rosie pushed from beneath. Ottilie huffed and whined but finally made it safely onto one of its branches.

There wasn't enough room for all of them, so Charlie and Rosie sprinted to different trees—one on either side. It took Rosie three attempts to pull herself up, the bark scratching her palms. By the time she'd made it, she was out of breath and covered in sweat. The Komodo dragon dropped the jacket and began to stride forward a little closer, still sniffing the air. It was heading toward the tree Ottilie and Jackson were in.

Where was Ms. Parr?

"Ahhhhh! Ow, ow, ow!" shrieked Ottilie, clawing at her arms and legs.

"What? What is it?" said Jackson.

"Ants!" said Ottilie. "There're hundreds of red ants all over me, *biting*." She seemed astounded that anything would be audacious enough to bite her precious skin.

"Move over to this side," said Jackson, holding out his hand.

"I can't, I can't," said Ottilie. As she leaned forward, her pink mini-rucksack fell, spilling lip glosses and makeup all over the ground.

Ottilie looked down after it and lost her balance, landing below the tree with a thump.

The Komodo dragon reacted immediately, running straight for her.

Oh no, thought Rosie. As much as she disliked Ottilie, she couldn't stand by and watch her get eaten.

Rosie leaped from the safety of her tree and ran to Ottilie. The Komodo dragon was coming at them fast, while Ottilie just stared at it from the ground, transfixed. Jackson reached down his hand, shouting for them to hurry.

"Get up," yelled Rosie, yanking Ottilie's arm.

Ottilie, roused from her daze, sprang to her feet. There wasn't time to get back onto Jackson's branch, so she let Rosie pull her through the trees. They sprinted away as fast as they could, the Komodo dragon continuing to chase them at full speed.

Jackson and Charlie were both out of their trees now, shouting and clapping to try to get the Komodo's attention, but the lizard was completely focused on Ottilie and Rosie.

A large oak came into view in front of them, with a perfect low-hanging branch. "That tree," said Rosie, pointing. "Get ready."

Ottilie nodded. As soon as they were within reach, Ottilie lifted both hands and grabbed hold of the sturdy branch, flipping her legs up. With Rosie pushing from below, she managed to get up, sitting with one leg on either side of the thick branch. Rosie then reached up her hand.

"Pull me up," she said, but Ottilie was too busy staring over Rosie's shoulder. She covered her mouth with her hands.

"It's coming!" Ottilie said.

The Komodo dragon was so close, tearing through the broken shrubs and frozen weeds. Its venomous tongue darted in and out. Rosie only had time for one more try. She jumped and wrapped her hands around the branch, but it was slippery with ice and her fingers couldn't keep their grip.

She fell to the ground and scratched her elbow down the trunk of the tree. The Komodo dragon was now less than a meter away, and there was nothing Rosie could do. She stared in horror as the giant lizard opened its jaws wide, ready to strike.

Teeth. Razor-sharp teeth. That's all Rosie remembered seeing. Hundreds of teeth like tiny crystal needles, coming toward her. A thick trail of poisonous slobber oozed out of the Komodo dragon's mouth as it salivated at the thought of its defenseless prey.

Rosie backed up against the tree as the deadly creature sprang.

Whoosh!

Something heavy swooped past Rosie's head, straight into the mouth of the Komodo.

A long tree branch. At the other end of it was Ms. Parr. The lizard bit down on it with its mighty jaws, its yellow eyes locked on the branch.

Ms. Parr gritted her teeth, heaving with all her strength to push the dragon back a couple of paces. Its whole body writhed as it battled her, its scaly skin crinkling like chain mail.

"Bah!" Ms. Parr was shouting to it. "Bah!" Her cheeks were flushed and her scraggy hair stuck to her forehead with sweat. "Stand up and grab a stick if you can find one," said Ms. Parr. "Show it you're not scared."

"I can't . . ." Rosie said, shuffling away.

"Yes, you can, Rosie. Take courage . . ."

The Komodo's jaws snapped Ms. Parr's branch in half, then it sneered at the groundskeeper, its tail lashing from side to side. Ms. Parr stumbled backward and lost her footing, crashing to the ground.

Rosie reached behind her for a sturdy-looking stick and staggered to her feet. She waved it at the dragon.

"Raaaaaaah!" she yelled, an animalistic roar. It felt good to scream. "RAAAAAAAAAAAAAHH! RAAAH! RAAAAH! RAAAAAAH!"

She swiped the stick down, blocking the dragon's route to Ms. Parr, and the dragon grappled it with its claws, but Rosie held on tightly. Ms. Parr got back on her feet too, the chewed-off branch still in her hand.

Between their combined stick-wielding and Rosie's raving shouts, the Komodo dragon eventually flinched back, hissing despondently. It had met its match. With one final flick of its tongue, it slithered backward, spun around, and scurried away. Ms. Parr chased after it, the broken branch held high above her head like she was some sort of Neanderthal warrior.

A calmness descended on the grasslands again.

Rosie was still breathing heavily. *What the hell just happened?*

"Just *wait* until my daddy hears about this," said Ottilie, who was still in the tree above her. Rosie had forgotten she was there.

Jackson and Charlie came running up to them.

"Are you okay?" said Charlie. "We tried to get it to turn around and follow us, but it was so fast."

"I can only apologize," said Ms. Parr, returning with the thick branch swung over one shoulder.

"We're fine," said Rosie. Her heart was still thumping, adrenaline still charging on through her body.

"Well done, Rosie, you showed real courage back there."

"Um . . . actually, we're not fine. All my cosmetics are smashed," said Ottilie, still clinging to the branch.

"We have to respect this is not our territory. You may

be more at home with the chimpanzees, who seem to handle their frustrations in a similar manner to you," said Ms. Parr, looking up at Ottilie.

"Whatever, I don't care. Anyway, what will my daddy think? He'll have plenty to say to you, and he has an amazing lawyer!"

"Everyone is welcome to learn from this island's inhabitants. Come down when you're ready, and then you can pick up your litter," Ms. Parr replied, looking over at the spilled contents of Ottilie's pink mini-rucksack.

Ottilie's eyes widened, and she opened her mouth, but no words came out.

Ms. Parr continued, "That dragon you just encountered was Ganas, one of the largest males on the island. If I'd thought there was any chance of an adult coming back to this side of the mountain this late in the year, I never would have brought you. In all my time here, I've never seen one this far east. I don't know what it signifies, but some change may be coming to Bloodstone Island."

"What do you mean by that?" Rosie asked.

"Let's walk and talk. I don't think he'll be back, but after what just happened, we shouldn't take any chances."

The four of them didn't need telling twice. Charlie and Jackson helped Ottilie down from the tree, and then the group set off in the direction of the school. Ms. Parr led at a brisk march, her eyes flicking from side to side as she went. She still held the tree branch in one hand.

"You said something about change coming to the island?" Rosie said to her.

"Yes," said Ms. Parr. "It's a possibility. Komodo dragons are highly instinctual creatures. Any change in their behavior may be the result of something upsetting the fragile ecosystem around them."

Rosie exchanged a look with Charlie. Could this be linked to Hemlock and whatever it was he was up to? Ms. Parr did say that Komodo dragons had an incredible sense of smell. Maybe they'd caught the scent of strange chemicals, or even explosives, in the air?

"Like if someone were to change the island in some way?" Rosie asked.

"Precisely," said Ms. Parr, setting a steady pace as she marched on.

"What, by, like, blowing some of it up or something?" said Charlie, trotting along behind her.

"That would certainly do it," said Ms. Parr.

"Is there a reason someone might do something like that?" Rosie asked, doing her best to keep up. "Use explosives on the island, I mean?"

"You kids certainly have some imagination," said Ms. Parr. "But unless we go to war, I think we're safe from any bombings or explosions. You've been watching too many action films."

"So there's no reason why anyone would have explosives on the island?" asked Charlie.

Rosie winced, thinking Charlie may have pushed it too far with such a blatant question, but Ms. Parr was unfazed.

"Not unless they were mining for bloodstone," she said.

"Bloodstone?" asked Rosie. "What's that?"

"Don't you know anything?" said Ottilie. "Why do you think it's called *Bloodstone Island*?"

"It's a semiprecious gemstone, known for its distinctive dark green and black coloring, flecked with specks of red," Ms. Parr explained. "Some people believe it has healing properties, but they're still researching it, so it's all a load of tripe until evidence is found otherwise. This island is enriched with bloodstone—hence the name— but it's not a valuable mineral. I doubt anyone would bother mining it. Besides, the island is a protected conservation zone. Miss Churchill would never allow it."

Rosie dropped back, lost in thought. Could it be bloodstone that Hemlock was after? If it was something that Miss Churchill would forbid, then it made sense to do it while she was off traveling. But why would he bother if it wasn't that valuable?

"You're shivering," said Jackson, who had fallen back next to her. "Here, have my coat." He took off his gray puffer jacket and offered it to Rosie.

"I'm fine," she said, but she *was* cold. The shock of the Komodo dragon attack was catching up with her.

"I'm a London boy from Putney Hill, but I spent a lot of time in Devon," Jackson said, "and it can get pretty wild down there, so I'm used to it. I don't really feel the cold. Go on, take it." He offered his jacket again.

"Okay, thanks," said Rosie. She could do with the extra layer.

Jackson put the coat around her shoulders like she was some sort of fragile princess.

She shook it off, putting her arms through the sleeves properly. It smelled of Jackson: clean soap, fresh and crisp. Nice. *No, don't get caught up in his cuteness.* Her mum's words rang in her ears. (She said this when they watched rom-coms together.)

As she zipped up Jackson's jacket, she caught Ottilie staring daggers at her. What had Rosie done wrong now? Ottilie wrapped her precious, mud-splattered Louis Vuitton coat around herself and stormed ahead without looking back.

How on earth was she going to get through the next challenge with Ottilie Aragon-Windsor as a teammate?

Chapter Twenty-One

IN THE BAND

Charlie has added you to the group "Falcon Rock Band WINNERS 🎸 🎤 🎶"

Charlie: Hey guys.
U recovered from the Godzilla attack yesterday 💥🚀💥
How bout we rehearse for this performance thing? You all free later?

Jackson: I am. What time?

Charlie: After lunch? 2?

Ottilie: I'm busy.

How did you even get my number?

Charlie: Jamila. Bribed her with doughnuts 👻

Ottilie: Urgh. So basic. Well don't ever phone me, okay? And you have to delete it as soon as this stupid thing's over.

Jackson: what time can u do, Ottilie?

Ottilie: Later on, I suppose.

Charlie: 4 o'clock then? Down in the rehearsals rooms?

Jackson: 👍

Ottilie: Fine

Charlie: Rosie?

Rosie: Yep. See you there

Charlie: It's a date

Ottilie: No it's not. It's a rehearsal.

Charlie: TEAM FALCON ROCK FOR THE WIN 🏆

Ottilie: And that is NOT our name

Rosie had never been in a group chat. The kids back home never really included her in much. She had to admit that now, every time a new message came in, she felt pleased. It was good to be part of something, although it took her a full ten minutes to decide what to reply, before settling on the pretty unadventurous "Yep. See you there."

She spent most of the morning staring blankly at the old, half-finished lyrics in her unicorn notebook. She tried to think of new lines to add to them, but nothing came to her. Her run-in with the Komodo dragon was still playing heavily on her mind, not to mention what Ms. Parr had said about change coming to Bloodstone Island. If the others were expecting her to come up with a new song before the rehearsal, they were going to be disappointed. She hadn't written a song since . . . her mum had . . . gone. The truth was every time she was stuck, every time she picked up a pen to write or play music, even if it felt good, she'd felt guilty, like she shouldn't do it without her mum.

A little before four o'clock, Rosie gathered up her books, then made her way to the music practice rooms in the basement of the West Wing. The first was occupied with a year seven student blasting his trumpet (badly), and a couple of girls were eating sandwiches and gossiping in the second. The third was empty, which was the room Rosie had been hoping for, because it was the only one containing a piano. It was a grand piano, walnut-colored and so highly polished, you could see your reflection in its lid.

Rosie sat on the stool, pulled out the small purple rule book, and flicked through its pages. *Hey, Queenie, have you got any words of inspiration? Lyrics, maybe? I'm a little dried up here.*

She read the second rule: *"United we stand, divided we fall." That's not helpful.* How the hell was she supposed to be united with Ottilie? More like they couldn't stand each other.

Rosie put the book back in her rucksack and sighed, placing her fingers on the cold, shining wood of the piano top. She then slowly lifted the lid, and for the longest minute she stared down at the glistening keys. Could she do this? *Mum, do you want me to play? Can I? Should I?* She placed one finger on an ivory key, the middle C. It had been her safest note on the piano. She pressed down and it hummed as if to say, *Come on, Rosie.*

She began to play a gentle, tinkling melody. The sound was like warm sunshine. It reminded her of her mum and their old flat in London. A wave of sadness washed over her; her head bowed, her shoulders slumped, then she paused. They'd only had a battered keyboard back at home, but her mum had been able to make it sound like the grandest piano in the world.

But then suddenly Rosie's fingers took over, her hands dancing over the keys like a wizard concocting a magic spell. She lost herself in the music, swept away by its rhythms. Her hands raced through the notes, pouring every drop of sadness and happiness she'd ever felt into the keys. Finally, she stopped, her eyes shining like she'd just been somewhere special. She looked up and saw there was someone else in the room with her.

"That's beautiful," said Jackson. "Maybe we've got a chance to win this thing after all."

Rosie lifted her fingers from the keys. "I've not played in a long time," she said.

"You can't tell," Jackson assured her. "Play that one you were singing earlier. How did it go? *Show me the way. What should I do?*" he sang. His voice was warm and soulful.

"Not quite," said Rosie. She played some chords on the piano as she sang. "*Show me the way. Where should I go . . .*"

"Yeah, that was it," said Jackson with a smile. "Again."

He took a seat right beside her on the piano stool. She had never been this close to him, shoulder to shoulder. He smelled like fresh lemongrass and leather.

Rosie played and sang the same line again, and this time Jackson joined in with a perfect harmony, his voice smooth and rich.

"This is gonna be awesome!" said Jackson. "What's the next line?"

Rosie's heart sank. "That's the problem. There isn't one. I never got finished writing it, and when I tried this morning, I was too distracted."

"Well, the song's about wanting to follow your dreams but feeling lost at the same time, right?"

Rosie nodded.

Jackson chewed on his lip as he thought. She noticed his dark eyelashes framing his light brown eyes, quiet in concentration.

"How about something like, *When the road ahead is dark, and I can't see a thing* . . . I'm just thinking out loud here." He laughed, then turned directly to her, all concerned. "Sorry, I'm treading on your words. Is it cool if we write this together? I get it if not; it's your song." Suddenly the cocky dude she'd first met was gone; no cool quotes, just a boy with kind, honest eyes, concerned that he might have offended her.

"No, it's all good," said Rosie, reaching for her unicorn notebook, then knocking it to the floor, flustered as she picked it back up. She tried to ignore the butterflies having a party in her stomach. "What about: *But the road ahead is dark, please shine down on me* . . . "

"That's it!" Jackson was getting excited again. He nudged her playfully. *"As I say goodbye to who I used to be . . ."*

"Yeah, cool," said Rosie, frantically scribbling.

"*And* it reflects the Anne Boleyn message. She was a powerful woman who believed in herself," said Jackson. "I like a strong woman. I'm actually a feminist." He smirked, elbowing Rosie again.

Just ignore the cute smile; focus on the writing, Rosie.

They joined the two lines while she bashed out a few more chords. Jackson slipped effortlessly into another harmony; even Rosie had to admit they were sounding really good together. A warmth spread through her. Jackson hit an off note. "Oops, can you blend with that?" he asked, and gave her a jokey side-glance.

She let out an awkward snort of laughter and almost slipped off her side of the stool, but he quickly grabbed her arm, pulling her back up sharply and inadvertently closer to him. With her face right up to his, almost nose to nose, she could feel him breathing. She shuffled back abruptly, cleared her throat, and looked down at the keys.

"Oh, sorry; am I interrupting?" said Ottilie from the doorway. "I didn't realize you'd planned a private rehearsal for just the two of you."

Rosie leaped up from the stool she was sharing with

Jackson as if shocked with a bolt of electricity. "No, it wasn't like that. We were just trying a few things out."

"Well, I'm here now, so we can begin properly," said Ottilie. "I'm the lead singer, after all."

She all but shoved Rosie out of the way and nestled herself in next to Jackson. He gave a polite cough and edged away from her.

"So what am I singing?" Ottilie asked, picking up Rosie's unicorn notebook.

"Don't touch that," said Rosie, snatching the book out of her hands. The last thing she wanted was for Ottilie to read the private letters she'd written to her mum.

"All right, touchy," said Ottilie. "BTW, you have serious anger issues, emo." She gave Jackson her wide-eyed "can you believe this girl?" look.

Rosie bit her tongue. Given that Rosie had jumped out of a tree to save Ottilie's life and nearly gotten herself eaten in the process, she thought Ottilie might be a bit more grateful. But no, apparently that would be asking far too much.

At that moment, Charlie bounded in with his customary gung ho enthusiasm. After saying a quick hello to everyone, he went straight to the instrument cupboard and started pulling out xylophones and kazoos, banjos and bongos.

"Not gonna lie, I can't sing to save my life, but how hard can it be to bash a bongo?" he said.

"We need to work out the main part first," said Ottilie. "I.e., my part."

Rosie and Jackson shared a glance. This was going to be unbearable, but they had all agreed that Ottilie could be the lead singer.

Rosie taught Ottilie the lyrics she and Jackson had come up with so far. Ottilie's voice wasn't *bad* as such, but it also wasn't that good. She was pitchy on the high notes and scooping on the low notes, neither of which was desirable.

"What do we do?" Rosie asked the others when Ottilie had left to go to the toilet.

"We'll just sing our harmonies really loud," said Jackson.

"Yeah, and I'll drown her out on my bongos." To emphasize his point, Charlie did a drum solo, bashing his bongos as loud as he could.

"Delightful," said Rosie.

"At least the song is good," said Jackson. He was right. Between them, by riffing off one another, they'd written a verse and a chorus of the song, building on Rosie's original lyrics. It was coming together really nicely. Ottilie had interjected with the occasional suggestion, but could sense she was out of her depth, so had mainly left the two of them to it, turning to her online shopping and giving them icy stares from across the room.

"Yeah, I'm really happy with the song," said Rosie. "And maybe Ottilie's singing will improve; we've still got eight days before the show."

"Let's hope so, or we'll be facing Crumwell's Shame Trap," said Charlie, putting on a creepy voice.

"So what's the Crumwell all about?" Rosie asked.

"It's based on 'Cromwell,' " Charlie replied. "You don't wanna mess with a Cromwell; they'll come getcha."

Ouuuuunk. The lower end of the piano keys clunked as Jackson accidentally leaned on them.

"Sorry," he said, biting his lip, but just as quickly, he was back to his usual smiling, composed self again. " 'Crumwell' was the name Anne Boleyn gave to Thomas Cromwell—the man who spread all the rumors about her," said Jackson.

"Oh, yeah," said Charlie. "Didn't she have her head chopped off 'cause of him?" He stuck out his tongue and sliced his finger over his neck.

Rosie felt a pang of grief at the thought of Anne Boleyn's fate.

"He destroyed the queen before she could destroy him," said Jackson flatly.

"I remember Hemlock prattling on about him in history one time," said Charlie.

"Okay, so that's who 'Crumwell' is," she said, "but what's his 'Shame Trap'?"

"No idea," Jackson replied. "And to be honest, I'd rather not find out."

As it turned out, Ottilie did get a little better at her singing over the course of the week, and no one could say she didn't have stage presence. She pranced around the room as if she owned the school and everything in it (no change there) and tossed her hair from side to side like she was auditioning for a shampoo commercial.

The four of them met all weekend and then every day after school and rehearsed for three hours before dinner and another two afterward. One thing that couldn't be disputed was their dedication; they all wanted to win.

By the following Tuesday evening, they'd finalized the lyrics, and by Thursday they'd perfected their harmonies. Even Charlie was sounding good on the drums. Then, on the day before the second Falcon Queen challenge, Ottilie dropped her bombshell.

Chapter Twenty-Two

CHICKEN CHOW MEIN!

Ottilie sauntered into the rehearsal room, waving several sheets of A4 paper in her hand. She passed them out and then stood in the middle of the room with her hands on her hips.

"There's been a change of plan," she said. "We're going to be doing *my* song instead."

"We can't just start again!" Rosie said. "The show is tomorrow. *Tomorrow.*"

"Are you even listening?" Ottilie looked down at her nails, then sighed. "This challenge is about reform—improvement," Ottilie said. "That means creative license to *change things* for the *bet-ter* . . . It needs more power, more strength. I refuse to squander this moment on mediocrity."

"Come on, you're not seeing things clearly," said Jackson.

"Er, it's you that's not seeing things clearly, with Rosie breathing down your neck and fluttering her eyelashes at you," she continued.

"I am not!" snapped Rosie.

"The song Rosie came up with is cool. It's about the power to change," said Jackson.

"Do you want to win this or not?" demanded Ottilie.

"Are you joking? We all want to win. That's why we're all here, isn't it?" said Jackson, frowning. It was the first time Rosie had seen him rattled.

Rosie rolled her eyes. "Yep, that's why we're here."

"Anyway, what the hell do you know about songwriting?" said Jackson, shaking his head at Ottilie.

"More than you." Ottilie practically spat the words out at Jackson.

The words kept on coming . . .

"Look, guys, can we work this out and get along?" Charlie interjected.

"There was only one Harry Styles in One D." She glared at Charlie. "Bottom line, either we do my song, or I walk. And if I do that, none of us win."

Rosie and Charlie exchanged a look. She could *not* be serious!

For some reason that Rosie couldn't quite fathom (but

presumably one that was grounded in Ottilie's narcissistic, green-eyed monster), Ottilie had written her own song, and decided—the day before they were due to perform in front of the *entire school* for a place in the finale of the Falcon Queen games—that they should abandon the song they'd spent all week rehearsing and perform hers instead.

"This is ridiculous! It doesn't make any sense," said Rosie, clenching her jaw.

"It makes perfect sense," said Ottilie with a flutter of her long eyelashes. "My song is better than yours. It's inspirational. That's what real power is about, inspiring others. Right?"

They all stood staring at one another for several seconds.

"We could at least hear it, I suppose," said Jackson. "And then have a vote on which we prefer?"

Ottilie wasted no time. She scanned through her phone and flicked on a punchy backing track, then grabbed the mic from Jackson.

She sang with her hand on her hip.

"With my vibe I will reign . . .

so off with your head like CHICKEN CHOW MEIN!"

She flicked her hair with the confidence of a stallion, then bowed theatrically.

The room fell silent. Charlie's mouth was slightly open,

while the others gave her an awkward round of applause.

"It was sort of good, and you excel at most things, but maybe you need to rethink . . ." said Charlie.

"What?!" Ottilie's hands were on her hips, and she was staring Charlie down.

" 'Chicken chow mein'?" He raised an eyebrow.

"What's the problem? It rhymes, and I'm being i-ro-nic." Ottilie shrugged. "Irony is a sign of intelligence, dumbo."

"Maybe we could blend the ideas together?" Charlie suggested.

"No, no time." Ottilie shook her head.

"Okay, then." He shrugged. "Let's just vote."

Ottilie was the only person who voted for hers.

"I don't care about some stupid vote. It's inspirational," said Ottilie. "I'm the lead singer and I get the final say. *You all agreed to that*, so that's what we're doing."

"Inspirational" was questionable. But she was right, they had agreed that she would get the final say, and no amount of reasoning or pleading would make her change her mind.

With no other choice, they dedicated the rest of that night and the following day to learning Ottilie's song, harmonizing "off with your head like chicken chow mein."

And with every "chicken chow mein" chanted, the

possibility of exposing Hemlock, or getting Rosie's case back, was slowly slipping away.

Luckily, the next morning they were excused from the Gutter Club since Ms. Parr knew they were competing that day, giving them a bit more time to work on it. God knows they needed it.

Chapter Twenty-Three

THE COURT OF REFORM

SATURDAY, DECEMBER 17TH. THE DAY OF THE COURT OF REFORM.

Before she knew it, Rosie was backstage at the school theater with Jackson, Charlie, and the other six teams. The only person who wasn't there was Ottilie, who'd left their final rehearsal early to go and get changed and hadn't yet returned. And Bina was acting as the band's PA, in case they needed anything. She said it would be good work experience for her CV.

"Right, everybody, listen up!" said Mr. Marcellus, the drama teacher. He had a slim build, brown skin, and a goatee. He put his clipboard under his arm and clapped his hands several times to get their attention. "It's twenty minutes until curtains up, so remember: What you are about to do has the potential to change lives . . . Be not afraid of greatness!" He spoke with such intensity it was like they were in a theatrical drama. "I want you to ignite— You, standing at the back." He clicked his fingers at Rosie. Rosie looked right and then left. Did he mean her?

Your doubts are your traitors.

Rosie frowned . . .

"Yes, you, young lady. I'm talking to you. With that attitude, you've lost already."

Rosie shrugged and gave a weak smile.

Mr. Marcellus's face crumpled in disapproval. "Is that the best you've got? The stage needs focus, energy, confidence," he said.

A heavy feeling weighed Rosie down. In truth, she was flat cola, two days old with the bottle top left off, not a drop of showbiz sparkle or fizz in sight. Everyone around her was chatting excitedly, brimming with confidence. But her team's new performance just wasn't good enough. There was no way they were going to get through to the next round. Like chicken chow mein, they were done.

"We've got this," said Jackson, placing a hand on Rosie's shoulder, his eyes warm and reassuring.

She didn't believe it was true—Mr. Marcellus was right—but she nodded at Jackson anyway. Her heart began to thump as she looked at him. Oh God, she was crushing on him?! Butterflies danced in her stomach. *Oh please!* That was all she needed right now. *Pull yourself together, Rosie Frost.* Anyway, what was taking Ottilie so long?

"We'll go in team order," Mr. Marcellus went on, glancing down at his clipboard. "I am the narrator on this sanguine stage, so you're in safe hands. I once shared a stage with Dame Judi herself, you know. So stay in your groups and start warming up. Breathe from your diaphragm, shoulders back," he said, breathing in with one hand on his stomach.

"What if one of our team's missing?" Charlie asked.

"Then you'd better hope they turn up, or you'll be disqualified," said Mr. Marcellus.

Twenty minutes later, a trill of regal trumpets blared out of the speakers onstage to indicate the Court of Reform was about to start. There was still no sign of Ottilie. Rosie peeked through the heavy curtain at the side of the stage. The auditorium was like a gaping mouth, ready to engulf her, just as the Black Lake had been before the first challenge. The whole school was there—hundreds of people, all waiting to judge their performance. In the center of the front row, not looking the least bit amused, was Mr. Hemlock.

"Okay, I'm going to open the show." Mr. Marcellus addressed the teams again. "Remember: performance energy!!" He beamed at them with a slick grin, then spun on his heel and walked out onto the stage. Rosie watched him from the wings, along with several other students. Next to her, Charlie hopped from one foot to the other.

"I need the loo," he said.

"Again? It's just nerves," Rosie replied. "You'll be fine."

"You know if you need to go while playing the bongos, it's hard to keep the rhythm. I should go one more time?" Without waiting for an answer, he dashed to the toilet.

Great, now they were down to two.

"I'll go find Ottilie," said Jackson.

"I'll go too," said Bina, following him. *Oh, you've got to be kidding, she's crushing on him too?!*

Now it was just Rosie. What the hell were they going to do if Ottilie didn't show up?

"Ladies and gentlemen, boys and girls, and everyone," Mr. Marcellus boomed at the audience from the center of the stage, with arms open under the spotlight. "Welcome to the Court of Reform—the second challenge of the Falcon Queen games!" His voice rose at the end of the sentence, then he opened his arms out even wider to the audience for them to applaud, which they dutifully did. It was as though he was announcing a gladiatorial battle in a Roman colosseum.

"Today we once again celebrate our school principles: *Animo, Imperium, Libertas.*"

"*Animo, Imperium, Libertas!*" the audience chanted.

"Seven teams. Only two survivors. Who will make it through to the final and who will fall victim to Crumwell's

Shame Trap? It's time to find out. But first, please welcome to the star chamber our own privy council—the real power behind the Court of Reform—your judges! All the way from Oxfordshire, give a warm welcome to the chief executive of the British Arts Council, the one and only Mrs. Barbara Warrington-Henley!"

The audience clapped as an austere-looking woman gave a regal wave from the "star chamber," the raised platform where she was sitting. She was plump, with cropped gray hair and lips so tightly pressed together they were almost invisible.

"Our second judge has flown in specially all the way from Vienna, and we are delighted to have him join us this evening," Mr. Marcellus continued. "Please give it up for the head of the Austrian National Opera, Herr Jung Wachter."

A tall, angular man, who was sitting next to the British Arts Council lady, stood up and gave a rigid bow.

How did they get such important people to come and judge? Rosie wondered. Maybe they were ex-pupils. Either way, knowing they would be watching only added more pressure. Beside each judge was a thick iron pole, sticking out from a metal box at their feet. Herr Jung Wachter tapped the one next to him with his long, bony fingers.

"And finally," said Mr. Marcellus, "due to a last-minute cancellation, we have a stand-in for our third and final judge. She's the woman who puts the *fun* in '*fun*damental particles'—all the way from the science department, let's hear it for Mademoiselle Curie Labouisse!"

"Thank you, darling," the science teacher purred at Mr. Marcellus from her seat as the pupils clapped politely once again.

"So you've met your judges—but will they pardon or punish? It's time to find out in the Court of Reform! Without further ado, please welcome to the stage your first act for tonight: the Dynamas!" The audience roared.

The first group was a mix of girls from years seven and eight who wore matching denim outfits and had their hair up in twin buns, which pulled their faces super tight. They performed a fast-paced hip-hop dance routine, complete with backflips and head spins. They were perfectly in sync and nailed the choreography. Rosie bit her lip. They were really good.

Next came a group of sixth formers who called them-selves Bard Knock Life, based on the idea that Anne Boleyn believed if you wanted to change your life, you had to work for it. They performed a dramatic play that included an emotional scene from Shakespeare's *Hamlet*, which brought some in the audience to tears. They were serious competition.

After them was a magic show by a group of hopeful year tens. It started off impressive—and they certainly had charisma—until, in their finale, they tried to make one of Miss Churchill's rabbits appear out of an old washing machine. When they opened the door for the grand reveal, the machine was still empty. The team left the stage deflated, with no one knowing where the rabbit had ended up.

There was only one more group to go before Rosie's team, but Charlie wasn't back from the toilet yet, and Ottilie still hadn't shown up, with Jackson and Bina still looking for her.

"Rule number two," a familiar voice whispered.

Rosie moved swiftly behind a large curtain at the back of the stage, where no one was around. She dug into her rucksack for the rule book, then pulled it out and started scanning through its golden pages. There it was: rule number two. She absorbed the words and closed her eyes, clasping her hands together. *United we stand, divided we fall.* She whispered the rule to herself, as though it was feeding her spirit. Feeling calmer, she then walked back to where the others were supposed to be waiting to go on.

Just then, the door backstage burst open and Charlie came bounding in, zipping up his trousers and looking a little flustered.

"What took you so long?" Rosie whispered to him.

"Sorry—I was sitting on the throne, laying a brick, you know," Charlie replied.

"What? I wish I hadn't asked . . ."

"Still no Ottilie?" said Charlie.

Rosie shook her head.

Jackson came back by himself, looking flustered. "I can't find her."

Bina returned a second later, shrugging. "Do you think she's bailed on you?"

"Don't know," said Rosie.

"What do we do if she doesn't show?" asked Charlie.

They'd be disqualified, that's what would happen. Farewell, Falcon Queen games and any hope of stopping Hemlock or ever getting back the red case and finding out what her mother had left behind for her.

The next act—a barbershop quartet featuring four boys from different year groups—came to an end, and Mr. Marcellus clapped them off the stage.

"Thank you, boys, for that delightful performance," he was saying. "You remind me of a young me"—he turned to the audience and gave a theatrical aside—"except *I* had more range. I'm joking! I'm joking! . . . I'm not . . . Anyway, up next we have our fifth team of competitors, so please welcome to the stage Ottilie and Her Squad!"

Rosie cringed as their team name was read out. It had been Ottilie's choice, and she'd thrown another diva strop when they tried to suggest alternatives. And now she hadn't even bothered to turn up.

United we stand, divided we fall. What a joke. They were living proof of that. Where the hell was she?

She gave Charlie a "what do we do now?" look. Jackson answered by walking out onto the stage. Taking his lead, Rosie and Charlie followed. Rosie squinted. The lights were so bright—especially compared to the darkness of backstage—that it took Rosie's eyes a few moments to adjust. Once they did and she had a view of the whole audience, her stomach turned to jelly. The theater was massive, with hundreds of eyes glaring at her through the darkness.

"It's that filthy sponger," someone whispered. Rosie flinched.

"Yeah, Frost girl, hashtag clean up!" sniggered someone else.

Oh God, they were still referring to that meme that went viral.

Focus, Rosie, focus . . . ignore them. Her heart was thumping. She lowered her head and stumbled toward the piano at the far side of the stage. It was different from the one they'd been practicing on and even more majestic. The glossy black lid glistened like an inky pond.

She took a seat, and Charlie and Jackson took their places. They looked at each other, and Rosie shrugged as she peered backstage.

"It looks to me like you're a person down," said Mr. Marcellus. "As you know, this challenge must include all team members, so I'm afraid unless the whole team is present—"

He stopped mid-sentence as Ottilie strutted onto the stage. She was wearing a sequined dress that shimmered every color of the rainbow, and her long, silky hair was colored with pink glittery stripes.

"You're late," Rosie mouthed.

"I was doing my hair," Ottilie hissed back. "I see *you* didn't bother."

Rosie frowned and smoothed down her own frizzy hair, which bounced back in protest.

Ottilie turned toward the audience, beamed her "all eyes on me" smile, then took center stage, where a microphone had been placed.

"Hello, Heverbridge!" she said into the microphone, as if she were on the Pyramid Stage at Glastonbury. "My name is Ottilie, and this is my debut single, 'I Came to Slay.' Hit it!"

Rosie presumed that was her cue to begin, so she started playing the introduction on the piano. But her fingers were shaking and, having only learned the chords yesterday, she kept making mistakes. This was going terribly, and they'd only just begun.

When it reached the point in the music where Ottilie was supposed to start singing, Ottilie shuffled about and cleared her throat, but didn't come in. Rosie played the introduction again, but Ottilie still didn't begin. Her bottom lip trembled and her eyes darted from side to side. What was going on? Was Ottilie *nervous*?

After playing the introduction for a third time, Rosie started singing the song herself, thinking it might encourage Ottilie.

"I can do it," Ottilie snapped. "I can do it!! I can do it . . ." echoed around the theater. She'd meant to say it just to Rosie, but the microphone picked up her voice. A few people in the audience started to snigger.

"She's got stage fright!" an older boy shouted from the crowd.

"No, I don't! It's just, it's just . . ." Ottilie stammered. At that moment, Ada—the rabbit that was supposed to magically appear from the magicians' washing machine—hopped onto the stage from wherever she had been hiding, going straight over to Ottilie's shoe and sniffing it.

"It's that rabbit!" Ottilie proclaimed, grateful for a diversion tactic. "It's putting me off." Ottilie snatched her up. "See, it's just *so* distracting! But it's okay; I love animals so—*oh my God!* It's peeing on me!" A stream of bright yellow liquid fizzled down Ottilie's front. "Not the dress, not the dress; it's Gucci!" she screamed. "Ewwwww—somebody stop it!"

Rosie and Jackson looked at each other and giggled as Ottilie shook all over, holding Ada at arm's length.

Mr. Marcellus strutted onstage with a towel, and Ottilie

practically threw the rabbit at him. "It's just a tiny tinkle," he said.

"It means she likes you," said Charlie.

"Or doesn't . . ." whispered Jackson, trying to contain his laughter.

"I need antibacterial wipes!" said Ottilie, snatching the towel from Mr. Marcellus and dabbing her sequined dress. "Why is no one bringing me antibacterial wipes?! I could get salmonella, listeria, pseudotuberculosis!"

Lots of pupils in the audience were laughing now, which was too much for Ottilie to take. She screamed, threw the wee-soaked towel to the ground, and stormed offstage. Mr. Marcellus scooped up the towel and followed her, with Ada tucked under one arm. There was no way they could win now; all Rosie's hopes were trickling down the drain.

As soon as they were gone, the audience fell silent. Rosie was aware of all those eyes waiting, watching her and wondering what was going to happen next. She looked at Jackson, who walked over to the microphone.

"Apologies for that . . . unexpected start," he said, which earned him a few laughs. "Mistakes happen, but we learn; we change and move on."

He picked up the microphone, carried it over to the piano, and angled it so Rosie could sing and play at the same time.

"What are you doing?" Rosie whispered.

"How about we go back to the original plan?" he said quietly.

Without Ottilie?

"You can do this; we can do this."

"Yeah, go for it, Frosty!" said Charlie.

Rosie didn't know. It was stressful enough playing the piano in front of the whole school, let alone singing. She hadn't mentally prepared herself for that.

What if—instead of singing—she just blurted everything she knew about Hemlock into the microphone, in front of the whole school? If enough people knew, he'd never be able to carry out his plan, surely?

But without proof, it'd almost certainly lead to her expulsion too, and then where would she go?

No, nothing had changed; she still had to win the games, and for that, she needed to sing. Her heart began to thump harder than ever, pounding relentlessly against her chest. *Oh God.*

"You can do it, Rosie!" someone in the audience shouted, causing another ripple of laughter. It was Bina, now sitting a few rows back. She beamed at Rosie and started clapping her hands, encouraging those around her to join in. Soon, the whole room was filled with the sound of applause.

A familiar smell enveloped the stage—velvet plum roses wrapped in cloves and spice. The ghost of Queen Anne had come to watch over the games once more. Rosie's mind flicked to Falcon Queen rule number two again.

United we stand? There was no denying it: they weren't exactly united; they were divided. But did they have to fall?? Maybe she could still try? For all at Heverbridge, for the Falcon Queens who had courage. Her friends believed in her, and that filled her heart with confidence. She would do this for them, and for the wildcats, and for Queenie *and* her mother.

Rosie took a deep breath, placed her hands on the keys, and began to play their song.

At first, her voice came out a little shaky, but then Charlie came in with the drums and Jackson joined her on the harmonies, and before long she was belting out the melody with a passion she never knew she possessed. She was carried away on the music, lost in its gentle ebb and flow.

"*I feel your star shining down on me . . .*" she sang with all her heart. She looked out into the darkness, envisioning her mother . . . her beautiful mum, laughing with her, holding her after a bad day at school, brushing her hair. Then standing at the back of the theater, smiling . . .

By the final chorus, everyone in the audience was swaying their arms from side to side, and when the song came to an end, the audience roared with applause, cheers erupting. Rosie pressed her lips together but couldn't prevent the broad grin spreading across her face.

Charlie leaped up from his seat and wrapped his arms around Rosie in an awkward hug from behind.

"Frosty! That was awesome."

Jackson was nodding next to them, and he also had a massive smile on his face. They'd done it. By the sound of the audience's reaction, their performance couldn't have gone better.

Mr. Marcellus sauntered onto the stage and snatched the microphone. For some reason he was still holding Ada the rabbit.

"Okay, everyone; hush now, please. Unless you're cheering for me, in which case feel free to continue." He smirked. The cheering stopped. "As lovely as that little bit of singing was, not all of the team members were present for the performance." He took a breath in. "I'm afraid this performance was a fractious emulation," he said, shaking his head. "So I have no choice, I'm afraid. This team is disqualified."

Chapter Twenty-Four

CRUMWELL'S SHAME TRAP

"D isqualified?" said Charlie. "You're kidding me!"

"It's the rules," said Mr. Marcellus.

"But, but . . ." Charlie was shaking his head.

United we stand . . . divided we fall.

Rosie cleared her throat. *Think of something, Rosie, say something.*

She looked up at the doors at the back of the theater where she had imagined her mother standing. There was no one there. She bit her lip. She then looked out in the audience . . . in the direction where the "filthy sponger" sniggering remarks had come from.

"Wait a minute," said Rosie. An idea had popped into her head. "Actually." She took the microphone out of Mr. Marcellus's hand. "I have a question . . . Who here has never made a mistake?" The audience fell silent. "I know I have . . ."

Her eyes were determined and focused. "Okay, then put your hand up if you're perfect, because I'm certainly not." She shrugged. Still silence.

"Yet, aren't we all so quick to judge, to make fun of someone when we see a flaw, a mistake? Well, that's what this performance was about. Yes, *one* performance with some improv acting," she declared. "We *did* all perform. The improv piece you saw was about truly inspiring change—when one person makes a mistake, we all learn from it. We don't scold; instead we respond and carry on. That's how we grow, that's how change happens. That's where real power lies, and that's what the Court of Reform is truly about." Rosie put her hand on her hip. *Imperium.* She was even convincing herself.

"Starting with some exceptionally special method acting by Ottilie Aragon-Windsor, the whole thing was staged, with an extra improvisation especially from Ada the rabbit." Rosie laughed. "But Ottilie made you believe it was real. Wasn't she fantastic? Are you still backstage, Ottilie? Why don't you come back on and take a bow?"

Rosie's heart was thumping as she looked into the darkness of the wings. She wasn't coming. The sidelights lit up the dust that drifted through the air. Suddenly Ottilie emerged through the haze. She walked out onto the stage as if her confidence had trickled onto the floor along with the rabbit wee, and the makeup under her eyes was smudged.

"A round of applause for our leading lady!" said Rosie. She widened her eyes at Ottilie, encouraging her to go along with it.

Ottilie was torn. On the one hand, she was desperate to sulk and let the whole world know how unfair her life was, but on the other hand, this was a chance to save face. Rosie nodded at her urgently, as if to say, *We could still make it through.* Ottilie looked at the audience and felt the warmth of the spotlight on her face, then finally smiled, raising her arms toward them all, and bowed right down to the floor.

The audience paused, unsure, then erupted into more applause.

"Bravo, bravo!" Mademoiselle Curie Labouisse was on her feet, cheering. The other two judges were clapping too, their faces a mix of smiles and speculative frowns. Hemlock just slowly clapped, with a mild scowl on his face.

Mr. Marcellus grabbed back the microphone. "Well," he said, "that was . . . erm, yes, an interesting interpretation of spontaneous ensemble theater. I guess it's true, with improv acting there are no mistakes, I'll give you that.

"Well . . ." he said again, "I shall leave it up to the

judges to decide what to make of that; they'll have the final say on the disqualification. For now, please give one last round of applause—although they've had their fair share already—to Ottilie and Her Squad!"

Rosie and her team gave the audience sheepish waves and left the stage.

"Nice one, Frosty," said Charlie once they were back in the darkness, huddled in the corner next to the costume rails. "You think we convinced them?"

"I hope so," said Rosie.

Ottilie was silent and glowering.

They had two more performances to wait through before the winner was announced. First was a balletic dance group called the Phenomenal Swans, celebrating Anne Boleyn's inner beauty and independence. They lived up to their name. From backstage, the first group to perform—the hip-hop girls with the tight buns—folded their arms and gave them death stares as the Swans floated smugly across the stage.

The final act was a string quartet that mashed up the Black Eyed Peas' "Where Is the Love?" with "Adagio for Strings," celebrating Anne Boleyn's dedication to providing relief for the poor (which worked surprisingly well). There was then an agonizing wait while the judges deliberated.

Finally, Mr. Marcellus called all the teams back. They were told to stand in their little groups on specific spots marked around the stage, forming a loose semicircle, with Mr. Marcellus in front of them.

"And now . . ." The Roman emperor voice was back. "The moment you've all been waiting for. It's time . . . to reveal . . . the winners! *And* the losers." He puffed out his chest. "Remember, our judges in the star chamber have the power to pardon or punish! As you know, only two teams will make it through to the third and final challenge of the Falcon Queen games, so this. Is. Everything!" Mr. Marcellus took a deep breath and raised his chin to the audience. "In honor of the late Thomas Cromwell, we have our own Crumwell's Shame Trap, and I can now reveal that the first team *not* to make it through to the final is . . ."

The male judge, Herr Jung Wachter, gripped the iron pole beside him. His eyes glistened.

"The Dynamas!" announced Mr. Marcellus.

There was a menacing clunk as Herr Jung pulled the iron lever, and a trapdoor fell open beneath the hip-hop dancers' feet. The four girls disappeared through the hole. The sound of their screams echoed around the theater for an uncomfortable amount of time before the trapdoor snapped shut again and the sound cut off. A stunned silence filled the auditorium.

"What? Where did they go?" Rosie whispered to Charlie. He shrugged in reply. His face had gone pale.

"Who will be next?" asked Mr. Marcellus. The

atmosphere among the contestants went cold. Everyone was looking at the stage beneath their feet, shuffling nervously, dreading they might be the ones to share the same fate as the Dynamas.

"The second group *not* going through to the final of the Falcon Queen games is . . ."

Rosie's legs trembled, as if they were about to give way beneath her. Charlie took hold of her hand and squeezed it tight. With her other hand, Rosie held on to Jackson's. Ottilie put her hands behind her back and stared straight ahead.

"The Magic Masters!"

Fear spread across the faces of the year tens. Herr Jung Wachter reached for his lever.

"Wait!" said Mademoiselle Curie Labouisse, raising her hand like a queen. "I pardon them!"

"*Was?*" snapped Herr Jung Wachter, asking "what" in German.

Mademoiselle Curie Labouisse pouted and raised her perfectly groomed eyebrows. "They were so adorable, with the little bunny," she said.

"I see a fracture among the judges," announced Mr. Marcellus. "It looks like Mademoiselle Curie Labouisse has shown the power of mercy!"

The Magic Masters let out a collective sigh, relieved they were going to be spared.

Then the third judge, Mrs. Warrington-Henley, leaned

forward. "Sorry, not good enough, and majority rules!" she trilled, pulling the lever beside her.

Another trapdoor opened up, and the whole group of wannabe magicians plunged into the darkness beneath them to the sound of their panicked cries. Mademoiselle Curie Labouisse frowned, placing a hand to her chest. She looked at Mrs. Warrington-Henley with disgust; meanwhile Mrs. Warrington-Henley kept looking straight ahead with her chin held high, as if Mademoiselle Curie Labouisse did not exist.

"It seems there will be no mercy shown from the star chamber today!" said Mr. Marcellus with obvious glee.

"This—is—brutal!" Charlie whispered.

With a clunk and then sudden screaming, each group fell as Crumwell's Shame Trap claimed one after another. The judges took turns pulling their levers. Rosie's brow was sweating, her heart pounding.

Soon, there were only three teams remaining: the sixth formers who'd performed the Shakespearean scene, the Phenomenal Swans ballet dancers, and Rosie's team. It all came down to this.

"It's the moment you've all been waiting for," said Mr. Marcellus, "as I now reveal the first team that *has* made it through the Court of Reform. And that team—the members of which will go on to fight for the title of Falcon Queen's champion—is . . ." He looked at each of the three remaining teams in turn. There was a long, dramatic pause, as if it were a Saturday night TV show. ". . . Bard Knock Life!"

The sixth formers high-fived each other as the audience cheered. Rosie felt sick. "Congratulations to you all," Mr. Marcellus went on. "A worthy win. And the second and last team to make it through to the final is . . ."

Another long pause. The judges nodded to one another, their hands on their levers.

Rosie's heart was beating so hard she thought it might explode. The ballet dancers were super talented, and there was still the possibility that the judges had disqualified Rosie's team. She squeezed Charlie's and Jackson's hands even tighter. *United we stand, divided we fall.* This was it.

"Ottilie and Her Squad!" Mr. Marcellus declared.

What?! The trapdoor beneath the ballet dancers opened up, and the whole Phenomenal Swans team disappeared.

"YES!!!!!!!!!!!" cried Rosie, turning to Charlie as he jumped in the air, whooping and hollering. Jackson raised Rosie's hand, and everyone in the audience was cheering for them. For her. And of course, Ottilie, who bowed gracefully. They'd done it. They were through. Rosie's heart flooded with happiness.

She had never felt joy like it.

After the show, there was a mini-celebration in the Sovereign Hall, where they served steaming hot chocolates and

Crumwell crumpets with jam. Rosie sat at a table with Charlie, Jackson, and Bina.

"You were all incredible!" gushed Bina. "Amazing!"

The amount of sugar Bina had added to her hot chocolate had probably added to her enthusiasm too.

Ottilie had refused their invitation to join them and was sitting with Jamila and Ishaan at another table. She'd changed out of her wee-stained dress and had a look on her face like someone had just vomited on her shoes. Her mood didn't improve, no matter how much her friends droned on about how *great* her performance was, how everyone thought she was *such* a great actress, and that the rabbit wee would *definitely* wash out of her dress.

"I'm just glad we avoided the Shame Trap," said Jackson, taking a big glug of his hot chocolate. "That did not look fun."

"Yeah, was that even legal?" Rosie asked.

Most of the pupils who'd fallen through the trapdoors had come out unscathed, but there were plenty of bruised knees and battered elbows, and one boy had landed at an awkward angle and broken his leg. Rosie wondered again how this school hadn't been reported to social services or sued by the parents.

"The rules are kinda different on this island," said Charlie. "Haven't you realized that yet?"

Rosie nodded. And the Falcon Queen's rules were

certainly helping—they were saving her at every challenge. She squeezed the little purple book in her rucksack and silently whispered a thank-you to the Falcon Queen, who she was sure would be somewhere nearby, watching over her.

"I think it was supposed to show how brutal Cromwell's judgment was, back in the day," said Bina.

"Is it really *that* important we keep being reminded about the past? History is history for a reason," said Jackson. "I wish we could just forget about it." He sighed as if a dark shadow hung over him.

Why was he being so moody? They'd just won.

"No! You should never forget who you are . . ." Bina gave him a side-eye. There was a frosty tension between them. She always acted so strange around Jackson—maybe she did like him, but wasn't letting on.

"Tough lesson, hard learned. But hey, let's just focus on our victory," said Charlie, chomping down a crumpet. "And bonus: Rosie, you're famous now for a *good* reason. And as for that flipping meme, I guess us filthy spongers cleaned up right!" He winked, then glanced over at Ottilie, who was still pouting.

Rosie was lost in thought, now wondering just how tough the lesson for the final challenge was going to be.

"In honor of your victory, I'm going to get more crumpets," said Bina, licking jam off her fingers. "Who wants more?"

"Is that even a question?" said Charlie. "I'll come with you. Rosie?"

"Yeah, sure. We are celebrating, after all."

"And for me, please," said Jackson. "I wouldn't want to miss out."

Charlie and Bina slipped out from their benches and headed off to the canteen end of the hall, leaving Jackson and Rosie alone, facing each other on opposite sides of the table.

For some reason, Rosie started to feel a little flushed around her neck.

"I haven't properly said it to you yet, but thank you. Our win tonight was mainly down to you," said Jackson. "Claiming Ottilie's tantrum was part of the performance was absolute genius! And the way you sang . . . you've really got something, Rosie, something special."

Rosie cleared her throat. She didn't know what to say, so she gave a small shrug. The heat on her neck was rising quickly and the butterflies were back. For something to do, she picked up her half-eaten crumpet and shoved the whole thing in her mouth, then began rigorously chewing. She tried to focus on something else other than Jackson, whose big brown eyes were looking at her, all cute and caring, waiting for a reply.

The crumpet got caught in her braces. She tried to dislodge it with her tongue, but just found herself chewing and licking, while Jackson continued to look at her, still waiting for a reply. As it finally came loose, Rosie swallowed, desperate to be rid of the piece of crumpet, but it was too large and next became lodged in her throat. Her eyes bulged and she started gagging into her hand. She couldn't breathe; she was choking.

"Are you all right?" Jackson asked. Rosie managed a little shake of her head. "Oh God, are you choking?"

He leaped around to her side of the table and gave her a sharp slap on the back. On his third attempt, the piece of jammy crumpet shot across the table and landed right in the middle of his plate.

Rosie coughed and took a massive breath of relief, then looked at the gooey blob splatted onto Jackson's plate. Her cheeks burst with color. Choking to death might have been less embarrassing than that smush of crumpet. Phlegmy mucus oozed out all around it. What was the polite thing to do in this situation? Reach across and pick it up? She bit her lip and gave Jackson an apologetic look.

"Sorry," she said.

"And there I was thinking Ottilie was the dramatic one." Jackson laughed and passed her a glass of water.

Rosie smiled and took a couple of sips.

"Correct me if I'm wrong, but I think I just saved your life."

Rosie frowned. She didn't want to be saved, especially by a boy, and especially not by Jackson Sterling.

"Don't worry, you'll save me back one day." Jackson winked.

"No promises . . ." said Rosie. "But thank you."

"Any time."

At that point, Charlie and Bina returned with a plate stacked high with crumpets. They looked at Rosie's flushed face, then down at Jackson's plate, which still had Rosie's projectile in the middle of it.

"Uh . . . what did we miss?!" said Charlie.

"Not much," said Jackson, "but I'm not sure I fancy any more of those crumpets."

"Wait a minute," Charlie said, looking down on the plate. "Did that come out of Rosie's *mouth*?!" He pointed at the gunky lump.

"I choked . . ." Rosie cringed.

Charlie started laughing like it was the funniest thing in the world. "Gross," he said in between breaths.

Jackson was laughing now too. Bina bit down on her smile, wanting to join in but not sure if she should. That's when Rosie realized they weren't laughing at *her*, but at the situation—and the situation *was* funny.

Rosie smirked, and the smirk turned into a laugh. Once she started, she couldn't stop; it was contagious. Soon, all four of them were laughing hard together.

It felt good to laugh. It felt really good.

Chapter Twenty-Five

THE BELL TOWER

A couple of hours later, most of the students—including Jackson and Bina—had left the Sovereign Hall and gone to bed, but Rosie and Charlie were still too pumped from the performance to think about sleep. They were on their third hot chocolate.

"Let's do something fun," said Charlie. "I've had enough of sitting here."

"Like what?" Rosie asked.

"Have you ever been to the top of the bell tower?"

"No."

"Then let's go! The stars at night are awesome." Charlie sprang up from his bench, still clutching his mug. "Bring your hot chocolate with you; it'll warm us up."

The bell tower was an ancient building, attached to

the central mansion via a cold stone passageway. Rosie had seen it from a distance, and heard the bell toll every hour without fail, but had never stepped inside. The ceiling was low and it was almost pitch-black. Charlie pulled out his phone to light the way, revealing a sign at the bottom of the staircase which had a picture of a person inside a red circle with a line going through it. NO PUPILS ALLOWED, it said.

"Are we just ignoring that sign, then?" Rosie asked.

"What sign? I didn't see any sign," Charlie replied with a mischievous smile.

Their footsteps echoed as they started climbing the stairs, which were damp and smelled of wet spinach. More than once, Rosie stumbled on the uneven steps.

"Do you think there are spiders in here?" Charlie asked.

"Probably," said Rosie. "Why?"

Charlie shuddered. "No reason . . ."

The walls were engraved with thousands upon thousands of butterflies that flickered in the light from Charlie's phone, making them look as if they were flying.

When they got to the top, they had to pull themselves up through a square opening—not an easy thing to do with a mug of hot chocolate in your hands—and then they were on the platform right next to the giant bell. Rosie gave it a sturdy pat. It was so heavy it didn't move one millimeter. Its surface was cold and dense.

Rosie sat on the edge of the tower wall with her feet dangling over the edge. Charlie sat down next to her.

There was a deep sense of calm in being so high, looking down on the world below. All was dark and still. She peered in the direction of Wildcat Woods. "I hope the wildcats are all right."

"They will be. Hemlock said he wasn't going to do anything until the winter solstice, remember, and that's still four days away. And thanks to you, we're one step closer to winning the Falcon Queen games, which means we're one step closer to stopping him. We'll get to make the rules this time."

Rosie looked up at the dark night sky.

There were two hundred billion trillion stars in the universe, but the sky was like an ink-black glass ceiling.

Was heaven up there? Was her mother hiding in the stardust?

"Let's make a wish," said Charlie, looking up.

"No stars out tonight; they're all hiding. Anyway, I don't believe in wishes," said Rosie flatly.

"Hold on, what was it you said in that song you wrote? *I feel your star shining down on me . . .*" Charlie half sang the words in a gruff, out-of-tune sort of way.

Rosie smirked. "They're just lyrics. Just words that rhyme," she said. Rosie wrapped her hands around her mug for warmth and took a big glug.

"Well, *you* wrote 'em."

That was then. Before everything happened. "Charlie, can I tell you something?" she said.

"Sure, Frosty. What's up?"

"I used to believe in fairy tales and dreams when I first starting writing that song, but I'm not sure anymore."

"Why?"

"Do you remember the first morning we met, at breakfast, you asked me why I was here at Heverbridge?"

"Yeah, you shot me down with a frosty glare. How could I forget?"

"Yeah . . . well . . . I've not told anyone this, because I just don't wanna be known as . . . as an orphan . . ." The word she dreaded. *Orphan.*

Rosie was staring into her drink, at the thick, milky liquid. "That's the reason I had to come here . . . My mum. She . . . died. She's dead."

Saying it out loud made it even more real somehow . . . Her mum was gone.

"Oh," said Charlie. "I'm so sorry. What happened?"

"I don't know, that's just it, I don't know," said Rosie emphatically. The words felt thick on her lips. "There are 'official procedures' in place, and I didn't even get to see her. I was just told she was dead. Then I was sent here, and I'm angry all the time."

"What about the rest of your family?"

"I've never known my dad and I don't have any other

relatives. But this lawyer turned up out of nowhere with all these official documents and letters, and next thing I know I'm in a helicopter being carted off to this super-weird island. I don't even know why I was sent here, or who's paying for it. The only thing I do know is that I'm an orphan, Charlie; I'm a lonely orphan."

Rosie choked on the words. They were bitter but true. She wanted to cry, but her eyes remained dry.

"I had no idea," said Charlie. "That's horrible."

Rosie scratched her head.

"I'm sorry."

"And then like I said, Mr. Hemlock took my mum's locked case from me. That's the real reason why I wanted to win the games, to make sure I had a chance to see Miss Churchill, make a new school rule, and get it back. It might help me find out more, explain things about who I am and why I'm here."

"What do you mean?"

Rosie explained the whole story behind the missing case—how she'd been instructed that only Miss Churchill could open it, but how Hemlock was still denying he had it for some reason she couldn't work out. And how she'd found this old Falcon Queen's rule book in Churchill's office that had been helping guide her. (She left out the ghost part.)

"I see, well, we're gonna win the games, we're gonna

save the animals, *and* we're gonna get your case back. Maybe there's treasure in it."

"Maybe . . ." said Rosie wistfully.

Charlie then pulled out something from inside his jumper. It was rolled-up scroll of hard paper.

"This is for you. I got this far thanks to you," he said with a shy look on his face. Rosie unrolled the paper and gasped. It was the most amazing drawing she had ever seen: a girl with wayward strands of hair in loosely sketched tendrils and a highly detailed face with a pensive expression and delicate features. It was a masterpiece, but there was something familiar about it. The girl in the drawing had a heart-shaped mouth, like hers.

She looked up at Charlie. "This sort of looks like me. Where did you get it?"

"I did it." He smiled.

"What?! Charlie! You're so talented. I had no idea!"

"I get it. Some people can't understand how I got a scholarship. They call me 'thick boy,'" Charlie said, then sipped his hot chocolate.

"You're certainly not that," Rosie said, still admiring the drawing. "You're a genius."

"It's okay. It's 'cause my spelling is bad, but I'm just dyslexic," he continued, then looked at the drawing. "I sort of based it on a Leonardo Definchy, the guy who inspired *The Celestial Rising*. He's the ultimate polymath—he was

an artist, scientist, inventor. I design things like him too."
He shrugged. "I got inspired by his work mixed with a bit
of you."

Written at the bottom of the page was *"The Frost Girl"*
by Charlie Saint.

Rosie's heart felt so warm reading these words. She
was lucky to know Charlie Saint.

"The Frost Girl" by Charlie Saint

"I wanna win the games as much as you. Gotta prove
myself." Charlie shrugged again.

"Charlie, we are in this together. You've really helped
me. Thanks for always being there, even when I wasn't

much fun to be around. Because of you, I'm starting to quite like it here. My mum'd be really happy to know I've got a friend like you."

"Oh, Frosty, stop it—you're gonna make me cry! I'm meant to be the tough guy."

"Girls save boys"—she shrugged—"and tough guys cry."

"Yeah, my nan says it's good to cry."

Rosie hadn't cried for so long she'd forgotten how it felt. "Your nan sounds nice."

She looked at him and saw that his eyes were wet. Then he flashed her that Charlie grin that made everything all right.

"She used to say, 'You're never too old to make a wish, Charlie.' Look up," he said. One lone star was now shining brightly as if to say, *I am here, I won't forget you.* "That'll be Regulus, the winter solstice star. My nan taught me that too. They say it's lucky; we should definitely make a wish. She's the one who believed I deserved to get into this school. She believes in me."

The sole star sparkled. With nothing to lose, Rosie wished for the safety of the wildcats, that she would find her mother's case, and that she might truly belong here at Heverbridge. A triple wish, just in case Charlie's nan was right.

A darkness swept over the star, and it disappeared

from sight. "Guess that's the stars over with, then," said Charlie.

BONG!

The giant bell behind them let out a mighty ring. It made Charlie jump so high he spilled hot chocolate all down himself. He leaped up, covering his ears. Rosie did the same.

BONG!

Even with her ears covered, the noise still rattled Rosie's head and echoed through her brain.

BONG!

"It's a bit loud!" Charlie shouted.

BONG!

BONG!

"Let's get out of here!"

They scrambled back down through the hole in the floor as the bell rang another six times. Once it had finally stopped, they collapsed in a fit of giggles. Charlie was drenched, his trousers dripping with brown splats.

"Looks like you've had an accident," said Rosie.

"At least I smell nice. Actually, that reminds me, you know you said that Falcon Queen's rule book was helping you? Well, my nan had her own rule she lived by which sort of helps me," he said, looking down at his chocolate-stained trousers.

"What is it?"

"Turn that poop to fertilizer," he said, grinning. Charlie laughed, and then took out his phone to lead the two of them back down the stairs. Rosie followed him, feeling different from how she had on the way up. Something inside her had lifted, and her heart was a little warmer. And maybe her mum's advice about keeping silent had worked for a while, but it was time to break her silence. She didn't want to shut out Charlie.

Thanks to Charlie Saint, things had changed. She wasn't lonely anymore; she had a friend.

Dear Mum,

Good news! I'm in the FINAL of the Falcon Queen games!!! Can you believe it? I feel like I'm dreaming. Do you remember that song we started writing together YEARS ago about following our dreams? Well, I finished it this week with a boy called Jackson and then we sang it in front of the WHOLE school. I was really nervous at first, but having my friends performing with me really helped. Then we nearly got disqualified, but I convinced the judges to let us through. Everyone was cheering and clapping. I couldn't believe it. We ate loads of crumpets to celebrate (although the less said about crumpets and Jackson the better . . .). Bina taught me this amazing wrestling move called The Rock's Rock Bottom! The trick is you stay tight together, but stay loose so you don't break anything, but go down and up together. She's big into wrestling, so she knows what she's talking about. You'd like her. And Charlie—he's always making people laugh. He drew me this picture. It's <u>amazing.</u> People don't realize how smart he is, he's so talented! Jackson's really nice too, cute and moody, and he saved me from choking— don't ask! I'm getting used to this place now and starting to quite like it.

That heavy feeling is lifting. I wish it could be you and me laughing about it.

Anyway, wanted to let you know it's been a good day.

Miss you,
Rosie x

P.S. I haven't forgotten about Hemlock and the wildcats— they're the main reason I'm trying to win the games. I'm starting to think I might actually be able to do it. With the help of the Falcon Queen, Anne Boleyn! AND OF COURSE I HAVE TO GET THE CASE BACK!! What's in it, Mum? Will I ever really know what happened to you?

P.P.S. Before you ask, Jackson is just a friend too. But I know, I know . . . I can hear you saying, "Never judge a book by its cover." Bina is crushing on him; she acts weird around him, but I keep my cool.

Chapter Twenty-Six

MURDER BY WORDS

TUESDAY, DECEMBER 20TH. THE DAY BEFORE

THE BATTLE OF BLOODSTONE.

It was the end of what had been a particularly excruciating math lesson (Rosie still didn't understand what Pythagoras was on about or what was so important about the hippopotenuse), but even that couldn't dampen Rosie's spirits. She was still riding high from their victory a few days ago, although now her thoughts were turning to the third and final challenge. They'd been told it would take place on the winter solstice, which was now just one day away.

That was also the day Miss Churchill would finally return for the Bloodstone Banquet *and* the day Hemlock planned to use his explosives for who knew what. The thought of all those things happening on the same day made Rosie's insides twist in knots. But on a positive note, the early mornings in the Gutter Club had dialed down a bit, as Ms. Parr was busy and the weather was shockingly cold. Snow was forecast.

Rosie's next lesson was geography, which was three floors up, on the other side of the main mansion building. Charlie walked with her, discussing the possibilities of what could be for lunch. As they climbed their third staircase, Rosie shivered, as though something cold had passed through her.

"Murder by words," the voice said, followed by the familiar smell of spiced cloves and velvet plum roses.

"Did you hear that?" Rosie asked Charlie.

"Hear what?"

"Nothing . . ." She had yet to tell him about the ghost of Anne Boleyn. Why had Queen Anne said this? It sounded like a warning. The rich scent of spices and cloves became stronger than ever.

She felt a cold chill tingle over her skin. Charlie was going on about the latest *Fortnite* game, but Rosie was only half listening. She was so lost in thought that she barely noticed the students who passed were all holding pieces of A4 paper and laughing at whatever was written on them. It wasn't until Rosie turned into the humanities corridor and saw similar pieces of paper plastered all over the columns and display boards that she started properly paying attention.

"What's all that about?" Rosie asked.

"Probably the Musical Society trying to get us to see their latest version of *The Miserables* or something," Charlie replied.

All along the corridor, people were snatching down the pieces of paper and reading them in small groups, mouths open wide.

"There she is," someone whispered, pointing at Rosie.

"Shame, girl!" someone else called.

What was going on?

Rosie walked up to the nearest board and pulled down a sheet. Her heart stopped. She recognized the handwriting at once, because the handwriting was hers.

Dear Mum,

No, no, no. How was this possible?

Someone must have gone through her private things, photocopied one of the letters, and plastered it all over the school. At least, that's what Rosie thought must have happened.

She read the letter in full, and as she did, her stomach sank. *What the hell?!*

Dear Mum,

I'm in the FINAL of the Falcon Queen games!!! I should be disqualified but the judges are just scared and have no power.

This place is so strange, filled with scratchy girls like Bina (my roommate), who's fat and a nightmare busybody, always talking. this boy called Charlie is Brainless. Jackson is my Prince Charming, it's true love! I dream for us be alone, to hug and kiss him.

Miss you,
Rosie x

P.S. Hemlock is a weird, lost dog who should be fired.

How? How? It was *her* handwriting and *her* words, but they were all mashed up in a different order. She hadn't said any of those things. Not in the way they appeared now.

Charlie was next to her and had also pulled down one of the letters. His face went ashen.

"So I'm brainless, am I?" he asked her.

"No, Charlie, of course not. I didn't—"

"Don't lie to me, Rosie, that'll only make it worse. I recognize your handwriting and I saw you writing letters to your mum in that notebook of yours."

"It's not—"

"So you're saying that's *not* your handwriting?"

"No, it is, but I didn't write that! I—" said Rosie, taking fast, shallow breaths. How could this happen? What *was* happening?

"Yeah, whatever," said Charlie. "You know what, forget

it. After what I told you the other night, you do this? I thought you were my mate. Oh well, go and get your kiss from Prince Charming."

He pushed the letter into her chest and walked off.

Rosie let the piece of paper fall to the ground. This couldn't be happening.

As Rosie ran back to her bedroom with her head down, she avoided the other students' dirty looks and murmurs. "What a traitor." "Nice 'friend.'" "Should be disqualified."

She paused outside the bedroom door. Soft whimpering was coming from inside. Rosie stopped and put her head to the door. Best leave Bina to it; she was probably furious. Come back later? What to do . . . She took a deep breath and opened the door.

Bina was facedown on her bed. When she heard the door open, she sat up and wiped her cheeks. She looked at Rosie, her eyes sad.

Rosie stepped into the room, letting the door close behind her, and sat down on her own bed.

"I'm so, so sorry," she said. "I can explain."

Bina wiped her face again but didn't say anything.

"I'm so, so sorry," Rosie said again, "but I didn't write those things."

"I get it. I am fat, so what; I'm down with my curves—but I talk too much?! I'm a busybody?? I was just being friendly! I guess you don't know what real friendship is, do you? And now everyone is laughing at me." Angry tears were running down Bina's cheeks. "I hate you," she said.

"But I'm innocent," Rosie insisted. "I've been set up. Don't I deserve a chance to explain? Look, I can prove it," Rosie said. She slid open her bedside drawer and rummaged around, but of course the unicorn notebook wasn't there. She checked her bag, her desk drawers, her wardrobe, even under the bed, but the notebook was gone. "It was here before, the same book that had the lyrics for the song me and Jackson wrote . . . so I had it with us at rehearsals . . ."

"Likely story. And you think Jackson is your Prince Charming?! You love him?! You think you know him? Ha! And I thought you were smart; what a joke."

"But it's all rubbish!"

"Don't say I didn't warn you." She laughed, shaking her head.

Is Bina jealous?!

"Just leave me alone," said Bina.

Rosie slipped out into the corridor. She leaned against the wall and slid down to the floor.

"This can't be happening." She sighed.

Okay, Detective Frost, think . . . Someone must have scanned in all her letters and then used some kind of design program to rearrange the words. Who had seen her notebook? Charlie and Jackson? They had no motive. Who really had it in for her?

It was obvious, from the minute she read the fake letter. She knew the answer . . .

Ottilie Aragon-Windsor.

Rosie looked around and saw her at once, at the far end of the corridor. She had a copy of the letter in her hand and was reading it, as if she didn't already know what it said. Jamila and Ishaan were reading it over her shoulder, giving theatrical gasps.

Rosie stood up, marched over to Ottilie, and snatched the letter out of her hand. "You did this!" she shouted, jabbing an angry finger at her.

"Uh, first of all, get out of my face. And second of all, no, I did not," said Ottilie.

"It is funny, though," said Ishaan.

"I like the bit about the dog . . ." said Jamila.

"I know it was you," Rosie said to Ottilie. "No one else would be this mean."

"Don't blame me just because you're dumb enough to write a letter slagging off all your friends."

"I didn't write it!" said Rosie. She felt like she was going to explode.

"If you wanted people to believe that, you probably shouldn't have signed your name at the bottom," said Ottilie.

"Yeah. You shouldn't have signed your name at the bottom," Jamila repeated.

Rosie didn't care about the damn rules anymore. All she wanted was for Ottilie to pay for what she'd done. She gritted her teeth and curled her hand into a fist.

"Rosemary Frost!" boomed a voice from the other end of the corridor.

Rosie unclenched her hand and spun around. Hemlock stood pencil straight with a look of pure disgust on his face.

"I think you and I better have a talk."

So here she was again, back in Hemlock's office. In serious trouble.

The stuffed dodo with the gray feathers looked at her with pity. If Rosie had been given the choice to switch places with it, she might have taken it. The dodo might have been dead, but at least it didn't have to face Mr. Hemlock's wrath.

Hemlock sat at his desk, peeling an apple with his knife. There was a copy of the letter in front of him. He slid it across to Rosie.

"Miss Frost, indulge me," said Hemlock with a sour smile. "Read aloud what you see in front of you."

Rosie gulped. "It's not—"

"Just read the letter, Miss Frost."

Rosie could feel the shame creeping over her once again.

"*Dear Mum,*" she spluttered. "*I'm in the final of the*

Falcon Queen games. I should be . . ." She hesitated, but Hemlock's eyes bored into her with the distinct impression that, if she stopped reading, lasers might shoot out of them and pulverize her into space dust. "*I should be disqualified but the judges are just scared and have no power.*"

Hemlock raised his eyebrows in mock surprise. Rosie kept going. Saying the horrible things she'd supposedly written about her friends out loud was like some form of torture.

When she came to the sentence about wanting to kiss Jackson, her face turned bright scarlet.

This wasn't fair. Ottilie was spreading lies about her. It was just like what had happened to Anne Boleyn—people gossiping behind her back and saying things that weren't true—and look what happened to her.

"*Miss you . . . Rosie.*" She finished reading and slung the piece of paper onto the desk.

"Oh, I think there's one more line at the bottom there," said Hemlock, raising his eyebrows. "Don't forget that; it's my favorite part."

Rosie stared at the floor for a few seconds, breathing hard, and then picked the letter back up.

"*P.S. Hemlock is . . .*" Rosie read.

"Yes? What am I, Miss Frost."

"*Hemlock is a . . .*" Rosie looked up at him. Would she really have to say it?

"Come on, spit it out."

"*Hemlock is a weird, lost dog who should be fired.*" She raised her chin and stared straight into Hemlock's eyes. She hadn't written this letter; she hadn't done anything wrong.

"'A weird, lost dog who should be fired'?" Hemlock repeated. He placed the knife in front of him so that it lined up with the edge of the desk, and took a bite of the peeled apple. He made Rosie wait as he slowly chewed and swallowed. "Interesting. I've been called many things in my time, but a 'weird, lost dog' . . . that is particularly eloquent."

"I can explain—" said Rosie.

"I don't want to hear it," said Hemlock. There was a dark fury in his eyes. He threw the remains of the apple into a metal bin, and it hit the bottom with a loud *thwack*. "No one, no one gets to slander my reputation. Not you, not anyone, Frost."

"I didn't write it! The letter was a forgery."

"Lying will only make it worse," said Hemlock. "I recognized your writing and have had your other teachers confirm it."

"But—"

"Not another word!"

It was so frustrating! He wasn't letting her speak.

"You have not been at this school long, and all I asked of you was to be a good girl, Rosemary Frost, yet you seem intent on disrupting. It seems I was too lenient on you last time; I will not make that mistake again." He paced the room. "Consider this your very last warning. As punishment, you will have detention every day after school for the next three months. And, in addition to the detention, you are also forbidden from going outside for the full three months—even at weekends."

Three months! That was ridiculous.

"And if you give me one more excuse to expel you, it's a fait accompli," Hemlock went on. "What happens to you then will be out of my hands."

Rosie swallowed. What *would* happen to her? Where would she go? She'd be homeless.

"Just step in line, girl. Remember who's in charge."

"I suppose with Miss Churchill away, you think you can do whatever you like," Rosie blurted out. " 'No one will suspect a thing,' right?"

Hemlock stopped and looked at her. "I see . . . what could you possibly mean by that?" he asked. He tilted his neck to one side and it let out a sickening click.

"Tell me, Rosemary Frost, what do you think is going on? Cards on the table."

Rosie bit her lip . . . Silence.

"There is something going on with you and that compound in Wildcat Woods. I saw . . . I know what you're trying to do."

He stared at her, his face like stone. Then the words tumbled out of her mouth. Without thinking, she said, " 'I don't give a damn about the wildcats, or anything else on this island for that matter.' "

She'd pushed it too far. He knew that she knew. Her stomach sank. *I should have been discerning with my words; it was my downfall*, Anne Boleyn had said. *Silence is your shield*, Rosie's mum had said. *Measured words.*

His mouth tightened, then he cleared his throat. "Thank you for sharing what's in that silly-girl brain of yours. It's good to get it off your chest." He smiled. "But just like your claims about the case, you have no proof. Are you forgetting who I am?" He sighed.

"Consider me your judge; so in your lovely letter where you said the judges have 'no power' . . . wrong again, Rosie Frost . . . *I* do have power, and with that power comes great responsibility; so therefore I am withdrawing you from the Falcon Queen games. You said yourself that you ought to be disqualified, and I couldn't agree more."

No, he couldn't do that. Rosie needed to be in the games. She needed to win. A seething rage boiled through her. First he stole her case, then he threatened the wildcats, and now he was enforcing the most absurdly harsh punishment for something she didn't even do. The tension thickened. Both stood resolute, glaring at one another. Her anger grew and the monster was back, tickling through her veins. Her power surged. All she wanted was to punish him back.

Hemlock bit his lip, now pondering. "Rosemary, why are you so angry with me? Is it because of your mother? Because of your missing case? I understand you're a sad orphan, which might make you imagine things that aren't really there. I honestly feel sorry for you. But are you going to say something you'll regret over a worthless case full of nothing?"

"My mother isn't nothing!"

Rosie dived for the knife on his desk and scrambled over to the large painting that hung on his office wall—the expensive Hockney that depicted the deputy head next to an ugly blue bird. She held the knife up to the painting.

"What are you doing?" Hemlock screeched, his eyes filled with panic.

"'Whoever has the power gets to make the rules,'" said Rosie. "Isn't that what you also told me?" She placed the knife edge across the exposed neck of the Hemlock in the painting.

"Don't touch that! Have you gone mad? It's worth a fortune," he stammered.

"Tell me the truth about what's really going on. I saw the explosives! What are you doing in Wildcat Woods? And with my case." She spat the words out, gripping the knife to his neck in the painting. "Or you can say goodbye to your precious masterpiece." Hemlock clasped his hands together.

"Okay, enough!" said Hemlock. His mouth was tight and his eyes still filled with panic. "I admit it, I did have your case, but it's gone. It was sent immediately to Miss Churchill's chambers located outside of Heverbridge. I apologize for not disclosing that information straightaway. I was just following orders."

Hemlock lied, pretending never to have had it. But why?

"It's out of my hands." He flapped them. "Until she gets back, I can't do anything to retrieve it." He cleared his throat, then sighed again.

"If you must know the truth about the woods, it's actually a highly confidential matter. There is a serious problem with soil erosion on Bloodstone Island. We have complicated geological conditions here." He paced the room.

"Yes, there are explosives. We are gently blasting the bloodstone rock, which is going to loosen a small amount of minerals into the soil. The bloodstone mineral has soil-enriching properties which benefit all the wildlife," he continued. "It's a very delicate matter which needs to be done with utmost care. We are keeping this a secret so the bloodstone mineral will be protected. Otherwise everyone will want it, but it's for the benefit of our land only. And it would be a disaster for Heverbridge's reputation if it wasn't handled with care and confidentiality. We pride ourselves on how special the conservation here is. Bloodstone Island's ecosystem is renowned, the best in the world." He shook his head sadly.

"I am Miss Churchill's loyal deputy. It's under *her* instructions we are working with the Isambard Foundation on this procedure with the soil erosion. Unfortunately, there may be a few little casualties. No one wants that, but we're doing this for the greater good. It will help the conservation of *all* wildlife here," he said flatly.

"So the wildcats will be the 'little' casualties?! You don't care? Tell me the truth!"

"I've worked at this school for over twenty years and always kept its best interests in mind. Quite frankly, I have no obligation to explain myself to you and shouldn't have told you any of this, so remember this is a private matter. And by all means, discuss it with Miss Churchill when she returns. I doubt she would believe some silly accusations from an overemotional little orphan anyway. Can you really start making these allegations when the whole of Bloodstone Island's reputation is at stake?"

Was it just soil erosion? Did Ms. Parr know about this too? She'd said Bloodstone had the most powerfully enriched soil on the planet, that the island was the most precious jewel on earth. So why would it need to be kept secret? Didn't she say the bloodstone mineral wasn't valuable enough to mine? Unless she was wrong, and it really is worth something?

Hemlock's explanation sort of sounded plausible, but something about it still didn't feel right. And he hadn't given her any guarantees that the wildcats wouldn't be harmed. There was also the issue of her mother's case. If he'd only sent it off to Miss Churchill, why would he have denied having it when she first confronted him about it and not explained this earlier? Was it just to torment her? Rosie wasn't buying it.

Her arm holding the knife began to shake, the blade still on the painting at Hemlock's throat.

"Perhaps you are what your name suggests, wicked and cold. Just like Avaline." Hemlock began to laugh, then drummed his fingers on the edge of his desk, glaring at the knife she was holding.

"What do you mean, Avaline?" she said, her voice shaky. *My mum's name.* Hold on . . . "Did you *know* her?" A strike of heat surged into her veins, the thought igniting in her mind.

Hemlock's face went cold.

"Tell me, did you know her?! Is that why you took my case?" she demanded.

"It matters not, child; she's gone, and so is the case. As I said, it's out of my hands." Hemlock flinched.

He knew her? How? Did she study here too?

Surely she would have said something? And told her all about this place. Maybe . . . but why hadn't she spoken more about it? Rosie couldn't be sure. One question led to another. It was like a puzzle rumbling through her brain, with too many jumbled parts.

"Besides, we're more alike than different, Frost. Now, if you're going to do it, just get on with it, because I'm bored of your little-girl rants. Or perhaps you wouldn't dare?"

Rosie raised an eyebrow. "Oh, really? I'm sick of your bull!" She pressed the tip of the blade a little more firmly into the canvas, then pulled it back, ready to strike.

Finally, in this moment, I hold the power, thought Rosie.

"Nooooo!" Hemlock screamed.

She struck the knife through the air, then stopped the blade millimeters away from the canvas.

The scent of velvet plum roses had tickled her nose, accompanied by a waft of cloves and spices. "Temper thy fire before thou strikest."

She dropped the knife on the floor.

"*Some* people are wicked and cold," she said. "But that's not me. Punish me, throw me out of the Falcon Queen games, torment me, do whatever you want, but know this: if anything happens to hurt those cats, I'll make sure you are held responsible. *And* I want my case back."

A serene peace settled over her. She walked past Hemlock's desk and made her way to the door.

"But you've made a hole in the painting!" Hemlock shouted after her. Rosie stood at the doorway, looking back at him.

"That's not a hole, it's a warning," she said, then closed the door behind her.

Chapter Twenty-Seven

A BLESSING OR A CURSE

TUESDAY, DECEMBER 20TH. THE NIGHT BEFORE

THE BATTLE OF BLOODSTONE.

When Rosie got to the bottom of the stairs that led down from Hemlock's turret, her whole body was shaking—so much so that she had to lean against one of the walls to catch her breath. She then forced herself to head out, rushing through the corridors. She couldn't believe what had just happened.

On top of that, everyone was still gossiping about her behind her back and giving her shady looks when they passed. The little whispers had moved like wildfire throughout the entire school. They say that lies spread faster than truth, and Rosie now discovered this couldn't be more right. No one wanted to hear her side of the story.

What about the Falcon Queen games? The wildcats? She couldn't just abandon them.

The image of Mercury and her cubs, with their silver eyes, haunted her mind. She had to save them, check they were okay.

And how the hell was she ever going to get her case back? Could he really have been telling the truth about having sent it away to Miss Churchill? *But he knew my mum.* The whole thing was so creepy and confusing. The ache of all the mysteries surrounding her mother and the case taunted her, the answers always just out of reach.

She had tried to do what was right, to follow the Falcon Queen's rules, but she was no closer to the truth. Now she'd let down the wildcats, none of her friends would talk to her, and she had to spend every day after school in detention.

Rosie sped on, head down, back to her room and stayed there for the rest of the day.

As the winter darkness began to set in, Rosie's hunger finally got the better of her and she decided she had no choice but to brave going down for dinner. As soon as she got to the Sovereign Hall, she filled her plate and sat down on her own. Then she saw him across the hall: Jackson. *Jackson is my Prince Charming, it's true love! I dream for us to be alone, to hug and kiss him . . .*

Her cheeks flushed. Cringe, it was so embarrassing.

He'd probably been getting loads of jibes from his mates. As soon as they saw each other, Jackson put his head down and quickly looked the other way.

Oh God, he was definitely mortified by her letter.

Rosie shoveled down a couple of mouthfuls but couldn't bear to be surrounded by all the judging faces anymore. Charlie and Bina were nowhere to be seen (they were probably avoiding her), so she had no one to talk it through with. She wrapped up the remains of her food and hurried out of the Sovereign Hall.

Having hidden in the library until it closed, she then decided to sneak out of the school.

Rosie swiftly headed down to Wildcat Woods, sticking to the shadows, out of sight, heart thumping with only the moonlight as her guide. Hemlock had forbidden her from going outside, but it was a risk worth taking.

She had to see Mercury—to apologize, if nothing else.

She pushed her way through shrubbery and went deeper into the woods, heavy and dense in the darkness, branches snapping under her feet. Rosie paused, her body tensed on high alert. The strange sounds of animal calls echoed through the trees.

Do Komodo dragons sleep at night? She breathed in the damp night air, walking quickly, stepping up her pace.

When she arrived at the compound, she tugged at the wide metal gate, but of course it was locked. Even if she still had her key card, she wouldn't have been able to get in without triggering the alarm. She peered through the slot in the gate. Beyond the metal walls, Wildcat Woods was deathly quiet.

"Mercury?" she whispered. She glanced over her shoulder and risked a slightly louder shout. "Mercury? It's me, Rosie."

Her breath disappeared into the darkness. She wished she could dissolve into the night sky too, along with all her problems. The moon shone down on her like a spotlight. She should head back; it had been foolish to come here. Rosie slumped down by the metal gate and leaned against the door. She dug her fingers into the soil, this strange magical earth, on an island she was now growing to love as her home.

Hemlock knew my mum. The thought rose up again, ricocheting through her mind.

Mum, where are you? She closed her eyes and sighed. After a hard day at school, her mum would always be waiting with a hug and say the right things. "Why did you want me to come here? I need you," Rosie whispered.

WORDS MATTER! her mum had said once over a cup of tea. *Bullies can use words to destroy, but words can be a voice for the voiceless . . . They can empower too . . . One day maybe you'll write a book. It will help others. That's why I write: words matter, Rosie.* Rosie could think of a person who had written a book to help someone else . . .

She pulled out the one thing she had come to rely on in moments of crisis: the little purple book. Words from a queen. The golden falcon on its cover glowed under the moonlight. Its wisdom had helped her find a way through every obstacle so far. Perhaps there was another rule, or something here, that could give her a clue about how to save the wildcats. She flicked through the pages and sighed. Tonight the words just blurred together as meaningless letters on a page, nothing sinking in. She started to read rule number three: *Never give up . . .*

"What?! No way! Are you kidding me?! Haven't I done enough? After all that's happened? How can I keep going when I don't know what to do? YOU'RE USELESS! I'M SICK OF YOUR RULES!" She threw the book hard to the ground.

Suddenly there was a crunching sound nearby. Rosie's body tightened. Was it Hemlock? A dragon? If she was caught outside—especially here, at the compound—she was going to be expelled. No more chances.

There was another crunch and the snapping of twigs. It was coming from inside the compound. Rosie peered through the slot again and met a pair of silver eyes, shining from inside the undergrowth.

"Mercury? Is that you?"

Mercury and her two little cubs stepped out of the bushes. With a gentle mewing, they approached Rosie and rubbed their tiger-striped bodies against the inside of the gate.

"I'm so happy to see you," said Rosie. "I don't know what is going on, but I wish I could get you out of there. I'm sorry."

She tugged at the metal handle, and even thumped the key card reader a couple of times, but it was futile.

When she next looked through the slot again, Rosie thought she was seeing double, or even triple. Mercury's mewing had attracted the attention of other wildcats, and there were now at least twenty more creeping out of the trees, all curious and—by the sound of their meows—all hungry. Their eyes looked different from Mercury's—more bronzy-gold, flecked with orange. They twinkled in the moonlight.

"Here, I brought you this." Rosie pulled out the remains of her dinner, tore up the pieces of bacon, and threw them over the gate to scatter them inside the enclave. The wildcats pounced and gobbled all of it up. Mercury had a little before ensuring her cubs got their fair share.

"I'm so sorry," Rosie whispered through the slot, once all the food was gone. "I let you down."

Just like I did with Muffin, my cat back home.

These woods were Mercury's home, and God knows she knew what it felt like to lose your home and who you love in a heartbeat. And if her hunch was right, what

Hemlock was doing could very well kill them all unless Rosie did something about it.

She needed advice, but who could she turn to? Her friends hated her, and if she spoke to any of the teachers, Hemlock would deny everything and discredit her, or even have them fired. She was utterly alone.

There was only one person who might be able to understand what she was going through. One person who knew what it was like to have lies spread about them, and to have everyone turn on them as a result. That's who Rosie needed to speak to: the ghost of Queen Anne Boleyn. She picked up the little book and dusted off the soil.

"I'm sorry," she whispered through the slot to the wildcats.

When she got back to her room, Bina was fast asleep, or was at least pretending to be. Rosie didn't bother to arrange her bed to make it look like she was sleeping this time; she didn't care if Bina knew she wasn't there. By the light of her phone torch, she threw a few essentials into her bag, including a packet of pickled onion Monster Munch that she'd stashed in her T-shirt drawer for emergencies, then made her way to the Falcon Queen gallery. As she pushed open the doors, she was surprised to see that there was already a woman standing in the middle of the room. No ghost, but someone very much alive. She looked at Rosie.

"Good evening," said Ms. Parr. "What could possibly bring you here at this time of night?"

"I . . . um . . . I just came to look at the paintings," said Rosie.

Ms. Parr eyed Rosie's rucksack and raised her eyebrows, clearly not convinced. The groundskeeper was standing by the largest painting—the one of Queen Elizabeth I—and Rosie walked over to join her.

"Quite the impressive monarch, isn't she?" said Ms. Parr.

"Yes," Rosie replied.

Once again, Rosie's eyes were drawn to the tangerine-sized red jewel that hung from a chain at the queen's waist.

"What's that orb thing hanging there?" Rosie asked.

"Ah, now, that's an interesting story. There are many theories about that piece of royal jewelry. I've done my own research, and although others may disagree, I am sure what I'm about to tell you is accurate."

Rosie was all ears.

"A long time ago, back in the time of Henry VIII, two dominant women vied for his affection—his first wife, Catherine of Aragon, and his second, Anne Boleyn. They were in opposition; essentially, they were enemies." Ottilie had told her about this when she first arrived.

"It was woman against woman, and they were encouraged to hate each other by friends who weren't real friends, spreading rumors behind their backs."

Smiling vipers, thought Rosie. She knew all about them.

"In the end, one of them made a gesture of friendship to the other," Ms. Parr went on. "As Catherine lay dying, she forgave Anne, remembering that she was once her lady-in-waiting and friend. She left her a gift of a ruby pendant. It was said to have ancient powers, and was given to Catherine when she first arrived from Spain to welcome her as the new queen of England. She gave it to Anne freely, to remind her that together women are stronger, that unity creates power. But five months later, when Anne faced execution, some said that the ruby had been cursed by Catherine.

"The truth is, Anne was just betrayed by Thomas Cromwell, her supposed ally and the man who had helped get her on the throne in the first place. When the time came, he was then the one who helped send her to her death.

"So it's up to your interpretation. What do you think the ruby represents? Friendship or power? Is it a blessing or a curse?"

"I don't know," said Rosie, unsure if it was a question that required an answer.

"Well, Queen Elizabeth agreed with Catherine of Aragon—that women *must* stand together; that's where real power comes from. So she must have considered the ruby a blessing. She must have worn it often, since she liked it enough to include it in this portrait. After her mother was executed, the ruby was passed down to her, along with a book called *The Falcon Queen's Rules*—a set of rules written by Anne Boleyn to guide her daughter through life. I believe Miss Churchill keeps the book in her office. Perhaps she will let you see it one day."

Rosie turned away, pretending to look at a different painting so Ms. Parr wouldn't see her blush.

The groundskeeper carried on talking, oblivious. "Queen Elizabeth's spirit was strong, all because she lived by the rules her mother had given her. So it's thanks to Anne Boleyn's *The Falcon Queen's Rules* that Elizabeth became one of the greatest monarchs in English history. That and, perhaps, the power of the ruby orb."

"What happened to the orb after Elizabeth died?" Rosie asked.

"No one knows," Ms. Parr said. "It would have been passed down to Elizabeth's child, had she had one, but she never did, so her bloodline stopped with her."

"Oh." If Queen Elizabeth hadn't had any children, there was no possibility that Rosie could be a direct descendant of Anne Boleyn. Rosie hadn't thought to look that up. She felt foolish for ever considering it might be true.

"However," said Ms. Parr, causing Rosie's ears to prick. "There are rumors of an illegitimate child. During the course of her reign, Queen Elizabeth had many suitors, but there was only ever one man who got close to her: Robert Dudley. Some historians believe she had a child by him, which was kept a secret because they weren't married."

Rosie knew about keeping secrets.

Who's my dad? The unanswered question reared its head again. *Sometimes it's best we just leave things as they are. It's for your own good*, was another one of her mum's replies.

"They speculate that the orb was passed down to this illegitimate child, and down and down through the generations. Which is kind of funny, when you think about it; it could mean there are direct descendants of Elizabeth everywhere. Research has shown there are secret royals all over the place, though. Each and every one of us, all the everyday people out there, could be a little bit royal. So it's not such an exclusive club after all." She chuckled. "But there's no real evidence Elizabeth had a child—in fact, she was said to be infertile—so it's more tripe if you ask me."

"Didn't the Aragons want it back?" asked Rosie.

"Yes, but it was never found. Wherever the orb is now, its location remains a mystery."

"How do you know all of this?" Rosie asked, looking closely at Ms. Parr. "Are you a historian as well?"

"Not as such. My family are descendants of the royal Parrs—Catherine Parr, the last wife of Henry VIII. Her mother, Maud Green Parr, was the head lady-in-waiting to all six of his wives. She made sure the rule book and ruby orb were passed down to Elizabeth. It was Catherine Parr who brought unity to the family—she invited Elizabeth back into the family fold, years after she had been excluded. So Elizabeth made sure *all* the families of Henry VIII's different wives and their children were always invited to study here at Heverbridge. Aragons, Boleyns, Seymours, Cleveses, Howards, and Parrs were invited here. She believed in inclusion, standing together."

Of course; that's why Ottilie Aragon-Windsor is here.

"I am a living descendant of that lady-in-waiting—in fact, I was named after her. Us Parrs have always been around, helping protect the crown. We've also taken care of this island and the estate for many generations."

Wow, so Ms. Parr was sort of . . . royal?

"What's it like?" Rosie asked her. "To be a royal descendant?"

Ms. Parr waved her hand, dismissing Rosie's question. "Parrs are the guardians of HRH's wishes. My family is a humble one. I learned from a young age that, regardless of any royal blood, everyone is important; everyone matters. It is the spirit of our ancestors that we carry forward, regardless of what their social status might have been."

Very true, thought Rosie.

"Anyway, there are bigger issues in this world than bloodline," said Ms. Parr. "Such as the future of our planet and everything that inhabits it. That's why Heverbridge was always such a special place for Queen Elizabeth; she would come here as a child with her mother. It was a place of peace. That's why they loved it so much."

Maybe this was Rosie's chance to tell her? She should surely know about the issue of soil degradation, if it was as Hemlock had claimed. But again, Ms. Parr wouldn't have the authority to stand up to Hemlock, even if she believed Rosie's suspicions of him. It would just get her fired. And what about Rosie's mother—might she know anything about *her*?

"Ms. Parr, did you know my mum? Did she come here?" Rosie stared up at her in anticipation, intensely focused.

"I'm getting old." Ms. Parr chuckled. "This school has been going for over four hundred and fifty years. There have been so many pupils here at Heverbridge, it's hard to remember. And now the Falcon Queen games final is upon us. It is such a special occasion . . . The games are really about transformation . . . reformation of hearts and minds, just like our bodies from the inside out. It's incredible to watch what happens to students who enter," she said, placing her hand on Rosie's shoulder. "They find the courage they never knew they had.

"The original Falcon Queen wanted that for her daughter, and Queen Elizabeth wanted the same for the students who entered. That's why the games were created. This will be our sixty-sixth games, if my math is correct." She then glanced down the hall to the end of the Falcon Queen gallery, where a glass cabinet was positioned with a golden trophy at its center, gleaming under a spotlight. Rosie hadn't really paid much attention to it before, having been so focused on the paintings.

On a framed parchment were the words:

Remember well, a deserving champion, a true sovereign, always acteth beyond the prestige of the crown. This person shall put others and our kingdom first.

"Queen Elizabeth was very proud of how all the pupils faced the challenges, with the winners' courage shining through. There have been some amazing champions." Ms. Parr smiled, enjoying the reminiscences. "I've witnessed quite a few. 1994 was a good year—one of the finest, a special win." She nodded. "Let's make this one just as good."

She obviously didn't know Rosie had been excluded from the games, and Rosie felt too ashamed to tell her right now.

"Anyway, you don't need to hear me prattling on all night, so I'll leave you to it.

"Would you like a biscuit to keep you going?" She pulled a scrunched-up packet of ginger nuts from her gilet pocket and offered it to Rosie.

"Thank you," said Rosie, deflating. Still no answers about her mother, and she didn't feel she could press Ms. Parr further. She took a biscuit, which was only slightly stale. The more time Rosie spent with Ms. Parr, the more she liked her, despite her rough exterior, and not just because she offered her biscuits.

"You know what, take the whole packet," said Ms. Parr, burying the remaining ginger nuts in Rosie's hand. "You don't want to go hungry if you're going to be here all night." With that, she bid Rosie good night and marched out of the gallery.

Rosie polished off three of the biscuits without really tasting them, all the while staring at the golden trophy. Did Ms. Parr also know about Anne Boleyn's ghost?

Rosie waited a few minutes to make sure Ms. Parr wasn't going to make an unexpected reappearance, and then locked the gallery's doors. It was a long time to wait until three o'clock—the time when the ghost usually appeared—so she set an alarm on her phone, ate her emergency bag of Monster Munch, and settled down to get some rest.

※ ※ ※

As it turned out, she didn't need the alarm but found herself waking from a deep sleep just before it went off. She spread out her arms and stretched her neck from side to side. Then, right on cue, the rich scent of roses and cloves spread throughout the Falcon Queen gallery, and the ghost of Anne Boleyn emerged through the wall. On the last two occasions, the ghost had stepped through assertively, but this time she walked slowly, staring straight ahead, her jaw clenched tight. She stopped when she reached the middle of the room and spoke as if addressing a crowd. Her face was ashen, frightened.

"I am come hither to die, for according to the law I am judged to die, and therefore I will speak nothing against it."

A shiver ran down Rosie's spine as she realized she must be witnessing the final moments before Anne Boleyn's execution.

"And thus I take my leave of the world and of you all," Queen Anne went on, "and I heartily desire you all to pray for me."

The queen knelt. Rosie ran over and knelt in front of her. As soon as Queen Anne saw her, her sad eyes filled with tears.

"My child, you shouldn't be here," she said.

"I didn't know where else to go," said Rosie.

"I am not long for this world, although it pains me to leave you. What plagues thee, my lambkin?"

"First, there's a girl," said Rosie. "Ottilie. And she's spread lies about me, and now all my friends hate me and I don't know what to do. Not only that, but one of my teachers is up to something bad, and he doesn't care who he hurts in the process." Rosie ran out of steam and lowered her head. "And most of all, I still don't have my case back. There are so many questions I have, but no one ever gives me a straight answer."

"Ah," said Anne Boleyn with a sage nod. "People plotting for their own gain. I know what it is like to be the victim of cruel rumors, but do not let the smiling vipers defeat you."

"But the letter . . . Everyone thinks—" said Rosie. Anne Boleyn silenced her by putting a ghostly finger to her lips.

"Keep your chin raised, my child, for you are brave and you are strong. You have the book, don't you?"

Rosie nodded.

"My heart and mind are always with you." Anne Boleyn glanced over her shoulder, then turned back to Rosie. "They are coming. This is the end for me," she said.

"No—please don't leave me," Rosie cried.

"I'm sorry, but I have no choice. Keep following the Falcon Queen's rules, and you will find your courage, power, and freedom, as I promised. You are on the right path . . ." Her eyes filled with sorrow, tears spilling down her face with such love and regret. It was the look of a mother to her daughter. "Oh Lord, have mercy on me. To God I commend my soul."

The queen closed her eyes as the sound of a heavy blade swished through the air. Rosie gasped, and the very next moment, the ghost of Anne Boleyn disappeared, leaving nothing but cool wisps floating in the air.

Rosie stayed where she was, staring into the blank space where the queen had been kneeling just moments before. She felt herself beginning to shake, the brutality of that moment sending its shock waves through her body. The queen had been executed, leaving a daughter without a mother, without anyone, alone in the world, just like Rosie.

Had Rosie's own mother thought about her, too, at the very end?

Rosie owed it to Anne Boleyn's memory to follow her parting advice. But how could she be on the right path when the final round of the Falcon Queen games were later that day and she wasn't even allowed to compete?

Keep following the Falcon Queen's rules, and you will find your courage, power, and freedom.

If only it were that simple.

Chapter Twenty-Eight

The Final Challenge

WEDNESDAY, DECEMBER 21ST. THE BATTLE OF BLOODSTONE.

Today was the day: the winter solstice. It was the shortest day of the year, yet Rosie knew it would feel anything but with all that was due to happen: the final challenge of the Falcon Queen games, the Bloodstone Banquet, Miss Churchill's return . . . not to mention the small matter of Hemlock using the occasion to cover up a massive explosion around Wildcat Woods.

The whole school had been requested to remain in the Sovereign Hall after breakfast for a special assembly, at which Hemlock was going to announce the details of the final challenge. Rosie sat on her own, staring out the window. She hadn't seen any of her friends this morning, not that they were talking to her anyway. She swallowed a yawn and rolled her neck, stretching her tired muscles.

Maybe going to the Falcon Queen gallery last night hadn't been such a good idea after all.

Outside the sky was stark white, and it had started to snow. The flakes fell like lost souls seeking their final resting place. Despite the roaring fire that had been lit at the far end of the hall, Rosie shivered.

There was a screech through the speaker system as Hemlock switched on the microphone. He was standing behind the lectern, one hand gripped firmly onto its side. Rosie scanned the room for any signs of Miss Churchill, but it looked like she still hadn't arrived. Not yet.

As soon as she's here, I'm going to tell her what's going on; games or no games, she deserves to know the truth.

"Good morning," Hemlock said. His voice echoed around the room. "What a day that lies ahead; tragedy for most and triumph for one. Today we find the real champion of Heverbridge, with the third and final, most ferocious challenge of these Falcon Queen games—the Battle of Bloodstone. It shall commence at eleven o'clock sharp, and you are all invited to attend. This challenge will celebrate the third Heverbridge core value: freedom. The winner of the Falcon Queen games will be honored. And they will be granted the chance to set a new rule for Heverbridge. Something they feel is important for the school, or perhaps a bit of wisdom for Heverbridge students to carry with them as they go out into the wider world. It will be the winner's legacy. So how far will our challengers go for this opportunity to make a change? And what will it cost them?

"There is no better place on earth to test our competitors' qualities than Bloodstone Island, with its cunning landscape, grueling heights, and treacherous weather. The Battle of Bloodstone will reveal precisely what they are all made of. As you know, this challenge will feature the contestants from the two teams who made it through from the Court of Reform, only this time everyone will be competing as individuals. There can only be one champion. It will take the form of a hunt, starting at the winter rose garden beyond the northern terrace. Would the seven pupils taking part please come up onstage? And let's give them a round of applause for making it this far," said Hemlock.

The school erupted into applause for those pupils left in the competition, including Charlie, Ottilie, and Jackson, as they walked up onto the stage. Rosie cheered with everyone else, but with a heavy heart. She should've been walking up on that stage too.

"The victorious winner of the Falcon Queen games will sit on the throne at tonight's Bloodstone Banquet, and from there they will announce their new Falcon Queen's rule."

Excited chatter rippled throughout the hall. With each of Hemlock's words, Rosie's heart sank a little lower. She'd wanted to win the games so badly.

"Before we begin, I would like our challengers to take

the penultimate step, to face your fears; facing your fears is the key to freedom . . . You will receive the 'fear card.' Only the Falcon Queen games' governing body will be allowed to see this."

Each contestant was handed the card, an envelope to put it in, and a pen by the school secretary.

"You will have ten seconds to answer one question, and you must be honest in your answer. It's designed to find out what kind of ruler you would be under pressure. If you don't answer honestly, you will be disqualified. And believe me, we have very effective ways of checking this. If you don't answer in under ten seconds, you are also out of the competition."

He glanced at the large screen with a digital stopwatch for all to see.

"In other news, sadly our eighth contestant, Rosemary Frost, has been removed from the games. Thank you," Hemlock said with a neutral expression while shuffling some papers, as if it was the end of delivering a weather report.

And as he did, every head in the room turned to look at Rosie. She stared down at her lap, feeling defeated, in a puddle of shame.

"Here is your question: What are you most afraid of?" He nodded and pressed a remote. The screen began to count down. Ten, nine, eight, seven . . . The school audience joined in, chanting the numbers.

Each contestant wrote something quickly and handed back their card in the envelope.

Three, two one . . . The screen buzzed.

"Oh dear, it seems we have another elimination."

A boy called Henry Percy was still writing. He looked up, his face shocked at being caught out.

"Rules are rules. If you can't handle pressure, you're no winner. Goodbye, Henry Percy; thank you for your participation."

The boy turned red, completely deflated, and stepped off the podium.

"We are now down to six contestants. I shall reveal the full details for the next challenge when I see you later."

Hemlock gathered his papers and was about to leave the podium when someone shouted, "Wait!"

It was Charlie. Addressing the whole room, he said, "Rosie doesn't deserve to be excluded. The letter you all read was a fake." He was holding her unicorn notebook.

Rosie's heart started thudding. Was Charlie coming to her defense, even after the mean things she'd supposedly written about him?

"Charlie Saint, be quiet," Hemlock said into the microphone.

"But Rosie *is* innocent," said someone else. Bina. She was standing up now too. "Doesn't she deserve a fair hearing?"

"This is ridiculous," snapped Hemlock.

"Er, actually, according to law," said Charlie, who was now pacing like a defense barrister, "it's 'innocent until proven guilty,' isn't it? I have evidence to support the truth." He lifted up the notebook for all to see.

Rosie sat watching, too shocked to process it all.

"What is going on?" Hemlock boomed.

"Please, sir. Look at the evidence," said Charlie, handing him the unicorn notebook, continuing in full barrister mode. Rosie could suddenly imagine him wearing one of those silly wigs in a courtroom.

"What is this?" Hemlock said with disgust. He picked up the unicorn notebook and frowned.

"Sir, would you please take a look at the marked pages," said Charlie, pointing at the bookmark in the unicorn diary.

Hemlock turned the pages, then stood reading them with an expression like a slapped weasel.

"What you are reading," said Charlie, "is a notebook with the original letters Rosie wrote to her mother, who recently died. It was stolen, with her *personal* letters, that no one had any right to share, let alone manipulate to look like something else."

He then handed Hemlock a sheet of paper with a copy of the fake note.

The crowd gasped, murmurs of concern spreading through the audience.

"Someone stole her private notebook, then scanned

in the letters and rearranged them," said Charlie. "And where would a person ditch something they didn't want to be found? In the kitchen bins." Charlie nodded profoundly.

"Now you all know the truth. But if anyone doubts this, it's all in the notebook. The actual details are very personal and private, but there is real proof." Charlie looked out at the school pupils, razor-smart and confident. "Mr. Hemlock, there is your evidence." He pointed to the unicorn notebook. "Rosie Frost is innocent."

The room fell silent. Rosie couldn't breathe. Her friends had found her notebook! Oh God. They all knew, the whole school, that her mum was dead. What would they think of her, that she was some poor Little Orphan Annie?

A girl from the year above who was sitting across from Rosie nodded at her with a warm smile. So did the student sitting next to her, and someone else leaned across and gave her arm a squeeze.

It wasn't pity, not that sort Rosie hated; it was kindness. She felt a bit lighter inside.

Rosie was breathing fast and her hands were shaking. She couldn't believe what was happening—what her friends had done for her. Up on the stage, Ottilie scowled.

"Heverbridge is about truth, honor, and justice, as I'm sure Miss Churchill would agree," Charlie added.

There was a murmuring of agreement among the pupils.

"Silence!" shouted Hemlock, who had clearly run out of patience. "You do not get to dictate what I should or shouldn't do. *I* am in charge." He glowered at Rosie, then scanned her notebook.

"You're absolutely right, sir; you are our leader, and a merciful one." Charlie was kind of turning on the charm now. Because it was true. Right now, until Miss Churchill got back, Hemlock was still in charge.

The room was tense. Would Hemlock allow Rosie back in the games? It didn't look good.

" 'The quality of mercy is not strained,' " Hemlock muttered to himself, still glaring. Then he turned to his audience. "Mercy is an attribute of God himself, so today, mercy will season justice," he declared with his chest puffed out like a proud king's. "Having read these letters, it seems clear to me that you have been the victim of a cruel trick, Miss Frost." He straightened his tie, looking like he'd just been forced to eat something foul. "Today I am feeling benevolent, and so it is *my* decision that you shall be allowed to participate in the games after all."

Rosie was back in! She could hardly believe it. Ottilie's plan had failed!

"But first, someone give her the fear card," he said, and then looked at Rosie with a sly smile.

"Frost, you must, like everyone else, answer the question.

Since you've been privy to what it was already, I will give you five seconds instead of ten. Remember to answer fast and honestly, or you're out."

She quickly headed up to the podium and was handed the card.

"What are you most afraid of?" He nodded, then pressed a remote. The screen began to count down. Five, four . . .

The school audience once again joined in with the countdown. Rosie bit her lip, then quickly scribbled down the answer, sealed the card in an envelope, and handed it back. Three, two, one . . . The screen buzzed.

"Now get out, all of you. This assembly is over." And with that, Hemlock stormed out.

Amid the bustle of pupils leaving the room, Charlie and Bina stood beside her, until they were the last ones left.

"How . . . ? Why . . . ? How . . . ?" Rosie seemed incapable of completing a sentence.

"Sorry I doubted you, Frosty," said Charlie. "I've been called stupid all my life, so it kinda hurt. Bina said she'd overreacted too, and that everyone deserves a chance to explain."

Bina nodded in agreement, smiling.

"But how did you know it was fake?" Rosie asked.

"Well, Bina told me what you said about it being forged, so I took a closer look and noticed something wasn't quite right. The sentence about me didn't start with a capital letter, but there was a capital letter for the word 'Brainless.' It all looked a bit fishy."

Bina nodded again.

"So I decided I needed to find the originals. We were lucky to find it in the bins. I thought confronting Hemlock with it publicly was the only way to properly clear your name, by putting pressure on him to reverse his decision," continued Charlie.

"No one can ever call you stupid—you're amazing!" said Rosie. "Thank you. So who do you think actually stole my notebook?" she asked.

"I'm not a hundred percent sure—probably someone desperate to win. I have my suspicions, but I need more evidence," replied Bina, like she was a real detective.

"We'd better get ready. We've got a competition to win, and it starts in less than an hour," said Charlie.

"But first, there's something I need to tell you." Rosie rattled off Hemlock's explanation about the soil erosion, and how the explosives were to be used to extract blood-stone mineral properties for the island's soil enrichment. And that it was all under Miss Churchill's instructions, as well as confidential.

"Mining bloodstone for soil enrichment?" Bina frowned.

"I don't know what to believe anymore," sighed Rosie.

Bina gave Rosie a very serious look. "This is utter

rubbish! I've been using my detective skills and did some digging online after you told me about the bloodstone mineral. Something didn't add up, and it turns out bloodstone really isn't worth mining—Ms. Parr was right about that. But it isn't the only rare mineral on this island. The other is axonite. And it's worth billions."

Bina pulled her laptop out of her bag and started clicking through all the various internet tabs she had open. "I don't know if you've heard of lithium—it's an element, and what they use in batteries. It's in really high demand at the moment, especially for 'clean' energy like electric cars, but scientists reckon the world's supply is going to run out by 2040, so all the big car companies are desperately looking for a substitute. Beneath the bloodstone on this island, there's a layer of this axonite, which is precisely that—a substitute for lithium that is ten times more valuable. I bet you that's what Hemlock's really after. The only problem is, mining for it releases toxic gases that disrupt the surrounding ecosystem and kill off animals for miles."

This was worse than Rosie could have imagined. "You're telling me that, if Hemlock goes ahead with the mining, *all* the wildlife on the island could die?"

Bina bit her bottom lip and nodded.

It would be a catastrophe. Rosie thought of all the animals she'd seen since she first arrived. Not just the wildcats, but also the birds, the deer, the Konik ponies, wolves, the Komodo dragons . . . All these endangered species that had been given a new home on this special island could be wiped out—everything Miss Churchill had worked so hard for, the heart of this school, gone just like that—because of one man's greed. She couldn't let that happen.

Hemlock was a lying murderer and she had to stop him.

"Miss Churchill needs to know urgently," said Rosie. "We have to win these games."

"One more thing . . ." said Bina. "I did some digging on Hemlock too and found out some things about him from the lovely chef. We met him when we were going through the kitchen bins, and he really isn't a fan. Hemlock used to be a pupil here at Heverbridge and, apparently, he entered the Falcon Queen games in 1994. It was particularly contentious as he was meant to be a sure thing to win, but then got beaten at the last moment by a girl three years younger than him. It's common knowledge that he threw a hissy fit, punching the ground and shouting, 'I won't let a girl beat me!' Bit of a sore loser if you ask me, and definitely not in the spirit of the Falcon Queens." Bina shrugged.

1994—the year Ms. Parr mentioned. A special win . . . Rosie turned and quickly headed toward the doors.

"Bina, you really are the best detective!" she called out.

"Where are you going? The challenge starts soon!" shouted Charlie.

"I'll see you at the starting line," Rosie hollered as she ran. "I need to check something . . ."

It couldn't be . . . could it?

Chapter Twenty-Nine

THE BATTLE OF BLOODSTONE

WEDNESDAY, DECEMBER 21ST. FINAL CHALLENGE TO START

IN THIRTY MINUTES.

Rosie ran as fast as she could down the hall, down the large staircase, down the long corridors, and burst through the heavy oak doors into the Falcon Queen gallery. She continued past the row of paintings, the stone fireplace, straight to the end of the gallery, then stopped.

The glass cabinet gleamed. Rosie walked slowly toward it and studied the golden cup inside. It was shaped like a falcon with extended wings as handles, shining as always under the spotlight. Rosie peered at it more closely through the glass. THE FALCON QUEEN GAMES CHAMPIONS was engraved at the center of it, with names and their corresponding dates swirled around the rest of the cup. The first name, right at the front, was Joshua Drake, dated

1567. There were over sixty names, tying in with the number of games Ms. Parr had mentioned. She couldn't see them all, though, as they were engraved on the side and back of the cup too. Damn it. She tried to open the cabinet, but it was locked, so she pressed her nose up against the glass and looked again, carefully scanning the names and dates. And there it was, just curled around the base of the cup: 1994. She couldn't quite see the full name beside it, except for the last bit, an *S* and *T*. Her stomach flipped.

"Such a worthy winner," said someone behind her, leaning over and unlocking the cabinet.

Rosie turned to see Ms. Parr.

"Take a closer look, Rosie."

Rosie stuck her head into the cabinet and touched the golden cup, taking the winged handles and gently moving the cup around. She closed her eyes and breathed, then opened them again.

Avaline May Frost—1994

Her knees almost buckled under her.

"My mum?!" she gasped. "Oh my goodness!"

She *had* come to this school! And she'd won the Falcon Queen games?!

"Yes, everyone said it was impossible for her to win. She was just a little thing, but with a huge heart. Avaline Frost was a testament that anything is possible when you truly believe in yourself."

This was amazing!

"Is that why *I'm* here?" *She wanted me to come here too?*

Her mother had never really spoken to her about her childhood, or school. She was always so vague. If she had beaten Hemlock at the Falcon Queen games, and he'd taken it badly, no wonder he had been so weird to Rosie since she arrived. It was all starting to make sense now.

"Do you know what really happened to my mum?" Rosie asked, more quietly.

"Those answers are not mine to give," said Ms. Parr. "But I believe this belongs to you." She smiled, reached into her jacket, and pulled out a small metal whistle attached to a silver necklace.

Rosie looked at her and frowned. She'd never seen that whistle before in her life.

"It was your mother's. As a Parr, it's my duty to give it back to you," she said adamantly. Before Rosie could protest, Ms. Parr unclipped the necklace and placed it over Rosie's head.

"Remember, any trouble you encounter on that mountain, blow this and she will come."

"Who will come?"

"Hildegunn. It means 'warrior,' or 'helpful battle maiden.'"

"Thank you," said Rosie, still unsure who or what

Hildegunn was, but amazed that she was holding a whistle that had once belonged to her mum.

"Now, Rosie Frost, get going," Ms. Parr said with a smile. "I believe in you, just as I did in Avaline."

Smiling, Rosie hurried to the winter rose garden, where the other remaining competitors in the Falcon Queen games were waiting already. She joined them, standing in the middle of the garden, positioned in a straight line.

Hemlock had given them strict instructions that they were not allowed to talk. Rosie found herself in between Charlie and Jackson, with Ottilie on Jackson's right, and then the three sixth formers—two boys and a girl—who all had a look of fierce determination in their eyes. Next to Rosie, Jackson couldn't keep still and kept biting his thumbnail. He couldn't seem to look Rosie in the eye. The Prince Charming thing had been cleared up, so what was wrong with him? It wasn't like him to be nervous.

As she looked at her competitors, something more stirred in Rosie. It was a spark of possibility that was ready to burst into a smoldering fire; she could win this. For the wildcats, for the wildlife on Bloodstone Island, and to give something back to Heverbridge in honor of the Falcon Queen Anne.

And, of course, for her mother. If she'd managed to win this, then maybe Rosie could too.

Rosie had the rule book with her in her rucksack, and she took it out, then opened it. She looked to rule number three again, and this time read the whole thing properly.

Never give up; be the light.

Serve your kingdom; you'll win your fight.

Okay, I'll do my best. Thanks, Queenie, thought Rosie.

All around her, roses bloomed in vibrant reds, oranges, and yellows, despite the fact that it was winter. Their delicate petals were heavy with snow. Behind them, the school glistened like an ice palace. The ground was now covered in a thick blanket of white, disturbed only by footprints that snaked across the lawn.

The rest of the pupils who'd come to watch had formed a circle outside the ring of rosebushes. Bina was there, wrapped up like a burrito. She gave Rosie a small thumbs-up.

Rosie returned the gesture and then stamped her feet, grateful for the boots Bina had lent her. The air was heavy with the smell of roses. The darkest red ones smelled just like Anne Boleyn. Or maybe the queen's ghost was already here, waiting for the finale of the games to begin.

"Welcome to the winter rose garden," Hemlock addressed the seven competitors, "for the final round of the Falcon Queen games. *Animo, Imperium, Libertas.*"

"*Animo, Imperium, Libertas!*" the crowd chanted back.

"You have passed the challenges of courage and power, and are about to face your final challenge, the Battle of Bloodstone. This will bring the ultimate reward: freedom. Real freedom comes when we confront our deepest fears, and this challenge is designed to ensure that each of you will personally face whatever it is you're most afraid of . . ."

He shuddered slightly. Rosie wondered if he was thinking about his own final Falcon Queen challenge.

"This also truly honors the late queen Anne Boleyn's fearlessness and love of adventure as a means to freedom. The roses around you, marked by beauty and thorns, are both innocent and duplicitous, and serve as a reminder not to be fooled. Make no mistake: this will be your toughest challenge yet, as you battle the elements *and* your inner demons."

He was holding a large tablet and pressed several buttons with a grimace on his face. He then made one final flicking gesture on the screen as each contestant was handed a GPS. All seven of them clicked on their gadgets, opening a white screen with a green infinity symbol on it, which kept redrawing itself and then disappearing, as if chasing its own tail.

"When the infinity symbol changes color, tap on it and a map will open showing the location of your own personal bloodstone medallion you must collect. Once you have it, it's then a race to the tippy-top of Bloodstone Mountain, the Volcan Crag. Remember, you can only proceed there once you have retrieved your medallion," said Hemlock. "The clock will be ticking. It should take approximately two hours, or an hour and a half if you're quick, and whoever reaches the top first should then press the large red button located there, and they will be declared the Falcon Queen's champion."

Rosie looked down at hers. The infinity symbol was still showing green.

"To those watching: you may observe from a distance, but absolutely no helping," Hemlock continued. "Anyone caught speaking to any of the challengers will face instant expulsion—which would make my day, if I'm honest. It's been a while since I last expelled someone and I'm feeling particularly in the mood for it, so feel free to break the rules should any of you wish to test me." He eyed the crowd. "There is nothing more to be said except good luck to those taking part. Let the Battle of Bloodstone begin."

The snow began to tumble out of the sky in abundance now. Rosie shut out the eager faces watching her and stared at the GPS screen as the infinity symbol continued its endless loop. Then, all at once, the symbol froze and turned bright red. Rosie tapped on it with fumbling fingers, wiping the snowflakes away. The screen dissolved to reveal a map of the island, not too dissimilar to Google Maps. On the screen there was also a flashing blue dot, which Rosie presumed was her current location. Now what?

A few of the other competitors were already on the move; Jackson ran in the direction of the main school building and Ottilie disappeared the opposite way, toward the wetlands where the Konik ponies were. The sixth formers had all dispersed as well, no one giving a second thought to anyone else. How did everyone know where to go?

Rosie pinched the map with two fingers to zoom out and a red dot came into view. That must be where her bloodstone medallion was hidden, but which direction was it in? She'd never been particularly good at map reading. On a hunch, she tapped the red dot, and the following words popped up just above it: *A Rose with Frost will never die.*

What the heck was that supposed to mean? She was Rosie, Rosie Frost, yes, and already standing in the rose garden—should she start looking here? No, the flashing red dot was miles away.

Charlie had worked out where he needed to go now too, leaving Rosie alone in the middle of the roses.

Suddenly a large bird flew over her head—Queen Nike, the white falcon. She made a harsh *caawk, caawk, caawk* sound, as if hurrying Rosie on.

"I know, I know, I need to be quicker . . ." Rosie muttered.

She turned back to the GPS and used her thumb and forefinger to twist the map, trying to get her bearings. If the blue dot was her, and the school was behind her, that meant she needed to head . . . west! Toward the cottages where the teachers lived. And hopefully nowhere near any Komodo dragons, or any other scary creatures. Clutching the GPS, she headed off as fast as she could, hoping the clue would make some sense once she arrived at her destination.

It wasn't easy to run at top speed while keeping an eye on the map to make sure she didn't veer off course, so her pace soon dropped to a heavy jog. The snow was coming down thick and fast. The blue flashing dot crept closer to the red one, so at least she was going in the right direction. She came to the teachers' cottages and went around the back of them, then almost stopped short when she realized where the map was leading her. The graveyard up at the base of the Volcan Crag.

She'd never been to the graveyard before but had overheard tales from other pupils about the terrors that haunted its crypts. She shook her head. She didn't have time to think about that. She had enough of ghosts lately.

The snowfall got even heavier, and the wind was whipping it up into a frenzy, making it hard for Rosie to see more than a couple of meters in front of her. She staggered on, head low, weaving around the pine trees. She felt like she was in Narnia.

A massive rush of snow swirled around Rosie, causing the GPS to slip out of her hands.

"Damn it," she cursed.

She scanned the ground, looking for where it had fallen, and rummaged through the powdery snow, but the GPS was nowhere to be found. To make matters worse, the blizzard had totally disoriented her, so not only had she lost her map, but she had no idea which direction she'd been traveling in.

"Now what do I do?" Rosie said aloud to no one. Inside her soggy gloves, her fingers had gone numb.

Caawk, caawk, caawk, came a cry from above her. Queen Nike.

Caawk, caawk, caawk.

Was the bird trying to help her?

Caawk, caawk, caawk.

Rosie didn't have a better plan, so she abandoned the search for her GPS and just followed the sound of the bird's call.

She walked with one arm bent in front of her face to try to protect it from the onslaught of the weather, but the snow still found a way into her eyes and nose.

Caawk, caawk, caawk. Queen Nike flew off into the sky, seeming to urge Rosie on. She couldn't be sure she was going in the direction of the graveyard, but the ground was sloping upward at least, and something instinctively told her that's where Nike was going.

She trudged on for another half hour, going higher and higher until, at last, she reached a creaky wooden gate. Through the snowy mist, she could just make out the spire of the chapel, and gray headstones poked through the snow. She'd made it to the graveyard at the base of the Volcan Crag, otherwise known as the Soul's Gateway.

"Thanks, Queen Nike," she shouted, although the bird was nowhere to be seen.

As soon as she stepped through the gate, the snowstorm softened, its temper calmed. The wind blew its last breath before dropping off completely, giving Rosie a much clearer view of the eerie landscape. Tombstones toppled over one another in a decrepit mess. Many were cracked and protruded from the ground at odd angles, like a mouth full of broken teeth. Rosie made her way between them, trying her best not to step on any graves, although with all the snow it was hard to tell where they were. She passed a huge tomb with a statue of a commanding dog guarding it. Another tomb had a two-meter-high stone angel balanced on top of it, which glared at Rosie with hollow eyes.

What was Rosie supposed to be looking for now? She might have made it to the graveyard, but the place sprawled in all directions; without the GPS, it was impossible to know the exact spot where she was supposed to search.

The air seemed thinner here, and she was starting to feel breathless.

A spattering of red drops stopped her in her tracks—claret-red splashes drenched into the white snow. It took her a second to realize what it was.

Blood.

She could barely breathe, and her heart began to race at a hundred miles an hour. Why was there blood? And who did it belong to? Was this part of the challenge—the Battle of *Blood*stone?

Of course it was blood. She'd written "blood" on her fear card. Her breathing intensified, and the ground began to move. She followed the trail, which soon led to a collection of dirty white-and-brown feathers. As Rosie made her way over to them, an overwhelming sense of dread filled her stomach.

In among the feathers were the remains of a bird, its two scaly claws sticking up out of the snow. The claws were huge, clearly belonging to a bird of prey, and they stretched up to the sky as if grasping for something they would never reach. Even more blood, defiant, angry red, sliced and drenched through the innocent white powder. She began to desperately pant, and then she realized that the body was headless. Beheaded. Just like Queen Anne Boleyn had been. Panic flooded Rosie. She was so dizzy the graveyard was spinning. Among the guts and blood spatters, she noticed that the feathers were also fringed with golden speckles.

"Queen Nike . . ." Rosie muttered, putting a gloved hand to her mouth. The falcon had led her here. How could she now be dead?

As the falcon flies, Heverbridge thrives. But if the falcon falls, judgment calls . . . That was what Ms. Parr had told them. And now Queen Nike was dead, in what looked like an execution. Was this an omen, that Hemlock was going to get his way and the island would fall?

The crimson continued to glare at her from the snow. She could not win the games, she could not save the wildcats, and she would never know what had happened to her mum. It was all over.

Thud. She hit the powdery snow.

Chapter Thirty

BLOOD AND DUST

The white sky gleamed above her. She must be dead—was she in heaven? *Mum?*

"Mama," called out a little girl with long red curls as she toddled along, giggling. A young woman wearing a long velvet dress with a hooded cape and a pearl necklace with the letter B hanging from her throat walked beside her. She scooped the girl up in her arms and kissed her forehead.

"Elizabeth! Look up, my child!"

A beautiful large white bird extended its golden-tipped wings majestically. It swooped down just above them. They were running, laughing, and the little girl cooed with delight as they followed the bird. The mother called out to the bird with scraps of meat in her hand. The bird swooped down and landed on her arm, then gratefully ate the reward. The mother lifted her arm and the falcon surged into the air.

"Look at this falcon, how powerful and strong she is, my darling! As the falcon flies, Heverbridge thrives!"

The lady pulled the heavy fabric of her dress around her and crouched on her knees, then held the little girl closer. She cupped her hands around the young girl's face . . .

"Daughter. Listen to me. Even when I am gone, whenever you are afraid, just look up at the falcon, and know I, your mother, am always with you." Her eyes flooded with tenderness as she spoke.

The little child nodded as if she had a spirit wise beyond her years.

"I am with you even in your darkest hour, to help you serve your kingdom. In my blood and even in the dust, I am with you," she whispered, holding the child tightly to her chest. "Mama must leave you now. I love you. Never forget me."

Tears tumbled down her face, as if her heart was literally breaking. She then placed a ruby orb the size of a tangerine in the girl's hand and handed her a little purple book.

The little girl frowned as her mother got up to leave.

"Mama, mama," the little girl cried out, dropping the book. She held on tighter to her mother's hand.

"Never, ever give up, my dear child. My Falcon Queen,"
said the young woman, then walked away.

Rosie opened her eyes, gasping for breath, then jolted backward. What had she just witnessed? A mother's farewell to her child. It was a young Queen Elizabeth's last moments with Anne Boleyn. There was a spattering of blood around the headstone right next to her. *Breathe . . . this is just you having to face your fear.*

Unlike all the other headstones, it was made of black marble, which stood out against its stark white surroundings. When she peered closer to read the words, she let out a pained gasp.

Queen Anne Boleyn
With God 1536.
Always in my heart, never forgotten.
Your daughter, Elizabeth
WE CANNOT CHANGE THE PAST,
BUT LEARN FROM IT.

She was laid to rest here, not in the infamous Tower of London. She was buried here by her daughter, Elizabeth, who loved her, here in dust beneath the earth, in a place she had loved, safely away from the treachery of court.

Her mother was lied about, shamed, and murdered.

Poor Anne had lost her life at age thirty-one, and her young daughter, Elizabeth, had lost her mother when she was just two years old. Two women lost each other, all because of a man's power and greed.

"I'm so sorry this happened to you," Rosie whispered.

I know what it feels like to be apart from someone you love.

Rosie wasn't sure how long she sat there in the snow, in front of the grave. She wiped her nose on the side of her glove and shook her head in an attempt to clear it. She breathed out, refusing the grip of the crimson continuing to taunt her from the snow.

Get up, Rosie; get up for your mum, for the queen. They believed in you; now it's time to believe in yourself.

Rosie Frost got up.

There was still a competition to win, and Anne Boleyn's grave had given her a renewed determination to succeed. But to do that, she needed to find the hidden bloodstone medallion. What had the clue said? *A Rose with Frost will never die.*

Rosie looked more closely at the engraving on the headstone and brushed her fingers over the queen's name. She then scanned the grave for more clues, but there was nothing.

Maybe she'd got it wrong and the medallion wasn't here after all.

She took a step back.

Just as she was scanning the graveyard one last time, wondering where next to search, a shaft of wind blew straight at her face, as if demanding her attention. She turned away from it, seeking shelter behind Anne Boleyn's headstone. The wind had loosened some of the snow, and a sliver of dark red appeared nearby on the ground.

Rosie dropped to her knees and brushed off more snow, revealing a single crimson rose growing at the base of the headstone. It had been buried so deeply in snow. *A Rose with Frost will never die.* The Deep Secret rose! Her mother's favorite—the one that grew in pockets of frost!

Us Frosts can endure the harshest weather. It was true. She was orphaned, and she had sniping bullies on her tail, but she'd got through this far in the games and hadn't crumbled.

The bloodstone medallion *had* to be nearby. But why would it be put here?

Rosie fumbled around the flower, being careful not to damage its fragile petals, and, sure enough, there was something hard buried in the snow behind it.

"Yes!" Rosie said as she pulled out a round dark green, black, and red stone the size of a flat orange.

"I have to go now, Queen Anne." She stood, placing her hand on the headstone. "You told me never to give up, and I won't. I'm gonna win this race for you, for my mum, and for all the Falcon Queens who have been hurt by cruel people. I will stop Hemlock once and for all, I promise."

Chapter Thirty-One

THE VOLCAN CRAG

Rosie was out of breath, panting. She'd been running full pelt since leaving the graveyard, and although she was totally focused on winning the games, questions swarmed her mind. Why would her bloodstone medallion have been placed by Queen Anne's grave? And how had Nike known to lead her to the graveyard?

She didn't have time to think about it right now, though. All that mattered was reaching the finish line. First.

From where Rosie had been in the graveyard at the foot of the mountain, the ascent was too sheer and impassable to climb directly up, so she'd been forced to make her way back down a little and then run around the mountain to find the most accessible route up. From the weeks spent in the Gutter Club, she knew the island better than most, and was confident she'd find the quickest way.

The Volcan Crag was the highest point of Bloodstone Island, as Ms. Parr had told them. She'd also happened to mention that this was where the Komodo dragons were occasionally spotted. *Let's hope they're busy elsewhere.*

Rosie glimpsed one of the other finalists, the female sixth former, running behind her in the same general direction. The girl was tall, with long legs, and at this pace would soon catch up to her. Rosie willed her body to move faster. The race was well and truly on.

There was also someone ahead of her—a small speck in her vision. Rosie couldn't make out who it was.

As she made it around to the other side of the mountain's base, her heart dropped. She spotted first one Komodo dragon, then another, and then a third. They were spread out, standing absolutely still, making it impossible for her to reach the path up the mountain without passing at least one of them.

I know exactly how to deal with you, thought Rosie.

Without breaking speed, she swooped down and picked up a long, pointed stick from the ground. She shook it in front of her and roared. The dragons watched her approach, their tongues whipping in and out as they tasted the air, but they knew better than to approach;

Rosie was wild and fast and fierce. The Komodo dragons scurried away and let her pass.

Once Rosie looked back, the venomous dragons seemed to have lost interest, and now that she was at least a hundred meters away from them, she ditched the stick and started her ascent. When she glanced back over her shoulder, she saw the female sixth former stopped in her tracks, unsure how to navigate past the Komodo dragons. It gave Rosie the lead she needed.

The mountain got steep fast, and Rosie had to use both hands to scramble up the slope. The ground was treacherous, with the snow hiding all manner of dips and rocks and loose stones. More than once, Rosie lost her footing and tumbled into the snow, but each time she jumped straight back up again and kept on climbing. To make matters worse, it had started snowing again, even heavier than before. Rosie couldn't see more than a few steps in front of her, so she had no idea who was ahead, or if there was anyone closing in on her from behind. The wind howled around her, nearly sweeping her off her feet. Even though she couldn't see much, she was sure she couldn't be too far from the top. Her thighs were really aching now, and her feet were blistered and sore inside Bina's boots. She closed her eyes against the stinging bite of the snow—which was when she bashed straight into something heavy and hard.

"Jackson?"

"Yeah, it's me. You charged straight into me!"

"Sorry, I can barely see a thing in this blizzard." Even though they were technically in competition with one another, Rosie was glad to see him.

"Got your bloodstone medallion?" he asked.

"Yep." She felt the stone in her pocket.

"Me too. Bit of a shocker. Certainly got me for a minute." Jackson took a large step forward. "See ya at the top!"

They both carried on climbing, the knowledge that only one of them could win simmering between them. Jackson was stronger, his body leaner, and he inched away from Rosie until she was a good few paces beneath him and struggling to keep up. The mountain was even steeper now, and a deep crevasse opened up on their left. One wrong foot and . . . Rosie didn't want to think about it. They shouldn't be doing this; it was too dangerous. They had to be nearly at the summit, surely?

"Don't take this personally, Rosie," Jackson called down to her. "It's every man for himself."

"Every person!" Rosie yelled back.

Drifts of snow and the occasional rock tumbled into Rosie's path, loosened by Jackson's scrambling feet.

"Ahh!"

Rosie looked up just in time to see Jackson lose his footing and slip down the mountain. She tried to grab him as he tumbled past her, but he was traveling at too high a speed and carried on down, then rolled off the edge of the icy crevasse, disappearing into the abyss.

"Jackson! Noooo!" Rosie screamed.

She crouched on her stomach and crawled toward the edge. She couldn't see a thing.

Was he dead? The hungry blizzard had swallowed him whole.

"Jaaaaaaaaaaacksooon!" she shouted into the void, so loud it made her throat hoarse.

As if responding to her scream, the wind softened and the blizzard seemed to subside a little, giving her a partial view into the crevasse.

"Oh my God, what the . . ."

A pair of bloody hands were gripping a thick branch that jutted out from the rock face on the inside of the crack. *No more blood.*

Rosie let out a sharp breath; at least Jackson was alive. He looked up, his eyes filled with dread as he strained to hold on.

"I'm slipping," Jackson said.

"Just keep holding on. I'm gonna get you out of there." Rosie lowered herself farther over the edge and reached out, but Jackson was too far away.

Jackson looked down and let out a pained yelp.

"I'm scared of heights . . . stupid me, I wrote it on the fear card," he said with a freaked-out sort of laugh.

"That's what this challenge is all about, remember: facing our fears."

"No. I can't, not again. I've been through enough back there."

"What are you talking about? Don't be ridiculous, just face your fear again. Mine is blood! We can do this!" Despite what she'd just said, she began to tremble.

Rosie edged a little farther out while digging her boots into the snow to stop herself from toppling over.

"Stop, or you'll hurt yourself. I've hurt you enough."

What did he mean by that?

"I can do it," said Rosie. "Just give me your hand." She reached out to him.

Jackson shook his head.

"Friends don't give up on each other."

"I'm not a good friend." Jackson shook his head again, his eyes filled with shame. "You don't understand. I'm not worth saving. We're bad people," he stammered.

"What?" Rosie reached as far as she could. This was not the time for conversation.

"I'm a CROMWELL! A Cromwell! Look at our reputation . . . you can't trust a Cromwell."

Rosie's stomach sank. A jumble of thoughts whirled around her brain; no, he was Jackson, who she had sung with, and yet here he was, with the name of a traitor, with eyes that looked so hurt. Ottilie had said there were

Cromwells studying at the school, and here was one.

The branch began to snap . . . Jackson gasped. Rosie blinked.

"So what? It's just a name," she said quickly. "Let me get you out of there, and then you can explain. Never give up!"

"Said like a true Falcon Queen. What your ghost queen taught you, I guess."

Rosie looked at him, stunned. *What? How did he know?* He was now dangling from the thin branch. He was about to fall to his death.

"It was me. I'm a traitor," said Jackson, his fingers trembling from the strain of holding on. "It was me who stole your notebook. I saw your letters, Rosie. I betrayed you."

Rosie's mouth dropped open and she gulped for air. His words were like a punch in the stomach with an iron fist.

Jackson had betrayed her. *He* was the smiling viper.

You think you know him? . . . Don't say I didn't warn you, Bina had said, and she was right. She wasn't jealous! She wasn't crushing on him; she was wary of him, warning Rosie about the snake he was. She must have known all along he was a Cromwell. When she followed him at the Court of Reform, she was keeping an eye on him.

But why would he do such a thing?

"I'm sorry, Rosie," he said, grabbing desperately on to the branch as his hands kept slipping.

"Look, right now, I don't care what you've done," she shouted out. "I'm not losing anyone else this year."

Her hands found a root buried deep beneath the snow. Praying that it would hold her weight, she swung her body over the edge, then pointed her legs toward Jackson. The root held, and Rosie used her feet to pin Jackson to the side of the mountain.

"Use my body to climb back up," she said.

"Rosie, I can't, I . . ."

"Just do it. Before this root comes loose and we both plummet to our deaths."

Jackson didn't argue further. As he dug his feet into the ledge and used Rosie's body as a makeshift rope, she tightened her grip on the root. It creaked and groaned beneath their combined weight.

With one final stretch, Jackson pulled himself back up to safety, then heaved Rosie up after him. Once they were both safe, he flopped into the snow, lying on his back as he let out several frantic breaths. Rosie lay by his side, looking up at the blank white sky. The wind was still grumbling around them, and gentle snowflakes landed on their faces.

"You're a Cromwell? So what? That's no excuse. Why did you do it, Jackson? The letter. How could you?"

"Look, I . . . 'The truth is rarely pure and never simple.'"

"Jackson, would you stop quoting other people? It's really annoying. How about just using your own words?" Her mother had warned her about boys like Jackson, with all their charm and chat. She looked at him and there were no butterflies anymore, just hollow disappointment.

Jackson opened and closed his mouth several times. "I did it because . . . he asked me to."

"What? WHO?" Rosie demanded.

"My uncle . . . Uncle Fenton. Fenton Hemlock-Cromwell," Jackson said.

"What?!" Rosie's mind was spinning. Mr. Hemlock was a *Cromwell*? And Jackson's uncle? "Your uncle?!"

"He's my godfather. He's actually a distant cousin of my dad's. Both are Cromwells and good friends too . . . They're different branches of the family—but they're still close. Cromwells stick together. We keep our name in the shadows. It's a traitor's name," Jackson said, not meeting Rosie's eyes. "It's better that way. He got me into the school; I owe him. He asked me to steal your notebook, so I did. But I didn't know what he was gonna do with it. I just did it because he asked me to," he explained. "I do know he was desperate for me, a Cromwell, to win . . ."

Of course Hemlock would hate another Frost girl beating a Cromwell.

"I just did what I was told. It got out of control . . ."

Jackson sat up and wiped some of the snow off his legs. "At the beginning, I saw you as just a competitor. Then I got to like you." He looked down in shame. "I'm a creep, and a lousy friend. You should have just let me fall."

"No, I shouldn't," said Rosie. "Don't you dare give up. This life, it's so precious. Don't you think people would miss you? You're hurting them too," she snapped.

"I'm not sure I deserve your friendship, but thank you. Thank you," Jackson responded, looking straight at Rosie's face now, his eyes warm and earnest.

"Well, you did say I'd save you back one day—the night I choked on that crumpet—so let's just say we're even."

"I read your letters. I'm sorry you've been through so much."

"It's been a lot." Somehow having people know her situation didn't feel as bad as Rosie had thought it would. In some ways, it was a relief not to keep all those secrets anymore.

"And the ghost queen thing? Is that real?"

Rosie nodded. "Yeah, I met a real ghost Falcon Queen, and she was amazing. I've learned a lot from her. Now, I don't know about you, but I've got a mountain to climb and the Falcon Queen games to win."

Rosie got to her feet, fully prepared to leave Jackson behind.

"Rosie, wait," Jackson called after her.

"What now?" She might have saved his life, but that didn't mean she'd forgiven him.

Jackson chewed his lip. "I can't do this anymore. It doesn't feel right. There's something else you should know. I should have told you before, but I don't know . . . I wasn't sure, and I was worried that, well . . . I was caught up . . . He said it won't be that bad, but I don't trust him."

"Just spit it out, Jackson."

Jackson looked her square in the face. "It's about Wildcat Woods. You know about the planned explosion, don't you?"

How did *he* know about the explosion? "Yes, it's happening tonight," said Rosie.

"No, it's not. That's what I have to tell you. It's been brought forward. It's happening right now."

"What?!" It couldn't be true.

"As soon as the first competitor reaches the top of the mountain," said Jackson.

"But I heard Hemlock say it would be tonight, during the fireworks after the Bloodstone Banquet." Rosie was sure that's what he'd said.

"He changed his mind. As soon as the first person reaches the top, cannons are going to be fired in some big display that lasts about ten minutes. He's going to use the sound of it to mask the explosion."

"But how do you know all this?" Rosie asked.

"I just do. You have to trust me," Jackson said, pleading.

"Trust you?" Rosie was almost screaming now. "Trust *you*? Trust you?? You stole my notebook and spread lies about me around the whole school!"

"I promise I didn't know this was going to happen, and I have no right to ask it from you, but if you want to prevent this from happening, you can't go to the top of the mountain."

"Oh, I get it. This is just some cheap ploy to stop me from racing. Low blow, Jackson. I don't know who you are anymore. You said it yourself, you can't trust a Cromwell."

Jackson lowered his head as if she'd physically spat at him.

"You're right. I'm not to be trusted, but for once I'm trying to do the right thing," said Jackson. "Sometimes we're so focused on winning, we forget what's worth fighting for. I'm as guilty of that as anyone. But right now, I'm telling you the truth, I swear."

Now Rosie was very torn. Could Jackson really be telling her the truth? The only way to find out meant giving up her chance to be crowned the Falcon Queen's champion. But if she ignored him and it turned out he wasn't lying . . .

"Rosie, one more thing," he said. "Your nose is bleeding. It must be the altitude. Here, use my bloodstone. It has healing properties that are said to help stop bleeding. Hold it on your nose." He pulled out his bloodstone medallion.

Rosie touched her nose, then stared down at the blood on her fingers. "I have my own bloodstone, thanks."

Something snapped in her.

Be the light . . . "Actually, I don't need this. I'm over it. I'm tired of being afraid." She swiped the blood from her nose, smearing it across her cheek. "Besides, I've got some wildcats to save."

She then turned and started sprinting back down the mountain.

Chapter Thirty-Two

HILDEGUNN

WEDNESDAY, DECEMBER 21ST. THIRTY-FIVE MINUTES UNTIL

CONTESTANT REACHES THE SUMMIT.

Jackson jumped up and followed Rosie immediately, which reassured her. *He must be telling the truth.* However, if he was, it meant she was dangerously low on time. One of the other competitors could reach the top at any moment. They hadn't passed anyone so far, but that didn't mean there was no one else on the mountain, including the female sixth former she'd seen trying to get past the dragons.

"What else do you know?" Rosie asked Jackson once he'd caught up with her. She kept trundling through the snow without breaking speed.

"Not much," said Jackson. "It was just something I overheard. About it happening now."

"Overheard *Hemlock* say?" Rosie asked.

"Yes," said Jackson, although he paused before he said it, which gave Rosie the impression he was lying. What wasn't he telling her?

"Do you know what's at stake here?" Rosie asked him. "The dangers of axonite? If that explosion goes off, it could release toxic gases which would slowly kill off the wildlife on this island."

"What?!" It was Jackson's turn to be surprised. "That's not what he said . . . I didn't . . ."

"You didn't know? Well, you do now, which is why we've gotta stop it."

About halfway down the mountain, they nearly ran straight into Charlie.

"Hey," said Charlie. "Aren't you two, um . . . going the wrong way?"

"You need to stop!" said Rosie. She revealed what Jackson had just told her.

"So we have to abandon the games? What about your plan for being crowned the Falcon Queen champion? What about your case?"

"I don't care about that anymore. We need to get to Wildcat Woods—now!"

Rule 3: Never give up; be the light. Serve your kingdom; you'll win your fight.

"I've got a better idea," said Charlie before letting out

a frantic scream. "Ahhhh!" He wiped his arm repeatedly, even though there was nothing there.

"What's wrong?!" Rosie asked.

"Sorry, thought I saw another spider. I was too honest on the fear card. My bloodstone was planted in the middle of loads of creepy-crawlies. Let's just say it was somewhere I won't be going back to in a hurry." He shuddered. "You guys go. I'll stay on the mountain and stop anyone who tries to reach the top. We can't have someone triggering those cannons."

Rosie looked him in the eye. Was this Charlie's way of ensuring *he* won the competition? No, she trusted Charlie; he wouldn't betray her for his own gain.

"Okay, good idea," she said. "Good luck."

"Same to you."

They left him there, on the side of the mountain, braced against the wind like a fearless snow warrior.

A little farther down, they encountered Ottilie, who pushed straight past them, her jaw tight and her eyes blazing. She was covered from head to toe in thick black sludge. Her bloodstone must have been buried in the heart of Bloodstone Swamp.

"Ottilie, wait!" Rosie called after her. She tried to explain the situation, but it came out all garbled. Ottilie spun around and gave her an icy stare.

"If you think for one second I'm going to believe your

pathetic story, you can think again," she said, wiping a smear of putrid slime from her cheek. "After what I've just been through, there is *nothing* anyone can do or say to stop me. Especially *you*." She flicked green algae off her eyebrow. "I am winning this race. End of!"

"Ottilie, please—if you cross that finish line, this whole island could be destroyed." Ottilie rolled her eyes, then adjusted her hat and earmuffs, turned away, and continued her ascent.

"Leave her to Charlie," said Jackson. "Hopefully he'll have more luck. And if not, we'll just have to be quicker than she is."

They picked up their pace. At the bottom of the Volcan Crag, they spotted the female sixth former Rosie had seen earlier, now clinging tightly to a thick branch high in a tree, with two dragons looking up at her. The other couple of sixth formers were running in their direction. They'd be climbing the mountain soon too. Charlie wouldn't be able to stop them all; someone was going to reach the top within the next thirty minutes. There wasn't enough time.

A large group of spectators had gathered on the plains overlooked by the Volcan Crag. They craned their necks, looking for any sign of a winner, even though the snow blocked the top of the mountain from view.

As Rosie and Jackson passed, several heads turned in their direction. No one could figure out why they were running *away* from the mountain at such speed. Perhaps the most confused expression of all was pasted on the face of the man in the very center of the crowd: Hemlock. He was sitting pompously in his field buggy, which had large gritted winter tires.

"Well, Hemlock is here," Rosie said between heaving breaths. "Didn't you say he'd be in the woods preparing to set off the explosion?" *Had* Jackson lied to her?

"He has help," said Jackson. "There's someone else in on his plan. It's that person who's going to set off the detonation."

Of course there was. She'd seen a couple of workmen with him before and had overheard Hemlock talking to someone about his scheme on two separate occasions but had never managed to work out who that person might be.

"Who?" asked Rosie. "Who's helping him?"

But Jackson kept his lips firmly together and wouldn't say another word as they ran. Was it someone she knew? And why wouldn't Jackson tell her?

"I reckon we've now got about twenty-eight minutes before someone reaches the top, so we're going to have to move more quickly," said Jackson.

"I'm going as fast as I can," Rosie replied, frowning, taking even bigger strides and breathing harder. After all the running she'd done during the last few hours, her legs were beginning to seize up and her feet felt like they'd been turned to stone.

"I don't know if we're going to make it. We're in trouble," said Jackson.

Trouble.

Remember, any trouble you encounter on that mountain, blow this and she will come.

"Hildegunn," said Rosie out loud, then pulled out the small metal whistle attached to the silver necklace.

"Hildegunn?" said Jackson.

"Hildegunn means 'warrior,' or 'helpful battle maiden,'" Rosie said, echoing Ms. Parr's words.

Rosie blew on the whistle. No sound came out, and she looked down at the whistle, puzzled.

Rosie blew harder, then once again with all the air she had left in her lungs, and this time it was met with the sound of a distant neigh. A few seconds later, a Konik pony came galloping toward them from the wetlands. Its long white hair flowed behind it in a glorious cascade.

"Is that coming for us?" Jackson asked.

Rosie replied by blowing the whistle again, without slowing her pace. The Konik pony came all the way up to them and then lowered her head, bending her knees like a humble steed ready to serve her queen.

"Hildegunn?" Rosie asked.

The pony snorted, as if confirming that was her name.

Konik ponies only serve the brave, Ms. Parr had said.

"Ever ridden a horse before?" Rosie asked Jackson.

"Yeah, but only when I was about ten."

He helped Rosie get up, and then pulled himself up behind her. Hildegunn shook her mane, as if to say, *I am Hildegunn the warrior, your helpful battle maiden!* and reared up with the strength of a mighty stallion. Rosie clung to the pony's mane and clamped her knees to stop herself from falling off.

"She's a unicorn on steroids!" Jackson held on around Rosie's waist.

"Go, Hilde, go!" Rosie said. "*Hee-yaaa! Hee-yaaa!*" she commanded Hildegunn. The pony, recognizing her cue, broke into a gallop.

They thundered across the open, glistening field as the sky rumbled above them, threatening more snow. Hildegunn surged forward, as if driven by a magical force; her hooves beat the ground in time with Rosie's heart.

Rosie looked back in the direction of the Volcan Crag. Time was running out—the cannons could go off at any moment, and then the explosives would blow.

"Faster," Rosie whispered to Hildegunn. "Faster."

Jackson held on to Rosie as she gripped Hildegunn's neck. The wind blew hard in Rosie's face and her hair trailed behind her as they charged across the island toward Wildcat Woods.

Chapter Thirty-Three

THE VIPERS' NEST

As Hildegunn slowed to a halt, Rosie and Jackson nearly flew over her neck. Rosie then jumped down and ran straight to the compound's metal doors. They were firmly closed.

"Damn it, I wish I hadn't lost that key card!" groaned Rosie, kicking the door. She thumped the keypad, getting no response, and tried to think what to do next.

"Jackson, lift me up," she demanded.

Jackson put his hands together for her to step on, then Rosie reached up to the top of the high metal walls. But it was no use; she was too short to get over.

"We have to find another way in," she shouted, slipping back down onto Jackson's shoulders and onto the ground.

"There must be something we can do!" She punched the keypad again in frustration.

"Neaaah." Hildegunn nudged her out of the way, then aggressively bucked her back legs, giving an almighty kick to the keypad. Miraculously, it whirred for a while, and then the little light turned from red to green.

Konik ponies respond harshly to anyone they consider wicked.

The gate of the compound swung wide open.

"That was amazing, Hilde, thank you! Can you wait for us out here?" Rosie said, giving her a pat on her warm neck. The pony whinnied softly, as if in agreement.

Rosie then turned and marched straight through the open gate.

"Wait," said Jackson. "Are you sure it's safe? If a bomb is about to go off in there . . ."

"Of course it's not safe," said Rosie. "That's why we have to stop it. Come on."

Jackson wedged a branch in the gate and then ran to catch up with Rosie.

The lights were on in the metal building—the one which Bina had peered into the last time they were here. Someone was inside, presumably the mystery person Hemlock was working with.

They crept up to the door, which was unlocked and slightly ajar. Rosie pushed it further open. Someone was sitting behind one of the desks, staring intently at the monitors in front of her. Her hair was a glossy brown flicked up at the edges. Rosie's shoulders dropped with relief. It was just Professor Isambard.

"Thank goodness you're here!" said Rosie. "We need your help."

Professor Isambard turned, her face full of surprise.

"Oh, hello," she said with a sweet smile. "How did the two of you get in here?"

"We're here to save the wildcats," Rosie spluttered.

"Save them?" said the professor.

"Yes, Hemlock's buried explosives all around the woods and they're gonna go off at any moment," said Jackson.

"Explosives?" Professor Isambard frowned. "No, you're mistaken. Small amounts of nitroglycerin are being used for some light excavations and very gentle drilling into the bloodstone for soil enrichment. There are no explosives here."

"That's a lie. We know what's really going on," Jackson said to the professor.

A hardness crept over her face as her jaw clenched and her cheekbones tightened.

"It's you . . ." Rosie said, realizing it for the first time. Professor Isambard was another smiling viper. "You're the one helping Hemlock. You're here to set off the explosives."

The professor sighed.

But Professor Isambard was a conservationist—she was supposed to be here to *protect* the wildcats.

"You shouldn't have come here. Neither of you should," said Isambard.

"We're gonna do what's right. Which means stopping you," said Rosie.

"And how exactly are you planning on doing that?" Hemlock laughed, strutting in behind them.

"Jackson, thank you so much for your services. You've been very useful. You may leave."

"ENOUGH! STOP THIS! YOU'VE TAKEN IT TOO FAR!" said Jackson.

"So my little spy is defecting? What a shame. So helpful too. You think you're so clever, don't you, Rosie Frost? But you didn't work that one out." Rosie was beginning to sweat.

"Spy?" Her mouth was so dry, the word barely came out.

"Oh," said Hemlock with feigned surprise. "You didn't think he really wanted to be friends with you, did you? You needed to be watched. He hung around with you because I told him to. Because you were shoving your nose where it didn't belong. We like to keep things in the family, don't we?" he said, looking directly at Jackson.

"And a Cromwell deserves to be the Falcon Queen's champion!"

"NO! I DON'T CARE ABOUT WINNING, not anymore." Jackson clenched his jaw.

Rosie's blood began to surge through her veins. "Thank you for clearing that up." She shook her head and looked at Jackson.

"At least the girl knows where she stands now," said Hemlock.

"This is Cromwell rubbish; it doesn't matter anymore!" said Jackson, his eyes full of shame and anger.

It was all starting to make sense. He hadn't just stolen her notebook, and it wasn't just about a Cromwell winning. All those times Jackson had stopped her from getting too close to the compound . . . He'd been spying on her this whole time for his evil gain; their entire friendship had been fake. Of course, they were Cromwells, what did she expect? Both were descended from the original smiling viper who betrayed Anne Boleyn. But . . . why did Jackson bring her here, then?

"Rosie . . ." Jackson said, his eyes filling with tears. "It's not like that, I promise."

"Really, Jackson," said Rosie. "What is it like, then? You tell me."

Jackson swallowed and looked at the floor. "At the beginning, I was just helping him—he said to keep an eye on the protected area for conservation, and I only met you by chance that first time. Then, yes, I was sent to the

Gutter Club to keep an eye on *everyone*, especially you, because he told me to, but I got to know you, and really like you . . ."

"Stop lying to me," said Rosie.

"I'm not, I swear!"

"You were working for him the whole time! You wanted to win and help him achieve this!" She spat the words out.

"Yes, it's true I was helping him, but I didn't know what he was really up to, I swear," said Jackson. "He'd told me to keep all pupils away from the compound because there was sensitive conservation work going on here. And I took your notebook because he said he wanted it to check where your head was at, because you were having a hard time after losing your mum and might harm yourself. And yeah, I wanted to win too, but I like you . . ." His voice trailed off. "All I did was take the book and bring it to him—it was him who made the letter and spread the copies everywhere. I didn't know he would do that."

Rosie looked at Hemlock in disbelief. "But that would mean you wrote that about yourself, that you're a *weird dog*?!"

Hemlock shrugged. "Weird, *lost* dog, I believe. It's quite amusing, and it would throw you off. You were getting far too inquisitive, so I thought it was time to clip your wings a little, as well as remind you who is in charge at this school. It also worked nicely to trip you into revealing just how much you

knew, which was very helpful for adjusting my planning."
Rosie thought back to when she'd lost her temper and confronted Hemlock about the wildcats in his office. See, there was her mistake. Silence had always been her best weapon, but she'd opened her mouth and blown it.

Jackson, Hemlock, and Professor Isambard. This was a vipers' nest of liars. She turned to Jackson. "How could you help this snake?"

"I'm sorry. I'm so sorry, Rosie," Jackson said, his eyes filled with regret and tears. "I was just doing it for my family and got sucked in. But I really didn't know about the planned explosions until last night. I never would have helped him if I'd realized the truth."

Hemlock looked like he was about to stride across the room and strike Jackson across his face. "I suggest you remember who brought you into this school from out of the gutter. *This* is how you repay me?" He scowled and Jackson recoiled, stepping back; Rosie barely recognized the scared boy before her.

"I'm grateful for that," said Jackson, "but this has gone too far."

"Boy, you have no idea what's really going on here," snapped Hemlock.

"*I* know what's going on," said Rosie.

"Oh, yes? Enlighten me, Little Miss Thunberg."

"Drilling bloodstone for soil enrichment is utter bull.

You're mining for axonite—a substitute for lithium that's ten times more valuable. And obtaining it will most likely destroy all the plants and animals for miles around, including the wildcats who live in these woods." She glared with contempt at them all. "Am I right so far, Professor Isambard?"

The professor nodded slowly.

"But how could you do something like this? You've spent your whole life campaigning for animal rights. I don't understand!" Rosie glared at her.

Professor Isambard pursed her lips and her expression was vacant. She picked up a black steel device from the desk, about the size of a walkie-talkie, with a long antenna sticking out of the top of it and a slick keyhole at the base.

"I'm sorry, Rosie. It's true, axonite is in high demand, and will become accepted as a global necessity very soon. We're talking about green tech here, and there's an argument to be made that getting this axonite will help decarbonize power generation. The world is going to run out of lithium for battery power, so we need an alternative solution. This planet is facing a global climate catastrophe, you know, so every little bit helps. Either way, it's happening whether we like it or not." She then picked up a key from the desk too.

As Rosie watched the defeated way the professor moved, she realized that evil didn't always happen overnight. It could seep in, like smoke under a door, slowly and silently poisoning you, until one day, without knowing how, you were doing something against your nature, against all you believed in. This was what had happened to Professor Jane Isambard, she was sure, but she still couldn't understand why.

The professor placed the key in the detonator and turned it. A red light switched on as though it was activating the electrics in a car, and a nine-minute timer popped up on the screen, ready to start counting down whenever it was triggered.

"And here comes the best bit," said Hemlock. "Rather aptly, whichever entitled brat reaches the tip of the Volcan Crag first and presses the button to become our Falcon Queen's champion will actually be triggering the detonator." Hemlock smirked.

"Wait," said Rosie to the professor. "Stop, please. You know this island's wildlife is too valuable to destroy, and for what? Some batteries? This is against all you stand for. You can't do this!" she pleaded.

"Don't be so hard on the poor woman. She just had a change of heart, that's all, and she knows what the right thing to do is." Hemlock went and patted Professor Isambard on the shoulder. "You're all so quick to judge, the 'entitled generation' who have never had to suffer, never had to endure the hardships of their elders. Professor

Isambard has responsibilities which have changed her priorities." He let out a long, exhausted sigh.

"You suddenly don't care about the animals on this island? I don't buy it," Rosie challenged her.

The professor only replied, "You should leave now. As soon as the Volcan Crag button is pressed, this device is triggered."

That could be at any minute. Charlie wouldn't have been able to stop all of the competitors. She looked at her watch—in fact, it should have happened by now. Rosie had to change the professor's mind before that moment.

"We'll tell everyone what you've done. You'll go to jail," said Rosie.

Hemlock laughed, a cruel, sharp sound.

"Be my guest," he said. "You see, we haven't done anything illegal. All the paperwork is in order, signed off and approved by the necessary authorities. We are just digging for bloodstone minerals for our soil enrichment program. If we unexpectedly hit some axonite while doing this, then that would be a very welcome bonus. People are greedy and selfish, and that includes politicians and government officials. They'll get their share of the money; that's all they care about."

What? No . . . no, this is disgusting. This magical island, the unique and special haven for endangered species, might be destroyed just so a few high-ranking people could get rich. Her blood began to boil, raging with anger.

"You're a monster," Rosie said.

"A cat is a monster to a canary; it's all relative." He shrugged. "Let me spell it out for you: mining for axonite is necessary and lucrative. It's happening all over the world."

"What about Miss Churchill? She won't stand for this, and she's back today."

"No. Wrong again. She's still saving orangutans; she won't actually be back for a while. So I'm in charge, and like I said before, I make the rules."

Jane Isambard stood up suddenly, holding the detonator and shaking her head. "I told him I didn't want to be part of this." Her face was suddenly ashen and worn.

"What?! It was your bloody idea, you found the damn stuff," snapped Hemlock.

"By accident! I was mining for bloodstone."

"Rubbish, you were happy to go ahead with this. You need the money for your delinquent son."

"Look, just turn it off, now!" cried Rosie.

BOOM!

Rosie was interrupted by the sound of a distant rumble. The cannons. Someone had reached the top of the Volcan Crag and pressed the button.

"We have a winner!" said Hemlock.

Professor Isambard held up the detonation device. The

digital screen clicked on, showing 9:00. "It's out of our hands now," she said softly.

"No!" Rosie pleaded. But it was too late.

The red numbers on the device started ticking down. 8:59, 8:58, 8:57 . . .

"Nothing can stop the countdown, so I suggest you use these last few minutes to get yourselves to a safer distance." Professor Isambard's face was resigned, her whole body deflated.

"You may not care about the wildcats, but I'm not giving up!"

Rosie bolted out of the metal building and ran straight into the heart of the woods, through to a large, flat open space where the trees had been removed.

"Rosie, what the hell are you doing? It's dangerous," Jackson called after her.

But she didn't care. She had to find Mercury and her cubs. Then she glanced back and saw the professor rushing toward her at a distance.

"Come back, you silly girl. You're standing right in the detonation area!"

Rosie took a deep breath and kept running.

I have a plan . . . thought Rosie Frost.

Chapter Thirty-Four

IF THEY DIE, I DIE

WEDNESDAY, DECEMBER 21ST. EIGHT MINUTES UNTIL

DETONATION OF WILDCAT WOODS.

J ane! What *are* you doing? Rosemary Frost, get back
here!" Hemlock called out, strutting after them.

"If they die, I die!" Rosie called out.

"Don't make me come and get you . . ." Hemlock ranted.

Rosie stopped. So did the professor, and they stared at
each other through the spindly trees.

"You will have zero chance of survival if you're there
when it goes off," the professor said, an edge of panic in
her voice.

"So turn the timer off!" said Rosie.

"I can't. I told you, it's too late. It's not possible to
override it."

Is that really true? I don't think so, thought Rosie.

There was always an override. It was a gamble she was willing to take. "Yes, you can—turn it off. Do it now or it'll be murder. You'll go to jail for life."

"If you think playing Joan of Arc is going to stop this from happening, you're wrong, you stupid girl!" shouted Hemlock, standing at the perimeter of the clearing. His face was twitching, eyes darting from side to side.

Professor Isambard breathed heavily, gripping the detonator.

"You're running out of time!" she shouted. "Come over here where it's safe."

Jackson ran to Rosie's side. "You can't do this. I'm with *you*, Rosie, it's my fault. I should have told you earlier," he said.

"Jackson! Rosie! Get away from there; you're just children!" Isambard cried.

"No, we're not going anywhere," Rosie said, standing firm.

Professor Isambard strode into the detonation zone, still keeping her distance from Jackson and Rosie, but holding up the activated detonator so they could see the numbers. 6:14, 6:13, 6:12 . . .

"Please, both of you, go back," she begged.

"You're being ridiculous!" called out Hemlock, who was still standing far back from the detonation zone.

Rosie stood firm, folding her arms. "These animals don't deserve this and neither do we."

"So bloody dramatic!" Then Hemlock began to walk slowly toward them, putting out his hands in a gesture of "I'm on your side; it's all good."

The four of them glared at each other like they were in some sort of Wild West showdown. In the distance, the cannons still rumbled from the top of the mountain.

6:00, 5:59, 5:58 . . .

Rosie held her breath and continued to stand her ground. Professor Isambard wouldn't go through with it, surely?

"Come on, Jane, pull yourself together. We can still do this. Let's just step away from the detonation zone. You give me the detonator and then get off the site. We still have a deal," said Hemlock.

Rosie watched her still hesitating. "Please listen to me. I know you care. You still have time to make this right," Rosie said softly, reaching out to Professor Isambard. "We all make mistakes. Everyone does."

"Please," said Jackson too, walking slowly toward Isambard. He then put a hand on her shoulder.

Her eyes filled with tears. "I'm sorry, I am a mother first. Before anything. Yes, it was for the money, but for my son, not me. He's in so much trouble." Her lip began to tremble.

"Desperate people do desperate things."

4:50, 4:49, 4:48 . . .

Hemlock was right: her priorities had changed. Her son's life was more important to her than the wildcats'.

"He's in debt to some very bad people. *He* said he would help us if I helped him." She glowered at Hemlock and stood there, frozen.

"Your son wouldn't want you to do this, would he?" Jackson looked into her eyes and smiled. "He loves you. I'm sure he wouldn't want this."

Jane Isambard looked at Jackson and something seemed to click. Her eyes spilled with tears.

Maybe it was because he reminded her of her own son, but she shook her head as though she'd been woken from an evil spell.

"I'm so sorry; I'm sorry . . ." She began to weep. "I can't do this," she said, looking at Hemlock.

Jane Isambard dropped to her knees. "I tried to make things right, but it didn't work, it never does. I'm not a bad person." She began to sob even harder, and the detonator dropped out of her hands onto the ground. Jackson put his arms around her.

Rosie didn't miss a beat, but neither did Hemlock. They both leaped forward for the detonator at exactly the same time. Hemlock got there first, though, and as soon as he'd grabbed it, he ran off, heading swiftly out of the detonation zone.

Rosie chased after him as fast as she could, darting through the trees, and then leaped in the air. She swung an arm over his shoulder, then with all her might, slammed him down on the ground.

"Aaaaah!" screamed Hemlock, landing flat on his back.

"YOU JUST SMELLED WHAT THE ROCK IS COOKING!" she screamed in his face.

(The Rock's Rock Bottom wrestling move that Bina had taught her really did come in useful!) He shook her off, scuttling away. They were both on their knees now, and both of them lunged forward for the detonator, which had landed on the ground. Their hands wrapped tightly around the black steel box. Face-to-face, they both held on to it tightly, refusing to let go.

Rosie stared right at him. "You will not hurt those wildcats."

"Let go, you silly girl, and no one will get hurt. We're all out of the detonation zone. Let's just get on with the job. Besides, you can't win this. You can't beat me."

"Oh yeah, like in 1994? When my mum did!" she declared.

His eyes nearly popped out of his head with rage. "No, no, no; she just got lucky. The whole thing was completely unfair!" he spat out like an aggravated child.

"She beat you, fair and square. Accept it," Rosie said through gritted teeth.

Then suddenly, as if all the pain and suffering of every Falcon Queen who had fought for what they believed in was surging through her heart, into her fingers, she gripped the box even tighter and screamed in his face, "I WILL NEVER GIVE UP!"

At that moment, something suddenly leaped out of the shadows.

"AAAH!" Hemlock screamed. That something, tawny with silver eyes, had sunk its teeth into Hemlock's arm, then scratched his face. A wildcat!

He let go of the detonator. Cradling his arm, he backed away from the wildcat that had bitten him, trying to side-step it, but it hissed and bared its teeth, its silver eyes shining like ice on fire.

"Great job, Mercury!" said Rosie, holding the detonator close.

The cat licked her lips and purred with pride. More wildcats bounded out of the woods and joined Mercury, forming a barrier between Hemlock and Rosie. She looked down at the clock. 0:35, 0:34, 0:33 . . .

How do I turn it off? How do I turn it off?

Rosie's hands were shaking. She turned the key at the bottom and flicked a couple of the switches, but the count-down continued.

0:21, 0:20, 0:19 . . .

"Looking for this?" said Hemlock, holding up a second

key. "It needs both keys to deactivate. Sorry, Rosie, but you're out of time."

"ROOOOOOARRRRRR!"

Someone behind Hemlock unleashed a mighty roar, as if scaring away a Komodo dragon. The wildcats scattered. Before Hemlock had the chance to look around, a large stick struck him over the head. He fell to his knees, dropping the key. Behind him stood the sludge-covered Ottilie, wielding the stick in both hands.

"Ottilie?" Rosie gasped.

"Told you I came to slay," she smirked.

Rosie scrambled for the key, picked it up, and tried to insert it into the device, but her fingers were trembling too badly.

0:09, 0:08, 0:07 . . .

Rosie took a deep breath. The smell of cloves and velvet plum roses hung thick in the air.

Never give up; be the light. Serve your kingdom; you'll win your fight.

It cleared Rosie's head and steadied her nerves. 0:04, 0:03, 0:02 . . .

She slid the key into the slot and turned it to the right. The device let out three short bleeps and the countdown froze.

0:01.

All the air fell out of Rosie's lungs. She wobbled

backward and Jackson caught her arm as she steadied herself.

Hemlock whimpered from the ground, cradling his bruised head. Ottilie stood over him, still holding the stick.

"What made you change your mind?" Rosie asked Ottilie.

"I was super close to winning . . ." said Ottilie. "But Charlie kept going on and on about what Hemlock was up to. I do actually care about the stupid animals too, all right? *You* helped me before, and anyway, I can't stand Hemlock's chauvinism; he doesn't really *get* Falcon Queen power. So I came to help. Whatever, all right? Did you really think you were the leading lady here? That you'd get all the glory?"

Rosie didn't know what to say.

"I was just about to turn it off," snapped Hemlock.

Suddenly they all heard the clip-clop of approaching hooves, and three Konik ponies cantered toward them. Riding tall on the central one was Ms. Parr, flanked by a couple of teachers Rosie didn't recognize.

Ms. Parr dismounted her pony and rushed over to them.

"Thank goodness you've arrived! That silly woman over there," Hemlock said, pointing at Jane Isambard, "has gone mad. She's reckless and nearly got us blown up! I just wanted her help with the soil." Hemlock continued to gush, "We were meant to be doing a soil-enriching exercise, gently mining for bloodstone, but she's really mining for axonite. She tricked us onto the detonation site and threatened to blow us all up. She needs to be locked up! Thank goodness I stopped her, to save these poor, innocent children." Hemlock looked at Jane and folded his arms.

"That is not true," shouted Rosie. "It was him!"

"Come, come, pupils, I'm in charge. I think they're still delirious from the high altitude on the Volcan Crag." He looked at Ms. Parr, shaking his head.

Ms. Parr frowned, obviously dubious of his claims.

"Let's discuss this later and get you checked over." One of the teachers led Rosie, Jackson, and Ottilie away.

Ms. Parr gave Hemlock a skeptical look, then said to Professor Isambard, "I think you'd better come with us."

The other teachers picked Professor Isambard up from the ground and started leading her out of the compound, along with the others.

"I'm sorry," Isambard said, looking at Jackson and Rosie as they walked away. Then she turned to Hemlock, the smiling viper who had betrayed his accomplice to save his own skin. *Just like Thomas Cromwell did to Anne Boleyn*, thought Rosie. Fenton Hemlock-Cromwell could not get away with this.

Chapter Thirty-Five

THE CROWN

FRIDAY, DECEMBER 23RD.

Today we crown our Falcon Queen's champion. It's such an honor for me to be here with you all, as the head of this mighty school on behalf of Miss Churchill, who unfortunately can't be with us after all. It is my favorite day of the year: the Bloodstone Banquet."

Hemlock addressed the entire school like a proud lion from his seat at the center of the top table, which was on a raised stage dressed in festive tinsel and candles. They were outside, on the lawn, all sitting at the long wooden tables that had been brought down from the Sovereign Hall. The pine trees sparkled with Christmas lights.

Hemlock had somehow wiggled his way out of any responsibility for trying to mine the axonite. So once again, Hemlock was right: they had no proof. It had been two days since the final of the Falcon Queen games; the banquet had been postponed while the compound was dismantled, allowing the wildcats to roam free once again and the explosives to be removed. The officials of Bloodstone were looking into the matter, and had interviewed both Rosie and Jackson, but Hemlock hadn't been arrested. As astonishing as it was to believe, Hemlock had been telling the truth: everyone involved had gone through official channels and no laws had been broken.

Any blame was still pointed at Professor Jane Isambard, and she was under investigation for misconduct. *The world is corrupt and unjust*, thought Rosie. At least for now the wildcats and their forest area were safe. But Hemlock and Rosie were locked in an uncomfortable stalemate. Until Rosie had the chance to tell Miss Churchill everything, they were stuck with him.

"Who's he trying to kid?" said Rosie. She was sitting next to Bina, with Charlie and Jackson opposite them. Despite the snow, which still lay thick on the ground, it wasn't cold, thanks to the enormous fires that had been erected around them on the lawn.

Fortunately, the world had also sat up and listened after some footage of "wildcats under threat" was released online. Thanks to Ottilie Aragon-Windsor.

She posted some amazing footage of the wildcats and their cubs in their habitat and it had set the internet on fire.

Rosie had written the caption to go with it, explaining the truth about mining for axonite. (And still maintaining the anonymity of Bloodstone, keeping the animals safe with their location undisclosed.) As the video spread, so, too, did the petition to make the mining of it illegal.

"And so I invite you to raise your glasses to our new Falcon Queen's champion, a wonderful young man, Otto Baldazar," said Hemlock. He raised his goblet high in the air, and everyone else followed suit. Otto—the sixth-form boy who had won the games—was sitting next to Mr. Hemlock on a grand throne, with a massive smile on his face and a crown on his head. The crown was made of metal feathers, interwoven to form a golden circle that shimmered in the firelight.

"Now, Otto, you know what this means. You must accept your prize and announce what your new rule is for the school."

What was it going to be?

Otto stood up, wrapped his thick fingers around the microphone, and smiled. "My new rule will be to—"

"Excuse me!" called out Ms. Parr, moving her way onto the stage. "Excuse me! Before we go any further, can I have a moment?" said Ms. Parr to Hemlock. "As protector of the Falcon Queen crown." She then handed him a phone, showing him an image.

The audience of eight hundred students broke into a

shocked muttering. What on earth was going on?

She said something to Mr. Hemlock, whose face showed no expression.

"Otto Baldazar, what did you write on your fear card?" asked Hemlock.

Otto looked left and right. "Erm, centipedes."

"Of course you did. As you know, it was imperative to tell the truth, and you bravely admitted you were afraid of centipedes. Isn't that right?"

"Yeah, can't stand 'em," Otto confirmed.

"Otto had to pick up his bloodstone medallion from beneath a mountain of centipedes. What a hero." Hemlock smiled, looking out to the audience.

Otto nodded.

"I'm curious; can you enlighten us as to why centipedes might be scary or dangerous insects?" asked Hemlock.

"Yes, although they aren't actually insects. Centipedes are arthropods. Insects have three body segments, whereas arthropods have many. Centipedes can also be poisonous," he said proudly.

"I see. You are very knowledgeable. Thank you for sharing this information. I suppose in your time working at your godfather's insect and chilopod zoo, you worked with them a lot? You are brave, aren't you, when you're so afraid of centipedes, hmm? Or are you just a poisonous little lying centipede?"

Hemlock pressed a button and an image appeared on the large screen. It was Otto, holding a centipede on his finger and grinning broadly.

Otto went red. *Boooooo*s hollered from the school of eight hundred pupils.

"Cheat!" "He's a cheat!" called out many of the students.

"Now, now," shushed Hemlock. "Poor little Otto did what was symptomatic of his entitlement. It's not his fault he's one of those children born into wealth. Everything handed to them on a plate, rules always bent. Otto doesn't know any better, but it's our job here to teach him," he said gently. Then his eyes hardened and he stared out to the crowd. "Otto's behavior is a disgrace to the competition, and to this school," continued Hemlock sternly. "Otto Baldazar, you're disqualified."

The crowd erupted in agreement. Then there were murmurs of speculation: "Who will be the champion now?"

"It's me! It's me!" someone squealed, jumping up and down. It was another sixth-form pupil, who had reached the buzzer at the top of the Volcan Crag just behind Otto.

Johnny rushed to the top table and grabbed the crown from Otto's head.

"No, it's not! It's me! I'm the winner," growled the third sixth former, a girl named Flinka who had also touched the button at the same time. She came bounding up and grappled for the crown.

"No, you're a cheat and an aggressive witch!" shouted Johnny at Flinka.

"*You* are the cheating fool. You pushed me out of the way!" She then shoved him hard, and reached to snatch the crown, wrestling Johnny to the ground.

Ms. Parr pulled Flinka off, and Hemlock stood over Johnny.

"Fighting is not permitted in the competition. Neither of you are worthy of the crown," said Hemlock. Ms. Parr nodded.

Then who would be the winner?

Ms. Parr and Hemlock began to argue.

"It should be Johnny!" "No, Flinka!" shouted the students.

Hemlock grabbed the microphone. "Order. I said *order*! I am in charge here and will make this decision!" He scowled.

Then the crowd gasped. A small old lady, hair in a white bun and wearing a green cloak, appeared next to Hemlock. Hemlock's face went ghostly white, his mouth dropping open.

"Oh my goodness, it's her! It's Miss Churchill!" someone said.

Hemlock trembled, lowering his head, and Ms. Parr smiled. "You're back. What a wonderful surprise," she said.

The lady nodded at Ms. Parr, ignoring Hemlock. Ms. Parr then handed her a microphone.

The old lady, who had hooded eyelids over piercing blue eyes and wrinkly soft skin, scanned the gathered school.

"Do we have a problem?" She turned back to Hemlock and smiled.

"No, no, Miss Churchill, of course not. All is under control." He smiled meekly back. "It's just that we have a little discrepancy with who should be our Falcon Queen's champion."

"So I've heard. But it's quite simple. Who has the courage, power, and freedom worthy of this title?

"Flinka Privalova, Johnny Levinson, Ottilie Aragon-Windsor, Charlie Saint, Jackson Sterling, and Rosie Frost—would you come up here, please," ordered Miss Churchill.

Hemlock's face darkened.

Jackson, Charlie, Ottilie, and Rosie all looked at one another.

"We have a dilemma," said Hemlock awkwardly. "None of these four actually reached the top." He nodded toward Jackson, Ottilie, Charlie, and Rosie. "Perhaps we should postpone?" He cringed.

"Or perhaps we have an opportunity to find a real Falcon Queen's champion." Miss Churchill smiled, looking at the six remaining.

"Let's make this interesting and test some old-school Heverbridge values. Ms. Parr, please give each of them a piece of paper."

Ms. Parr handed Johnny, Flinka, Ottilie, Jackson, Charlie, and Rosie a piece of paper and pen each.

"You have twenty seconds to answer the question I am about to pose. If you're not honest and fast, your vote doesn't count. This is a competition, so you may vote for yourself. Whoever has the majority will be named the champion." Miss Churchill pulled out an old pocket watch. "Tell us who your own champion is, and one reason why. Who has the real courage, power, and freedom? Three, two, one, go . . ."

Seconds later, each of them had passed their paper back to Ms. Parr, who then handed them on to Miss Churchill. She opened each and read them to herself.

"It looks like we have a very clear majority of three out of six votes. Would you one by one step forward and tell us who your winner is and why," said Miss Churchill.

Flinka stepped forward. "Me. I deserve it. I got up that mountain the quickest but was cheated by the others."

Johnny stepped forward. "I vote for me. *I* got up the quickest."

Charlie stepped forward. "She saved me in the Black Lake—I pick Rosie Frost."

Ottilie stepped forward. "Even when I made a mistake,

she united us in the Court of Reform, *and* she *even* slayed a dragon for me. Rosie Frost," announced Ottilie with her hand on her hip.

Jackson stepped forward. "Even when I betrayed her, she helped me conquer my fears and showed me what's really important on Bloodstone Mountain, so it's Rosie Frost."

"It looks like we have a clear winner!" announced Miss Churchill. "The champion of the Falcon Queen games is Rosie Frost."

The crowd erupted into applause.

"Rosie Frost, would you please step forward." Rosie gasped. Was this really happening? Miss Churchill placed the golden feathered crown on her head, and the crowd cheered again.

Charlie, Jackson, Bina, and Ottilie whooped and clapped. Flinka and Johnny folded their arms in disgust.

Miss Churchill put her finger to her lips, shushing the crowd.

"I have a question for Rosie too. Tell me what you wrote on your paper. Who did you vote for?"

Rosie's cheeks flushed the color of a Deep Secret rose. She bit her lip and looked out at the hundreds of faces staring at her.

Remember, silence is your best defense. No one can

judge you. It went so quiet that she could hear her own heart thumping against her chest.

"Don't be shy," Miss Churchill prodded. "Tell us, Rosie. Read it out. Who is your deserving winner?"

It was like a flashback moment in a movie, and all the things leading up to her arrival at Heverbridge popped into her mind. Losing her mum, finding it so difficult when she got here, deciding to keep silent and not get close to anyone. Then the love and support she'd found. It was clear: when the going gets tough, you find out what you're made of and who is really there for you.

She looked at Charlie, Bina, then Jackson, and even Ottilie. None of them were perfect; they'd all made mistakes. They sometimes didn't like each other, or even agree, but each of them at different times had helped Rosie.

In that moment, Rosemary Regina Frost conveyed something more than words, something more true and powerful than she had ever had the courage to say in her whole time at Heverbridge. Warm, hot tears filled her eyes and trickled down her cheeks. *Tears are the words the heart can't find,* her mother used to say. And finally they had come.

Rosie cleared her throat. "My friends," she said. That's what she had written. "They all helped me find my true courage, power, and freedom. They are all the deserving winners."

"Said like a true Falcon Queen." Miss Churchill smiled. "Now tell us what you propose for the new school rule." A warm scent of mixed spices and deep red roses washed over Rosie. She looked out to the blood-orange evening sky and, somehow deep within herself, she felt the courage and power of all the Falcon Queens who had gone before.

She looked out at the crowd. What would be her new rule?

"More holidays! No homework!" someone shouted.

Finally, she could get her case back . . . *All pupils' confiscated belongings returned*, yes. Her mum's case, finally!

"My rule would be . . ." Rosie paused again. The silence stretched on for so long, it felt like a lifetime.

Rosie looked at the Heverbridge students. The school went quiet . . . All the faces staring back at her. All the faces she knew and loved. Bina nodded with encouragement.

Remember well, a deserving champion, a true sovereign, always acteth beyond the prestige of the crown. This person shall put others and our kingdom first.

That's what was written on the parchment.

"I am with you," the voice whispered as a faint smell of roses wafted over her.

She looked at Jackson and Ottilie, Mr. Hemlock, Ms. Parr. Rosie cleared her throat, swallowed, and then took a deep breath.

"Before I say my rule, I need to tell you something.

When I first came here, I was scared of all of you. I was scared that you would see exactly who I am: just an ordinary girl with ginger hair, old boots, and a broken heart." She cleared her throat. "And then I got to know you. Yes, we come from different places, and we make judgments because of the way we look, or our different accents or family origins. We are given labels, good ones and bad ones."

Rosie looked out into the crowd, taking in every single person standing there.

"But I learned we might look fierce, or happy, confident. We may keep quiet or do silly things, but really, underneath, the story might be something different. We might be sad or lonely, or afraid. We never know what's going on with someone until we actually really get to know them."

Her voice grew intense, stronger, like a young, determined queen.

"We all have our own ghosts that follow us, names we carry . . . Sometimes we say nothing because we're hurting, or because we don't want to hurt others. We have different faces, with different lives. But I know deep down we all want to belong, so that's why my rule is pretty clear. It's what my mum once said to me. I thought it was a boring cliché when I first heard it, but I didn't really understand it, until now."

Rosie breathed in with her shoulders back.

This one's for you, Queenie . . . Queen Anne Boleyn,

a smart young woman with a whole life ahead of her, a mother who was misjudged, and murdered.

" 'Don't judge a book by its cover . . . Look deeper. There's always more on the inside.' And it's thanks to the original Falcon Queen that I learned that." Rosie smiled, then squeezed the purple book in her pocket. *Thank you, Queenie.*

"*Animo, Imperium, Libertas!*" she declared.

"*Animo, Imperium, Libertas!*" the whole school chanted, louder than ever, then broke into applause.

Caawk, caawk! A loud screeching came from above.

Is that . . . ?

"Queen Nike!" said Rosie, looking up to the sky. "She's alive." The regal white falcon swooped through the air, her chest flecked with bronze.

As the falcon flies, Heverbridge thrives. But wasn't she dead?

"Let's celebrate! Let's eat!" someone shouted.

No one needed telling twice. Throughout the lawn, hungry hands reached for the various dishes that had been placed down the center of the tables: fresh breads and hearty stews, spicy curries and loaded fries. Rosie and the others left the stage to join the banquet. She would get to sit on the throne next to Miss Churchill later.

"Guys, you saved the island from exploding. That was a pin," said Bina, striking a new wrestling pose.

Rosie, Charlie, and Jackson laughed. Jackson had explained things to everyone, and they had all decided to let what happened go for now and move on. Hemlock could wait for another day, and the main thing was that Miss Churchill was back. Rosie looked at Jackson and could feel things slowly mending between them. He had stood up for her in the vipers' nest and had kept professing how sorry he was. As for her butterflies, they were back, still gently fluttering around, but she ignored them. Being good mates was enough, for now.

" 'Friendship is more tragic than love; it lasts longer,' " Jackson said, back to his usual quoting of Oscar Wilde. Rosie rolled her eyes at him with a half smile.

"So majestic, isn't she?" said Ms. Parr, who had walked up beside Rosie.

"I thought she was dead," said Rosie, looking up to where Queen Nike was still swooping above them. "I saw blood and a headless body on the mountain. *If the falcon falls, judgment calls*—isn't that what you told us?"

"Interesting . . . Perhaps what you saw on the Crag was your fear," Ms. Parr replied.

"What do you mean by that?" Rosie asked, scooting over on the bench to face Ms. Parr.

"The Volcan Crag is a strange place. It's also known as the Soul's Gateway, remember? Whether because of the altitude or the volcanic gases it releases, people have reported seeing all kinds of inexplicable things on its slopes."

But the carcass had been real, Rosie was sure of it . . . This island *was* strange, it never stopped astounding her. Well, at least Queen Nike was still alive and Heverbridge was still standing.

"How did you know to come for us the other day?" she asked. It was the first time she'd had the opportunity to speak to the groundskeeper since.

"You have your friend Ottilie Aragon-Windsor to thank for that. She came racing down the mountain to find me. Insisted that's where she was going and that I should go straightaway too."

Rosie glanced down the table, to the far end where Ottilie was sitting, gossiping with Jamila and Ishaan. Ottilie had given up her chance of winning the games to help them stop Hemlock—and she'd worked afterward with Rosie to spread the truth about axonite—but Rosie still wasn't sure where she stood with her. Ottilie met her gaze for the briefest of moments and gave her a look that could have been a frown, but could also have been a smile. You never quite knew with Ottilie. There really was more to the first-class mean girl than Rosie would ever have expected. This island was definitely miraculous.

Caawk, caawk! The falcon soared above them once again, then released a stream of white liquid. The muck landed directly on Hemlock's head, splattering his tailored suede coat.

"You disgusting flying rat!" Hemlock's eyes nearly burst out of his head.

Laughter spread throughout the lawn.

"Mother Nature is in charge!" called out Ms. Parr.

Barely retaining his composure, Hemlock excused himself from the top table and hurried inside.

"Well, I'll leave you to it," Ms. Parr said. "But I wanted to let you know how proud I am of you. Your mother would be too." She gave Rosie's shoulder an affectionate squeeze.

With that, Ms. Parr walked away, and Rosie wiped a happy tear from the corner of her eye. It *was* good to cry.

"You know what, Charlie? You were right," said Rosie. "Well, your nan was. That night we went up the bell tower, I made a wish. And most of it came true."

"Oh yeah?" said Charlie. "What did you wish for?"

"To save the wildcats, and to feel like I really belonged here at Heverbridge with you guys."

"Aww, all mates together!" said Charlie, pulling Rosie, Jackson, and Bina into a big group hug across the table.

"We have to hold it for seven seconds!" said Bina.

"One, two, three, four, five, six, seven!" they all said in unison, before falling back off their benches, laughing into the snow.

As Charlie struggled up, Bina threw him back down with her Rock's Rock Bottom move. "Okay, I think I surrender! I'm okay getting beaten by a girl!" laughed Charlie as Bina grinned back at him.

Then she smiled at Rosie. "And surprise! I got you pineapple upside-down cake—your mum's favorite, right?" She handed Rosie a plate.

Once they'd all eaten as much cake as they could, Bina turned to them and asked, "Who's up for a game of *Miracles and Monsters?*"

"Why not," Charlie said. "I could do with a win." He gave Bina a wink.

"Sounds fun," said Jackson.

"Rosie? What about you? You gonna play and slay?" asked Bina. Rosie looked at their smiling faces and didn't even need to say a word; she just nodded. Because they were her friends.

"I'll be right there, just a minute," Rosie said as she walked over to the edge of the Heverbridge lawns. She looked out to the amazing landscape of Bloodstone Island, crisp under the night sky. One lone star was now shining brightly above, just as she'd seen it before from the bell tower, and once again she felt it was saying, *I am here, always.* She clutched the little purple book in her pocket. The familiar smell of rich velvet plum roses wafted over her.

"Thank you, Queenie, I'll never forget what you've taught me."

For the first time in a long while, she felt everything was going to be okay. She still didn't have her case back, or all the answers she needed about her mum. It didn't matter anymore; she knew who she was no matter what. If this was to be her future as an orphan here at Heverbridge, knowing that fairy tales don't come true, and that Prince Charming wasn't coming to rescue her, that was okay. Because with a little help from her friends and the Falcon Queen's rules, Rosie Frost knew now that she could always save herself.

Epilogue

THE CASE IS CLOSED. OR NOT . . . ?

SATURDAY, DECEMBER 24TH. CHRISTMAS EVE.

Dear Mum,

We saved the wildcats!! <u>And</u> I won the Falcon Queen games—
can you believe it?! Just like you.

I can't believe you actually beat Hemlock. He can't be happy to
have been beaten by both of us! I wonder what his fear card was?

Most important, the animals are safe now.

I understand now why you sent me here. I'm not angry
anymore. I just hope you're okay, wherever you are. Anyway,
it's Christmas! My first one without you . . . It's going to be a
bit weird . . . No making gingerbread biscuits together. They
were delicious, the best! And no heavy Christmas cake that
you make with way too many raisins—it was like a brick! No

singing Christmas carols all morning, and remember that pressie I gave you, the rainbow scarf I knitted? Even though it had holes in it, you smiled like it was the best thing ever . . . Your smiling face. I'm going to miss that the most. But Miss Churchill has invited everyone who's not going home for Christmas for a special dinner. She's also asked me to go see her. I wonder what she wants.

I love you, Mum. MERRY CHRISTMAS!
Rosie xxx

Rosie took a deep breath, then blew out. She squeezed the little purple book she was holding and knocked on the door.

"Come in," said a voice from inside.

Rosie opened the door and stepped into Miss Churchill's office. The plants that crawled up the walls and cascaded from the bookshelves had all been resurrected since Rosie was in there last, making the room look more like a jungle than a headmistress's office.

"Ah, Rosie, I'm so glad you came. Sorry it's taken me so long to see you—I've had a huge amount to sort out since I got back, as I'm sure you can appreciate. Please take a seat."

Rosie sat on the armchair opposite Miss Churchill, sliding the little purple book surreptitiously down its side, out of view.

"Would you like some tea? I've just made a fresh pot."

"Yes, please," said Rosie. "That'd be lovely." Her foot started tapping with nerves. Rosie placed her hands under her thighs and bit her lip.

"I trust you enjoyed the Bloodstone Banquet yesterday?" Miss Churchill asked as she picked up a fancy teapot.

"Yeah, it was great," Rosie answered.

Miss Churchill poured the tea into a bone china teacup on its matching saucer and handed it to Rosie.

"Thank you," said Rosie. She blew on the steaming liquid and took a sip. It was unlike any tea she'd ever tasted, spiced nutmeg with a whisper of citrus and something else she didn't recognize, but it was like a sweet comfort when she swallowed it.

Rosie couldn't believe she was finally here, in Miss Churchill's office, talking to her. Yes, she looked old, but the glint she now had in her eyes assured Rosie that her mind was still youthful and alert.

"It seems rather a lot happened while I was away," said Miss Churchill. "Including a near-detonation which would have been catastrophic. And I believe I have you to thank for preventing that from happening?"

"Um . . . well . . . as I said, my friends helped, but, yeah, I suppose . . ."

Speak with pride, Rosie Frost.

"Number four, the rule of most importance: *To thine own self be true*," said Miss Churchill.

Rosie swallowed. *The rule book.*

"The Bard borrowed that one from our original Falcon Queen." She smiled.

"The Bard?" Rosie asked.

"Our dear William Shakespeare, of course. One of the greats who studied here at Heverbridge. A Falcon King."

William Shakespeare came to Heverbridge! That is amazing!

"The Falcon Queen's rules were used by all of them. And creating a new rule is inspired by rule number four: the freedom to be yourself. I've decided that your rule will not only be an official school rule, it will also become part of the Heverbridge principles." She pulled out a red leather book and flicked through the pages. "Only a few Falcon Queen's champions have rules that made it into this leather book." She gave Rosie a smile. "And actually, in addition to that, I believe it even deserves a place in the original Falcon Queen's purple book. This would be the first time a champion's rule has ever been added to Queen Anne's founding principles." She smiled again. "Maybe you'd like to write it in there yourself, since you just tucked it down the side of my armchair . . . ?"

Rosie's cheeks burst with heat.

"I brought it here to give it back to you," she said. She pulled it out and offered it to Miss Churchill. The headmistress waved her hands.

"Keep it. I'd say it's found its rightful owner for now. You will know when it's time to pass it on to the next person worthy of it."

"Oh. Thank you," said Rosie, practically speechless at being given such a valuable gift.

Miss Churchill handed Rosie a pen, and she added her rule on the first empty page, wondering what her mother's rule was, whether it had become a Heverbridge principle. Rosie was on the verge of asking, when Miss Churchill leaned back in her chair and sighed, like it had been a long day.

Maybe I'll ask her another time, thought Rosie.

For a while neither of them spoke, and Rosie took another sip of her tea. She forgot to blow on it first, though, and scorched her lips. From her seat opposite, Miss Churchill watched her with round hooded eyes, like an owl settling down to roost.

"There are some things you need to know," said Rosie. "About Mr. Hemlock . . ."

Miss Churchill shook her head. "There is nothing you can tell me about Mr. Hemlock-Cromwell that I don't already know."

"But he's the one who—"

"Yes." Miss Churchill cut her off. "I'm well aware of the role he played in all of this."

"Then why is he still here?" Rosie asked, then bit her

lip. Would she be overstepping the mark? But she had to ask it anyway. "Can't you fire him or something?"

Miss Churchill pulled at one of her wispy strands of hair. "Sometimes it's better to keep certain people close to you."

For the first time, a stern edge had crept into Miss Churchill's voice. "We have no proof of matters, and I would appreciate you not spreading any sorts of rumors. Let's talk no more of the subject." It was clear the case was closed.

Rosie sank a little deeper into her chair, with the distinct impression that she'd just been told off. Why was Miss Churchill protecting him?

"You are very like Avaline was," she said more gently, with a smile. Rosie's heart pounded.

Miss Churchill knew her mother. Well, it seemed. *I miss you, Mum.*

"She was an incredibly impressive student. One of the best in the time that she was here. But even as a young girl"—Miss Churchill lowered her gaze—"trouble followed her . . ." She sighed heavily. "How much do you know about your mother's death?"

Rosie looked at her blankly as Miss Churchill leaned forward in her armchair. Clasping her hands together, she lowered her head slightly. "Nothing, really."

Rosie had thought about it constantly. Had it been a serious illness her mother hid from her? Or could her mum have even faked her death, like in the movies? But that felt too far-fetched and painful to believe. So she had done her best to push those thoughts to one side whenever they reared up. She hadn't imagined anyone on Bloodstone Island would have information. But now it seemed like Miss Churchill knew something.

Rosie's body tightened, anticipating what would come next, the unspoken words that had been kept from her until now. She stared down at her worn-out boots and bit her lip. What was coming?

"I'm sorry, there's not more I can tell you at the moment," Miss Churchill said, looking at Rosie intensely, as though studying her to see if she was ready.

"But . . . but I need answers!" The words burst out of Rosie. "I'm her daughter! She's my mum. I deserve to know what happened. Was it my fault?!" Angry tears tumbled down her cheeks. "I've waited long enough." Her breath heaved out of her chest. "How come no one will tell me anything?"

"There is still an ongoing investigation, and it would be irresponsible to draw any conclusions without the hard facts being verified. You're a minor, in our care, and your well-being is our priority." Miss Churchill raised her eyebrows, tilting her head. Was this sympathy? Then she cleared her throat, as though she was about to say more, but stopped.

"What is it? Please tell me, I beg you. Was she really sick? Could I have done something?" Rosie's face contorted into as pleading an expression as she could manage. "How could she just leave me?" If Miss Churchill had had a visible heartstring, Rosie would have literally pulled it.

"Your mother loved you very much, and there was nothing you could have done."

Rosie grabbed Miss Churchill's arm. All the confusion and doubt began to boil up inside her. Feelings she had buried alive now seemed about to erupt.

"Please . . ." She couldn't take any more of this not knowing.

Miss Churchill sighed again. "Very well, but as I said, there is not much more I can tell you. And it's all highly confidential. We hadn't wanted to say anything until you were settled, and until we were sure, but there is evidence of . . . something." Miss Churchill's blue eyes were serious.

"What?" Rosie stuttered.

"Suspicious circumstances . . ." said Miss Churchill softly.

Rosie's hands began to tremble.

"You mean she could have been . . . murdered?!" Rosie couldn't believe she was actually saying it. The word hit her like a punch in the stomach.

Miss Churchill nodded, her mouth in a grim line. The shock of the suggestion hung in the room.

Rosie's skin felt clammy; her heart began to race. Miss Churchill then leaned farther forward and squeezed her hand.

"I just don't understand, who would want to hurt my mum? I thought maybe she was ill or something, and I just didn't know." Rosie shook her head in defeat, then put it in her hands.

"Nobody really understands," Miss Churchill said, patting Rosie's shoulder. "Not yet. Let's see what conclusions the investigation comes to. That's all I can tell you for now."

The warm, familiar liquid began to drip down from Rosie's nose. A warning her old "friend" was back. Miss Churchill handed her a hanky to mop up the blood, and Rosie leaned slightly forward, pinching the bridge of her nose.

They sat quietly like that for a while, until the bleeding stopped. But the tears continued to stream down Rosie's face.

"I will do my best to support you, Rosie, and we will get to the bottom of it." And then Miss Churchill stood up slowly and walked over to her desk.

"I've got something for you," she said. She slid open the middle drawer and pulled out an object which clunked heavily as it hit the side of the desk. She held it up for Rosie to see.

Her burnt-red briefcase!

"You *do* have it!" said Rosie. "Mr. Hemlock—"

"—as instructed, was kind enough to send it straight to me," said Miss Churchill with a look that told Rosie she should leave it there.

It was now obvious to Rosie that Hemlock resented anything to do with her mother, who in his eyes had achieved an impossible win. Beating *him*, a Cromwell, in the Falcon Queen games was simply not fair—and the fact that she was a younger girl was humiliating to him. It seemed that in lying about the case's whereabouts to her, he must have just wanted to torment Rosie. But Miss Churchill was clearly not going to discuss any further details about Hemlock's twisted behavior—not today, anyway. The main thing was that she'd got it back now.

"It was for *me* to decide when to return it to you, as soon as I felt it was the right time for you to have it. You had to learn what's important before you opened that case." She paused. "Your mum and I both wanted you to find out exactly who you are, to draw on your inner strength and discover your true power. It was Avaline's hope that you would enter the games."

Her mother had wanted her to enter the Falcon Queen games?!

"Then, after the tragic loss of your mother, I thought it would be exactly what you needed, but there had to be some incentive for you to compete."

What was she saying? Miss Churchill had told Hemlock to withhold the case from her on purpose?

"I am sorry to have caused you distress, my dear. But I have a question . . . Would you have entered the Falcon Queen games, *and* competed with such determination initially, if you hadn't wanted to get your case back?"

Rosie shook her head.

"It was a gamble. I didn't know how much pushing you might need, but Ms. Parr informed me that you'd entered the games, and kept me updated on your progress. And I wondered whether you might have received encouragement from some other quarter too . . ." Miss Churchill raised her eyebrow but said nothing more. Could she be referring to the ghost of Anne Boleyn—did she know about her?!

Before Rosie could question her further, Miss Churchill moved swiftly on. "Of course, everything that followed came from you, as we hoped."

Rosie sat with a confused frown on her face, wiping any remaining tears away as she absorbed everything Miss Churchill was telling her.

"So my mum is the one who sent me here? But how? We only ever lived in a tiny flat, always struggled—we never had enough to pay for a fancy place like this," said Rosie.

"She was part of the alumni, which can give your

children automatic entry if they can keep up with the academic standards—and you certainly can. Your mother sent me the songs you'd written; they're outstanding. Your school fees have been covered by a private trust. We made sure you would be eligible to come here when the time was right for you to start.

"Now, I think you have shown yourself more than ready for this," she said, pushing the case across the desk toward Rosie. "It's not just about winning a trophy, as I said before. By putting others before yourself, you have shown the courage, power, and freedom of a true Falcon Queen. The struggle was just as important as the reward itself. Open it."

Rosie leaned forward in her chair, her lip trembling. There it was, the little red case. The last thing she had from her mother. What would it hold, and what more could it tell her?

"Do you have the combination number?" asked Rosie.

Miss Churchill wrinkled her brow, then said, "You know it."

Rosie frowned, puzzled. What did she mean?

Miss Churchill raised her eyebrows. "Think carefully, child."

Rosie stared at the numbers and ran her fingers over the coarse cover of the briefcase.

It smelled of old leather, just like she remembered.

She had already tried meaningful birthdays when she was first given it. She looked back up at Miss Churchill with eyes like saucers, pleading. What could it be?

Queenie, help me now . . .

No, it was up to her to work it out. Her fingers trembled as she slowly touched the dials. It was impossible to guess . . . *Impossible*. Her mother had always said, *Nothing is impossible*. That was it! Her heart began to thump as she slowly rolled the first number, then the second, the third, and the fourth . . . Barely able to breathe, she placed her fingers on both buttons. Had she got it right? Rosie then pressed the buttons to the side, and with one small flick, the latches sprang open. 1994! The year a Frost had proved that everything was possible. When a young girl had beaten all the odds to win the Falcon Queen games.

Thank you, Mum! You inspired me too!

Rosie lifted the lid.

What? The case was empty. Almost. There was just a flimsy piece of paper in the middle of it, folded once. It must have been the case itself that had made it feel so heavy, rather than its contents.

Rosie took out the piece of paper and unfolded it. It was a letter, addressed to her, written in her mother's handwriting.

Dear Rosie,

If you are reading this, I know you are on a path that was unexpected. But one thing you must be sure of is this: I am not leaving you by the roadside. I will always be with you, in your heart, in the wind, in the moonlight . . . When the sun beams on your face and when the birds sing in the sky. I will always be there, watching over you. My heart and spirit live on in you, and love never fades. Now you're going to feel sad, maybe angry. That's okay. Cry a little—or even a lot—but then I want you to keep going.

Bloodstone Island is a magical place—I hope you love it as much as I did. I longed to tell you more about it, but I wasn't ready to let you go yet, and it's only when you come here you understand how special it is. It is a place where you will come to appreciate your true power and worth. Live life to the fullest, for the world we inhabit is a wonderful one. If ever you're feeling lonely or like you don't belong, just imagine me by your side. People may say things about you—and judge you—but do not let negative thoughts muddy who you are. Believe in yourself. You are beautiful, brave, and strong, and I am so very proud of you. Your best is yet to come.

I love you and I always will,
Mum xx
P.S. Keep it safe . . . protect your flame.

Rosie read through the letter once, twice, three times. More tears streamed down her cheeks. This wasn't just a letter; it was the voice of her mum speaking directly to her. In that moment, it was the most precious item she could ever have received.

She read the final sentence again.

Keep it safe . . .

What did that mean?

Rosie looked in the briefcase one more time. There was something she'd missed. Tucked into one corner was a small square of cream silk fabric, folded over several times. She gingerly unwrapped the silk, her fingers gliding over the beautiful thread. Nestled inside it was a shining slice of a red ruby crystal, about the size and shape of a tangerine segment attached to a little gold chain. She held it close to her face, examining it, and it glimmered in the light. It looked like it came from something much larger . . . a slice from an orb. Like the orb in the painting in the Falcon Queen gallery . . .

"What's this?" Rosie asked Miss Churchill. The old lady's eyes glimmered.

"That, my child, is a reminder of the spark within you, of who you really are."

Rosie stared at the slice of ruby and frowned.

Who I really am? Rosie bit her lip. So far, it had been

one hell of an adventure finding out, but there was still more to discover. And what had *really* happened to her mother? Whatever it took, she would find out the truth. Because whatever it was, she was a Frost, and just like the Deep Secret rose, Frosts could endure the harshest weather . . .

The Falcon Queen's Rules

Animo, Imperium, Libertas.

Rule 1: Have courage; make the choice thou fearest the most.

Rule 2: United we stand, divided we fall.

Rule 3: Never give up; be the light. Serve your kingdom; you'll win your fight.

Rule 4: To thine own self be true.

If you likest not these rules . . . make up thine own.

Rosie's Rule

Don't judge a book by its cover . . . Look deeper. There's always more on the inside.

·FAMILY TREE·

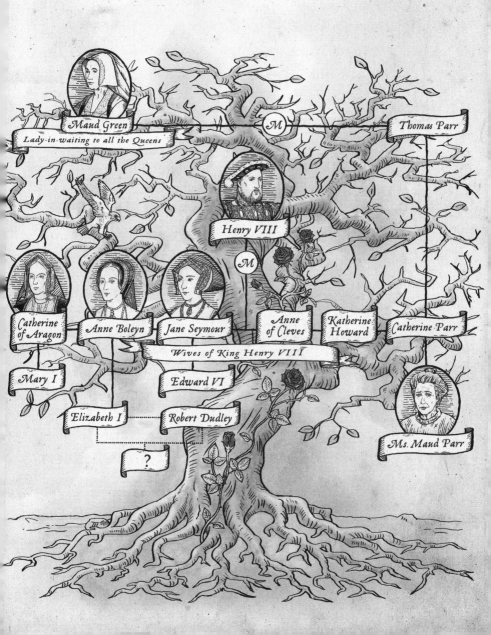

Maud Green

Lady-in-waiting to all the Queens

Ⓜ

Thomas Parr

Henry VIII

Ⓜ

Catherine of Aragon

Anne Boleyn

Jane Seymour

Anne of Cleves

Katherine Howard

Catherine Parr

Wives of King Henry VIII

Mary I

Edward VI

Elizabeth I

Robert Dudley

?

Ms. Maud Parr

Acknowledgments

To William Boyd, legend! The game changer. Thank you for your guidance and support.

Jacqueline Wilson, you deserve a medal; you read the first-ever draft! And then introduced me to *Jane Eyre*.

Rafaella Barker—you've been such an encouragement.

Christopher Little—RIP. Thank you for honesty; you were there right from the beginning. "Start again!" you said.

Jeff Frasco, who never stopped believing in me.

Jason Weinberg, all these years later . . . wow . . . thank you.

Anthony Mattero. Your faith in Rosie—thank you for being so supportive.

Then my amazing, amazing publishers!!

Jill Santopolo and all at Philomel and Penguin Random House. What a woman—so talented, the biggest heart, with courage and kindness—and thanks to you I wrote my first-ever prologue!

Linas Alsenas and all at Scholastic—wow, smart, honest, and brave.

And of course, thank you to my darling husband, Christian, for your patience and support as I would disappear with Rosie.

This is a dream come true . . . eight years.

Thank you to you all for your belief in Rosie Frost.

GLOSSARY

barrister: lawyer/attorney

blimey: an expression of surprise

football (footie): soccer

full-on: very enthusiastic

full pelt: as fast as possible

gobby: loud, offensive

jumper: sweater

loo: restroom

loo roll: toilet paper

mash: mashed potatoes

mobile: cell phone

pillock: an unintelligent person

pudding: dessert

quiff: a hairstyle brushed up and back from the forehead

Rombard: Anne Boleyn's executioner

rubbish: garbage

rucksack: backpack

scratchy: mean-spirited

sixth form: final two years of school before university, when students are sixteen to eighteen years old

slow coach: slowpoke

strop: temper tantrum

torch: flashlight

trainers: sneakers

tuck in: eat heartily

twigged: clicked (was understood)

wee: urine

wellies: rubber boots

To hear original Rosie Frost music
by Geri Halliwell-Horner,
use the code below
or visit RosieFrostBooks.com